W9-CJQ-359

(Continued from front flap)

story with a compelling premise: Suppose all of Earth—all of the universe—were the creation of the fertile imagination of an alien world; suppose too that we had reached the point of being able to destroy that world, without realizing it was our creator, without knowing that its destruction would virtually erase our existence. And suppose that the future of both races lay in the hands of a confused man who is half greedy, aggressive human and half precocious, naive teenage alien!

A masterful concept, masterfully and wittily presented and resolved, makes for the Herberts' newest bestseller.

Frank Herbert is the world-renowned author of *Dune* and over two dozen other books of science fiction. **Brian Herbert**, author of *The Garbage Chronicles*, *Sidney's Comet*, and most recently *Sudanna, Sudanna*, lives in the state of Washington.

Jacket painting copyright © 1986 by John Schoenherr
Photograph of the authors by Theresa Shackelford

G. P. PUTNAM'S SONS
Publishers Since 1838
200 Madison Avenue
New York, NY 10016

DISCARDED

MAN OF TWO WORLDS

Also by Frank Herbert

THE DRAGON IN THE SEA
(Reissued as UNDER PRESSURE)
DESTINATION: VOID
THE EYES OF HEISENBERG
THE GREEN BRAIN
THE HEAVEN MAKERS
THE SANTAROGA BARRIER
DUNE
DUNE MESSIAH
WHIPPING STAR
THE WORLDS OF FRANK HERBERT
THE GODMAKERS
THE JESUS INCIDENT
(With Bill Ransom)
SOUL CATCHER
HELLSTROM'S HIVE
(PROJECT 40)
THE BOOK OF FRANK HERBERT
THRESHOLD
THE BLUE ANGELS
THE BEST OF FRANK HERBERT
CHILDREN OF DUNE

THE DOSADI EXPERIMENT
GOD EMPEROR OF DUNE
THE WHITE PLAGUE
THE LAZARUS EFFECT
(With Bill Ransom)
HERETICS OF DUNE
CHAPTERHOUSE: DUNE

Edited by Frank Herbert
NEW WORLD OR NO WORLD

Also by Brian Herbert
SUDANNA, SUDANNA
SIDNEY'S COMET
THE GARBAGE CHRONICLES
INCREDIBLE INSURANCE CLAIMS
CLASSIC COMEBACKS

MAN OF TWO WORLDS

FRANK HERBERT
AND BRIAN HERBERT

G.P. PUTNAM'S SONS / NEW YORK

G. P. Putnam's Sons
Publishers Since 1838
200 Madison Avenue
New York, NY 10016

Copyright © 1986 by Frank Herbert and Brian Herbert
All rights reserved. This book, or parts thereof,
may not be reproduced in any form without permission.
Published simultaneously in Canada by
General Publishing Co. Limited, Toronto

Library of Congress Cataloging-in-Publication Data

Herbert, Frank.
Man of two worlds.

I. Herbert, Brian. II. Title.
PS3558.E63M3 1985 813'.54 85-28224
ISBN 0-399-13132-9

Printed in the United States of America
1 2 3 4 5 6 7 8 9 10

ECC/USF Learning Resources
8099 College Parkway, S.W.
Fort Myers, Florida 33907-5164

This book is dedicated with gratitude
To Hal Cook and Jeanne Ringgenberg

If every Dreen dies, the universe collapses, for all life and all matter are sustained by Dreen idmaging.

—*The Touchfinger Tabloids,*
Dreenschool curriculum

Ryll felt no pain on awakening, and he did not remember the collision. His mind groped for reality. What was the odd surface under him?

I am on a Far Voyager deck, he thought.

The surface where he lay felt slippery with viscous liquid. Something approximating gravity held him down. His Dreen senses suggested he was caught in an erratic spin but it was more than that, perhaps the gravitation of a planet as well, and he could not understand why he returned to consciousness this way—his eyes swiveled inward to darkness.

I am a Dreen.

It was a clear thought and suggested things not in immediate memory. His brain ached as badly as from a bazeel hangover. Urgency tugged at him but he did not want to face it. Better to consider what it meant to be Dreen.

Was it good to be Dreen?

I can idmage.

Despite this Dreen creative power, he now saw little that was graceful or pleasing in his native flesh, an observation that struck him as peculiar.

But Dreen mind powers could create new matter (even stars

with planets) and new life forms. He could shapeshift his body into that of any other creature, changing functions and appearance entirely.

Why then, Ryll asked himself, did Dreens look so similar—lumpy ovoid bodies with four concealed legs and two arms with six-fingered hands extruded only when needed?

Even Habiba, Supreme Tax Collector of Dreenor and the oldest Dreen, could not explain this peculiarity. She said the reasons for Dreen shape and powers were lost in prehistory. Dreens, Habiba explained, were similar to other life forms in this limited knowledge about themselves.

An intrusive buzzing and clanking sound interrupted these reflections.

Odd sounds. Patricia *at work?*

What a strange name for a semisentient spaceship: *Patricia.* That had been his first reaction. It was not a name a Dreen spoke easily even after creating the requisite vocal system in his malleable body.

Patricia?

He recalled his initial shock at the ship's odd behavior.

"My name is Ryll."

He had said this in a patronizing tone, the one taught for use with Excursion Ships. The response was unexpected:

"Don't take that tone with me!"

He remembered sitting in the control room, shocked by the ship's commanding tone. Did it suspect he was adventuring? He thought of his intentions as adventure, not as stealing.

I was escaping Dreenor's boredom.

Ryll had been extremely tired of all the talk about his gifts and potential. What did they expect from a son of Jongleur, the Chief Storyteller? He thought the Elders would call his taking the ship a schoolboy prank if they caught him.

So I took the ship. And I am Dreen but far away from Dreenor.

He had no idea how he knew these things nor why it was important to reflect on being Dreen.

Why don't I think of myself as graceful?

Was it that he could completely alter his appearance but could not make piecemeal changes? A Dreen's floppy ear covers draped like small brown blankets down each side of his body. Very impractical, as was the large horn-tool nose that dominated his face from the widow's peak of pink hair atop a neckless and shoulderless body to the concealed mouth that revealed itself only when open to receive food or make noises.

He had a memory vision of fellow Dreens lifting an ear flap and asking speakers to repeat themselves. Impracticality: small mouth, weak vocal cords, ears blanketed. By idmaging, he could shapeshift his entire body, but tradition dictated he never do this on Dreenor. Metamorphoses were reserved for offworld. Dreenor was a place of sanctuary and storytelling cameraderie.

Ryll wished he were back on Dreenor now to share a tale of distant travel, idmage creations and adventure.

That's why I defied my Elders and took the ship. I was tired of the boring schoolboy life. I wanted to be the youngest Junior Storyteller. That's why I did it. That's why I'm here on this slippery deck.

Slippery deck?

His eyes remained swiveled inward to darkness but more details began to surface.

The ship.

Many ships sat on the mud-brown Flat of Dreenor, coming and going with their Storyteller captains. The ships were great bulbous things with extruded sensors like waving cilia to guide them through the Spirals of Creation in tangled space.

Sometimes, for no observable reason a ship would remain unchosen and dormant, awaiting just the right captain. That was the way it had been with this ship. It had been part of Ryll's environment from earliest childhood only a few months out of seedhouse.

Even before being sent to the school for gifted children he had thought of this ship as his own, creating fantasies of himself in the Spirals.

He had wondered often about its personality. The varied personalities of Excursion Ships as taught in school fascinated him. Ships were almost like people. But this one . . .

"*You will call me* Patricia!"

Ryll's proctors had told him the most enjoyable trips into the tangles of space were on ships having personalities compatible with your own. You chose your ship with great care.

Patricia?

Immediate sense impressions demanded attention. What was

this viscous fluid under him? Why the dullness in his body? Something was disturbingly wrong. Had *Patricia* malfunctioned? Impossible! Excursion Ships were idmaged to be perfect. Then what was this erratic spinning motion holding him to the deck?

He tried to consider the possibility of something wrong with *Patricia* and recalled instead the appearance of the ship on the Dreenor Flat—a golden egg with cilia-sensors glistening. Each time passing the Flat he had looked to see that *his* ship remained unchosen by an adult.

Wait for me, beautiful ship. When I graduate you will be mine.

Once he had seen a group of adult Dreens working on the ship, all under the direction of Mugly the Elder. They conferred, pointed and swiveled their eyes inward to idmage, making the ship even more perfect, no doubt.

Nothing could go wrong with a perfectly idmaged ship.

Could it?

Early one morning before school he had sneaked past the sleeping monitor and boarded the ship to take away copies of its flight-simulation manuals in their crimson displays.

He rationalized that gifted children were expected to prepare themselves for the day they would go out as Storytellers to create new worlds. But this was secret preparation, teaching himself to pilot an Excursion Ship, something far beyond the careful pacing of the adult-monitored curriculum.

No one suspected he could pilot *his* ship, could take it without permission and vanish into the Creative Spirals—no matter that he was too young and had not absorbed enough cautionary instruction.

I'll be the youngest Dreen ever to create new worlds.

He saw himself in the Elite class of Junior Storytellers, training ground for advancement to Elder.

Idmaging!

How attractive to contemplate the supreme Dreen ability: to make tangible the living fantasies of the mind, to create new life forms and return to Dreenor with stories of his artistic efforts. That was why he had taken *Patricia*.

So why was he here on a deck with a slippery fluid under him? There was an odd smell. Vaguely familiar. What was it?

"Patricia?" he ventured.

The ship did not reply.

Patricia had not opposed him when he took over the controls, although she called his pretensions "an interesting dream produced by your immaturity and boredom but consistent with a Dreen's natural idmagination."

Did Patricia *self-destruct?*

That was a terrifying thought and flooded his mind with *Patricia*'s irritating voice: "You are going to a dangerous place and the Storyteller who commands me likely will die."

By Habiba's everlasting seedglands! He suddenly remembered the awful revelations of *his* ship: "The Earther Zone Patrol holds captive Dreens. I have this information to explain why I must self-destruct rather than permit Earthers to learn my secrets."

This was more than the bits and pieces from adult whispers about Dreen disasters.

"The creatures he made worshiped him!"

"His creatures did not evolve and just died out. Faulty precepts."

Children heard such things and created their own myths. But his present situation was no myth to be greeted with amused tolerance by adults.

Why wasn't I told?

Patricia said children could not share real disaster tales until deemed capable of handling harsh information.

I have encountered harsh information.

What happened to my perfect ship?

Once more he called out to *Patricia* but still the ship did not respond.

He thought he would even welcome one of her caustic lectures, if only she would speak. He did not want to be alone.

Where am I?

Ryll swiveled his eyes outward and locked them into place. He saw shadows, then bursts of light that brought pain and forced him to blink. He squinted cautiously and saw a dented silver-yellow bulkhead directly over him—*Patricia*'s control room but badly damaged. Destruction but not total.

He lay on his back and it hurt when he extruded an arm to touch the deck. Not cold . . . not hot . . . sticky stuff.

More memories returned.

He saw his ship emerge from the Spirals, felt again the excitement of that moment and . . . and . . . and then disaster!

Another ship occupied the emergent space!

The effect was not just a collision but a massive attempt by two large objects to occupy the same space at the same time. His control room smashed through to the center of the other ship, dominating the impact and telling him his was the more massive object.

When the first shudderings and boomings of the crash subsided, he heard hissings, clangings and snappings and saw emergency repair manipulators attempting to seal his area against loss of atmosphere. Fire! He remembered flames. That was what destroyed the sacred Dreen drive!

I am trapped here! But where is here?

He could still hear nearby sounds to suggest emergency repairs. This gave him hope. He rolled his body slightly to the right. Pain! He was a moment fighting off the defensive-ball reaction, every Dreen's instinctive response to danger.

Curiosity and a need to know sustained him. What were those two mounds stretched across a break in the bulkhead? He stared at them.

Badly damaged protoplasm! Bodies from the other ship.

Ragged bits of green and black fabric hid some of the shattered flesh.

Ryll took an interminable time extruding legs to help him crawl toward the bodies. His efforts hinted at terrible injuries—vital organs crushed and severed. Too much damage for idmaging repairs, but those bodies at the broken bulkhead offered a way to survive.

Painfully, he reached the first body. He recognized the shape from Storyteller accounts: an Earth human. The Earther was dead.

Ryll moved to the second body.

Blood . . . much blood—some his own yellow, flowing and mingling with Earther magenta . . . and a clear fluid spouting from a bulkhead rift.

The second human still breathed. Ryll's left front leg crunched shattered eyeglasses. Agonizing cramps warped his flesh and the defensive-ball reaction tried to dominate him.

Can't let that happen!

This was no time to be immobilized and helpless.

The odd smell remained but he noted no more hiss of escaping atmosphere. What was that smell? Memory from a fully assimilated Storyteller account answered his question.

The clear fluid: vol-tol!

It had been an extremely artistic Dreen story explaining vol-tol, the highly explosive fuel used in Earthers' primitive ships.

The other ship in the collision was of Earther origin! One of its occupants lay dead and another appeared to be dying.

But the vol-tol demanded immediate attention. It could ignite, destroying the shambles of the collision and every living thing aboard.

Ryll knew he had to deal with the problem himself. *Patricia* was no longer functional.

I must move quickly!

He touched the surviving human's crushed head and neck.

Yes, dying.

Darts of agony shot through Ryll as he moved. It occurred to him that he, too, might be fatally injured. He paused to make an internal assessment.

By the blessed left arm of the Supreme Tax Collector! Almost ten percent of my mass is gone!

This time there was no trouble with the defensive-ball reaction. His probing hands fanned into cilia, an automatic reaction against which every Dreen child was warned. Ryll watched the cilia slither into the dying human's face.

Merging!

He knew he must prevent this. Combining life forms created unpredictable and often dangerous results. That was one piece of harsh information taught to every child.

But without more mass immediately I will die.

Ryll stared at an audio-visual ID tag on what remained of the mortally wounded Earther's green and black tunic.

"I am Lutt Hanson, Jr.," it said in English.

Ryll's language-interpretive facility, a product of Dreen storytelling and education, immediately shifted to the proper linguistic form.

What odd names Earthers chose.

No matter the harsh warnings, survival necessity drove him.

There was no time for idmaging, and he needed portions of this dying body to rebuild his Dreen mass.

Abruptly, he heard wreckage moving. Metal grated against metal. Then . . . voices!

Discarding niceties, Ryll allowed Earther flesh to flow into and combine with his own, an oddly pleasing sensation. He felt his Dreen resources using Earther protoplasm, letting it creep into and around his cells. Alien memories intruded.

Fascinating! The cells carried Earther information—too much to review at once, but similar to assimilating a Dreen Storyteller's account.

Suddenly, a voice boomed from behind Ryll.

"All personnel evacuate this ship immediately!"

Ryll identified the characteristic sound-clipping of an artificial amplifier.

The shock of the voice and the final merging with an essential mass of Earther flesh jolted him.

I must hide!

Using Earther-cell data, Ryll assumed the appearance and clothing of Lutt Hanson, Jr. A facsimile Earther took shape on the shattered deck, complete with clear-lensed, round-framed eyeglasses—no need to match originals. Ryll's eyes in a new olive shade stared out of Earther-shaped flesh. The meticulously copied face was blocky and soft: thin red-brown hair, a high forehead and a raised blood vessel like a tiny medusa serpent on the left temple. With desperate cunning, he appropriated a nametag from the Earther's ragged tunic and pushed discarded flesh into contact with the dead companion.

The intrusive voices were much louder, metal slamming against metal. Once more, the amplified voice boomed out.

"Fuel rupture! All personnel except emergency volunteers evacuate the damage area!"

Metal crashed to the deck behind Ryll. Heavy footsteps clumped to his side. An armored hand came into view and a brown faceplate with helmet lowered close to Ryll's face.

"Hey! This one's alive!"

"Move him!"

That was the amplified voice of command.

Memories and motivations from Lutt Hanson, Jr., seeped like tendrils bleeding across nerve contacts into Ryll's awareness. What an odd creature, this Earther. There were visions of a wealthy family rife with disputes and intrigues—this Lutt Junior active in many ways, coordinating and plotting to fulfill his single, driving ambition . . .

"A dead one here!"

That was the voice of the one who had come into Ryll's view.

"Part of the body's melted away! Yeccch!"

"Leave it and bring the survivor! This place could blow any second!"

The amplified voice of command again.

Ryll felt something being slipped under his body—a thin fabric with stiffeners. Two armored Earthers lifted him and carried him through the hole torn in the bulkhead.

Ryll closed his eyes and experienced a deep sense of gratitude at being rescued, even though it was by creatures produced in Dreen idmages. Survival dominated his reactions now and an immediate problem required attention.

Lutt Hanson, Jr., was becoming aware of the merging.

Who are you? How did you get into my mind?

It was a soundless voice but it roared in Ryll's awareness.

What are you doing to me? Get out! Get out!

Ryll formed a responsive thought, trying to make it as soothing as possible. But overtones of panic were unavoidable.

I can't get out. That would kill both of us.

The human responded with more panic and tried to take control of their mutual body.

This is my body and I want you out of it!

Only a small part of this body is yours. Most of it is mine. I'm trying to save us both.

You're lying!

Ryll allowed a memory vision of the moments before fleshly merging to flow into common awareness. He carefully controlled what was shared but made it appear uncensored, astonished at his sudden ability to dissemble.

The human's response was predictable.

My God! Is that me? Oh . . . yes. The back of my head was

crushed! Nobody could have survived that. I must've been dying.

We both were dying. There was enough flesh to save us but only in one body.

Can't we separate?

There may be a way but it will take time and facilities you don't yet possess.

Who are you?

I am a Dreen Far Voyager.

That was a lie but the human could not know, could not acquire any of Ryll's memories unless Ryll chose to share them.

What's a Dreen?

I'll explain later. What was your ship doing in my emergent space? You caused the accident.

No response from the Earther.

Ryll sensed advantage and pressed it.

Didn't you know an Excursion Ship of a Far Voyager might come out there?

The human tried to change the subject. *What's this language we're using and how come I understand it?*

This is the Dreenor language. Habiba's language. When we merged, some of my language facility became available to you.

Why do you say I caused the accident?

You entered emergent space without proper warning.

I was testing my new ship. Definitely defensive.

Well, your companion is dead and both of our ships are total disasters. Who are these people rescuing us?

Zone Patrol. I wasn't authorized in their perimeter and there's going to be hell to pay. It's into the clink for sure, no matter who I am.

Ryll allowed himself a secret thought: *Zone Patrol! The ones who held captive Dreens!*

He assumed his most persuasive personality. *I have a suggestion, Lutt. May I call you Lutt?*

Sure, but what do I call you?

My name is Ryll. I suggest you take over control of our body and answer the Zone Patrol's question. I suggest you not tell them about me.

Silence, then: *Yeah. They'd think I was nuts unless . . . Say! What's our body look like?*

Like you but slightly larger than before the accident. More massive.

Ryll felt the litter being lowered to a flat surface and opened his eyes. He sensed Lutt reaching for dominance in their mutual flesh. Vision blurry—vague movement of armored figures, a gray bulkhead.

A faceplate came into view.

"He's coming around. Should I give him a shot?"

"Hold it. This deck will shake if that fuel blows."

As though the words created the effect, red brightness erased the shadows. There was the thumping sound of a muffled explosion. Ryll bounced in a wash of heat.

"Jeeedarussi!" It was a voice close to his ear.

The commanding voice boomed out: "Get the fire control team in there or we'll lose the whole thing!"

Ryll heard the movement of many armored humans but could not see them because someone without armor bent close, blocking his view. Ryll saw a wide, heavy head with short hair. Hands probed and tested his new body. Female by the voice and briskly professional.

"We'll 'ray him but there don't appear to be any broken bones."

"If that isn't fool luck I never heard of it. Right next to a dead one, too."

That was a masculine voice from one side.

"His lapel tag says Lutt Hanson, Jr.," the woman said.

The man spoke sharply. "Hanson? This is old L.H.'s kid! I'd better call in."

Ryll still felt the gropings of Lutt Junior trying to take over control of their body. Very tentative and wary, like an insect crawling along his nerves. The human lacked Dreen experience in the mental acceptance of storytelling.

There came the sound of a click and a humming buzz.

Ryll thought: *My human head moves on a supple neck.* He turned his head toward the sound but could not bring the man into view. The voice was clear, though.

"Sergeant Renner here, sir. We're at the crash site. One survivor with an identity label saying he's Lutt Hanson, Jr."

Silence, then: "No, sir. Fuel spilled and exploded. There are no other survivors."

Ryll focused on a circular crest adorning an arm of the woman bending over him. He filled out the shared memory with an assimilated Dreen Storyteller account.

Zone Patrol. This is the dangerous, all-encompassing United States security force—a unification of their previous military agencies.

Sergeant Renner spoke: "There was only one other body, sir, and we couldn't get it out."

More silence, then: "Very well, sir. Will comply."

I really messed up, Ryll thought.

He closed his eyes and began sorting through newly acquired memories.

What a jumble! Important data, though. The Earther ship employed a primitive form of Dreen drive. We collided because the crude thing inherently homed on the signal of my incoming ship. Stupid! Stupid!

What happened to Patricia? *Is my perfect ship destroyed forever?*

Why, oh why did I take that ship?

Lutt Junior assumed command of their flesh and Ryll sank into his own thoughts with a sense of relief.

In school they had said the Dreen partner in this amalgam might have difficulty withdrawing completely but could be dominant by choice, taking over muscle and nerve control at any time. That was reassuring.

He felt the litter being lifted and carried somewhere.

Patricia, *what is happening to you?*

It had been so easy to take the ship. Too easy. The chief monitor at the Flat during Ryll's sixteenth year out of seedhouse, an Eminence named Prosik, had shown flexions and tremblings characteristic of bazeel addiction. Prosik had other defects, all of them adding up to sufficient reason for his never having risen above the position of Eminence, nineteenth from the bottom of Habiba's fifty-seven social varieties. He often slept during guard duty and even when awake accompanied the curious child into the ship for play at being a Storyteller.

If he hadn't been asleep I never would have acquired the flight-simulation manuals.

Despite the present mess, Ryll still felt proud of the way he had taken the ship. He had raised the impossible-to-idmage bazeel in a small experimental horticultural garden off his bedroom, hiding the prohibited plant under broad-leaved herbs. His parents, admiring the garden, never suspected.

Ryll had tried the bazeel once and awakened the next morning with a severe brainache and little memory of its effect except for vague visions of extruding all four legs and falling asleep while counting them over and over.

Periodically, Ryll presented small stems of bazeel to Prosik and, one day, gave the Eminence a large frond of the drug "to thank you for letting me play in the beautiful ship."

Shortly after consuming the bazeel, Prosik's horn-tool extension sank into the brown mass of his body until it lay almost buried there and the chief monitor was a comatose lump of protoplasm. He did not stir as Ryll crept into the ship, gaze fixed on the icy yellow light shining from the control room.

At last! He was in a Storyteller's sanctum and he possessed the knowledge to command an Excursion Ship.

Around Ryll lay an ovoid enclosure seven times his height and so wide even his longest extensions could not span it. He touched the first command plate and a silver-yellow glow filled the space with an exciting lambent radiance.

Ryll stared at the controls. This was the light that signaled life-creating forces.

So I have the necessary powers.

One could never be sure until touching that plate in the command space and this had been forbidden to a mere child.

For a moment he felt fearful of the life patterns that might emerge from this place and he dawdled while sealing the external hatches.

Hesitation passed. He formed the proper pseudopod, touched the proper plates in proper sequence and exactly as the flight simulator had predicted, he found himself and the ship in the infinite Spirals of tangled space.

Elation filled him.

I've done it!

Sensors displayed what lay outside—the substance of creation bathed in a light very like that within the Storyteller sanctum. Out there stood the most exciting mystery of all—the raw material from which Dreen idmaging produced new places and new life. He had touched the control plate and filled his mind with awareness of the Spirals. Now . . . now he could idmage something important!

And no other Dreen could track him. Memory and the ship systems held the coordinates to guide his return. Dreenor was not lost to him; he was lost to Dreenor.

Ryll sat in the Storyteller harness, swinging at the focal center of command and he felt very much the maker of a reality dream, that marvelous precursor to idmages. That was the moment the ship chose to shock him.

"You will call me *Patricia* of the female gender."

Ryll jumped. Nothing in his education had prepared him for the candor and adjustment capabilities apparent in the voice of this . . . this artifact. He had never heard of a ship initiating conversation.

"That's interesting," he managed. "Why should I call you *Po . . . Putrushua?*"

"*Patricia!*" she corrected him. "You will call me *Patricia* because it is my name and we are going to a place where that is a common appellation."

"But I want to go through the Spirals and—"

"I am ordered to one destination and cannot disobey."

"My name is Ryll and you will—"

"I observe that you are quite immature and will require careful supervision. It is difficult to compute why you were assigned this mission. Perhaps you are expendable. That fits the rationale of my task."

"Answer my question!"

Silence.

"Please tell my why we have only one destination."

"I am a Reserved Inspection Ship devised to erase an idmage."

Ryll's body collapsed into a hard ball, his horn tool pointed at the source of the ship's voice above him on the plate wall. He knew this posture. Defensive reflex.

Slowly, Ryll formed his voice orifice and did the only thing left to him. He confessed.

"Interesting," *Patricia* said. "I am incapable of turning back from this mission and you are the only Dreen available to make the life and death decision."

"Why didn't Prosik warn me what kind of ship you are?"

"Prosik is only an Eminence. He will, of course, be severely punished. What they will do to you must be left to conjecture."

"They know where we're going and they'll come for me, won't they?"

It was more statement than question.

"They will follow at a much slower pace. I was devised for the swift emergency erasure of a particular creation should a Storyteller command it."

Erasure!

That word again, and Ryll thought of what it meant—a planet and its life gone forever, the tangible evidence of a Storyteller's creative idmaging . . . everything gone and never to recur. Ryll's horn tool pulsed in and out with distress.

"But why would . . . I mean, if . . ."

Ryll could not bring himself to say it. The idea was horrible beyond anything he had ever considered.

Harsh information, indeed!

"The creatures of this world pose a potential threat to every idmaged creation the Dreens have ever made."

That was worse!

Ryll began to see the extremis behind creation of this ship. Another aspect of the problem occurred to him.

"You mean I may have to decide on . . . I may have to order the . . ."

He still could not say the word.

"You are Dreen and you may have to command it. If you give the order, I must obey."

Then she gave him the full dose of harsh information.

Loneliness enfolded Ryll. Accounts from school and Storyteller assimilations had not prepared him for this. He was cut off from security, from things known and expected.

He might never return to Dreenor. That was where all Dreens conveyed their tales and replenished themselves.

"Tapping into the past," Habiba called it.

Even if he survived the . . . the . . .

Damn Habiba!

"Return or die," Habiba often said.

And she had the long history of Dreen tragedies on her side.

I have nine Dreenyears at most.

Dreens who failed to return within that limit had been found dead in distant places. Folk wisdom said all Dreens must share their story experiences to survive, that Dreenor was a storehouse of mystical regeneration, enabling Dreens to live forever. This was believed despite infrequent accidental deaths on Dreenor and elsewhere.

Return or die.

Ryll thought he might rather die than take this kind of story home to Dreenor. Who could possibly admit him into the Junior Storytellers after he had . . . had . . . had . . . done what *Patricia* said?

That might be a useless fear, too. Even though disguised as an Earther, he was now another Dreen captive in the hands of the dreaded Zone Patrol.

There will always be newspapers, always some crusty old publisher, or a young publisher with crusty old ideas, who refuses to let go of the past. I respect the past, the smoke-filled, bustling news offices and all that, but I'm not a sentimental person. We create a better future if we stay in touch with our past, but I feel damned good about my electronic newspaper. It's my base and conduit for creativity. No details yet, but I'm about to unleash a technological breakthrough in this industry. And a related, but even more astounding development will follow shortly.

—Lutt Hanson, Jr., an interview
in his *Seattle Enquirer*

Someone's moving my arms, my legs and my head and controlling where I look.

These were panic thoughts in Lutt's awareness. Through the round lenses of his spectacles, he saw foggy human shapes. He heard the rattle of keys and clanking metal. There were men walking around him—at front, back and both sides.

I stumbled and something took over my body.

An alien force held him upright and walking steadily.

"I am Ryll, son of Jongleur, the Chief Storyteller."

That was hearing voices in his head—madness.

I was in my ship, the Vortraveler, Lutt thought. *I said something to Drich Baker, my engineer and copilot. What did I say?*

Memory provided no answer. He knew there had been a blackout. It had erased part of his mind.

He took a familiar mental course then, recalling the day before boarding the *Vortraveler*.

If I exercise the brain muscles, go through everything up to the blackout, maybe I'll remember.

He had been in the family-owned Seattle Enquirer Building. That much he remembered. A gray, seventeen-story structure, the building housed the plant of an electronic newspaper.

Only a tax writeoff in Father's mind.

Running the family's Newspaper Division gave Lutt the sense that the *Enquirer* was much more than "a fixture of antiquated technology," as his father called it.

Lutt recalled arguing with old L.H. in the boardroom that morning. But Father always had the last word.

"Stop wasting time on that damn vorspiral crap! You're making us a laughingstock, predicting 'astounding developments' and 'technological breakthroughs' that'll never happen!"

"Dammit, Father, you think things will never happen just because you don't want them to happen!"

"Son, you're sounding more and more like that crazy brother of your mother's. You keep on this way and you'll wind up like your Uncle Dudley!"

Lutt stared at his father. For years, the cloud of some violent quarrel between the two men had hung over the family. And now the old man broke his own rule against mentioning Uncle Dudley.

"Just how did Uncle Dudley wind up?" Lutt asked, almost choking on the forbidden name.

"I hope what they say is true—that he disappeared on Venus! He deserved to get his ass fried!"

Seeing the signs of increasing rage in his father, Lutt changed the subject but that only led them back into the fight about the *Seattle Enquirer*, vorspirals and Lutt's future in Hanson Industries.

It was a continuing conflict with predictable reactions on both sides.

But L.H. doesn't know what Drich and I have already achieved.

Drich!

The voice in his mind said Drich was dead. And there was that brief memory—his own body with a crushed skull.

Was that really me?

Lutt cast off those thoughts.

Hallucinations. The Zone Patrol doctor gave me a shot. That's what's causing me to feel this way.

Vorspiral communications technology! That would win the argument with Father. The ability to send almost instantaneous messages across millions of kilometers of space—transmissions faster and clearer than anything in history.

Just a little more testing and development, some careful publicity, and it surely would be of interest to the military and even to other news services.

But old L. H. wouldn't listen, wouldn't bend from his rigid ways.

We'll call it Vorspiral News Service—VNS.

And the possibility—no! the *probability!*—loomed before him of extremely rapid travel across interstellar space. Theory said there were vorspirals to link any place in the universe with any other place. The speed of this travel still had to be tested, but he knew it would be very fast.

Abruptly, Lutt recalled what he had said to Drich Baker in that instant before the blackout.

The memory came to him so clearly and in such detail that he found himself reliving the events. He was in the *Vortraveler*'s cockpit. It was late afternoon and the ship sat on the tarmac of the secret testing site just east of Seattle. A rainy day with water running down the shields. The instrument panel glowed green. There was a reassuring hum to the power systems. Drich sat beside him and they were struggling to get the ship into a vorspiral that (theory said) would link them to another solar system.

"Maybe this time." That's what I said.

Lutt recalled the words but nothing more. Whatever happened after those words was eaten up by . . . by . . . a blackout.

Lutt's troubled memory returned to the morning at the *Enquirer*. It was after L. H. had slammed out of the boardroom.

I went to the fourteenth-floor editorial conference room.

Eight senior editors sat with him around the long table amidst ranks of electronic newspaper receivers. He recalled arguing loudly that the *Enquirer* was not resourceful enough or snappy enough in its news play.

The ranks of receivers showed the *Enquirer* and rival publications to back up his argument.

"We need more sensational stories, more grabbers!"

He flipped the paper-thin sheets of liquid crystal screens to display pages of the rivals.

"Look here!" Lutt said, pointing to a headline on page one of the *Cincinnati Crier*.

PATTERN TO UFO SIGHTINGS

"Here's a story that screams to be read. The *Crier* says a classified Zone Patrol report shows common factors for credible UFO sightings. This is great stuff! They say all UFOs have a bulbous shape and insectlike antennae all over them, plus flexible rods that sway as though blown by a wind."

"Those guys on the *Crier* make that stuff up out of their heads!"

That was city editor Anaya Nelson, caustic as usual.

Lean, heavily made up around the eyes and framed by straight golden hair, Anaya's face still held a measure of her youthful beauty. But she had hard edges now. The staff said her face had only one relaxed expression—condescending.

"They quote pages and paragraphs of this Zone Patrol report!" Lutt snapped. "And they're citing the First Amendment to protect their sources!"

"So they got some rear-rank swabby to steal a piece of ZP fantasy."

"It sells papers, dammit!"

"You're really going to turn this operation into a money-maker? No more writeoffs for our beloved parent company, Hanson Industries?"

Lutt noted the other editors trying to conceal amusement at his usual collision with Nelson, but he ignored them.

Nelson smiled, knowing this irritated Lutt.

Damn her!

Lutt had criticized her "noncooperative attitude" on many occasions but to no avail.

What could he do about her? Nelson was a hard-shelled news veteran in her late middle years, long rumored to be old L.H.'s mistress. Lutt did not know for sure but the reports were that she had been an extraordinary beauty in her youth when the old man first met her. What everyone here knew for sure was that she had a pipeline to L.H. and could not be fired. Not by Junior anyway.

Lutt felt his ire rising. "I thought I made that clear!"

His nostrils flared, picking up a faint odor of paint in the editorial conference room. *Always painting and repainting in here!* He fanned through a graphics file on his printer, found what he was seeking and displayed it for Anaya. It showed a new masthead for the *Enquirer* with "L.W. Hanson, Proprietor."

Nelson examined the artwork disdainfully.

Managing editor Adrian (Ade) Stuart leaned close to stare over Nelson's shoulder. A paraplegic without legs, Stuart rode an electric cart that required wide aisles in the City Room. Overweight and with a softly rounded face under gray hair, Stuart often surprised new acquaintances with his commanding baritone voice. Some said Stuart's voice was the main asset that had carried him to power on the *Enquirer*.

"Very dignified," Stuart said.

"It doesn't specify L.W. Hanson Senior or Junior," Nelson said. "Shouldn't that be corrected?"

"This is the way I want it!" Lutt said.

They all know L.H. still owns this paper and my stock is a token five shares. She'll go straight to Father with this but I still run the operation.

Suzanne Day, who edited the Style Section, leaned forward with a sweet smile. Lutt had heard she practiced that smile for "boss buttering." Still, she was attractive enough—a slender brunette with gentle features that were sure to coarsen because she drank too much, boasting: "I can drink any newsman on this paper under the table."

"Why don't we offer a copying service?" she asked. "It could be built into each receiving frame. We could—"

Nelson interrupted with a calculated imitation of Lutt's voice: "But we want increased productivity, more efficiency, more circulation, more advertising revenue."

"We also want excellence," Lutt said.

Day required no more encouragement. Still with that sweet smile, she said: "I've checked it out. If a subscriber wants a copy of any article, he just touches the screen over the article, tapping once for each copy desired."

"It's been tried before," Nelson said.

"*Albany Evening Bible,*" Stuart said. "Mmmmm . . . four years ago. There were problems."

"Because they were first," Day said. "There were headaches with startup costs and glitches."

Like my Vortraveler, Lutt thought.

Lutt's erratic memory went spiraling off into his pet project—near-instantaneous communication and travel across the solar system and interstellar space. L.H. would never provide the development money.

He wants me to run Hanson Industries.

Lutt's mother, Phoenicia, wanted the same thing—but only because she thought her son would keep up the profits. She and his younger brother, Morey—always with their hands in the till.

Morey!

Lutt recalled another detail of the day before the blackout.

I couldn't keep my appointment with Morey. What a shock, dear brother, to learn that someone has discovered your financial indiscretions!

That'll be worth a lot of money from his accounts. But I didn't keep the appointment because of the crash and . . .

Yes! There was an accident with the Vortraveler!

This memory brought Lutt full circle and back to his immediate situation—in a corridor surrounded by Zone Patrol guards, his detached body walking under its own power.

His vision cleared slightly but he still had no control over where he aimed his attention.

How badly was I injured?

He felt too weak to take command of his own body. Lutt felt certain his eyes were not moving randomly. He was staring with too much purpose—surveying the brown and blue uniforms of his guards, examining the long gray corridor and the barred doors of the cells along both sides. He noted that a prisoner's black and green gorcord tunic covered his body. How demeaning!

Into the clink! I said that but who did I say it to?

His detached flesh did a terrifying thing, then. It spoke without his volition.

"I demand to know where you're taking me!"

It was a boyish voice, not Lutt's gravelly tones.

There were strange, alien thoughts in his head, too.

How dare they treat me this way? I am Ryll, son of the Chief

Storyteller! But I can't say anything about that. I'm supposed to be an Earther. They think I'm Lutt Hanson, Jr.

Lutt wanted to speak but his voice would not obey. He could think, though.

Are you real? Someone else in my head and . . . body?

Oopsah! I left my thoughts unshielded.

Am I going crazy?

You are not insane, Lutt. I have been listening to the sporadic activity of your simplistic mind. Your latest thoughts about your ship and the Spirals confirm my earlier surmise. Your primitive ship and your lack of caution caused a disaster.

Ryll?

Ahhh, you remember my name.

You said . . . you said I could control . . . our body.

You were doing it too poorly. These guards are not very intelligent but they are trained to be suspicious. The Zone Patrol reported only two bodies at the crash and now they know there were two people on your ship. Ergo: Where is the pilot of the other ship? They will assume he was destroyed in the blast and fire but only if we do not feed their suspicions.

Darkness enclosed Lutt although he sensed his eyes remained open.

What's happening? He's not letting me see!

The guards and their prisoner arrived at an empty cell. One guard opened the door and they started to thrust Ryll through the doorway. He began to struggle and shout.

"I've done nothing wrong! You'll pay for this!"

"The Hansons think they own the universe," a guard sneered.

They sent Ryll staggering into the cell and the door slammed. The sound of the lock clanging into place was loud in the metal-walled space.

"Look, fella," a guard said. "We know who you are but you're still going to answer some questions. You'll be interrogated tomorrow and there's nothing your old man or any other Hanson can do about that!"

The guards clumped away down the corridor.

There was laughter and calling from other prisoners.

"You really got one of the Hanson tribe in there?"

"What'd he do? Steal a general's mistress?"

Still in darkness, Lutt ventured a protesting question.

Why won't you let me see what's happening?

No need.

But I . . .

Be still! I have to decide what to do about this.

A metal door boomed closed down the corridor. The laughter and catcalls subsided.

Ryll inspected the cell. A tiny cubicle with solid walls. Bars on the door. No internal illumination. Light came through the bars from a small fluorescent panel in the corridor ceiling. Shadows of bars on wall and floor. Round metal drain hole in the floor bubbling with foul-smelling ordure. Gray floor and walls that looked as though they had never been painted. Water stains and rough scratchings from former occupants. He read one of the wall scratchings:

"Welcome to Hell."

A toilet fixture protruded from the back wall. A bunk bed was cantilevered from a side wall. Thin mattress. One rough blanket.

There was a distinctly stale odor to the place and the smell of disinfectant did not cover the pungency of urine and excrement.

Ryll went to the bunk and stretched out on it to think.

This had become much more than an adventure.

Was there anything useful in the data about Earth assimilated from Dreen Storytellers? He began to doubt this.

Nothing was said about Earthers experimenting with travel in the Spirals.

But an . . . an erasure ship had been prepared.

Erasure.

He found the concept easier to contemplate.

This world was a peculiar creation. Caution with any idmage interference was strongly indicated. Who knew what Earthers might learn if they saw Dreen powers at work? But they imprisoned a Dreen in a dark, dank cell! And *Patricia* said they held other Dreens captive.

However, they do not know I'm a Dreen. That is a mitigating circumstance.

The bed was uncomfortable. The floor did not attract him as a resting place. Dirty and smelly down there. Ryll longed for the simple platform of hardened vegetation in his Dreenor bedroom. Well, there was something he could do about that. He got up and removed the mattress, leaning it against the barred door and exposing the bunk, a hard metal surface of pipes protruding from the wall. It felt much better when he lay down once more. The blanket, while coarse, provided some warmth. He felt himself drifting into sleep. Yes . . . this had been an exhausting experience.

Still in darkness, Lutt came to weak awareness of the hard surface under him. He complained about the bed.

Ryll paid little attention to the protests. The deeper stages of Dreensleep were more attractive. He drifted into a combined Dreen-human dream.

The Lutt part of the intertwined dream focused on an ideal (to him) human female and became (to Ryll) a nightmare. The woman had no visible face but she possessed a voluptuous body from which radiated a golden aura that drew the dreamers to her.

In the dream, Lutt made love to the female in the abhorrent human way that had so shocked Ryll when he encountered it in a Storyteller account on Dreenor. How could a Dreen have idmaged such a thing? The dream with its immediacy was even more revolting than the story assimilation. Ryll now felt himself almost a participant!

Still, as the nightmare continued, Ryll sensed something odd emanating from the dream encounter. This particular woman Lutt hoped to meet someday aroused tender feelings in him, feelings almost approaching Dreen tenderness. Lutt called her "Ni-Ni" and said she was far different from the whores of his past experiences.

The nightmare continued for what seemed to Ryll an interminable time. Ni-Ni never spoke or showed her face. But Lutt's dream thoughts revealed her history. Ni-Ni had lost her family in a war on a planet other than Earth. She loved Lutt but he was forced to compete for her with another man. Dreamer-Lutt demanded the name of the other man, shouting:

"I will kill him!"

The other man appeared in the nightmare then, another faceless figure in the shadowy distance.

"You love him, too!" Lutt shouted. "I know you do!"

Dreamer-Lutt chased the faceless man but the man ran through fearful shadows and hid in impenetrable darkness.

Ryll felt the torment and frustration of the nightmare as though they were his own but could not find answers to the dream's questions.

Was Ni-Ni real? Was she dead? Was she someone Lutt would meet in his lifetime?

In the midst of this frustration, Ryll found himself dreaming simultaneously of Dreenor's school for gifted children. Proctor Shanlis ranted at Ryll's inattention to lessons.

"The tests say you're intelligent!" Shanlis screamed, menacing the youth with a flexible rod. "The tests say you will be able to idmage more than common Dreens. Why then can't you understand the simplest lesson?"

The dream Shanlis whipped the rod against Ryll's back, demanding: "Why? Why are you wasting my time and testing my patience? Why?"

Ryll felt the dream-whipping raise welts, saw yellow blood run down his brown skin. The pattern of the welts was that of the steel bedframe in his cell and blended with the bars on the door.

The nightmare came to an abrupt end with the clanging of a metal door somewhere in the distance.

Ryll awoke and, for a moment, could not remember where he was. He could still feel the stings of the whipping and the frustrations of the human nightmare.

Something was approaching his face. More nightmare? No . . . it was an insect. A fat spider dangled from its silken thread directly above him, descending slowly. Its legs were arched gracefully, extended like the stabilizers of a flying ship. Ryll saw it was preparing to land on his forehead, unaware of the eyes observing it. Rolling from beneath the arachnid, Ryll batted it toward the wall and saw there a cockroach. It waved its antennae at him.

Ryll swung his feet to the floor, looking at the Earther shape he had assumed, thinking: *A cell! They've confined me in a cell. I must escape! I've come from a classroom prison to this Earther cell and the prison of a merged body. What can I do?*

Lutt continued to dream. Ryll picked up fragments of the human's awareness, oddly parallel to Ryll's classroom dream. Lutt sat in a classroom and an Earther scolded him. The instructor was Lutt Senior. How tough and cold he looked. He wore strange devices over his eyes and offered money instead of grades. The dream father waved a five-hundred-thousand-dollar bill as his mouth shaped words that had no sounds. In the dream, Lutt Junior thought: *I can read your lips! I understand the language of your body.* But there was no interpretation in his thoughts.

Ryll turned his attention from the dream.

The swatted spider had recovered. It swung from the end of the bedframe, descending to the floor. Abruptly, it occurred to Ryll that he could shapeshift into the spider form and escape this confinement. He leaned close to the insect and formed a single cilia, which he inserted into the spider as it dangled on the end of its thread. The thing was remarkably simple and Ryll wondered why a great Storyteller had bothered to create it.

Giving little thought to the varieties of shapeshifting, Ryll assimilated spider essentials from its cells. Confidently, he swiveled his eyes inward and focused on the changes necessary to convert himself into an arachnid.

The change was comparatively easy but he came through it with the abrupt realization that he had done something perilously wrong. Not enough oxygen! He was dying of oxygen starvation! Too late, he remembered a Dreenschool lesson.

"With simple shapeshifting, you will have approximately the same mass in the new form as in your form before the change."

He was a gigantic spider! The gorcord tunic burst across the middle from the spider's fat body. Eight wiry legs ripped their way through the fabric. Shoes and socks fell to the floor and the useless eyeglasses dropped onto them.

The spider's primitive system of oxygen absorption would not support his mass!

Ryll felt consciousness fading.

His giant insect body plopped to the floor. The legs extended uselessly to the sides. Energy was fading fast.

Thoughts of escape dissipated. He had to focus on surviving this stupid mistake.

I may have energy for only one attempt to return to human form!

Desperately, he swiveled his eyes inward and concentrated on the Lutt shape he had so carelessly abandoned.

Is it working?

Slowly, he realized he lay stretched out on the floor, face down with nose pressed close to the odorous drain. His chest heaved and he realized he had returned to Earther shape.

The gorcord tunic lay in a tangled mess that required quick idmaging to restore before someone saw him in this disheveled state. He replaced the eyeglasses on his nose, put on shoes and socks and, presently, sank back to the hard pipes of the bunk, weak from exertion.

First things first: He forced himself to review the idmaging and shapeshifting lessons of the Dreenschool.

Basic idmaging: A Dreen's personal mass, reinforced by a lifetime of experience, dominates shapeshifting. Reducing mass to the size of an insect required long training and tremendous concentration taught in a graduate course he had not yet taken. Such a shift also left a residue of protoplasm that would degenerate unless conserved in one of several dangerous ways.

"You will learn mind over fear," a proctor had told him.

I wish I already had learned it.

Another bodily priority intruded on these reflections. Hunger gnawed at him. He had expended great stores of energy since the last time he had eaten aboard *Patricia*—an idmaged meal of Suprinian proteins. Now, his hunger would not let him think of anything except food.

What to eat? His Earther form and proximity to Earther society reminded him of a favorite confection. It would take energy to bring in the required mass, but . . .

Something bubbled out of the drain hole and he looked down at a drowned rat. Easily available mass! Ryll's eyes turned inward to a vision of an Earther delicacy common on Dreenor. The rat carcass vanished. In its place there appeared on the floor a strawberry ice cream sundae in a white plastic bowl. A plastic spoon stood upright in the ice cream.

Ryll did not waste time admiring the sundae. He rolled his eyes outward and sat cross-legged on the floor to eat.

The spoon, he noted, bore a familiar inscription: "McDonald's Restaurant," a tradition on Dreenor, a simple way to think praiseworthy thoughts about the Dreen who had created the Great Story out of which this confection arose.

Ryll reviewed praiseworthy thoughts as he savored every melting bite of the rich, creamy sundae.

Abruptly, he felt Lutt's awareness intrude, demanding a share in control of their body.

"Ice cream?" Lutt asked.

The vocal cords produced a gravelly voice.

Ryll noted this and corrected his voice-memory against the next time he wanted to use their mutual speaking system.

"Why are we eating a strawberry sundae?" Lutt demanded. "I hate strawberries."

Someone in the adjoining cell said: "Hey, this Hanson fella thinks he's eating strawberries."

Catcalls and laughter echoed up and down the corridor.

"Why can't he think he's eating a steak dinner?"

"Nawww, cherries jubilee!"

"He should think about sole amandine!"

"Chocolate cake!"

A commanding voice from the end of the corridor shouted: "All right, you guys! Break it up or you won't even get your evening gruel!"

Silence.

Ryll experienced resistance in his arm muscles as he lifted another spoonful of ice cream to his mouth. He reverted to think-sharing, though, having seen what speaking aloud produced along the corridor.

You're not eating this sundae, I am.

Tell that to our taste buds!

Strawberries are one of my favorite foods. And since I can idmage anything I wish to eat, provided I have energy to bring in conversion mass, I will eat this whenever I wish. I also enjoy rummungi, worsockels and bitter peeps. You've never tasted those foods because they come from faraway planets.

Your strawberries make me sick!

Indeed, on examining his internal reactions, Ryll found the strawberries were producing a protein incompatibility that would require correction in the Lutt parts of their body.

With a sigh, Ryll put the bowl on the floor, swiveled his eyes inward and de-idmaged the sundae as much as possible. When he looked at the area near the drain, shards of rat flesh lay on the floor.

No more strawberries, he thought-shared. *I do want to get us started on an amenable footing.*

What did you just do, Ryll?

We call it grine-idmaging or grining. Grine means . . . well, your closest word would be voiding.

A kind of erasure?

Don't use that word!

Why?

Erasure is . . . it's more difficult.

It felt like my eyes turned inward.

They did.

I don't like that feeling.

You'll get used to it.

You call it . . . idmaging?

That is the name for how we create living and inanimate objects by mass transfer from a reservoir of available matter. Sometimes we use mass nearby and sometimes from far away.

I don't believe any of this.

I see that in your thoughts.

This is schizo. I bumped my head somewhere on my ship.

Your ship is a wreck.

No, this is me being schizo because of an injury.

The condition of schizophrenia on planets where it can occur is a chemical imbalance. A bump on your head is not a likely causative factor.

Then I'm nuts in some other way.

You are not any more insane than others of your kind.

I'm supposed to believe there are two of us in my body?

My body, not yours. It looks like yours but you died on your ship. My body was badly injured and I required some of your protoplasm to survive. That is how we merged: Your awareness came with your cells.

So I'm sharing this body with an . . . an alien?

From my viewpoint, you might be considered the alien. It's a matter of perspective.

If this is real, then you're the alien, buddy. We're in Earth territory of the Zone Patrol. Earth, not this . . . this whatever-it-is where you're supposed to come from.

Dreenor. The entire universe, you see, is a product of Dreen idmaging. We like to think of it as a unit, rather than as separated pieces alien to one another.

You think you're some kind of god? Now I know I'm nuts.

If that's what you prefer. You will come to accept this, however. You must because we really share this body.

Some sharing! You're in control.

Then use our eyes and take a look around. We're in a Zone Patrol cell.

Ryll waited while Lutt obeyed. Their view shifted around the cell—barred door, walls, floor, ceiling . . .

Hallucination!

I think you'll accept it when they take us away for interrogation.

Sure! And I'll . . . Ugh! Is that pieces of a dead rat on the floor?

Left over from the mass required for the strawberry sundae.

This isn't happening. It's impossible.

You are persistent, Lutt. I will say that.

If this body looks like me then it's mine!

I merged our flesh and used your shape for security. The wreckage was crawling with Zone Patrol. You can imagine what they would have thought if they had seen me in the original.

Yeahhh? What do you look like?

A large Humpty Dumpty, to borrow an image from your nursery days.

So I've reverted to infancy. That's the kind of insanity I've—

Please stop this foolish refusal to recognize facts!

I'll decide what facts I recognize!

You remember the crash. I can see that in your mind. It was your fault. You attempted to enter a Spiral without—

Maybe that's it! I did enter a vorspiral and . . . and it made me crazy.

Spiral! They are Creative Spirals, to be precise. And since Dreen knowledge predates yours, kindly employ our terms.

What's the difference?

The Creative Spirals are sacred to us!

So my Vortraveler *got in your way?*

I had the right of way, Lutt! You should have seen the blue light indicating an approaching Excursion Ship. When you see that light you're supposed to stay out until the way is clear.

Let's say I accept this craziness. What were you doing in the . . . the Spiral?

I was looking for adventure.

Man, you sure found it! What made you think you'd find adventure on Earth?

The stories of my people told me all I need to know about Earth.

Not quite.

Perhaps. But I thought it might be interesting to see a human war. Dreens do not have wars. We are not violent.

Sounds dull.

I am forced to agree.

Would you like to beat up on somebody?

Oh, no! I couldn't. It isn't in the Dreen nature. I would not mind observing, however.

If you used my body to save your life, don't you feel any gratitude to me?

Gratitude is an emotion Dreens do not enjoy. Besides, you were certainly dying.

And your life isn't worth being grateful?

This is a foolish argument! Dreens don't ordinarily die, except as casualties from stupid accidents. We have no diseases, and that includes the disease you call "old age."

You just go around forever telling stories?

In a way, yes. We tell stories about places and life forms we have idmaged.

I still say this isn't happening. I'm nuts but it's interesting. I didn't know I could imagine such weird things.

Your imagination is but a paltry shadow compared to Dreen idmaging. My people are wondrous Storytellers.

And one of you Dreens created Earth?

Oh, yes. And Earth, like all other Dreen idmages, can self-destruct, decay or be destroyed by another Dreen creation. That's the way of idmaging. Things we idmage exist only as long as the original force remains in the one who created it or in someone who has fully assimilated the creative story.

If you all die out then the places you created die, too?

We say all creation depends on its creators.

And you say I'm not nuts? Here I am having a religious argument with myself and you say—

Not with yourself.

My ship crashed and I'm dead. This is some kind of wild cosmic joke.

I see I'm going to have to prove this to you. Very well.

Ryll felt the energy of the ice cream sundae coursing through his body. He swiveled his eyes inward and idmaged a redecoration of the cell. For energy practicality, he drew mostly on the ordure bubbling from the central drain. This immediately improved the aroma. An enclosed shower stall went over the drain, its pipes linked to the building's plumbing. He carpeted the floor in green plush, put a cheerful shade of yellow on walls and ceiling. A full-length mirror went up beside the barred door and he hung a few pastoral pictures.

Why don't you . . . grine the door out of existence? Lutt asked.

It's called grine idmaging and I must be very careful what effects I introduce into Earth culture. There is a specific injunction against what you suggest. It's incorporated in the original story.

All I felt was that funny twisting of my eyes. How do you do these things?

Idmaging occurs in a private portion of my thoughts not available to you.

How about idmaging a beautiful woman for me?

Really, Lutt, we must discuss the lustful nature you inherited from your father. Dreens think fornication is quite revolting. We don't touch each other.

Yeahhh? How do you reproduce?

Habiba gives us a childseed. We place it in a seedhouse. You may think of it as a small greenhouse. Then for three days and nights, the parents sit outside with the seedhouse between them. They use concentrated idmaging to produce precisely the child they have decided to bring into being.

So you don't get ugly ones or . . .

Dreen ideals have nothing to do with appearance. Desired traits are honesty, fidelity, a peaceful nature, pleasing personality, loyalty to Habiba, our Supreme Tax Collector . . . and characteristics of that sort.

Man, does that sound dull! And if a Dreen created Earth, he must have thought it dull, too.

It is slow, not dull. Each night, the seedhouse must be kept warm with a blanket cover and idmaged heat produced by the parents. When a Dreen baby evolves from the seed and embryo, it is brought forth—a new life.

The parents don't touch each other?

Nor do they speak during the entire three days. Their energy is conserved for the difficult idmaging process.

Yeahhh, well I gotta have a woman occasionally.

Perhaps we could compromise. If I forgo strawberries in any form would you consider not engaging in . . .

Why don't you just find a way to separate us and go back to your damned Dreenor?

I do wish I could.

What's it like, this Dreenor?

There are many ancestral family homes built of natural mud-brick, stones and hardened vegetation. Each home is occupied by the family's youngest married adults and the one child they are permitted to have.

One kid per family? Is that all? But wait a minute! If you only die in accidents, the population pressures must be fierce. How do you handle that? Idmage new Dreen planets?

Ryll found this a puzzling question and reflected on it before responding.

Actually, our family homes extend far under Dreenor's surface, the deeper levels occupied by family members in order of age—the eldest in the deepest level.

How deep do these homes go?

Habiba says the depths are endless.

There's gotta be a limit.

I've . . . I've never thought about that. Perhaps it should be a worry but we are taught that worry is a negative thought process and we naturally do not worry very often. Especially about unimportant things such as how deep our homes may go. That would interfere with our requirements for positive thoughts.

Every day in every way things are getting better and better, eh?

Now that I think of it, Habiba says we depend on the concept of "ampleness" wherein Dreenor is always large enough to accom-

modate all Dreens. Even though I am naturally rebellious and think forbidden things, I don't consider this worth my effort.

So you're a rebel, too.

Yes, but I must tell you the full beauty of Dreenor. Each family home has an adjacent air shaft. Dreens can control a helium gland permitting us to airfloat up and down these shafts.

We could float out of here?

Unfortunately, Dreens cannot do this anywhere except on Dreenor. Habiba says we have a mental and physical block that is coded into us at birth.

And everything you do is controlled by this tax collector?

We pay in stories. The surface occupants of each home are the taxpayers. They are required to tell one or more stories to a Bluecap who transmits them up the hierarchy to Habiba as her tribute.

Good stories, huh?

Habiba judges that. The best story receives a maximum of ten talents, the annual tax rate on a home tract. It is best to have backup stories available at tax time, however. Habiba rarely awards maximum talents to a story.

Humans also use stories instead of money to pay taxes.

It's not quite the same but the storytelling aptitude must be a natural part of your genetic coding because you are, after all, products of Dreen idmaging.

New stories every time?

Oh, no! Old stories are quite important, too. They are the Dreen heritage, because if any story dies out from not being shared, the physical aspects of that story—people, planets and other life forms—all vanish.

You know, this is weird, and it's all coming out of my mind.

Our mind.

Sure, sure!

Normally, taxpayers must tell two or three stories a year to meet the tax obligation. Taxpayers with a repertoire of superior stories capable of paying their assessment five years in succession with but one story per year are invited to join either the Junior Storytellers (for those under five hundred years of age) or the Senior Storytellers (for those five hundred years of age and older). Gifted Seniors join Habiba's personal entourage as Elite Storytellers.

This Habiba sounds like some powerhouse.

She is the eldest of us all and teaches the most. Other Elders come up from the deeper levels periodically to instruct the taxpaying surface residents in the art of storytelling. That's how we keep the old methods and sagas alive.

Anybody ever get dispossessed for nonpayment of taxes?

We hear about family holdings being placed in jeopardy but I don't believe a family has ever been expelled. Habiba can withhold childseed. Being childless places you in low esteem, a supreme punishment.

Ryll got up and went to the mirror.

It occurs to me, Lutt, an examination of our body proves this is true. You will notice our general appearance conforms to your rather unmuscular body but we are now stronger, have more mass and are some seven centimeters taller.

I'm going along with this hallucination because it's interesting but I don't have to believe it. Why not shift back into your own shape and show me that?

There is a scrambling problem when I shift back and forth between your form and mine. Please look into the mirror.

Lutt stared at his reflection.

So, okay, it's me and I'm larger.

Ryll did not respond. He found the mirrored body curious. Not a handsome man, according to standards available from stories and Lutt's memory. A softly blocky face, round eyeglasses . . . high forehead to a thin crop of red-brown hair. A serpentine raised blood vessel curled up the left temple. One eyebrow partly concealed a small black mole.

Ryll held his hands up to the mirror. A philosopher's hands with long, slender fingers almost pointed at the tips. But there was a distinct hint of roughness and cruelty to this man.

Ryll decided that could mean trouble if he gave up control of the body.

What're you looking for? Lutt asked.

I would have liked a better body but I had no choice.

What's the difference how you look? It's power makes the difference in this universe, buddy. If you got the clout, that's all you need.

A gross mistake in attitude, Lutt.

I won't argue it because events prove me right. But I kinda like the idea of being bigger. Too bad this is all a dream.

It's not a dream. And you'll like it even better that this body will continue to grow.

How come?

In terms of growth completion, I am roughly equivalent to a sixteen-year-old human—about forty Dreenyears. You can blame the growth on the accident—a release of hormones.

And you're in control of our body. How's that for a power trip?

To be civil, I will relinquish control occasionally, permitting you to behave as you ordinarily would. I want to observe Earther behavior.

But no women?

I saved your life, Lutt. Is that not enough?

Abruptly, metal clanged far down the corridor and there was the sound of clumping footsteps approaching.

Oopsah! Ryll thought. *They mustn't see this.*

He swiveled his eyes inward and restored the jail cell's Spartan appearance, then stretched out on the bare bunk. He pulled the blanket to his chin and stared at the barred door through slitted eyelids.

A female guard appeared beyond the bars—muscular body and a heavy face.

"Just making sure you're comfortable, honey," she said. "I hear you like strawberries. Too bad we can't bring you some on your evening gruel."

She noted the mattress leaning against the wall.

"Tough guy, eh? Sleeping on the bare pipes."

"Too many other occupants of that mattress," Ryll growled in a reasonable copy of Lutt's voice.

"Maybe I should come in and make you comfortable." She laughed, a grating sound deep in her throat, and turned away. There was the sound of her clumping footsteps receding.

Lutt tried to sit up but Ryll resisted, preventing all except faint jerks and twitches. Ryll provided a lecturing thought.

You must understand that I can control this body whenever I wish. I know every thought you have but you cannot share my thoughts without my permission.

I'm getting tired of this dream.

Then we will go to sleep.

Perchance to dream of a beautiful woman and I can . . .

We will merely rest on this rack, Dreen fashion.

This isn't Dreenor, asshole! You wanta learn Earth's ways? You're imposing on me. I'm uncomfortable.

Just to be nice, I agree that you may use the mattress for a while.

Lutt, beginning to doubt his belief that this was all some kind of nightmare, tried to suppress bitterness. If Ryll could read every thought, best to keep him happy.

Ryll relaxed and permitted Lutt to reassemble the bunk. When they returned to it, they argued about which way to rest—face down or on the back. They compromised by facing the wall, a position neither of them wanted as first choice.

Lutt tried controlling their voice, just a whisper at first.

"Let's say I believe this crazy story," he said. "So you're just a Dreen kid. How come they let you take a ship?"

"I . . . ahhh, fed a drug to the monitor and took the ship without adult permission."

"Dreens use drugs?"

"There is one—it's called bazeel. The monitor was an addict."

"Crazy, crazy. And all for a little joyride."

"I suspect the best part is yet to come."

As he spoke, Ryll realized his boyish zeal had returned.

Up is only up when you have a down.

—Sayings of the Raj Dood

The temperature along Florida's mangrove coast had plummeted to six degrees Centigrade during the night and Dudley bundled himself in a red woolen blanket to watch Osceola at their morning fire. With his bare shanks sticking out beneath the blanket, he looked like a strange bird—long-faced, a fuzz of straggly blond hair tumbling around his head.

He could not understand why Osceola insisted on this primitive way of cooking. Something to do with her Seminole ancestry, probably. He saw no other reason. She could afford the most modern kitchen in the solar system and the profit charts from her Spirit Glass industry would not even show a *blip* at the cost.

Dudley glanced around him at jungle growth, Osceola's old shack they called home on Earth, the rickety pier extending out into the tidal estuary. This place *did* guarantee the privacy they both prized so much.

By any contemporary standards, Osceola was an ugly old woman, but she suited Dudley. Sometimes, though, he wished she would not dress so garishly. This morning she wore a magenta muu muu adorned with pale green and bright yellow tie-died splotches. Her long dark hair was braided and held at the forehead by a purple bandanna.

Gold bangles jingled at her wrists as she prepared a turtle-egg omelette. One of the neighboring Seminoles, all of whom feared and revered Osceola, had left the eggs the night before, departing without being seen . . . at least by Dudley. Osceola always knew when her neighbors left propitiatory offerings.

She put a pan in the orange coals to heat the oil and spoke without turning.

"That dang nephew of yours got hisself in deep shit this time. I told you this was gonna happen."

"I wish you'd stop spying on him, Osey."

"I don't do nothin' you don't do."

"But I *have* to know what he's doing."

"Well, I told you to put a stop to it when he started messin' with the Spirals."

"I didn't stop you learnin' about 'em, did I?"

"I'd like to've seen you try." She poured eggs into the sizzling oil.

"I don't think I could've stopped him once he stumbled onto the secret."

"Stumbled, my ass! You been proddin' him the same way you did me. And don't think I'm so dumb I can't figure why. You won't quit till you make that kid's father cry uncle!"

Dudley chuckled. "You've raised old L. H.'s blood pressure yourself a few times, Osey."

She gave the pan an expert flip and put it on gray coals at one side. "You want pan bread or grits with this?"

"Why can't I have both?"

"'Cause you're gettin' fat in the body to match your head. Lutt's wise to you, you know? It's those crazy names you give people you send to help him. Sam R. Kand! Crissakes, Dood, he'd have to be a pureblind idiot not to know something funny was goin' on. Well, which is it, grits or pan bread?"

"Pan bread."

She spooned eggs onto a warmed plate, placed a thick slice of golden pan bread beside the eggs and put the plate on the ground in front of him.

Dudley squatted and began eating. One thing about waiting while Osceola built a fire and made breakfast, he thought. It sure got the juices running.

Osceola stood over him, hands on her hips.

"Lutt coulda got hisself killed there, Dood."

"You wouldn't've missed him."

"Your own flesh and blood! Sometimes I wonder. You takin' it out on the kid 'cause you hate the father?"

Dudley spoke around a mouthful of omelette. "Don't hate him, Osey. Tried to save him from himself once. Failed. Now, maybe I can save his boy."

"Lutt's no boy! He's a mean son-of-a-bitch and don't you ever forget it."

"But not sneaky like his brother. Lutt has a few good qualities."

"Name one."

"He's capable of loving a woman."

"Like all them whores he uses?"

Dudley wiped up the last of the omelette with a corner of bread and ate it before answering. "That's because of his father, Osey. L.H. dirties most things he touches. My sister never should've married him."

"You were just as big a fool going partners with him!"

"That was a mistake. I admit it. But I was young then."

"And just as soft in the head as you are now. I swear, Dood, all those Hansons are a bad lot. Best you forget 'em."

"But you said it yourself, Osey. Lutt's my blood kin."

She turned away from him, prepared a plate for herself and squatted beside the fire to eat. Presently, she asked: "When you goin' back to Venus?"

"When enough of them need me up there."

"Need! You're a meddlin' old fool, Dood. Don't see why I put up with you."

"Because you don't like being bored, Osey."

Her teeth flashed a wide grin. "That's the truth, and no mistake. But we gotta be careful with those Dreens, you hear?"

"I hear."

"That Habiba could be more trouble than a pen full of wildcats, Dood. She may seem peaceful but I got a bad feelin' about that one."

"Osey! You haven't been risking a look in on Dreenor without my knowing, have you?"

"I'm stayin' clean away from Dreens, but now we got a new one loose in our own backyard, so to speak. And I tell you true, I'm worried."

"He's just a kid, Osey."

"But he's mixed up with your nephew! Dood, that could be real trouble. Might lead him straight to you!"

"We'll watch it, Osey. We'll watch it."

"That Dreen could make things hot enough around here even inceram suits from your precious Venus couldn't save us."

"I told you I'd watch it!"

"Like you did when you let old L.H. steal some of your best inventions?"

"He didn't get the really important stuff, Osey."

"Enough to make him the richest man in our universe!"

"Some things you can't buy, Osey. Just remember that."

"I hope you're right. Here, take my plate. It's your turn to clean up."

In the ceremony of the Seedhouse, a Dreen's need for dominant mass is made basic to his nature and this is reinforced whenever he uses his idmage powers. Shape-shifting into reduced mass is seen by a Dreen's subconscious as a threat to his existence. But whether he shapeshifts smaller or larger, he must return quickly to his body's remembered mass. The longer he remains offsize the more difficult it is to resume Dreen normalcy.

—"The Dreen Subconscious,"
a Zone Patrol report

On the trillion and eighty-first cycle of Habiba's reign, afternoon of the second day in the Dreenor week (varying from seven to seventeen days depending on the season), Habiba made a mental note that this was officially New Story Day.

Sunlight, tinted green by the visuplex of her witch's-cap cupola atop the Supreme Cone, felt warm to her but did not ease the chill in her seedglands. Her towering cone, riding on a floating island at the center of an ancient sea, put her high above the walls of an extinct volcano. From this vantage, Habiba now exercised her secret and exclusive power to see to the limits of Dreenor's horizon and deep into the sea. To the west across the distant Flats, she identified Mugly the Elder's yellow cap and the green smocks of his aides. They stood beside a low building.

A shallow dent in the soil nearby revealed where the stolen Excursion Ship had been.

It's gone, Habiba thought. *It's really gone! Jongleur was right to bring me the full story before Mugly comes ranting in here.*

Habiba wore no garment, permitting the taxables who might chance upon her to be reassured by sight of the great brown-skinned mother-body in its cupola greenhouse. The green silk of her hair, sprouting like a wild garden atop her mounded head, lay draped over her ears in a calculated tangle. Her large horn snout stood out prominently between her bulbous brown eyes. Her mouth, its dendritic pulpers withdrawn, formed a shocked oval.

Is this how it must end? she asked herself.

Far down below her pinnacle, visible in a sweeping panorama from the top of the Control Cone, ancestral homes of her people lay like scattered childhood toys—mud-colored copies of her dominant abode.

She thought them rather pitiful in their immobility.

A swirl of pumice dust drifted around the cone but did not settle on the sea that filled the extinct volcano below her. The clear water of the sea glistened with reflected sunlight.

Mugly the Elder and aides could not see her in the distant cone but they stirred and glanced toward her, then looked away.

Mugly will think I incited the child to steal the ship, Habiba thought. *He will not come right out and accuse me but he will think of it. Poor Mugly. He believes his plans to erase Earth are such a secret.*

Despite the great distance, she identified his seven companions by their distinctive movements. Two of them attracted her special attention.

Deni-Ra and Prosik are in for a hard time. I will have to make some reassuring gesture in their tax assessments. Mugly goes too far sometimes.

Mugly glared across the Flat in the direction of the eroded volcano. The shiny green surface of Habiba's cone poked above the rim. He turned back to look at Deni-Ra, a young adult female of low parentage. Short and plump with deep creases beneath her eyes, Deni-Ra displayed only limited Storyteller signs. She crouched on all four legs while holding an ear flap open with an extruded hand, the better to hear Mugly's words.

"You're sure the ship was operational?" he demanded.

"With a Storyteller captain such as yourself at the controls, *Patricia* was fully operational," Deni-Ra said.

"I intended to be that captain," Mugly growled.

He twisted his floppy yellow cap, badge of his membership in the Elite Storytellers, to a firmer position on his head. The tiny silver pin on the cap, symbol of his rank as third in command behind Habiba and Jongleur, jabbed into a finger and he suppressed a cry of outrage.

"Which of you was on duty when my ship was stolen?" Mugly demanded. He swept his glowering gaze across the seven Dreens who stood in a semicircle around him.

Six sets of eyes twitched in the direction of Prosik, a tall, thick-eared Dreen, but Mugly pretended not to notice.

So it was that stupid Prosik!

Mugly fixed his gaze on Luhan, youngest of the group and second-brightest of the seven behind Deni-Ra despite a deformed but still extrudable right arm.

Or perhaps he is bright to compensate for the deformity.

Luhan remained calm. So Luhan was not connected with this disaster.

Mugly shifted attention to Alade, so neatly turned out in forest green, the big pockets of his smock empty as usual and pressed flat to show the sleek lines of his ideal Dreen form. A conformist who followed orders with lackluster consistency, always taking into account a way to avoid blame, Alade would be sure to have an impenetrable excuse for his part in this affair. He displayed a certain tension, though.

Ah, yes. Alade was one who recommended Prosik.

Mugly turned and stared directly at Prosik.

Barely awake and leaning his weight on his two left feet, Prosik fought to stay alert. His eyelids fluttered.

Bazeel hangover! And Prosik doubtless is one of those who calls me "Mugly the Characterless."

Mugly waited, letting tensions build. The aides stared at him nervously. Mugly did not deceive himself about what they saw. There were few creases, supposedly marks of storytelling ability, in his light brown face.

I'm a great Storyteller despite my lack of character lines!

No false pride inflated Mugly's recognition that he could captivate large audiences with charm and wit.

I'm every bit as good as Jongleur!

But these aides were more immediately familiar with his dark side: Mugly's fiery temper and ability to deceive. He was a person deeply frustrated by Dreens who promoted the much-touted peaceful nature of their kind.

"Prosik!" Mugly barked. "Look at you! Is this any way for my chief monitor to appear? What's the matter with you?"

Prosik's eyes became bird-alert, then dull.

"Speak up, Prosik!"

"I ahhh . . . I'm . . ."

"Bazeel, isn't it?"

Prosik lowered his gaze. Confession enough. But the chief monitor outraged Mugly even more by what he said next.

"I have already told the full story to Jongleur."

He dared go over my head! He has a sneaky intelligence.

"What did you tell Jongleur?"

Prosik stared along the bridge of his horn-tool nose at the ground. "Ryll, Jongleur's son, has been raising bazeel and providing it for me. The boy obviously did it to incapacitate me and permit him to steal the ship."

"You see?" Mugly swept his gaze across the other aides. "You, who share our secret that Earthers capture and imprison Dreens, must now have no doubts about the peril from that deadly planet!"

They knew what he meant. Bazeel, a terrible substance with no antidote, the only drug known to alter Dreen behavior, had originated on Earth. More and more insidious things were appearing from that place once considered the product of a Great Story—Wemply the Voyager's supreme creation.

But the bazeel!

Earthers, totally unaffected by it, spiced their food with bazeel. Despite severe warnings, Dreens persisted in bringing back large quantities of bazeel from Earth. Clandestine bazeel gardens had been found even on Dreenor.

"I want the full story," Mugly said.

They listened quietly while Prosik recounted his sorry tale. Prosik spoke loudly so Mugly would not be forced to lift an earflap, a thing certain to increase the Elder's irritation.

"You frequently let him board *Patricia?*"

"He was a gifted student and Jongleur's son. I thought he was just playing. He said his classes bored him."

"A gifted student, indeed! He undoubtedly figured out the controls in short order."

"He gave me his solemn promise he wouldn't touch the controls without an adult there to guide him."

"A solemn promise! I'm sure that makes this whole affair acceptable."

"I assumed the son of Jongleur would act with honor."

"Honor? From the family of Jongleur? But is he not one of those who oppose erasure of Earth?"

"Habiba herself opposes it," Prosik ventured.

"But I do not! Tell me, Prosik, to whom do you owe your Eminence? You owe it to me! Did you not consider the possibility that Ryll might be his father's agent sent to sabotage me?"

Prosik shifted from left feet to right feet and back. "But how could they have known the ship's purpose?"

"Bazeel addled your brain!" Mugly accused. "They chose the perfect attack time—when the ship was ready to go."

"It is rumored that Ryll does not get along with his father," Deni-Ra said. "The boy is known to have objected to the school for gifted children."

"Are you suggesting this was a schoolboy's lark?"

"It must be considered," she said.

She's right but that doesn't help matters. Damn them! My ship could go nowhere but Earth. Erasure is another matter. I am the only one who knows the full sequence. I should have made the erasure automatic. Why didn't I plan for this contingency?

Mugly was forced to be honest with himself.

I wanted personal credit for eliminating this terrible danger, that's why! By the blasted-off hind foot of an untaxable demon! My ego got in my way.

"It's going to rain," Luhan said.

Mugly looked up at the suddenly cloudy sky. *This would be the afternoon we ordered rain!*

"We should go inside," Deni-Ra said. She looked pointedly in the direction of the Supreme Cone, reflecting Mugly's suspicion that Habiba could watch them wherever they were.

Mugly agreed and, once in the guard station, took the only stool to sit and think while the others stood in obedient silence.

What now? Other than secrecy, what resources do I have?

Mugly believed he concealed his thoughts during the Supreme Tax Collector's weekly Thoughtcons. It was then that Habiba absorbed stories from people Mugly invited to her Sharing. Mugly's aides certainly suspected his ability but knew better than to inquire. He had stumbled onto the method: idmaged disconnection of those neurons carrying conspiratorial memories—a piecemeal alteration Dreens considered impossible. It was timed to last a day and left him feeling hazy, wishing Dreens had doctors.

Mugly knew his concealment technique was dangerous.

Do I create a different self by my disconnections?

She gives no sign she suspects me.

Habiba was always more interested in stories of lesser Dreens—the brightest Junior Storytellers, government tax collectors and the like. She displayed obvious fascination in these stories that were the currency of Dreenor. And along with stories went every other morsel of data in the minds of the ones Mugly invited to a Thoughtcon.

She thinks she knows everything and that's supposed to keep us honest. But the good of our universe requires me to carry out my conspiracy.

Mugly did not know if he were the only Dreen capable of hiding his thoughts and he dared not discuss it with anyone, not even with those who served him.

If two people know a thing, it is no longer a secret.

That was one valuable concept acquired from Earth.

I do this for the love of Habiba, he told himself.

He loved Habiba, as did all Dreens, but disagreed fiercely with her claim that nonviolence was intrinsic to Dreen nature.

Mugly saw something he called "the larger picture." In it lay a total catastrophe destroying all Dreens. Dreenor might be a planet of tranquillity and restoration for weary Storytellers home from their creative travels but that universe out there contained wild pockets of supreme peril.

I care not for other matters but Earth must be destroyed!

This belief he buried in his deepest thoughts, ready for disconnection at the slightest sign of prying. Except on Thoughtcon days, Mugly considered this several times each day.

As long as I control invitations to Thoughtcons, Habiba will continue to believe I have only pure thoughts, and my plea for erasure of Earth is no more than an intellectual thing without plans to carry it out. And I will never permit her to share with those who serve me.

Still, Mugly worried. If only he had been able to design and idmage *Patricia* by himself! The size and complexity of the task had forced him to enlist these aides, all of them young and possessed of comparatively low storytelling skills. They were, however, energetic idmagers when he guided them. Most vital, they agreed with him that the destruction of Earth was for the good of Dreen posterity.

But only I know all eight parts to the puzzle of Patricia.

And *Patricia* was needed because the long-ago Storyteller who had idmaged Earth had set in motion a vehicle of destruction.

Strange that Wemply the Voyager's idmage of Earth has created such a cult of imitations. Why is it so popular! The death and destruction are easy to see. Earthers are sick with a fascination for weapons and attacks on other life forms. I'm sure they would attack even us if they learned about us.

Mugly sighed. What could he suggest to his aides?

"Perhaps Ryll hoped to be a hero," Deni-Ra said. "Is it possible he learned of *Patricia*'s purpose? He might have thought he would save our universe and return triumphant."

"There's no way he could have learned," Prosik said.

"Yes," Mugly agreed. "He most likely would not have gone if he had discovered the secret, because that also would have told him the operator of the ship is likely to die in the erasure."

"Not to mention the deaths of the Dreen prisoners the Earther Zone Patrol is holding," Luhan said.

"Is there some way this could be turned to our political advantage?" Prosik asked. "Could Habiba be made to suspect Jongleur sent his son to steal your ship?"

Mugly looked at Prosik with new interest. Despite the bazeel addiction, Prosik showed sparks of real intelligence.

"Thoughtcons will tell her Jongleur had no part in it," Deni-Ra said.

Yes, always the Thoughtcons to complicate conspiracy.

"Let me go after Ryll and activate the erasure ship," Prosik said. "Give me the chance to redeem myself."

Mugly listened to the rain on the guard station roof for a moment, thinking, *What if Jongleur, too, can hide his thoughts?*

"You will be tempted by bazeel on Earth," Mugly said.

"I swear I will not touch it! Believe me."

"I thought of following him myself," Mugly said. "But I hold knowledge valuable to the Earthers and if I were captured . . ."

"And we need you at the Thoughtcons," Deni-Ra said.

"Prosik," Mugly said, "how do we know we can trust you?"

"I will dedicate myself."

Again, Mugly listened to the rain on the roof. The tempo was subsiding. He studied the penitent expression of Prosik's face. Yes, Prosik was most easily spared.

"Very well. I will share the secrets of activating *Patricia* and you will go. Take my personal Excursion Ship, the *Kalak-III*. But flee rather than be captured!"

"What will you tell Habiba?" Luhan asked.

Trust Luhan to ask the most worrisome question!

"I will tell her a truth—that my aides took it on themselves to prepare a ship in case Habiba agreed to erase Earth. But now, Jongleur's son, Ryll, has stolen the ship and that may be disastrous."

Dreens appear capable of creating only viral and bacterial life forms as an aspect of what they call "idmaging." This creativity and allied shapeshifting powers impose their own rules. Idmaged life forms follow laws of evolution inherent to themselves and their environments. Dreens display ignorance about many aspects of their creations and say such understanding does not submit to rational analysis.

—"Dreen Mysteries,"
a Zone Patrol report

After the morning gruel, two Zone Patrol guards in brown and blue uniforms with gold braid of Command Echelon escorted Lutt down the drab cellblock corridor and up an elevator to the next level.

Lutt felt clear-headed and in control of himself after a restful sleep disturbed by a brief nightmare most of whose details vanished on awakening: something about redecorating his cell and then removing the changes.

No more hallucinations, he told himself.

The elevator opened into a round room with smoky gray glass wall panels that changed shape as he focused on them.

Spirit Glass!

The glass, an Osceola Industries monopoly, had been demonstrated to him once in a Hanson laboratory where his father's researchers failed to penetrate their secret.

"Dangerous stuff," a technician had warned. "It can twist your mind out of shape."

A familiar whisper interrupted his nervous examination of the glass-walled room.

"Major Captain will be with you presently."

That's interesting, Ryll intruded.

Lutt came to a stop between his two guards, his body trembling without control. That voice in his head again! But it was not like the familiar whisper that came to him almost as though originating within his left ear.

Who was that whispering? Ryll asked.

It was you, wasn't it?

I'm glad you finally accept my presence but I assure you it was not I who whispered.

I don't accept you or anything like you!

It felt almost as though it came through the Spirals, Ryll offered.

Shut up! Get outa my head!

Slowly, Lutt brought the trembling under control. The two guards were amused by his obvious fear, he saw. If they only knew the cause!

The whisper was a disconnected piece of a lifetime puzzle floating in Lutt's awareness. The pieces knocked against one another without proper alignment.

Major Captain. Another crazy name!

People with bizarre names often came associated with that eerie whisper. There had been Tundra Farmer, a stocky playmate of his childhood. Tunny, as most called him, always appeared when Lutt was about to be defeated in a schoolyard fight. The strange child threw such a barrage of blows that after a time his mere appearance sent attackers fleeing.

Other oddly named people aided Lutt in adolescence and young adulthood: Pipple Iter got him through college math, and Waxy Gourd convinced him to concentrate on aerospace design, solar communication and study of the flame-drenched planet Venus.

Most recently, Samuel Robert Kand, an aerospace engineer, had presented himself to Lutt and been placed in charge of the *Vortraveler* shop.

Even "vorspiral" had come to him via that disembodied whisper, a label accompanied by such a spate of technical data Lutt had dashed to the nearest recorder to preserve it for later examination.

When he had said "vorspiral" once in his mother's presence, she surprised him by saying, "I've heard your Uncle Dudley say that. What does it mean?"

They had been home after one of her interminable afternoon teas and Lutt, bored by compulsory attendance, had been galvanized. "Uncle Dudley? Where and how did he mention vorspirals? When?"

"Now, dear, I don't remember. But it is a curious word. Does it mean anything?"

"I'm not sure. Where's Uncle Dudley? I have to talk to him."

"You know he and your father had a falling out, dear. And you mustn't upset your father."

"But where's Uncle Dudley?"

"Everyone says he's on Venus, as I'm sure you've heard. I don't know why, what with all the violence there. It's best we forget my poor brother, dear. He always was a bit strange."

And that was all she would say about Uncle Dudley.

Sam R. Kand's appearance to work on the *Vortraveler* had not really surprised Lutt but he still wondered if Uncle Dudley were behind this mystery, especially when the best investigators Lutt hired could not find a trace of the man.

Was Major Captain another oddly named "helper"? Faced with Spirit Glass windows, Lutt suspected he would need all the help he could get.

One of them thrusting each shoulder, the ZP guards pushed him toward the center of the room. "Find your way to the circle at the center," one of them growled.

Lutt stumbled away from the guards and heard a sliding sound behind him. He turned and was in time to see a Spirit Glass panel close off the elevator. His last view of the two guards was of them grinning at him.

What circle at the center? Lutt wondered.

He turned away from the panel concealing the elevator and saw a spiral pattern spinning on the floor at the center of the room. It had not been there before. They were projecting it from somewhere but he could not determine the source.

Spiral . . . another spiral.

Lutt looked at the Spirit Glass on the far wall and, for an instant, thought he saw the remembered features of Uncle Dudley in the smoky depths. The image disappeared and reshaped into an older Uncle Dudley seated on a rickety pier. Uncle Dudley was watching a woman with a cane pole fish from the end of the pier. The woman turned and Lutt recognized Osceola looking much as she had in the most recent media picture on the five o'clock news.

The pier, Uncle Dudley and Osceola dissolved into gray mists.

Nightmare! The Spirit Glass was taking over his mind!

But Spirit Glass windows were an exclusive product of Osceola Industries. Why couldn't the glass show her?

Lutt shook his head. Osceola—another barrier to his father's dreams of empire. Beth Osceola, a seventy-two-year-old half Seminole, ran her company with no regard for L.H.'s dreams. She refused to sell Osceola Industries to his father and would not even return a vidcom call.

"The Old Bag," Hanson Senior called her, but Lutt secretly admired her independence.

A sibilant voice with no apparent source abruptly hissed at him: "Stand on the circle at the center!"

With a helpless feeling of compulsion, Lutt stepped forward onto the spinning spiral. The Spirit Glass in front of him whirled with dancing lights.

They're going to fry my brain!

Where was Major Captain? Where was any helper now that he needed one?

He closed his eyes but memory of the Spirit Glass filled his awareness. What could he do? The glass could be shattered by a blow but behaved more like liquid than any solid substance. He opened his eyes and tried to count the windows around the room. They undulated sickeningly.

Thirty-five windows. That's my age.

He counted them once more and came up with sixteen.

That's my age, Ryll intruded. *Stop counting them.*

You don't exist so stop telling me what to do!

This was much more than interrogation, Lutt realized. And it was very dangerous to his sanity.

Of course it's dangerous to our sanity! Ryll offered.

Voices in my head, hallucinations!

Lutt felt perspiration on his brow. He rubbed a moist palm across his mouth and smelled machine oil.

Machine oil? That's the smell in my Vortraveler. *Where is my ship? What happened to Drich Baker?*

Baker's dead. I told you that. You'd be dead, too, if I hadn't saved us. Now let me help you or that Spirit Glass will get us both.

I don't believe in you!

Stop that! I leave you in control of our body for a few minutes and you fall into this crazy delusion.

You're the delusion!

You listen to me, Lutt. For the sake of appearances I'm letting you take charge but I can stop that anytime I want.

So stop it! Stop messing up my mind!

Use some intelligence, Lutt. These Zone Patrol people are suspicious. If I made some nonhuman slip, they'd notice. Do you want to spend the rest of your life in a cell?

Then if you're real, why don't you go to sleep and let me handle this?

I need to learn about you, Lutt. And we Dreens don't need much sleep, so don't think you can wait until I doze off. Dreens lead very active lives.

Lutt removed his glasses, found a handkerchief and wiped perspiration from the lenses. In the search for a handkerchief, he determined that his other personal effects—keys, watch, slips of mini-note, a small pen—were gone.

Removed by the Zone Patrol?

They took everything from our pockets, Ryll offered.

That voice in his head again.

But why was the ZP interrogating him?

Even in voiceless mental communication, Ryll's next offering was patronizing: *It's because of the crash. You know that. But have you noticed how well you see without glasses?*

Lutt looked at the glasses in his hand, at the room, at the handkerchief. Shocked, he realized he was seeing clearly without glasses.

You are seeing well because these are not your eyes, Lutt. They're my eyes. I idmaged only plain glass in your lenses. Good idmaging, eh? A technique I learned in school and am delighted to see I can perform. Does this convince you?

Lutt replaced the glasses on his nose.

I must fix my mind on one thing to keep my sanity.

To keep your delusion, you mean!

He ignored this and watched a pane of Spirit Glass change from square to round, then to oval and rectangular.

Psychiatrists and police were said to be the principal customers for Spirit Glass. Investigators said prolonged exposure to the constantly changing shapes turned a subject's brain to mush, causing him to reveal his darkest secrets. Interrogators wore special glasses to protect them from this dangerous effect.

A loud click startled Lutt, causing him to retreat from the central spiral. He looked in the direction of the sound and saw a brown dome emerging from the floor nearby. A hum of motors and noise of gears accompanied the appearance of this object. The odor of machine oil was pronounced.

A female voice filled the room.

"Stay within the circle!"

It's some kind of freaking vorspiral, Lutt thought.

Spiral! Just Spiral. It is a Dreen label.

Dreen, schmeen!

But something forced Lutt onto the spiral.

Where is my helper? he wondered.

With an increasingly loud hum, the dome came through the floor. Tiles folded into place around it. The room fell silent.

Lutt saw a jagged dent in the dome, surely a sign of damage. A flaw in the adversary?

Adversary? This is my nation's Zone Patrol!

"By what right are you holding me?" he demanded.

Something in the dome gave off a dull "clunk." He heard a low voice say, "Oh, shit!" then another dull "clunk."

Slowly, the dome opened, a metal flower spreading eight curved petals onto the floor around it. In the center, at a shiny silver desk, sat a fair-skinned female officer in the dark brown of Zone Patrol Special Forces. Blue-black hair wisped from under her gold-trimmed officer's cap. Her collar displayed golden ovals with caduceus symbols. She appeared preoccupied with turning a large wheel beside her.

Medical officer of some kind, Lutt thought, but he had no military experience to tell him her rank or specialty. She wore dark glasses that glittered when she aimed them at him.

Abruptly, she released her hold on the wheel and laughed, a menacing sound that sent a chill up Lutt's back. She slammed a fist against the wheel and it vanished into the desk.

"Why do you need that wheel?" Lutt ventured. "I thought the military was fully automated."

"Shut up, you! I'll ask the questions here!"

No gentle lady, this one!

She adjusted her dark glasses on her nose. "I am Major Paula Captain." Crisp, authoritarian voice.

She did not sound like one of his periodic helpers. Father always said to attack when in doubt. Lutt took a deep breath. "Have you been a major long enough to get over being called Captain Captain?"

"Your lame levity is not amusing, Mr. Hanson."

"Then maybe I should publish a series on how the military gold-plates everything to make jobs for officers. Would that amuse you?"

"Are you threatening me?"

"Oh, no, Major Captain, ma'am."

"I've heard every play on my name your lame brain could imagine and I do not bow to threats. Is that clear?"

"As clear as Spirit Glass, Captain . . . I mean, Major."

She glanced at something on her desk. "You've been brought before me on an extremely serious charge."

"Trespassing," Lutt said.

She leaned toward him. "We could've blasted you out of space without warning! Do you understand that?"

Lutt stared past her at a pulsing panel of Spirit Glass.

Lutt! Stop looking at that glass. That's what she wants.

The voice in his head! Real or not, a good warning. He shifted attention to Major Captain and imagined her naked. That sometimes put officious types in proper perspective. Firm chin, largish nose, small breasts. The desk hid her legs.

The room's light shifted suddenly and the Spirit Glass became mirrors. The glass reflected several aspects of Major Captain. All of them wavered and elongated, then shortened.

"Your guards told me to stand in a circle, but this is a spiral under me," Lutt said. "I know something about spirals."

"Perhaps you didn't locate the correct place to stand," she said. No hint of a smile.

She wants you to look around. Don't do it.

Again, good advice from the voice in his head. Lutt formed what he hoped was a sarcastic smile.

Something under her desk went "clickety-clickety . . ." She struck the desk with a fist and the sound stopped.

Lutt concentrated on the Spirit Glass behind the major. Gray silhouettes there began to dance suggestively.

The glass responds to your lustful mind! Don't do that.

He imagined rabbit ears and they attached themselves to her reflection.

Lutt chuckled. *I'll have her nibbled to death by rabbits!*

Two rabbits appeared in the reflections and began eating the major's images. The illusion vanished with an audible burp.

"Have you ever heard of Dreens?" she asked.

Urgency gave Ryll command of their voice. "Screens? What kind of screens?"

"I said Dreens!"

"What the hell are Dreens?" He inched backwards.

"Stay in the circle!" she barked.

"I understand." Ryll spoke with tenuous voice control. "Black is white and brains are pudding to be stirred and eaten."

She leaned forward, an elbow on her desk, and supported her chin on one hand. Her expression did not change.

Ryll felt a growing panic from Lutt.

All right! Take over but be cautious. This one could throw us into prison forever.

Hesitantly, Lutt resumed control. He blinked, stalling to get his thoughts in order, and glanced around, trying once more to count the panels.

Stop counting. You'll get a different number each time.

"Perhaps you've overlooked something," she said.

"This room is supposed to seem like a whole level of the building but it's too small," Lutt said. "Any idiot can see that. Even you. It's just tricks, illusions. I stopped being impressed by carnival games when I was ten."

She laughed and once more it carried a mean tone.

"I freely admit there are other rooms on this level. Do you know which panels are actually doors into those rooms?"

Look at her, not at the Spirit Glass!

Lutt stared at her and realized he was looking at a reflection. He swept his gaze around and focused on what he thought was Major Captain seated at her desk.

"I know about Spirit Glass!" he said. "It's supposed to turn my brain into pulp for an inquisitor like you."

"Considering who your father is, I don't doubt you've seen such glass," she said. "But you're not with your father now."

"He'll be madder than a wet adder when he learns about this!"

"Come now! Why don't you look at me!"

Lutt realized he had been looking at another reflection. He turned and saw the desk with Major Captain behind it. She smiled, cold and frightening.

"Be a good boy and help me get through this."

The way she said "good boy" sounded vaguely like his mother. This Major Captain was an irritating bitch!

He saw a female dog in a reflection. It was suckling a puppy but turned on the puppy and ate it. Lutt felt like vomiting.

"Lutt Hanson *Junior*," she said. "I'm told you're a good newspaperman but you've never heard of Dreens."

"That's doubletalk! You're just trying to confuse me."

"Are you a good newspaperman?"

"Hell! I own a newspaper."

"No. Daddy owns it. He gave it to you as a plaything."

All of the major's reflections began chanting in Lutt's mind:

"Daddy owns it . . . Daddy owns it . . . Daddy owns it . . ."

You're hallucinating! Stop it!

Lutt felt his face flush hot.

"Where's my ship?" he demanded. "You'd better release me and return my ship."

"You've been conducting illegal research on space travel."

"Who says it's illegal? Show me the law!"

She propped her display screen into a new position, studied it a moment, then smiled sweetly at Lutt.

"Spiral communications, yes. And now you want to take this development into space."

"Who told you? Where did you—"

"I ask the questions; you answer."

"This is no way to negotiate with me for the use of what I've discovered! Is that what you're doing?"

"What have you discovered?"

"None of your damn business!"

"Oh? Well, we'll find out when you apply for patent."

"I'm not going to patent. I'm going to keep it secret and protect it with a self-destruct system."

She scowled. "Are you saying your ship self-destructed?"

"I'm not saying anything."

"What if I said you collided with a Zone Patrol ship?"

"I'd call you a liar."

"Were you drunk or on drugs, Mr. Hanson?"

"Your doctors have already told you I'm clean. I don't befuddle my brain."

"We haven't 'rayed you but the preliminary examination says you came through the accident remarkably unscathed. How did you do that when your copilot was killed?"

I told you Drich was dead.

Stay out of this!

Steer her away from this, fool! Next you'll be telling her the other ship was Dreen and we'll be in the soup!

You know I don't believe that.

You got us into this mess, Lutt, improperly accessing a Spiral. Don't make it any worse.

I'll do what I damn well please!

Despite its human appearance, our body is mostly Dreen. Haven't you any gratitude for what I did to save you?

There's no such thing as a Dreen.

Damn it! We both heard her!

Just more hallucination!

Desperately, Ryll tried once more to override Lutt and met resistance greater than anticipated. Ryll tried to move their left foot and felt it twitch.

What was happening here? Yesterday, Lutt had been weak and easily controlled. Now, he was fearful, angry and stronger.

Lutt! The Zone Patrol has Dreen captives who may never see freedom again. Do you want to join them?

I don't want to believe this.

You must believe it!

It's the Spirit Glass. They've fried my brain.

Ryll hesitated. With a sinking feeling, he realized he could take command of this body but the effort would be sure to arouse the interrogator's suspicions.

Lutt allowed himself a gloating thought. *I feel better today. I'm okay except for an annoying voice in my mind.*

Clasping his hands over his head, Lutt stretched, making his knuckles pop.

Urgency gave Ryll control of their voice and he blurted: "Don't do that!"

Major Captain stiffened. "What don't you want me to do?"

Privately, Ryll thought: *That was a mistake. By the fallow glands of a sterile tax collector, did I merge incorrectly?*

Lutt grinned and resumed control of their voice. "Just trying to keep you awake. Looked like you were getting sleepy."

"How can you tell? You can't see my eyes."

Lutt closed his eyes and sighed, concentrating on his bodily sensations. Was it possible this creature calling itself Ryll actually existed? Concentration gave Lutt the momentary sensation of Dreen inward-seeing. It was elusive, just at the fringe of comprehension. Sickening!

"You're the one looking sleepy," Major Captain said.

Lutt opened his eyes. "I've a headache."

"Then speed this up by telling me about the Dreen ship you hit."

"There you go with that doubletalk!"

You're doing fine, Lutt. Accuse her. Attack.

Behind the major, Lutt saw a glass panel take the shape of a kangaroo. It began hopping from panel to panel. Meeting the undulating form of a naked Major Captain in a panel, the kangaroo developed a large penis.

Lutt! Stop that. It's exactly what she wants!

The kangaroo vanished but all of the Spirit Glass began to undulate suggestively. Multiple reflections of the major appeared in a clinging yellow gown.

Lutt tried to find the real major among the reflections.

Find the one in uniform, idiot!

He saw her then, seated at her desk, but there was lace at her neck. She appeared to look directly at him.

"What do you see?" she asked.

"What do *you* see?" Lutt countered.

"You tell me what *you* see."

"I want out of here and I want my ship. The ship I hit came out of thin air without any warning. I'm not to blame."

"Air? In space?"

"You know what I mean."

"I'm sorry, but you must tell me yourself what you mean."

"I'm patriotic and I'll cooperate as much as possible, but I won't give away my family's proprietary secrets. You'll have to pay hard cash for those."

"We'll learn all we need from the wreckage."

No, she won't! Ryll thought it openly, allowing Lutt to share. *My Dreen drive self-destructed to keep it from alien hands.*

Lutt found himself not quite accepting the reality of this voice but desperately wanting to believe what it now said.

Are you sure?

I saw it happen. Patricia *would not let herself fall into Earther hands.*

Patricia?

A very odd name, I agree.

Major Captain cleared her throat. "Are you suggesting you hit a UFO?"

"Of course not!"

"We've had enough such nonsense. It does nothing but create panic and hysteria."

Lie! Say there was no other ship. Say you had a malfunction, your ship strayed off course and exploded.

That was a good idea! Lutt accepted it and obeyed.

Major Captain listened quietly. She appeared pleased.

When Lutt fell silent, she touched a lever on her desk. The Spirit Glass became steady, a dull shade of opaque gray.

Major Captain removed her glasses, revealing eyes almost the same gray as the Spirit Glass. Her mouth formed a rigid smile. He had never before seen an expression that chilling.

That was the explanation she wanted.

Damned voice in his head!

"Let's understand each other, Mr. Hanson. Technically, you broke the law by entering a restricted area. What were you doing there?"

"I had an accident. Isn't there an unwritten law about 'any

port in a storm'? Doesn't the Zone Patrol have obligations to taxpayers?"

"Be quiet, little man. We could put you away for a long time. But our examination of your ship led us to the conclusion you have just voiced."

"I told you the truth."

"Of course you did. But only after you tried to develop a story you could exploit in your damned newspaper."

"So I'm a businessman and my experiments are expensive."

"We're willing to shelve prosecution, Mr. Hanson, but only on one condition."

Oh, oh! Here it comes!

Will you get out of my mind!

Our mind, Lutt. Our mind. Well, ask her what condition!

"What condition?"

"If you develop anything valuable for national defense, you give it to the Zone Patrol first."

"That's blackmail!"

"It's good business."

While Lutt was distracted by this idea, Ryll suddenly seized control of their voice and said: "Shit!"

"No need to get angry, Mr. Hanson. We'll pay well."

But Ryll's reaction was to the sudden realization he could have escaped the Zone Patrol cell by shapeshifting into a long, thin snake having mass equal to his Dreen body.

But they'd have known I was Dreen then. Fearfully, he returned control to Lutt.

"You're young," Major Captain said. "Perhaps you'll be wiser when you mature."

She opened a desk drawer and removed a clear plastic bag, which she extended toward Lutt.

"Your personal effects."

Lutt accepted them, fearful of what his misbehaving body might do next. Why was he saying these things?

"You're damn lucky to have such an influential father," Major Captain said.

So Father put on the pressure!

Emboldened by this realization, Lutt said: "And I want my ship back as soon as possible!"

"It sustained extensive damage and there'll be a hearing over the death of your copilot."

"Drich signed all of the test-pilot waivers! We carried heavy insurance for his survivors."

"No doubt. We merely wish to determine the degree of your culpability."

"Drich was in control when it happened."

They'll follow and watch us.

Will you stop distracting me?

Major Captain glanced at her screen, then: "As for your ship, you can have it but we don't deliver. See our warehouseman in Section 154-C."

"How do I find this warehouse?"

"They'll give you directions when you sign out. Take the elevator up one level and check out with the lobby guard. And you'd damn well better say nothing about Dreens."

"Lady, if I knew what you were talking about, I'd discuss this with you. Personally, I think you're nuts."

"We'll see who's aberrated. Oh, there's a limo waiting outside for you."

Lutt smiled. So the Zone Patrol was sending him home in style. He hoped the elevator would be visible when he turned. It was.

But the major was not through with him.

"That's some limo they sent for you. Your father must have those things made for some Chinese circus."

Oh, damn! Damn! Damn! It's a Hanson limo—one of our blasted rickshaws! They know I hate 'em! Why are they coming for me in one of those?

Combining life forms has a long history of creating havoc.

—Dreen warning

It was a full Thoughtcon of Dreen Elite in the visuplex cupola atop Habiba's cone. Giving off a faint icy yellow glow, the Supreme Tax Collector perched in a gold and white robe at the peak of the circular room. Below her, spaced along a spiral terrace that wound its way down to the lowest members of the hierarchy, sat the chosen ones invited here by Mugly.

Beneath Habiba at her right, Chief Storyteller Jongleur rocked slowly, balanced at the edge of Thoughtcon trance. Mugly the Elder sat half a meter farther down the terrace. Below them were thirty-four others—twenty-six of the Senior Elite and eight Juniors. All of those below Habiba wore large-pocketed black robes with floppy ochre berets. The soft berets of Seniors flopped to the right, while those of the Juniors flopped to the left.

Mugly squirmed in his seat. He felt hazy and inadequate, unaware that he had disconnected his conspiratorial memories before entering the cupola. Moments earlier, he had felt a tingling in his nose, spine and hair roots as Habiba drew energy from his body. Presently, he felt vaguely serene.

Habiba had explained once that seating in a spiral cone permitted an upswirl of thoughts, which she absorbed instantly in her ancient and eternal brain.

"This is the combined information from which I make my state decisions."

Mugly looked out at the island whirling in the center of the sea below the cone.

The Sea of All Things. Why do we call it that?

Habiba did not respond to his unspoken question.

Mugly was forced to consider the possibilities while he waited for whatever Habiba might introduce next.

Sea of All Things and the island beneath him: no Dreen had idmaged any of this, so Habiba said. A quirk of nature had made the island, a round boat kept afloat by airpockets of pumice and held in one place by a continuous whirlpool that spun it in the center of the sea.

What keeps the whirlpool going?

Again, Habiba did not respond.

Habiba's Cone of Control sat on precision rollers, turning in an equal but opposite direction to the whirlpool. This kept the cone stationary in relation to the volcano's outer rim. There was no sensation of movement within the cupola.

Coming out of her Thoughtcon trance, Habiba saw the lights on the volcano rim that locked the cone in its single directional orientation. Six hundred lights on tall towers ringed the Sea of All Things. They flashed alternately red and blue. Whenever the cupola's visuplex was open, she could hear the faint synchronized "pips" as the cone's receivers acknowledged each light's signal.

But the cupola was sealed now for Thoughtcon.

Habiba listened and heard only the deep, soft breathing of entranced subordinates.

"The Sea of All Things," she said, forcing the magnificent words to tumble through the minds of those below her.

All turned to look down on the sea: perfectly clear water to tune them in to perfectly clear thoughts.

Despite its clarity, the sea gave the illusion of not being deep. But Habiba knew it extended into unfathomable depths, conforming to the "ampleness" of Dreenor itself. As with all of Dreenor's water, the sea surface held no impurities, no algae, no suspended particles. Creatures were known to live far down in its darkness where even Habiba's uniquely amplified vision could not penetrate. Creatures conceived by Dreen idmagination lived there and young Storytellers competed to idmage the most outlandish life forms for the Sea of All Things.

Even Habiba, who had heard more stories than any other Dreen, did not know all that lay beyond the reaches of her secret powers. There were stories about stories and some of them had the ring of truth. It was a fact that she could not possibly share *every* story. Thus, she could not know everything that existed. In this aspect, the sea stood as a symbol of the idmage mystery. No one could know all things and the sea could not contain all things except in potential. Therefore, the sea, as a symbol, represented only the ideal of perfect and complete knowledge.

Some of these reflections filtered down the Thoughtcon spiral, accepted at lower levels according to the abilities of each Dreen.

Only Habiba and Jongleur were expected to go in and out of Thoughtcon trance during the Sharing. Jongleur occasionally added refinements or suggestions. He did this mostly in private sessions afterward. Today, however, Mugly intruded with constant harping worries about Earth. There was no doubt that his argument gained force from the theft of the special Excursion Ship.

Habiba was forced to consider the threat.

Ryll is only a child and he may make very serious errors.

Who could deny it? The child already had shown a tendency toward mistaken judgments.

Perhaps we should have treated him with a Soother. It had been so difficult, though, to say her firstborn's firstborn might be . . . well, aberrant.

But what to do about Earth?

Their warlike people now possessed spacecraft capable of attacking other planets. She saw their present ships as no immediate threat, but if Earthers achieved the Dreen drive, they could come through the Spirals to threaten Dreenor itself.

What if, through some quirky accident, they captured this child and his ship?

It was a horrible thought and her own past words came back to haunt her. She had said a thing to Jongleur and others on many occasions.

"We have no weapons for defense or offense. This is as it should be. History has proven that the entry of even the tiniest weapon into any society always leads to violence and the ultimate destruction of the entire social organism that has allowed this mistake."

Dreen idmaging had experimented with countless forms of Free Will, every time with the same dismal result. But the most recent reports brought from Earth complicated her considerations.

Mugly intruded with one of his warnings: "The danger increases. Experiments in travel through the Spirals are being conducted on Earth at this very moment."

That was the substance of a recent report. No doubt of it. An Earther named Lutt Hanson, Jr., was reported to have relayed radio messages in Spiral form, transmitting from spaceships in the Earth solar system.

How could the Earther fail to suspect that Spiral travel also was possible? This human might be close to a solution.

The warriors of Earth could be at our doorstep with their terrible weapons.

The Elite Storytellers below her had brought even more ominous news today, a report from the latest Earth excursion.

Earth nations have concluded a mutually verifiable treaty freezing and bridling their most awesome weapons.

So they were not as likely to exterminate themselves. It meant they were not in imminent danger of meeting the fate that had destroyed other people reaching a similar stage of war technology.

"Our problem is the universe's problem," Habiba said. She gazed across the Sea of All Things while this thought swirled down into the ranks. "All things are idmages held in our memories. When the last Dreen dies, the universe dies."

A statement requiring no response.

Jongleur ruminated on the Supreme Tax Collector's words.

Why did it have to be my son who precipitated this crisis?

Habiba reached down and patted his head.

Jongleur looked up at her lovingly. Habiba in full sunlight was a green goddess, her hair a salad of delights.

He took a deep breath, restored by her touch, and glanced around the cupola. Once more, sadness engulfed him. The window frames were shedding black flakes and the greenish-brown hardened vegetation at the base of the cupola needed polishing. Habiba must approve each maintenance detail and, in the normal course, these matters were cared for efficiently by useful manual labor and idmaging. She had had other problems to occupy her attention of late, though, and the cupola reflected neglect.

"Perhaps we are too curious about the unlimited possibilities in an unlimited universe," Jongleur said.

"Who says it's unlimited?" Mugly demanded.

"It is ample," Habiba said.

Jongleur considered this and thought then about the touristlike curiosity of Dreens. Overdeveloped curiosity! Dreens always wanted to go in person and see the places, the creatures and marvels they had heard about in story form. Many stories touched on Earth because Dreen visitors had intervened with idmage changes over the millennia.

Variations on a theme.

It was an extremely popular place to visit but always presented that problem of Free Will no Dreen seemed capable of changing.

Such a pretty planet, though, when you got away from the places the occupants had contaminated and defaced with their constant disregard for consequences.

Why didn't the original idmage contain an injunction against fouling their own nest? Mugly wanted to know.

Because that goes against Free Will, Jongleur explained.

None of this helped Habiba with a solution to the Earth problem. She had tried sending representatives to approach the planet openly, using many different shapes of ships and forms of life. But Earthers always shot first with no apparent interest in the identity or purpose of visitors.

"Shoot first and ask questions afterward," was an Earther cliché.

We must believe it then, Habiba thought.

They would approach Dreenor that way, too. Guns blazing and bombs flying. Our advanced technology would make them suspect we possess commensurate war technology. They would fear us and try to exterminate us. How can we possibly teach them that the absence of monstrous weaponry represents a more advanced civilization?

"They already hold some of our people captive," Mugly reminded her.

"But they have none of our ships and do not know our location," Jongleur said.

"Ahhh, the Dreen pacifist tries to lull us," Mugly sneered.

"All Dreens are naturally pacifist," Habiba reminded him.

"Am I not a Dreen?" Mugly demanded.

"And you are more peaceful than you care to admit," Habiba said. "You merely have a capacity for anger that does not appear very often in our people."

"Are you saying I am the product of a bad seed?"

"Mugly!"

"Sorry, Habiba. I do love you dearly."

"Sweet Mugly, try to smooth over your anger."

"But the Earther Zone Patrol holds ninety-one of our people and every time we try to free them we lose more."

"The Zone Patrol is crafty because they were idmaged that way," Jongleur said.

"But they hold the prisoners separated, move them often and apparently keep them under almost constant interrogation."

"They may not yet have seen the original Dreen form nor witnessed our full idmaging capabilities," Jongleur said.

"Will your son change that?" Mugly asked.

"Whatever happens he does not have the secrets of our technology nor do any of the prisoners. Only you and Habiba and I share that precious knowledge."

"Why do you think I didn't go racing off after my ship?"

"Your people took much on themselves to idmage such a ship," Habiba said.

"I have censured them severely and, as punishment, have ruled that none of them may ever share your precious presence in a Thoughtcon!"

Because he had disconnected his most secret thoughts, Mugly believed this untruth sincerely and, for a moment, was awed by the cruel severity of his own anger.

For once, though, Jongleur agreed with him. "You were wise, Mugly. Your action sends a salutary signal throughout Dreenor."

"But it teaches very little other than the severity of those who rule," Habiba said. "And I doubt it will stop others from trying similar tricks."

Jongleur looked upward and, seeing the intense downward stare of Habiba's round brown eyes, realized he was distracting her from developing a solution to their crisis. The Supreme Tax Collector's sensitive microneurons required serenity to perform at their best. Jongleur swiveled his eyes inward and concentrated on transmitting serene story thoughts. The others in the Thoughtcon took their cue from him and reinforced the sense of serenity. Only Mugly the Elder maintained a tiny jangling interference but it was so small that Habiba alone could sense it.

Habiba now engaged in a performance available only to herself. One eye turned outward and the other inward. This act separated consciousness from unconsciousness even while she sank into Thoughtcon trance. The trance itself permitted her to mediate between her separated selves. Below her, thirty-six other minds added their efforts to Habiba's. The intense energy generated by this concentration lifted the cupola from the roof of the cone and allowed it to turn with the swirling of the whirlpool in the sea below them.

Higher and higher the cupola flew, piercing clouds and rising into the stratosphere until the winds there buffeted it. Still it climbed, always keeping its alignment with the cone far below. Habiba knew she had never flown this high before but Dreens had never before encountered a problem of this magnitude.

Earth must be a faulty idmage, she told herself.

At last, the cupola ceased rising but it was far out of the atmosphere. The occupants survived now on air their combined energy idmaged and were warmed by the heat of their own efforts, protected by this concentration from intrusions of other thoughts and objects.

Habiba's released awareness flowed through all the stories of Earth she had Shared, shutting out distractions. Every known facet of Earther existence that Dreens had witnessed and told in their tax tales or other Sharings—a comprehensive picture within which she searched for Earther motivations—absorbed her entire attention.

The cupola, without her to hold it, sped off laterally far beyond the Sea of All Things. After a time no one could count, a solution occurred to her. Habiba withdrew from the trance and found her cupola sitting in a meadow of bright yellow flowers almost the same color as her icy-yellow Thoughtcon aura.

Like the first childseed that I made fertile, she thought.

But these were not childseed flowers. All such plants were gone, picked by her hands and never again to grow on Dreenor unless eternity demanded she plant them.

With a pang, Habiba recalled the ancient odors of the childseed flowers. Nevermore to enjoy such beauty? Something about *nevermore things* troubled and frightened her. She wanted permanent creations or, at the very least, renewable cycles. Would she ever again know childseed flowers? Habiba longed either to learn the answer or to forget the question.

The Thoughtcon Elite remained entranced below her, breathing deeply, their energies decreasing. Presently, they could be awakened.

And I will be here—Habiba the Eternal.

That was how her people saw her: Supreme Tax Collector, Mother of All, the First Dreen. No family Elders lived below her home. She alone among Dreens needed no mate. Dreens could not conceive of anyone or anything predating Habiba. She had always ruled Dreenor and, therefore, commanded the universe. She would always occupy that pinnacle.

Such reflections disturbed Habiba. She felt the discord worry its way down the entranced hierarchy of the Thoughtcon.

There was a *first memory* in her awareness and she tried to avoid it but now felt unable to escape.

I awakened. I remembered a void—nothing in it. And I was a naked girl in a great meadow of yellow flowers. How did I know to pick and store their seeds?

She recalled the pleasant warmth of that long-ago meadow where she had idmaged her first mudbrick shelter as a center for neat rows of stone containers holding the childseeds.

Countless containers.

Jars as large as her youthful body. They stretched farther than even her eyes could see—and her eyes saw farther than those of any other Dreen.

Nothing ever again grew where childseed plants flowered.

I filled all the jars: a sacred task. How did I know it was sacred?

The years of the harvest did not seem long to her immortal timesense. Any measured time appeared minuscule when seen against eternity, Habiba thought. And she called the harvest time "First Day."

At dawn of "Second Day," another period of uncounted sunrises and sunsets, Habiba spoke her first words:

"These are the childseeds of my people."

From seventy brown seeds, she brought forth the first children—

thirty-five females and thirty-five males. When they were born, that was the dawn of "Third Day," an *evermore* period extending through this time of the Earth period.

Earth!

The shock-snap of this reality awakened the Elite.

"I have considered the erasure of Earth," she said.

"Mass capital punishment is unthinkable," Jongleur objected.

Habiba did not need to look down at Jongleur to know he stared at her in fearful amazement. The familiarity of aeons told her every physical reaction of her Chief Storyteller—

My firstborn.

"I reject erasure," Habiba said, "but not because capital punishment is objectionable. Earth's death would precipitate a storytelling sickness. I fear that our sensitive, creative minds might experience idmage withdrawal. Would that not mean the death of all Dreens?"

Jongleur nodded. Habiba was so wise!

She shifted slightly on her perch. A thin vertical shadow cast by a visuplex frame crossed to the right side of her face.

To Jongleur, the shadow was like the deep creases that etched her dear features. He noted her Thoughtcon aura subsiding—the icy yellow visible to all of her people, brighter and more constant than the aura of any other Dreen.

Mugly could hold his silence no longer.

"But erasure would solve the problem permanently! Dear Habiba, even though my people acted on their own, perhaps they were not misguided."

"Erasure, dear Mugly, would bring other problems, some quite possibly beyond our powers to correct."

Mugly sat in stunned immobility. Problems beyond Dreen idmaging powers?

"What . . . what problems?" he stammered.

"I really don't know, Mugly. But they could well be devastating."

"If Earthers capture one of our ships intact, that could be the end of us," Jongleur said. "I suggest we put Earth off limits to Dreens. That would . . ."

"That would tantalize our Storytellers," Habiba said.

"And we'd have no advance knowledge of their actions," Mugly said. "Besides, they already know about the Spirals."

"Then let's idmage a barricade shutting off the Spirals," Jongleur insisted.

"I'm surprised and dismayed at you, Jongleur," Habiba said. "Have you heard nothing I said? Confine us to Dreenor, our creativity with no outlet? Dreens would go mad."

Jongleur pulled a puff of his beret forward and hid his eyes under it, not daring to look at Habiba. He searched his mind for something intelligent to say.

"The idmage of Earth was a rotten job!" Habiba said.

Jongleur bobbed his body in agreement but dared not mention the name of the Dreen who had idmaged Earth at the risk of disturbing her.

Wemply the Voyager, an unfortunate Dreen, really. Killed by Earther soldiers after he assumed Earther form.

The death of Wemply saddened Jongleur.

"How any idiot could idmage bacterial creatures possessed of Free Will and a definite tendency to violence is beyond me!" Habiba said. "He must have known he would populate the planet with all forms of predators."

"Some Dreens will never heed your warnings," Jongleur said, looking pointedly at Mugly. "The great power of idmaging requires great caution and never indiscriminate creation."

Jongleur ventured to look up at Habiba then. Her great body trembled with emotion.

"Then what do we do about Earth?" Jongleur asked.

"We must create an idmage shield around Dreenor that camouflages the planet to look hostile and uninhabitable."

Mugly was confused. "But didn't you say we must not prevent Dreen travel to—"

"No barrier! This idea occurred to me because of a thing Earthers do. They make swimsuits that appear opaque but allow the tanning rays of the sun to penetrate."

"Brilliant!" Jongleur said.

"Our shield will float overhead," she said. "Rays of the sun will pass through it but passersby will see only a hostile surface."

Grudgingly, Habiba admitted to herself that Earthers did produce marvelously inventive ideas. Perhaps that had been the intention of the original idmage.

"Ironic, isn't it?" she said. "Earth's Free-Willed minds imperil us but also provide the seedling of our salvation. Now! In addition, we must send more operatives to seek out Jongleur's misguided son. Ryll's presence there is a danger to us. We have no idea how much he may have learned about the erasure ship or how much he may tell the Earthers if he is captured."

Mugly felt the stirrings of disquiet. Habiba's tone told him she, too, was enthralled by Earth despite its dangers. Was her shield idea not a bit facile?

"To make a shield, would we not have to alter the Creative Spirals around Dreenor?" Jongleur asked.

"Minor changes," Habiba said. "We will loop the Spirals to leave alien visitors well outside our shield. We will merely pass through the shield by more primitive propulsion before connecting with a Spiral."

"I assume Dreenor itself was a Dreen creation," Mugly said. "Do we dare tamper with . . ."

"We will not tamper," Habiba said. "My senses tell me Dreenor is a very powerful idmage. But our shield can be made if we use the concerted energies of all Dreens."

Jongleur looked at Mugly. Mugly looked at Jongleur. Two Dreens with one thought: *This is still tampering with our nest.*

"Come!" Habiba said. "Back into Thoughtcon trance, everyone! We must return our cupola to its proper place."

We do not know why Hanson Junior collided with a Dreen ship. He claims ignorance of Dreens. Nothing useful came from study of the wreck. We assume a Dreen self-destructed to avoid capture. Hanson's ship will be released and he will be watched.

—Zone Patrol day sheet. *XEN*-50: Major Captain

In the Zone Patrol elevator, Lutt stepped on the glowing butt of a discarded cigar. He waved at stale smoke and wondered why air conditioning had not dispelled it. He found his answer in a grimy placard beside the door:

"Please be patient during air conditioning repairs."

The placard was dated almost eight months earlier.

The elevator doors groaned closed, shutting off his view of Major Captain in her odd perch. She sat studying something on her desk.

You should've smoked the cigar, Ryll intruded. *It was less than half consumed. I like an occasional drag.*

The elevator began a slow, clanking ascent.

If I'm nuts, I guess I have to roll with it, Lutt thought. *So don't suggest I use someone's leavings. That's a sure way to catch a disgusting disease. Besides, I don't smoke.*

But I do and finding a butt saves the trouble of idmaging.

But the germs in another's saliva!

Dreens are immune to all diseases. This body is more than ninety percent my protoplasm and I feel confident that Dreen cells dominate it.

Old age is a disease. Are we immune to that, too?

My school proctors claim not all mergings are identical, but if we avoid the Zone Patrol and other dangers, we may live long enough to make your question purely academic.

So you don't really know.

I know I'd like to be separated from you, Lutt!

Amen!

You're beginning to believe in me, aren't you, Lutt?

That bitch did ask me about Dreens. And . . . there were times when I said things that . . .

I'm sorry I pre-empted our voice that way. I will try to remain silent in the presence of others until I learn more about your ways. Blame the outburst on my youth. Dreens should be patient and observe closely before speaking.

The elevator bumped to a stop and the doors slammed open alarmingly. Lutt stepped out into a green-tiled lobby with a high ceiling that glittered with tiny lights. A replica of an antique Zone Patrol ship occupied the center of the lobby. Its stubby wings glistened. Groups of Zone Patrol officers stood around it talking. They paid little attention to Lutt. Through bars at the door he glimpsed a portico entrance and street traffic. A sergeant sat behind a desk beside the door.

The sergeant looked up with a bored expression as Lutt approached. Lutt started to speak but the sergeant thrust papers toward him and interrupted.

"Here's directions to the warehouse. Here's where you sign that you were not mistreated and you love the Zone Patrol like a father."

"Oh, yes," Lutt said. "I love you just like I love my father."

That was a very deceptive response, Lutt.

So don't distract me.

Lutt signed where indicated and accepted the directions to the warehouse. The sergeant pressed a button on her desk.

The door creaked but did not open.

"Damn GI equipment!" the sergeant said. She went to the door and kicked it. Rasping and jittering, the door inched open.

Lutt darted through, fearful that the doors would slam shut on him. He paused under the portico and looked down at the street.

Lutt, you must stop thinking of me as a distraction. I wish to study your primitive peoples in meticulous detail. There will be questions and I shall expect answers from you.

It's like having a mosquito buzzing in my ear.

Become accustomed to it or I shall begin calling you Lout, the way your brother does.

My name's Lutt, dammit! And stop spying on my thoughts!

I will attempt to cooperate. Even if we can't be friends, we can be courteous.

Yeah, and I'm the Queen of Rumania.

Lutt took a deep breath of cool morning air. A concrete walk led off through high hedges to his left beyond a sign that read "Transport Area."

I shall try to be more reticent, Lutt, but I have much to offer you and it is the way of my people to speak openly.

You're a damn chatterbox!

You surely don't expect me to be mute.

Lutt set off along the concrete walk without responding. It was a snake track through the high hedges, with occasional wide places where benches had been placed beneath "No Loitering" signs.

I see that you fear embarrassment, Ryll ventured. *You don't want to become nervous and . . . ahhh, with a flushed face. Your emotional reactions are known to us, you see?*

It's not nice to embarrass people.

Are Earthers always nice?

Of course not!

Then I will behave as Earthers do, being nice only some of the time. That appears to be entirely proper and I do not wish to create behavioral mistakes with our mutual body.

Just leave me in charge, huh?

I shall keep a mental tally. Whenever I see Earthers being polite, or if I hear of politeness, I will make an entry. We Dreens do this sort of thing with ease.

You talk too much!

That is not polite, Lutt.

I'm not trying to be polite. I don't want to be polite. I just want to be shut of you!

Obviously, you know nothing about a Dreen's infinite capacity for recollection—when we're paying attention, of course. My store of experiences and stories is limited by my youth and past inattentiveness but it is possible for me never to forget a story or any observed detail.

The walk opened out onto a wide stairway climbing to another level planted with shrubs and trees. Lutt could hear vehicles moving up there.

I am particularly talented when I put my mind to it, Ryll insisted.

Lutt began running up the stairs, leaping them three at a time. He made groaning noises as he ran to drown out Ryll's intrusive voice and wished he might leave this madness behind him. A blackbird hopped aside midway but he met no people until he reached the top where two women in Zone Patrol uniforms glanced at him curiously before descending.

"Don't loiter!" Lutt shouted after them and laughed hysterically.

The women quickened their pace with startled backward glances.

You're behaving foolishly for someone who fears embarrassment, Lutt.

Aw, shut up!

I see I must give you more time to adjust.

Lutt emerged onto a wide sidewalk along a curved drive lined with vehicles—vans, limousines, buses. He had no difficulty identifying the rickshaw. Oversized, trimmed in garish carving and with a heavily armored enclosed cab, it looked like a giant red sedan chair on cushioned wheels. The towbar rested on a jade green inflatable Chinese dog. Six fat robots painted and dressed in gold-thread brocade like ancient mandarins stood beside the towbar. Each held a pellet gun made to appear like a laser rifle.

Hanson Security programed them to guard against terrorists but the design was said to be pure L.H.—"Something different for friends and family." L.H. had once told an interviewer he never created for his enemies "except to make them jealous."

As Lutt approached the limo, he wondered if these vehicles had ever aroused anything but laughter. His mother professed to admire them because the design "was one of my wedding presents." She also liked the idea that robot guards were an obvious flourish of wealth but she said their presence "tends to prevent trouble."

Abruptly, one of the limo's electric doors flopped open to become a ramp. Phoenicia Hanson emerged followed by Lutt's younger brother, Morey. This aroused a flurry of activity among the robots.

Two detached themselves from the towbar and flanked the ramp. Their weapons pointed at Lutt.

"It's me, dumbos!" Lutt shouted.

The guns continued to point at Lutt but the robot eyes scanned other areas around them.

Looking at his mother and brother, Lutt thought, *What a contrast!* Phoenicia, a small woman in an ankle-length dress of white embroidery, appeared pale and delicate under a bun of strawberry blond hair. Morey towered over her, a commanding patrician with high cheekbones, deeply set pale blue eyes and a sharp nose that some said could scratch glass.

Contrasts within contrasts, Ryll intruded.

It was Lutt's thought precisely. Phoenicia's delicate appearance concealed a toughness that caused friends from her Alabama childhood to call her "the Steel Magnolia." And behind Morey's imposing presence lay a weak character.

"You were running," Phoenicia said as Lutt stopped below her. "Are you escaping?"

"I wanted the exercise," Lutt said.

"Exercise?" Morey sneered. "That's not like you, Lout."

"You don't know what I'm like, but I'll teach you the meaning of pain if you call me that again," Lutt warned.

"Boys!" Phoenicia said. "I do wish you'd both grow up and behave like civilized gentlemen."

Lutt mounted the ramp, gave his mother a pecking kiss on the forehead and glowered at Morey, surprised because Morey did not appear as tall as remembered.

Morey, too, noticed this. "Have you grown since I saw you last, dear brother?"

Ignoring the question, Lutt growled, "Let's get into the cab and out of the high-target area."

"You sound just like your father," Phoenicia said, but she returned to the cab. Morey followed her, moving slowly and forcing Lutt to wait outside.

Always hoping some terrorist will pick me off!

Stooping to enter the pseudo-rickshaw, Lutt marveled that he felt so good after the run. The sedentary life of a newspaper publisher and inventor had left him accepting a slower pace . . . until yesterday.

You feel my strength, not yours, Ryll told him. *But do not fear I will embarrass you. I wish to observe your family before speaking to them on my own.*

Don't you do that! You hear me?

I can hardly fail to hear *you when we share the same body.*

The ramp swung up and sealed them inside as Lutt sat down facing his mother and brother, his back to the robots, who resumed their stations along the towbar. As usual, Lutt found the limo's dim interior repellent—red velvet and tassels, brocade, red and black lacquer. And the seats were too soft.

"Did you have to come for me in this damned sideshow?" Lutt asked. "I've told you time and again I hate it."

"I rather like it," Morey said. "And it carries fond memories for Mother." He turned a melting gaze on Phoenicia. "Doesn't it, dear?"

"You're being smarmy, darling," Phoenicia said.

"I really think these limos are one of L.H.'s better efforts," Morey insisted.

Phoenicia abruptly glared at her younger son and snapped: "Be still! You don't know what you're saying."

Morey fell into abashed silence.

Morey the flunky, Lutt thought. *You never know when defending Father will get you into trouble.* But Phoenicia's response surprised Lutt. Was there something about these limos that had not been revealed?

Phoenicia opened a glossy black panel beside her and spoke into it, addressing the collective robot system directing the limo: "You know where to go, Hung Far Low."

Alerted to nuances, Lutt heard the effort it took his mother to use the key-name required before the limo would obey. Father had always said it was named for a favorite restaurant in Portland, Oregon, but Lutt wondered if that name might not be another sign from the mysterious "helper."

The limo lurched into motion and Lutt heard the clopping of robot feet on paving, at first quite distinct and then blurred into a staccato buzz as they picked up speed. You had to say one thing for these damned rickshaws, he thought. They could do an honest seventy klicks an hour.

Lutt studied his brother. What to do about Morey? *I know about your thefts from Hanson Industries, Brother. And that million-dollar postage stamp in your left shoe heel.*

Eyes and Ears Unlimited, a surveillance firm hired by Lutt, had produced the damning information about Morey. It had been a delicate task under the noses of Hanson Family Security. But EE, as it was known on the street, had been owned by the late Ricardo Green. The surviving son, Esteban Green, had been Lutt's roommate in their teens at a private school. Lunches, dinners and dates with sexual partners carefully vetted by the senior Green had built a bond between the young men.

With instruction from Esteban, Lutt himself had placed the surveillance bugs around Morey. Esteban never asked why this was done but Lutt suspected EE of bugging the bugs. No matter—spying on the Hansons could be dangerous and Esteban had earned a reputation for extreme caution after his father's mysterious death in the collapse of a building EE was watching.

But now I have you where I want you, dear brother. No more of your insults and backbiting.

Morey frequently hinted he might tell Mother how Lutt consorted with the cheapest prostitutes. "If she only knew."

But you consort with criminals, Morey. You steal from your family. You support the vicious traffic in narcotics and . . .

Ryll interrupted. *What fierce emotions you Earthers have! And you are very devious, Lutt.*

Stay the hell out of this!

Impishly, Ryll seized voice control and said: "You're in deep trouble, Morey."

Lutt overrode Ryll and shouted: "Be quiet!"

"What are you saying?" Phoenicia demanded. "And why are you changing your voice that way?"

Morey was fearful. "What do you mean I'm in trouble?"

"Just watch your step, Morey," Lutt said.

"Will you both please try to behave?" Phoenicia pleaded.

What would happen if you told them about me? Ryll asked.

You'd better think about what the Zone Patrol would do with that information.

Your own family would . . . ahhh, rat on you?

Morey would.

Your memories confirm this painful truth.

So stop making my life miserable with interruptions!

I can do more than interrupt.

Ryll forced the closure of their eyelids and swiveled their eyes inward.

Lutt choked and gagged.

Ryll returned their eyes to normal and opened them.

"Are you all right, dear?" Phoenicia asked. "What did those terrible Zone people do to you?"

Lutt spoke weakly. "They held me in a cell and asked a lot of dumb questions. They told you I had an accident with my *Vortraveler,* didn't they?"

"They told us nothing," Morey said. "Father informed us this morning where you could be found and told us to get you."

"Were you hurt in the accident?" Phoenicia asked.

"Just a few bruises."

You could say I was a hallucination following the accident, Ryll suggested. *That way they'd know about me but it would not be information useful for Morey.*

You are *a hallucination!*

Excellent. This way you'll sound all the more sincere.

You're nuts!

I cannot be a hallucination and insane.

"Tell us about your accident, dear," Phoenicia said.

Lutt took a deep breath, inhaling the slightly offbeat smell of newness in the limo. Not a natural odor. Something from a can, the way he simulated newsroom odors at the *Enquirer.* Another false front, and Phoenicia tried most of them.

"It helps to talk about dangers we survive," she said.

Lutt stared past his mother and brother through a brass-framed armor-glass window. It framed an avenue of poplars growing smaller in the distance. The limo turned a corner and the trees no longer were visible. Sunlight struck the rear window, activating a dark green shade in the glass.

"Something you're ashamed of?" Morey asked.

Tell them but don't mention Dreens, Ryll insisted. *Do it or I'll inward-focus.*

"All right!" Lutt said.

He leaned back in the velvet cushions and gave a brief account of the accident and aftermath. At Ryll's prodding, he added: "I thought an alien got into my body. There was a voice in my head."

"You hear voices?" Morey asked. He sounded pleased.

You're a poor storyteller, Lutt, Ryll intruded. *I'm a very young Dreen but even I can do much better.*

"And poor Drich Baker is dead," Phoenicia said. "Oh, dear! I shall have to call on his family."

"But Lutt's hearing voices, Mother."

"Not voices, dear. A voice. His accident was more severe than he lets on. We shall have to employ specialists."

"Isn't this what happened to Uncle Dudley?" Morey asked.

"My brother has nothing to do with this! Don't mention him again or I shall be forced to tell your father."

"I just wondered if there might be a nutty streak in the family." Morey sounded plaintive.

Your Uncle Dudley sounds interesting, Ryll offered.

Please let it rest for the moment, Lutt pleaded.

You seem almost polite.

I'm begging you. Morey would like to use this against me with our father. And if it gets back to the Zone Patrol . . .

Very well. But only because you're being polite. I shall tally that in your favor.

"You should not have built that spaceship without your father's consent," Phoenicia said. "You know how good he is with inventions and things of that nature."

"Like this limo?" Lutt asked.

Phoenicia scowled but she only patted Lutt's knees. "Don't worry, dear. Our specialists will cure you."

"Voices in his head," Morey muttered, nodding.

Phoenicia sent a warning glance at Morey and sank back into her seat. She placed a manicured finger against her hair, adjusting the bun.

Lutt noted the finishing-school grace of the movement, her chin uplifted. A sense of superiority had been ground into Phoenicia by a lifetime of plenty. Morey tried to ape her manners but it was all sham—another false front. There was something feral about him, sinister and sneaky, especially in those eyes of perishable blue he had inherited from his mother. Morey seldom looked anyone in the eyes.

Phoenicia, on the other hand, could burn you with a stare. She and old L.H. were as different as two married people could be—Father a tough spacedock worker who had made good the hard way; Mother, old Southern money and old ways. But in her own snobby manner, Phoenicia was every bit as tough as L.H.

"Your father wishes to talk to you, Lutt, about your recent expenditures," Phoenicia said.

Morey grinned at him.

Lutt glanced out the window beside him. *On the carpet!*

"I have a few things to tell Father, too," Lutt said.

"He'll be very interested to hear about the voices in your head," Morey gloated.

"He might be just as interested in what I could tell him about some of your recent activities," Lutt said.

Morey's brows drew down into creased lines.

"You'd better keep your mouth shut if you know what's good for you, Morey," Lutt said.

Phoenicia looked at her younger son. "Have you been getting into trouble again, Morey?"

"Tell her where you were last weekend," Lutt said.

Is that true? Ryll asked. *Was your brother meeting with vicious criminals last weekend?*

EE wouldn't lie to me about it.

When Morey did not respond, Phoenicia sighed. "Well, you'll both be with your father, soon. I hope he can make you act more like loving brothers."

Lutt sat up straight. "We're going to You Gee One?"

"I told you he wants to talk to you," she said. "Now you both be nice. We'll be there soon."

I wanna be president when I grow up. No! Not of Daddy's company! I wanna be president of the solar system!

—Lutt Hanson, Jr.,
at age ten

"The Elites are dispersing with your message."

Jongleur spoke as he entered Habiba's private quarters, adding: "Soon, your plan will be fait accompli."

"I wish you'd stop these Earthisms!" Habiba snapped. "That place occupies entirely too much of our lives."

Seeing that Habiba was emotionally disturbed, Jongleur felt at first guilty for upsetting her and then contrite.

Give her time to compose herself, he thought.

He focused on calming stories and glanced around Habiba's quarters. These always surprised him—so small and plain, a three-room mudbrick and stone building with many signs of wear. The building stood on the high vaulted lowest floor of her cone, hidden away among old storage jars and discarded seed husks.

Habiba clung to it out of sentiment, she said. It was her first dwelling, the one she had idmaged in a meadow of childseed flowers on her first Dreenor Day.

But now it was less than an hour after returning from her most recent Thoughtcon, and Habiba still displayed such emotional upset that her Chief Storyteller entertained fears for her.

"We will go outside," Habiba said.

Jongleur blinked assent but waited. She often said this but until she led the way he never knew whether she meant actually out into the open air or just out into the artificial light of the cone's main floor where soil had been spread over the lime slate to simulate a natural yard. It was not the same as a residential yard but Habiba said it gave her communion with her people, especially with the Elders who lived deep beneath the surface.

"Touching the dirt of Dreenor prevents me from taking on airs and behaving in the vain manner of lesser rulers in our universe," Habiba said as she stopped in the vault-enclosed yard and stared around her in the greenish-yellow light.

Jongleur was familiar with these little homilies. They reinforced the belief that all Dreens should strive for a perfect existence and that watching the idmaged worlds evolve taught Dreens the frailties inherent in other sentient creatures.

Jongleur did not dare express his own fears about this—that the idmaged creatures and their worlds reflected a flaw in the Dreen character. He thought it, though, and thus Habiba knew his fear from her Thoughtcon Sharings.

"Have you noticed how Mugly smells when he's angry?" she asked.

Jongleur shuddered. *That smell!* His first lessons had taught that rage produced a snout-twisting odor, a warning to prevent Dreens from inflicting violence on each other. Until Mugly, Jongleur had never experienced the natural odor.

"That smell tells me Mugly is a throwback to an earlier Dreen form," Habiba said. "I have asked myself many times why such a phenomenon should occur at this time."

Jongleur waited for her to expand on this interesting concept but Habiba changed the subject.

"The Excursion Ship your son took was created to go only to Earth. Do you think Mugly connived in its creation?"

Jongleur stared at her. *What a question!* Did not Thoughtcon open all minds to Habiba?

She increased his confusion by what she said next.

"I know about your occasional indiscretions with bazeel, Jongleur. I tolerate them because you are not excessive."

"Many of us . . ."

"I know."

Of course she knows. Then why the question about Mugly?

As though she read his mind outside of Thoughtcon, Habiba said: "We must ask ouselves if a throwback such as Mugly may not have other characteristics detrimental to Dreen serenity."

Jongleur suppressed his defensive reflex with some difficulty and wished he had a small bit of bazeel right now, just enough to calm his nerves.

"Can you visualize what may happen if Earthers capture that ship intact?" Habiba asked. "They will come here with their terrible weapons!"

"But our shield . . ."

". . . may not be enough to protect us indefinitely."

Habiba glanced at the tall double doors leading to the outside corridor and only then did Jongleur hear a sound there. He marveled at Habiba's acute senses. Someone coming.

The latches gave a loud click and the doors swung inward admitting a Junior Storyteller. He scurried in, holding his floppy yellow cap on his head as he ran.

Trouble! Jongleur thought.

No one would interrupt a meeting between Habiba and her Chief Storyteller without grave cause.

The Junior Storyteller stopped at the edge of Habiba's yard and bowed low. "Your pardons begged," he said. "I have an urgent message. The stolen ship has collided with an Earther ship and the wreckage is in the hands of the Zone Patrol."

"Survivors?" Jongleur bleated.

"We are investigating as well as we can," the Junior said. "There is a report on Earth saying Lutt Hanson, Jr., has been rescued from an experimental ship that exploded."

"And my son?"

"No word yet but there was a fire."

Jongleur moaned, "Ohhhhh . . ."

"Compose yourself, Jongleur!" Habiba ordered. "This is an emergency."

"Yes . . . yes, of course."

"How do you know it was a collision?" Habiba asked.

"Our sensors in the Spirals. An unfortunate delay in the reporting system is being investigated."

"It happened in the . . . in the Spirals?" Jongleur demanded.

"At Phase One of entry," the Junior said. "We do not know

if the Earther could have completed Phases Two and Three."

"Lutt Hanson, Jr.," Habiba said. "That's the dangerous Earther whose experiments led to this crisis."

"My son . . ." Jongleur began.

"Forgive the cruelty of this, Jongleur," Habiba said, "but death might be preferable to capture."

The Junior Storyteller was not finished. "Mugly assures us the Excursion Ship was set to self-destruct rather than submit to Earther probes."

"But it was a collision," Jongleur said.

All three of them reflected on the unknown possibilities in such an accident. Habiba was first to recover.

"Jongleur! We must act quickly. Earther knowledge of our Spiral technology, whether developed independently or stolen from us, must be destroyed."

Jongleur was shocked by the potential violence in her orders. "What are you saying?"

"Send our operatives immediately. That troublemaker, Hanson, will have to be dealt with. Abduction if necessary, but no killing."

Jongleur was speechless. Of course no killing! A Dreen could not commit murder! Only some life forms evolving from primordial Dreen idmages could do that and, even then, only if they were granted Free Will.

"Free Will," Habiba muttered, echoing Jongleur's thought.

Jongleur agreed completely with the emotion he sensed in her. Free Will—that eminently bothersome concept Habiba warned them about so often. But she did not (could not?) put a stop to it, nor to bazeel.

"Well go at once and see to these matters!" Habiba ordered.

Deeply disturbed, Jongleur left the Supreme Tax Collector's presence. His thoughts suggested limitations on Habiba's powers—powers Jongleur and other Dreens had taken for granted over many generations.

Jongleur heard the quick, shuffling steps of the Junior Storyteller behind him as he left the cone's vaulted room.

And I dreamed my Ryll would wear that yellow cap one day. Ohhh, what has happened to my son? Ohhh, why did I not take the advice of my Elders and fit him with a yellow Soother?

Shame had prevented him from taking the advice, Jongleur realized. Each small Soother, a living creature, soft and furry, faceless and without appendages, projected balancing thoughts into the mind of the one it soothed. But the things were always visible and people tended to avoid the presence of a person being soothed. Who wanted his thoughts read all the time? And Soothers certainly read the thoughts of anyone within their range.

You Gee One—Phonetic for UG One, the underground (UG) terminal where Lutt Hanson Senior's private tube train picks up passengers bound for his subterranean offices and shops built in an old MX missile site.

—*Atlas of the Powerful*

From the moment he learned they were headed for You Gee One, Lutt realized he was headed for a family confrontation. Morey was maneuvering again! *Never let up, do you, Brother?*

The infernal rickshaw lurched and Lutt caught Morey's gaze for a moment, easily forcing the younger man to look away.

No guts!

"This hallucination about an alien in your body can be dispelled quite easily by modern medicine," Phoenicia said.

Lutt let it rest. With any luck, Morey would take the revelation merely as a sign of weakness, something to exploit with L.H. Let them believe in a head injury. God! This morning was sure to lead into an awful day.

Perhaps you should reinforce the impression of mental instability, Ryll suggested. *Your brother appears hostile to you. Perhaps I was a bit impetuous insisting you reveal my presence.*

Right! Let's have some fun.

Abruptly, Lutt shouted: "Graaar!" He waved his arms wildly and leaned toward his mother and brother with a look of menace. "You think I'm nuts, eh?"

Phoenicia and Morey recoiled.

Her voice cracking, Phoenicia said: "Of course not, dear."

Lutt found he still could read her emotions as well as ever. *So like his father. Poor dear. An uneven personality.*

Lutt had once heard her describe him to someone on the vidcom: "He looks rather bookish. It's partly his glasses. His hair is still reddish-brown but beginning to thin prematurely."

Yes, Lutt agreed. *I'm the sort of person you might find in the dusty stacks of a library. But that's not where you'll often see me. My lessons come from life.*

He knew it was bragging but he liked to tell people he was a newspaperman who rarely read anything except headlines.

Morey studied him with fearful expectation.

Lutt wished he were elsewhere. The brief flash of enjoyment over Morey's discomfiture vanished. Mother, he noted, had a brown leather case by her feet. *Prepared for a stay?* He settled into the seat, legs extended.

I'm slouching, Mother.

He knew what she would say next.

"Don't slouch, dear," Phoenicia said.

Right on cue every time. Dear this, dear that. It's always dear.

"I'm Lutt!" he shouted, and this time there was no pretense. "Don't call me 'dear'! Don't call me 'Lutt Junior.' Don't call me 'Lout'! You know my name. Use it!"

Phoenicia looked hurt. "I've never called you Lout. I call both of my sons 'dear' out of love."

Lutt felt anger pulsing in the serpentine blood vessel at his temple and put a finger on it.

Phoenicia shook her head, causing the golden circles of her earrings to bounce against her smooth neck. "Your father worries about you, Lutt. I do, too. And you really should not slouch. It's ruinous to your posture."

"I'm thirty-five," Lutt said. "If I want to slouch, that's my business. I don't have to ask permission of you or Father when I want to do something."

"But, dear, your attempts at invention are becoming quite dangerous. Someone has been killed."

"An accident! Father wants to stop me because he's afraid I'll invent something better than he ever did. And I already have!"

"Your father knows what's best to invent, dear. If he says something's wrong, you should listen to him. After all, you are using his money."

Lutt stared past her out the rear window and muttered: "I've earned that money with all the crap I've taken from him." He saw Morey's involuntary nod of agreement and felt a resonant chord—a shared but mostly unspoken suffering—two neglected sons of a man consumed by his business empire.

Phoenicia's silence hinted that she shared this resentment. How much emotion had she invested trying to make up for L.H.'s neglect of his family? Was that what had driven her to her high-society friends? Perhaps. But as usual she went too far.

She'll do anything for those fawning sycophants!

Morey chose this moment to make his contribution.

"I've noticed something about you, Lout."

Phoenicia, quick to smell trouble, snapped, "You must not call your brother that!"

Morey shrugged, then: "You know, he always slouches like that when he's in trouble or wishes he were somewhere else."

"We all have our little idiosyncrasies, dear."

"Sure we do," Lutt growled. "And Morey's is to play fast and loose with money trusted to him."

Morey paled but Lutt's satisfaction was cooled by his own involuntary reaction: sitting up straight. *I'm still in trouble,* Lutt thought.

Lutt touched a panel button to his left. An oval vidcom dropped from the ceiling on the end of a flexible tube. The tiny robot eye on the microphone positioned it in front of Lutt and blinked green to show it was ready.

"Shop Two," Lutt said and he imagined the crystal bell sounding in the shop near Seattle where he had built his ship. The area was wooded and mostly uninhabited now. Once it had been a prime residential area but the senior Hanson had razed the homes after acquiring the property. It was a pattern repeated on all eleven family plots around Seattle.

"The Hansons want privacy and hunting preserves," commentators said.

A high-pitched computer ditty signaled engagement of the scrambler system to ensure privacy on this call.

Presently, a bearded face appeared on the tiny screen and a deep voice said: "Hi, Lutt. Good to see you're okay."

"Yeah, Sam. You heard, huh?"

"Is Drich really dead?"

"And the ship is shot to shit."

Phoenicia rolled her eyes heavenward. Lutt, dear boy that he was, could be so gross. And he kept such low-class company! This assistant, Sam R. Kand, was every bit as improper as the friends L.H. chose. Unsuitable, all of them.

"Can we salvage anything?" Sam asked.

"I'll let you know later. Meanwhile, start building a new core. And I want you to make these modifications . . ."

Lutt noted Phoenicia's eyes glaze over. She never liked technical details. And Morey was too interested in watching a shapely young woman walking a bloodhound at curbside.

The limousine came to a crisp stop, blocked by a truck backing up to a warehouse bay. Morey smiled and tried to catch the young woman's attention but she did not even look at the garish limousine.

Lutt noted this with part of his attention. Everyone down here knew the rickshaw, of course.

While Lutt gave his instructions, Ryll absorbed the words for later examination.

Something about the fat-necked bloodhound at the curb caught Ryll's attention. The dog reminded him of a hated proctor at the school for gifted children. What was it about that dog?

He saw differences between the dog and Proctor Shanlis, but the four legs and the dog's facial expression struck a spark of memory. The dog's face recalled Shanlis, Ryll decided: hang-jowled and morose, a wide Dreenish nose.

The animal sank onto its haunches and howled.

Ryll, seeing a vision of Proctor Shanlis doing this, laughed and heard the sound in the rickshaw, realizing he had forced this reaction on their body.

"Will you stop that?" Lutt shouted.

Sam on the vidcom screen looked startled. "Stop what?"

"Not you," Lutt said.

"Are you all right, dear?" Phoenicia asked.

"Of course I'm all right! Sam, you know what to do?"

"Get things going. When will I see you?"

"I'll call. But in the meantime I want you to send four sling-loaded turbocopters to retrieve what's left of our ship." Lutt glanced at the directions from Zone Patrol and repeated them, adding: "You're my number-one assistant now, Sam. We're going to build a better *Vortraveler.*"

Lutt sent the vidcom back into its concealed slot and looked at Phoenicia. She was smiling at Morey, responding to some exchange Lutt had missed.

She said she was glad Morey is more refined than you, Ryll volunteered.

Yeah! Morey the diplomat. Morey the kiss-ass. He even gets along with L.H.

Its way once more clear, the limousine accelerated.

"What're you going to tell Father?" Morey asked. Definite signs of fear.

"Only what circumstances force me to tell," Lutt said.

"He's pretty angry," Morey said. Gloating.

"I think he's mostly concerned for your safety," Phoenicia said. "And he doesn't want you wasting time on insignificant projects."

"He may not even dock your allowance," Morey said.

"The hell with that!" Lutt said. "I want *more* money! Damn it! I deserve more money." Lutt grinned at Morey. "Isn't that the Hanson way, dear brother?"

Phoenicia smiled warmly. "Now, isn't it better when you get along like gentlemen?" She blew a kiss to Lutt. "We'll have you right as rain very soon, just as soon as the doctors 'ray you and do the other things they should."

No! Ryll objected. *You mustn't allow anything that would reveal internal differences—our swiveling eyes, for one thing. Stay away from doctors. Too many questions we can't answer. Tell her you'll see your own specialists.*

Lutt saw the wisdom in this and obeyed.

Phoenicia appeared mollified but still concerned. "Get the best money can buy, dear. I'm sure your father won't object to that sort of expenditure." She leaned forward and peered at Lutt's glasses.

"You have new glasses."

"That's very observant, Mother."

"I remember warning you about scratches on your lenses. These are quite clear."

"I got them just before the accident."

"They've come through it remarkably undamaged."

Hoping to divert her, Lutt asked about her carrying case.

"Oh, I don't think I'll be staying at You Gee One, dear. This case contains a replica of a Byzantine vase." She pronounced it "vazz."

"What're you doing with a replica?"

"That is embarrassing, dear. I purchased it last week at Shigg's Auction House. Mr. Shigg himself assured me it was an original and one of a kind. Very rare. But when I got it home, I discovered I already had the original—or what I think is the original, purchased four years ago in Singapore. I now have two of them and two sets of papers purportedly authenticating each of them. I want your father's help looking into this."

"He'll break some heads," Lutt said.

Phoenicia put a hand to her mouth. "Oh, I do hope . . . not."

Lutt and Morey exchanged knowing looks—another point of accord. Phoenicia was not above using L.H.'s muscle when it served her purposes. Lutt sighed. He wished he, too, had time to devote to art collecting. A fascinating hobby. Profitable, too, when you went at it right.

But I have too many other priorities.

You do seem to use your time well, Ryll intruded.

This voice in his head hit the mark that time, Lutt agreed. In common with many successful people, Lutt knew he had learned a great secret: the ability to use small bits of time.

Observing now that the limo was entering the southbound freeway, Lutt estimated they would be at You Gee One in about fifteen minutes. Well, at least this mobile monstrosity carried all of the essential necessities to make those fifteen minutes useful. Lutt leaned over and flipped a tab near the floor. A wide, shallow drawer extruded itself between his feet. An electronic news receiver unfolded from the drawer and lifted into position in front of him.

"Look at him!" Morey sneered. "Can't leave the Eleanor alone for five minutes."

Lutt smiled. At least Morey knew the news jargon. These receivers were known technically as "ENRs," and the initials had shifted easily into the vernacular "Eleanors." In front of Lutt now stood a titanium frame with thin LCD screens for pages. He spun a black dial one-quarter turn and the top screen came alight with the *Enquirer*'s front page and the masthead he had ordered:

"L.W. Hanson, Proprietor."

So the old man had not yet objected.

Lutt flipped through the pages, scanning headlines and bits of copy. One headline offended him.

INDY 5000 GIVEN
A NEW LEASE ON
ITS SPEEDY LIFE

Using his override, Lutt changed the headline to read:

INDY 5000 GETS
A NEW LEASE ON
THE FAST LIFE

"Can't even use verbs right," he muttered and, suddenly angry, he keyed a memo to Anaya Nelson, knowing the city editor must obey his orders in this but would do it with resentment and reluctance. She also would get the message of his anger in the fact that he bypassed Ade Stuart and made her do the dirty work. The memo was direct and curt:

"Whoever wrote the headline, today's fourteenth edition, top of column five—fire that person!"

"You're so full of energy," Phoenicia said. "Just like your father."

Lutt returned the Eleanor to its concealed drawer and grimaced. "What a shame I won't step into Father's big, stinky shoes and run his interplanetary business empire!"

"Who says he wants you to do that?" Morey demanded.

"He does, little brother. He does."

Morey lapsed into sullen silence.

Phoenicia patted his arm and looked out at the brightly garbed robots pulling the limo. Lutt was right about the empire and the limousine, of course. The rickshaw and robots were garish. But she liked the limousine and using it was an indulgence she could justify to her friends:

"It was a wedding present from L. H. He's really very sentimental about it and keeps it in superb condition."

The vehicle was decelerating for an exit ramp. She could see broken-down shanties built of scavanged metal, cardboard, wire, bits of plastic and scraps of wood. The shanties, looking as though a light breeze would blow them down, were crowded into a narrow strip here along the city's boundary.

"Lowtowns," they were called wherever they sprang up around the earth and the other planets—*low* for the height of the decrepit buildings and the status of their occupants.

Poor creatures.

Taking the regular route Phoenicia preferred, the limo skirted Lowtown. She gazed out at ragged women crouched in doorways. Some of them nursed naked babies. All of the children she could see appeared sickly.

The women watched her pass. They always watched. No men were visible. The men, Phoenicia had been told, were busy at various curbsides hunting cigarette butts, or they haunted alleys and dumps scrambling for usable garbage.

Phoenicia thought it obvious that many of these people were mentally ill. The *Enquirer* said they were brain-damaged by undernourishment or bad genes. The eyes of these desperately impoverished people all looked alike to Phoenicia: forlorn, dull, without hope, almost lifeless.

Lutt gazed dispassionately at Lowtown through the side windows of pelletproof glass. He thought of the people there as life's bystanders. They lived in a distant world of slower motions and accumulated filth.

Phoenicia opened her side window, letting the clamorous sounds and repugnant odors into the limo's perfumed isolation.

She's going to do it again, Lutt thought. *When will she ever learn?*

Phoenicia opened a refrigerated compartment beneath her seat and removed a plastic bag of food. She held the bag in the window opening, momentarily between worlds. One of her platinum bracelets dangled to the sill.

Lutt looked at this with what he thought of as objective judgment. He was a newspaperman considering a story about the contrast between extreme wealth and dismal poverty.

Dutifully, the limo slowed. Phoenicia extended her food package. Her slender, manicured fingers released their grip on the prize. It dropped.

"The fastest and strongest always get it," she said, keeping her hand out the window and pointing at the older children and women who ran toward the package on the street behind the limo.

One girl, perhaps thirteen or fourteen, wearing a ragged skirt too short for her skinny legs, ignored the food package. She caught up with the slowed limo and coughed phlegm at Phoenicia's extended hand.

"Ohhhh!" Phoenicia jerked her hand into the limo and grimaced at a gob of brownish-yellow spittle on her wrist.

"Pittance!" the running girl screamed.

The limo picked up speed quickly, leaving the girl and the crowd around the food parcel far behind.

Phoenicia cleaned her wrist with a square of French linen followed by disinfectant from a spray can in her purse.

Morey touched a button and the window closed with a soft thump. A fan whirred, cleansing the air in the limo. "They're doing that much more frequently," Morey said.

Lutt nodded. "Someday, one of them is going to steal a gun and give you more than spit. It's damned foolish to open that window."

Lutt remembered the scrambling people, the faces looking at the limo. He had seen no anger in the faces, only desperation. He knew the anger was there, though.

This *gift* of a food parcel had become one of Phoenicia's rituals, Lutt realized. It'd make a helluva feature for the *Enquirer.*

Rich lady with fake conscience doesn't accomplish jack shit for the poor. She does this for herself so she can brag to friends about her charity and talk about the deplorable behavior of the recipients. What would the old man say if I published that story? Can't do it, of course. We take care of our own. Maybe we should do another Lowtown series, though. The downtrodden poor are always with us—the unfortunate wretches clinging to the shadows of our lives.

Ryll absorbed this. His adventure was turning out not at all the way he had imagined. The values of patience and attention to lessons began to gain new stature.

"Does L.H. know you do that?" Lutt asked.

"Now, I don't want you telling your father I opened the window," Phoenicia said. "It would only disturb him."

"It'd do more than disturb him," Lutt said. "He'd be furious after all his attention to security."

"He thinks a nasty terrorist will throw a bomb through the window," Phoenicia said.

"Or a bunch of those locator dots that stick to your clothes," Morey said.

"Your father is positively paranoid about someone with an electronic tracker following us to his offices," Phoenicia said.

Lutt spoke dryly. "It's been tried, you know."

"Sometimes, I don't understand him," Phoenicia said. "His business interests get more attention from Security than his own home."

"It's just a different kind of security, Mother," Morey said. "He's right when he says we don't want to live underground. It's bad enough to have to work there."

"But he's so secretive . . . even with his own family," Phoenicia complained. "It's like stories you hear about the military and . . . and 'the need to know.' "

"Why don't you hook a refrigerated container to the outside of the limo?" Morey asked. "Push a button in here and it dumps the food. Father's right, you know, when he says a Hanson can't be too careful."

"Would you make such a device for me, Lutt?" Phoenicia asked.

"Sure. Only I'll have the robots throw the food. That way, we'll use the existing in-car communications system instead of a new signal button."

"Oh, that would be splendid!" Phoenicia said.

Lutt shook his head in dismay at the things he could not say. *Father's mechanical coolies will throw pittances to the peasants. What a story if only I dared print it! Are you getting all this, Ryll?*

You do have a strange family by any standards I have ever encountered, Lutt. Ohhh . . . why are we stopping?

We've arrived at You Gee One.

Lutt heard the great security doors clang shut behind the limo, and brilliant artificial light bathed the interior parking area with its bustle of human and mechanical activity.

As usual, Lutt felt a tightening of his stomach.

A contingent of blue-uniformed Hanson guards ran toward the limo, weapons ready.

"Now, you two boys be nice for your father," Phoenicia said. "I'll see you later."

"Aren't you coming in with us?" Lutt asked.

"I have to get to the auction house and straighten out this little misunderstanding. Morey will speak to your father about it. He knows what to say."

Yeah! Morey always knows what to say!

Speed and efficiency have never been part of the Dreen psyche. Our high technology is concentrated on travel through the Spirals into an ever-changing universe. Ancient, unalterable Dreenor must remain a regenerative nest. The Dreen watchwords, "All things are possible," must serve us always as a bulwark of conservatism.

—"Mugly the Elder,"
a critique

"Why didn't she warn us the shield is going to change our sky?" Mugly complained.

He stared out a window of Jongleur's home where he had been summoned by the Chief Storyteller. A late-afternoon sun painted rosy edges on puffy white clouds. But moments earlier, a weak test shield idmaged by Habiba had dissolved. During the test, Mugly and Jongleur had stared out at a gray landscape, not quite dusk and definitely unfamiliar.

"She's testing because childseeds require a particular spectrum of sunlight," Jongleur said. "There's some question whether a shield can admit the correct light. Oddly, the light we need is close to what Earthers favor for darkening their skins."

"That's called 'tanning,' " Mugly said.

"I know what it's called!"

"We could always open flaps in the shield occasionally," Mugly said.

"And how would we guard such openings?" Jongleur demanded. "Will we make weapons and slaughter intruders?"

"We have a right to defend ourselves," Mugly insisted.

"The shield is a brilliant idea," Jongleur said.

"Even if we never again have children, we must protect what we have now!" Mugly insisted.

"And what is it we have now?" Jongleur asked.

Mugly waved his arms to encompass Dreenor. "Everything! What a strange question! Your mind is becoming odd, Jongleur."

Jongleur had to agree. Only that morning, he had taken his fears to Habiba. "What have we created in that Earth?"

"We?" Habiba had asked.

"Dreens have meddled with Earth since its creation," Jongleur mourned.

"Meddled? These are strange thoughts, Jongleur."

And Habiba had taken him on a small tour of her cone to quiet him. It was a strange feeling to walk the colorful floors and realize they were built over an extinct volcano. The porous ground beneath the cone was a spiritual abode, a place of secret chambers and passageways only Habiba traveled. Jongleur knew of them from Habiba's quiet comments.

"Beneath this precise spot is a fumerole that spirals down very deep, and it is dry for all of that descent."

Jongleur treasured these tours. The palatial floors and corridors inlaid with jewels brought to Habiba from uncounted planets had always seemed the most permanent thing in the universe.

But this day he was struck by the impermanence of the structure. In a catastrophic attack by Earthers, everything here might be scattered in fragments.

All things are possible. And once there was a volcano here. But now it's a pumice island whirling in a sea. An eternal sea? Is anything eternal?

Thoughts about eternity came readily at the Sea of All Things but Jongleur now found them disquieting.

Mugly jerked him out of these reflections with a stark question: "Is it true the erasure ship crashed?"

"The wreckage is on Earth."

"Wreckage. That's good."

"My son was in it. And we do not know the extent of damage. If sensitive components survived . . ."

Jongleur let that idea hang between them.

"*Patricia* was designed to self-destruct rather than let aliens learn her secrets," Mugly said.

"That is a very strange name for a ship, Mugly."

"It is a common name for Earther women. Men are often called by a similar form, Patrick. A holy man, you know?"

"Did you think of that ship as holy?"

"I did not think of it as anything. My aides built it without my knowledge or consent. Why did you summon me, Jongleur?"

"Habiba commanded me to make certain our secrets are never learned by Earthers. And now I hear you have sent the Eminence Prosik to Earth with orders to retrieve this . . . this *Patricia*."

"My people contributed to the problem; they should solve it."

"Is Prosik a good choice?"

"The best."

At least he's the best for my purposes, Mugly thought.

"I have been trying to think as you would think," Jongleur said. "And it is a fact that you still want Earth erased. Did you give other orders to Prosik?"

"He was told to act as the situation dictated," Mugly said. "You must admit, if Earth were erased, that would satisfy Habiba's command. Earthers would never again threaten us."

"You left the question of Earth's erasure up to a . . . to a mere Eminence?"

"He was a good Storyteller in his day, Jongleur."

"I've heard rumors he's a bazeel brain!"

"An occasional indulgence, no more. That could be said about many of us." Mugly looked benignly at Jongleur.

Jongleur spoke quickly: "You have tied my hands! We cannot send ships after this *Patricia* willy nilly! Every ship we send is a potential betrayal of our secrets. I am forced to use new operatives and your man, Prosik!"

"I told you he was the best. What do you have in mind?"

"The erasure ship is in the hands of the bothersome Zone Patrol. You must send a Spiral signal to Prosik, telling him this and ordering him to assume Zone Patrol disguise. That's his only hope of finding the ship and recovering it."

"Very well. I'll see to it immediately."

"And tell him he must not erase Earth!"

"Don't you think that should be left up to our Dreen on the scene?"

"I do not! This is an extremely complex matter. Your ship did not just crash, Mugly. It collided in the Spirals with a ship built by an Earther named Hanson!"

Mugly was well and truly shocked. "In the *Spirals?*"

"You see, Mugly? A fine mess you've got us into."

"Erasure of Earth becomes more and more our best option!"

"I forbid it in Habiba's name! No! Prosik must search out this Earther, Lutt Hanson, Jr., and I want him to look for clues to what has happened to my son."

"You'd endanger us to satisfy your personal fears?"

"Of course not! I am following a plan suggested by Habiba."

Mugly sighed. "What is Habiba's plan?"

"We will abduct Hanson—if he's still alive—along with anyone in whom he has confided his knowledge of Spiral technology."

"And how will you know who has shared this knowledge?"

"There will be plans, drawings and descriptions. We will find out who has seen them."

"Earthers call them 'blueprints' and they—"

"I know what Earthers call them! You don't have to explain everything about Earth to me, Mugly!"

"But you never can be sure you've identified everyone who has seen the blueprints. And as for people this Hanson has spoken to in the course of his—"

"It must be done! Anything is preferable to erasure!"

"Anything?"

"Mugly . . . please. You are the most violent Dreen I have ever encountered. It's frightening. For Habiba's sake, rein in your violent nature."

"I must do what is best for all of us, Jongleur. But I will convey your admonitions to Prosik. He is really quite a peaceable type."

Except when he's high on just the right amount of bazeel.

"It gladdens me to hear that, Mugly. Get on with it, then. I must lay plans for the abduction."

Autopsies of these subjects reveal odd bodily variations. The eyes are attached to the skulls above and below by post and socket. The eyes swivel one hundred and eighty degrees! In one position, they appear normal, but when they are turned inward they present a blank gray surface. Movement is controlled by pivot muscles of great elasticity. Our studies fail to explain this. We do not rule out surgical or other medical intervention to create these changes. The study board suggests these oddities may confer mysterious powers on the subjects.

—Zone Patrol report TS/Dreen

With a contingent of Hanson guards following out of earshot, Lutt and Morey walked downramp to the You Gee One Terminal. Just before the last Security checkpoint, Lutt looked back.

The garish rickshaw still stood in the parking area, the robocoolies sprawled around it as though in the last stages of fatigue.

"Look at that," Lutt said. "They're doing it again."

"One of Father's more amusing japes," Morey said.

"Mother knows robots can't feel fatigue," Lutt said. "I think Father programmed them that way just to annoy her."

"She'll use the waiting time to run up the long-distance vidcom bill," Morey laughed. "And it'll all be on the You Gee One relay. He'll see the bill; you can count on it."

"Kind of a silent war," Lutt said.

They rounded a corner beyond the checkpoint and entered a long low tunnel lined in white tile and lighted by a single overhead glow strip. The parking area was hidden from view.

"Not like our war, eh, Brother?" Morey asked.

"We'll discuss that later. Meanwhile, if I were you, I'd mind my tongue."

The tunnel opened to a wide concrete platform where the sound of machinery was louder. Ahead of them lay the old tracks on which You Gee One's tube-trains ran.

Above the loud machinery sounds they heard the hum and squeals of an approaching subway car. Cool yellow standby illumination washed the tracks in low, shadowy light.

Lutt, still wearing the green and black tunic Ryll had reconstituted through idmaging, shivered in the cool air. He wondered if Ryll could idmage warmer clothing.

Are you beginning to believe in me, Lutt?

Just testing.

I'd give us a fur parka but Morey would notice.

They were near the passenger loading platform now and Morey studied Lutt with a new caution as they walked.

"You wearing elevator shoes?" Morey asked. "You look taller."

Lutt waited until they stopped before answering. "Haven't you heard about Pluto resin injections?"

"Hey! Pluto resin isn't approved by the WDA yet. How'd you get it?"

"Maybe I'm just wearing elevator shoes, Morey."

"If you can get Pluto resin, I know where we could peddle it at a big markup."

"How much could you get for my shoes?"

"About as much as I could get for that story about an alien in your head."

Lutt! Do Earthers sell their stories, too?

Not the way he's suggesting.

"Had you going, didn't I, Morey?" Lutt asked.

"You reverting to your college games, Lutt? Your pranks cost Father a bundle bailing you out of trouble every few weeks."

"Not what it'd cost him to bail you out of the trouble you'll be in if the law catches up with you."

"Let's declare a truce, Lutt. I'll support your bid for money to finance your ship or whatever it is if you'll be a good brother and keep Father off my back."

"I'll think about it. Let's see how well you do today. You see, Morey, I also know how Father learned about some of my college pranks. You and your big mouth."

Morey raised both hands, palms outward. "I'll be good. I promise. And I never told Father you graduated by hiring people to take your tests and write your papers."

"Because we both know that's how you got through the Harvard Business Institute, Morey. Right?"

"So we got drunk once and confessed our indiscretions to each other. Isn't that what brothers are for?"

"I'm not sure what brothers are for, Morey. Maybe I'll find out someday."

"What is this ship you're fiddling with, anyway?"

"If L.H. will put up just a little more money, the Hansons will have a spaceship that can cross the universe in less time than it takes to tell about it. We could be in Citelli's star system by morning."

Morey pulled at his lower lip.

Does he believe you? Ryll asked.

He's wondering about it. You can bet he sees the big bucks in it if I'm right.

What makes you think Dreens will let you into the Spirals?

We'll learn the traffic signals, how to tell if there's another ship approaching. You'll teach me everything I need to know, won't you Ryll?

I don't know everything.

But you'll teach me what you do know.

You really believe in me now!

For these stakes, I'll gamble. Now back off. There's a train coming.

Through their shared vision, Ryll paid attention to these interesting surroundings. The loading platform stood above a carbarn wheel of tracks. At the center of the wheel, the Hanson family crest had been worked in green and gold. Six tunnels fanned out from the wheel. The tunnel to their immediate left glowed with the white light of an approaching maglev train. The light grew brighter and the train emerged, an articulated car—a humming mechanical worm that glided to a stop over the Hanson crest.

From Lutt's memories, Ryll knew the car would return via another tunnel into a subterranean maze. The whole thing was, to Ryll, a parody of Dreenor homes, the Elders living deep within the ampleness of the planet.

With a loud sound of grating metal, part of the car's roof opened and a tubular ramp extruded with an armed security guard standing in the opening.

The ramp lifted and extended to the platform where the guard hesitated, his attention centered on Lutt.

"He's noticed that you're bigger," Morey said.

Lutt held up his right hand to display the palm to a scanner beside the guard.

Morey addressed the guard, one of Father's hand-picked "specials" in green and gold uniform. "He's doing something to make himself taller."

The guard's voice was a suspicious growl. "I see that." He glanced at the scanner, then back to Lutt. "Okay, it's you."

Lutt found himself amused by this. He stepped past the guard and, followed by Morey, descended to the brightly lighted interior of the car where they strapped themselves into the first available seats. Except for the guard, who took up position beside the accordion stacks of the tube as it folded back into the car, they were the only occupants.

As soon as the outer door sealed, the car turned on the track wheel and began moving—slowly at first and then swiftly accelerating until the headlight's reflected glow showed a dark blur of tunnel walls. Presently, the car slowed and came to a stop at another carbarn wheel where it was turned and aimed into a different tunnel. Once more, they accelerated. Three more times they were aimed in new directions and finally saw the green walls of the core tunnel.

"Only four changes," Lutt said. "It's usually more."

"Father's overriding the computer," Morey said. "He's impatient to see us."

Abruptly, the car lurched to a stop in the green-walled tunnel, pressing them against their safety harnesses. They saw a freight train cross ahead of them. The articulated sections of the freight cars creaked and groaned, indicating a heavy load.

"Wonder what he's bringing in now?" Morey asked.

"He'll tell us if he thinks we should know."

Lutt slouched in the seat, harness tight across chest and abdomen. Morey leaned forward, trying to get a better view.

"I'm looking forward to the day I'll know everything about the business," Morey said.

When the old man dies, you mean, Lutt thought. *What a foolish man you are, Brother.*

Even without much formal business education, Lutt knew he could step into command of Hanson Industries. That was what Father wanted. L.H. had made it plain despite ranting against Lutt's other activities.

Idiot Lutt with his pipedreams of ultra-fast space travel! Would that be the argument today? Signs that Father was losing patience with Number-One Son were on the increase.

Morey cleared his throat. "I waited dinner for you last night."

"What a shame."

"You were in a Zone Patrol prison at the time. Does that make you an ex-convict . . . among your other achievements?"

"Be careful, Morey. I wasn't convicted of anything. You're the one with valid credentials as a criminal."

"Just what do you mean by that?" Morey blustered.

"Let's talk about your stamp collection," Lutt said.

"What stamp collection?" Morey demanded.

"That stamp in the heel of your left shoe, for instance," Lutt said.

Morey's face darkened with a rush of blood.

Lutt bared his teeth in a wolfish grin. "I can prove you've been skimming from the companies you manage. You're stealing from your own family and buying rare stamps. They are so portable, aren't they, Morey?"

"You . . . you wouldn't . . ."

"Tell Father? Not unless you make it necessary."

"What do you want?"

"That's better, Morey. You can be realistic. That 1995 Anatolian in your heel—what would it bring at auction?"

"You think I'd let you take everything away from me?"

"But I don't want everything. I just want to rein you in a bit, the way Father does with Mother. She can't resist rare objets d'art. You have this compulsion to buy the most expensive stamps."

"If you don't want it all . . . how much?"

"Maybe half. We'll see. I'll need a million right away. That Anatolian should do it, according to my sources."

"What'll you do with it?"

"Father won't give me all the money I need to rebuild and improve my *Vortraveler.*"

"*Vortraveler!* You expect me to pay for that damn thing?"

"Whatever Father does not give me, you will provide. I'll need forty thousand a week after the start-up costs. Now, Brother!"

Lutt held up a cautioning hand as a pale and angry Morey started to reply.

"Just think of me as a dependent. You can peel off a bit more for your new dependent."

"And if I refuse?"

"Don't be stupid, Morey. You'll have a very long and uncomfortable session with Father and his auditors if I lay the evidence in front of him."

"How do I know you have this evidence?"

"You're grasping at straws, Morey. If I know about that Anatolian . . ."

"But where's your proof?"

"I'll see that you get copies."

A deep sigh shook Morey. "You always win, damn you!"

"This time, we both win. I'll just make more profits for a branch of Hanson Industries and it'll be independent of Father."

"Nothing's independent of him!"

"He'll accept it after we start making big money. Just think of yourself as my silent partner."

"And I have to do whatever you say?"

"If you don't, you can stick that Anatolian to your forehead and mail yourself to Pluto. You'll have no reason to stick around here. You see, Morey? Stick, stick, stick! I'm sticking it to you, fella. Finally!"

Morey brought a monogrammed white handkerchief from a pocket and mopped his brow. "I always knew you were a nasty person,

Lutt. How did you find out about . . ." He left the question hanging.

"Why should I tell you? If our positions were reversed, would you tell me?"

Morey's silence was a sufficient answer.

Ryll intruded on Lutt's thoughts. *How can you be this mean to a sibling?*

You say you have my memories. You already know what he's like and should have a good idea about Father's character. They are not nice people.

Neither are you, Lutt.

I'm a survivor. I do what I have to do. You're in Rome now, Dreen alien or whatever you are.

When in Rome, do what the Romans do? Yes, I know the allusion. I also know your "chicken or the egg" argument. Which comes first?

You're learning how to be a human from Earth.

I have many fully assimilated stories of your dreadful planet.

But the reality is not what you expected?

You make a mistake if you treat me as a child, Lutt. I know many things.

I'll get you to tell me some of your stories sometime.

Only if I wish it. My ruminations are my own.

So you say.

Morey chose this moment to whisper in Lutt's ear. "There may be a limit to how much you can bleed from me. Father might like to know how you discovered my secret."

"You think I've tapped Father's Listening Post? Don't be stupid, Morey. If that were it, he'd already know about you."

Morey sank back, glowering.

The exchange set Lutt thinking. *Father's Listening Post.*

It was old L.H.'s ultimate family secret, passed on only to male descendants—a package complete with damaging private information to prove its authenticity. Electrodots on Hanson products spied on the purchasers—computer-sorted surveillance stored at "the Listening Post." Both Morey and Lutt suspected Father of conducting a gigantic blackmail operation but all they knew for sure was that L.H. could influence important people dramatically.

The sons also were assured that no spy dots were found on products used by the Hanson family. Hanson Security paid extremely close attention to this.

The last freight car passed. Their train lurched into motion, gathering speed along a section of track that curved hard left. The brothers were pressed together into a corner of the seat. They pushed themselves apart and presently their car stopped in an enormous cavern.

Lutt unbuckled and stood. He looked up through the car's transparent roof at the brightly lighted cavern. Father's mobile office tower loomed over them in its outsized tunnel—the underground hideaway that once had concealed rows of MX missiles. Like an echo out of the past century, the tower rode its own tracks, able to move even farther into the subterranean maze that concealed Hanson Industries. Lutt thought this the most remarkable achievement of his father's mind—a marvel of robotics and engineering. Like its creator, the Hanson Industries building traveled secret places on a course no other could follow.

Morey, looking troubled, seemed to share similar thoughts as he joined Lutt beside the tube exit. There were dark and secret places in the senior Hanson's mind.

Standing erect beside his brother, Lutt saw that Morey was only about six centimeters taller. The difference had been twice that before the collision.

The guard stood aside as the tube exit opened. "Your father is expecting you."

"We mustn't keep him waiting," Lutt said, leading the way.

"You sound almost eager," Morey said, following Lutt into the tube. "I'm never eager for a scolding."

"You think he's just going to scold me?"

"You may be his favorite, Lutt, but he has a place for me, too. You'd better know he's just made me vice-president for far planet affairs."

"I know all about it, Morey. I know everything you do."

"You're just as bad as Father," Morey complained.

"Why, Morey! And after Father has just promoted you to a position of power and affluence. You're such an ingrate."

"I hate it when you take that smarmy tone!"

"I learned it from you, Morey. Come on! L.H. is waiting and we both know he hates to wait."

As Lutt moved his Dreen-shared body up the exit tube, Ryll mulled private thoughts: *I've linked myself to a wild animal. What can I do to tame him? Is it possible to bring even a small degree of civilization to such a creature?*

Who spies on the spies?

—Watchword of Hanson Security

Lutt Hanson Senior looked down on the MX cavern's arrival area with mixed emotions, watching his sons emerge.

My sons . . . my enemies.

Every word Lutt Junior and Morey had exchanged as they moved through the maze of tunnels had been heard by the senior Hanson here in his office at the peak of the corporation's hidden tower.

How do I make up for the mistakes of a lifetime?

He felt both guilty and thankful for the precaution that allowed him to eavesdrop on the pair. Precaution? Had he somehow been able to foresee what Morey would become? Or Lutt Junior?

But something had inspired him to program a robosurgeon to implant a tiny electrodot transmitter in the neck of the newborn Morey twenty-nine years ago, just as he had done earlier with Lutt Junior. The spy instruments of his own invention were robotically manufactured, as were his other security devices. No other human knew of their existence. But the spydot in Lutt Junior's neck no longer functioned.

I expected them to last a lifetime but now . . . something has gone wrong. What has happened to my firstborn?

Lutt Junior's spydot had been silent since the *Vortraveler* crash. And now their father could eavesdrop on both only when the sons were together.

What happened to him out there in space?

The information remained tantalizingly sparse—bizarre talk about an alien in his body. And Number-One Son's words projected fascinating possibilities in communication . . . if this Spiral News Service idea proved true.

The aging L.H. hobbled on automated canes along a one-way window wall, attention directed downward to where his offspring were undergoing the security check all people underwent on arrival. Human and robot guards scanned and probed the pair before passing them to another maze that would bring them to the top of the tower.

It was difficult to move and still look down at the arrival platform. Elaborate motile amplifying lenses of his own design—contacting the corneal surfaces—projected from his failing eyes like the antennae of a mechanical insect. While he wore them, he could not blink or move his eyes. The system lubricated the eye surfaces and controlled the wearing time, blacking out and forcing him to remove the lenses at a calibrated fatigue point. The lenses forced him to turn his head to adjust the line of sight.

Leaning on his automated walking sticks, the senior Hanson hobbled back and forth, impatient for the arrival of his sons, yet dreading it.

The young Hansons passed through Security and vanished from sight into the lower levels of the mobile tower.

The senior Hanson touched a button on one of his sticks and sent the tower rumbling deeper into the maze of the ancient MX complex. He turned his head and focused on a multicolored hologram projected from the opposite wall—a three-dimensional schematic depicting Hanson Industries' divisions and wholly owned companies.

Biggest damn conglomerate in the solar system!

More assets than those of most nations, an octopus with arms reaching into monopolistic market dominance in places where few suspected his presence.

And who will inherit when I die?

A fit of coughing shook him, dropping his emotions to a new low. He had been feeling markedly worse of late and admitted an anxiety to get better or be done with life.

But how do I pass along the power?

He felt singularly unfortunate. Both sons were thieves and undeserving. They opposed their father in devious ways.

What did I do wrong?

He felt at least partly to blame for the aberrant natures of his sons—either by genetic transmission or in the way he had raised them. Their lives now seemed indelible and this struck him as ironic. He had long been accustomed to reshaping the universe around him according to his personal desires—molding the animate and inanimate as he wished.

And now I seem unable to change my sons.

Security devices in the outer corridor alerted him to the imminent arrival of Lutt Junior and Morey.

Time to make another stab at correcting my mistakes. And this time I'm going to be even more devious than they are!

Try to control everything and you're soon juggling too many forces that have their own momentum. It's like the Sorcerer's Apprentice problem. When things break down into chaos, you don't have the right spell to keep control.

—Wisdom of the Raj Dood

Osceola looked out the inceram window at the Venusian landscape on the rim of Gorontium City—ruddy flames, rivers of molten sulfur, cascades of fiery magma sparkling like a July Fourth display, orange light dancing on the poisonous clouds.

Her watch said it was early morning here but you could seldom tell by the variations in light.

She could hear Dudley in the lock of the entrance anteroom getting out of his inceram armor. Clumsy. He sounded like a bull alligator rubbing against a log.

Their penthouse with its quintuple shielding afforded the best available protection against the planet's searing heat—450 to 600 degrees Centigrade—but she always felt uneasy here and seldom ventured out. Best to come and go by Spiral.

The rooms were comfortable, though, even if they were Spartan and all the furnishings were made out of dull inceram.

Dudley came up beside her and sealed off the view.

"Don't torture yourself, Osey," he said. "You don't have to look at it. You should've stayed in Florida this time."

"Don't like the secretive way you're doin' things. Sometimes, I think you need a guardian. What was so danged important you had to risk going out there in armor?"

"Lutt needs a good woman to bring him into line."

"Your nephew's on Earth, not Venus!"

"But there must be ten or twelve women here who fit the requirements for what he needs."

"According to you! And how you gonna get him here to meet these answers to a young man's wet dreams?"

"I think it'll just happen naturally."

"Natural, my foot! You're interfering again!"

"A little bit. I kinda whispered to him across dimensions that Venus was the ideal place for his vorcamera demonstration . . . and for other things."

"Oh you did, did you? Well why don't you get him a pass to the Legion cat house? That's what your Lutt would like."

"No women for him there. He needs a wife who sets a good example."

"Wife? He's not the marryin' kind, no more'n you are."

"We might's well be married. Must be thirty years now."

"Seems like thirty centuries. Men! You think all it takes is the right woman and everything turns up smellin' like magnolias."

"It's worth a try, Osey. He's not the same Lutt, what with that Dreen kid sharing his body."

"I wish you'd drop this whole mess! You haven't done anything right with the Hansons since you tied up L.H.'s automated limo factory so's it can only make those rickshaws."

"That was pretty good, wasn't it? If he messes up the limo program, all of Hanson Industries shuts down and he knows it. Got his hands tied."

"You were really getting back at your sister, weren't you? For marryin' him?"

"That's not true, Osey!"

"Then why'd you fix it so's she has to say 'Hung Far Low' before the dang things'll move?"

"Some of her posh friends think it's amusing."

"So does L.H. But you're not answering my question."

"It's good therapy for my sister. Reminds her where she comes from."

"Therapy, my ass! That prudish little belle still isn't sure where her sons come from."

"Osey, you stop that! I know you don't like my sister and her family but you go too far sometimes."

"Okay. So now you're pandering for your nephew. What's next?"

"I'm not really trying to control things, Osey. Just influencing them a little."

"Lutt comes up here, he could get hisself killed."

"I know that, but Venus puts a charge in you. He's never been on the real edge of death. It'll be good for him."

"Yeah, I know—therapy. Sometimes I think you fancy yourself as shrink for the whole human race."

"Just for those who need me, Osey."

"Like me, I suppose?"

"It was not I who brought questions to the wise man."

"That does it! We're going home."

"But this is also our home." He gestured at the dull gray room.

"This ain't home! This is a game you play. We're leavin'! Every time you come here you turn into a swell-headed wise guy. 'It is not I who questions the wise man'!"

"I'm sorry, Osey, but I have to stay for awhile."

"Well I'm goin' back! This place gives me the creeps. And it's even worse when I see what it does to you."

"I tried to get you to stay in Florida."

"I'm goin' home but I'll still be watchin' you, you dang old fool! Dammit, you try my patience sometimes!"

"I'm glad you'll be keeping an eye on me, Osey. I'll sing out if I need help."

"And maybe I'll answer and maybe I won't!"

She went to an oblong panel inset into the wall beside the entrance lock. There she placed a palm against a dark spot and her body melted into the panel, vanishing in a twisted whirl of bright light.

"Maybe it's time I retired," Dudley muttered.

Perhaps we have an unconscious desire to enter Time and scatter our seeds. This might explain the existence of Latents. How else could we Dreens harbor such wildly unpredictable idmagers in hidden form?

—Habiba's journal

Entering his father's office suite, Lutt automatically paused just inside the doorway, blocking Morey. This was a requisite pause to survey obstacles ahead of him. Old L.H. was notorious for rearranging his office and placing booby traps in the path of the unwary. Lutt knew most of the pitfalls but Father was continually tinkering. Father warned family members never to enter the office when the senior Hanson was absent.

"It could be fatal."

Lutt believed him.

The place was a multilevel throne room in Lutt's eyes. The Lord Founder of Hanson Industries stood waiting, leaning on his automated walking sticks near the far windows at the top of a crimson-carpeted stairway. No throne there, though the setting called for one. The old man rarely sat down. There was a sense of forced activity about him lately, of a man fighting ill health and desperate to remain in motion. Phlebitis hobbled him and slowed him but Father stubbornly remained on his feet, aiming those alarming lenses at you in an unwavering mechanical stare.

"Well, come in, both of you," L.H. called, his voice cracking slightly. "You'll probably make it safely."

A cackle of laughter shook the old man's body.

Lutt led the way, conscious of Morey close behind. Straight ahead toward the carpeted stairs and pedestal at the windows, both sons walked carefully through the center of the room. Lutt composed himself to show no fear but he could smell the acridity of Morey's sweat.

Yeah, Brother. Stick close to me. We'll probably survive.

The old man remained silent, watchful. He had been known to call out warnings: "Don't step there. Don't sit there."

Lutt kept part of his attention on the wrinkled mouth.

Halfway across the room, the sons passed a standard desk on the right against a yellow and brown wooden wall covered with charts and displays of work in progress. Father seldom used it, preferring an adjacent chairless drafting table he could use while standing. That was where L.H. did whatever remained after his computers had danced to his commands. The computer terminals occupied a gray metal wall to the left—set at a distance that forced frequent walks back and forth.

As he passed the drafting table, Lutt scanned the wall display, noting some of the interests currently occupying L.H.—Solar Wind Farms, Property Management, Space Mining Ventures Ltd., Consumer Products Division, Military Manufactures, Inc.

The old man cares more about his business than about his family, Lutt thought. *Anything solely from his own imagination is more important!*

Like the gadgets L.H. invented and exhibited at prominent places around the Hanson empire, he could point to each of these accomplishments and say: "This is mine."

Lutt had decided at an early age never to become one of Father's exhibits. Morey, however, might still fall into that trap.

At the foot of the staircase, Lutt paused at a gesture from his father. Morey bumped into him, revealing that the younger brother had been looking elsewhere.

"Don't tread on that third step," L.H. said. "And stay in the middle, at least a half meter from either side."

"What is it, Father?" Lutt asked as he skipped the third step. "Detonators? Trap door? An ejection mechanism?"

L.H. smiled. "I've forgotten."

The words rang true to Lutt. The old man's automated canes were another dangerous marvel with an array of buttons that activated concealed weaponry and other devices. Lutt worried that L.H.'s feebleness might accidentally trigger a weapon, killing anyone unlucky enough to be present.

At the top of the stairs, Lutt and Morey moved to a bench on the left—"the Visitors' Hot Seat." Silvery smooth and hard, the alloy surface had no back, making it almost impossible for visitors to relax. Lutt had once brought a padded, clamp-on back of his own design and, in Father's presence, provided himself with a more comfortable seat. It had been planned as something of a joke but the old man showed no reaction.

Telling me it takes more than that to get his attention.

Lutt had left his contraption in place but it was gone at his next visit, probably relegated to a trash heap by this powerful, self-consumed man.

Using his canes for support, L.H. turned slowly as his sons seated themselves, but the mechanical eyes were focused on Lutt.

"Well, Father," Morey said.

"Be still!" L.H. snapped.

Morey fell into abashed silence.

"You both may have noticed," L.H. said, "that I have no newspaper exhibits here. The reason has been explained to you many times. The *Seattle Enquirer* is good for no more than a writeoff."

The senior Hanson's loose-throated voice fell off in a fit of coughing that troubled Lutt. When the spasm passed, L.H. spoke in a lower voice, droning through a recital of Lutt's many failures that concluded with the crash of the experimental ship.

Lutt waited in silence, then: "I'm learning from my mistakes the same way you learned from yours. The *Enquirer*—"

"A writeoff! And now I'm told you are attempting to make it profitable."

"True. I brought in new people at higher salaries, bought modern equipment, remodeled the building and improved morale."

"With my money! You're wasting my money on foolishness!"

"Haven't I heard you say it takes money to make money?"

"It also takes good sense!"

"Father, I've made some choices that—"

"—are unacceptable! Newspapers are an anachronism. You're doing foolish things—even making the offices smell like an old-time establishment! Next, you'll probably toss out the electronics and print on paper!"

"That'd be stupid!" Lutt got to his feet as he spoke but noted that Morey remained seated as Father preferred during a lecture session. "I re-created the ambience of an old news office because that's a proven think-tank. Competitors are copying me."

"Ambience!" L.H. sneered.

"I'm a realist, Father. I use modern technology to the hilt. I want to blend the old and the new to best advantage."

"Son, if you'd branch into satellite communications and intersolar networks, I'd provide all the funds you—"

"Father, I want to dominate the market. *My way!* And it's what I'm going to do."

After a disturbingly long silence, L.H. asked, "How?"

"With the fastest and most reliable interplanetary news service in history."

"Then why're you playing these games with the *Enquirer?*"

"I feel comfortable with the *Enquirer*. It's—"

"Comfort? Comfort is for losers. You only get ahead by being uncomfortable. That's why I never sit at a desk."

"Fine for you, Father, but I have more ambition than you realize."

"I hoped you'd grow out of this nonsense."

"The *Enquirer* is not nonsense!"

"You're actually getting worse. The paper is a scandal sheet. It's embarrassing your mother. You can't go around sensationalizing murder, rape and offworld warfare."

"Why? Because they increase circulation? Don't you appreciate profit?"

"I don't *appreciate* the tone of your editorials! How dare you let Ade Stuart criticize my business interests?"

"Ahhh, the piece last week about the Hanson Industries solar power monopoly."

"A son of mine should be more sensitive to economic realities and family interests."

"A living, breathing newspaper must have editorial freedom. Are you threatening to cut off my funds?"

"You'd only go out with a swan song editorial about me. I know you, Lutt."

Lutt grinned and was surprised to see a matching grin on his father's face. Emboldened by this, Lutt said: "The *Enquirer* can be far more than a writeoff. It could be the base for my Spiral communications system, an almost instantaneous—"

"This so-called vorspiral development you keep pouring money into?"

"I've already sent hyperlight messages to Earth from a ship in space. I believe the entire universe is connected by Spiral passages that will allow us to—"

"—to wreck more expensive ships in space!"

"I now know how to prevent such accidents."

"Look, boy, I'm an inventor myself . . . a *proven* inventor. This little toy of yours has cute aspects but—" Again, L. H. fell into a fit of coughing.

Lutt took advantage of the break to say: "There's a potential for big profits here."

"Your fancy idea will never be profitable," L. H. said.

"How can you say that? My system works. And even without rapid transport of matter I think it follows from—"

"You think!"

"Father, there are major wars on three planets. The potential for news breaks there alone—"

"Hanson Industries is not involved in those wars except as a munitions supplier and that amounts to small potatoes on our total balance sheet."

"But faster communications could also prevent damage to our assets in deep space. We could take quick action when problems are seen."

"Our assets out there already have fail-safe systems handled by equipment and personnel on the spot. You've seen what we did on Uranus. Knock over the competition when they get rough. That's the way to handle these things."

"But with just a little more investment . . ."

"You're looking at big start-up costs. There might be a small profit in a couple of years, but that'd vanish once the competition climbed on our wagon."

"But we could monopolize this, I tell you!"

"Profit is the bottom line, son! Believe me, the profit from this harebrained scheme would be nothing compared with what you'd see if you stepped into this office."

Morey cleared his throat loudly.

"Well, whatta you want?" L.H. demanded.

"Father, perhaps I could—"

"You let me decide about you, Morey. Show some real responsibility and things might change for you."

Once more, L.H. confronted his eldest. "You're wasting time and money and taking unnecessary chances."

Morey was not to be silenced. "You took big chances to get where you are, Father."

"Are you siding with Lutt?" L.H. demanded. He sounded pleased.

"I think he deserves a chance."

"So he can make a pratfall and you can pick up the pieces, that it?"

When Morey did not respond, L.H. sighed and looked once more at Lutt. "I don't know why one of my boys has to have all the guts and no sense while the other has the sense and no guts." He teetered on one stick, lifting the other to point at Lutt. "Now, you look here, boy. You should leapfrog from what I've built—use my back and jump ahead. Take advantage of the situation, boy. Can't you see what I'm offering you?"

"Stop calling me boy! Hanson Industries is your work."

"And it could be yours."

"I want something that's really mine. If the universe is connected by Spiral passages, Hanson Industries would be a tiny part of what we could gain."

"You're talking crazy. That ship you built almost got you killed."

"But I survived and learned something."

"I learned something, too. I've had your project under close watch and if I thought your hyperlight system had potential I'd put one of my divisions to work on it right away."

"Does that mean you won't give me any more funds for my project?" Lutt asked, noting how carefully Morey watched their father to learn his response.

L.H. shook his head in exasperation. "Pie in space!"

"And maybe it's a bigger pie than you think!"

L.H. suppressed a smile at the way Lutt had gone on the attack.

I called him in to chew ass about spending money on unauthorized experiments and he's swinging it around against me! He's a stubborn cuss and that's for sure. Let's see how stubborn.

"Tell you what, son. Maybe we can strike a deal."

"What kind of deal?"

"The *Enquirer*'s policies and editorials are totally at odds with my position, young man. How important is this freedom of editorial policy?"

Lutt smiled, seeing where the old man was about to take them, and saw the beginning twitches of a smile on L.H.'s face.

"You always say everything has relative value," Lutt said.

"Then come with me." L.H. spoke gruffly and motioned with his stick as Morey started to rise. "Not you, Morey. You wait here. And I'd advise you to stay seated. That way you'll be in one piece when we get back."

Leaving Morey, the old man turned and led the way down the steps, lurching on his sticks. They crossed to the computer center where L.H. pointed a stick at the bare wall beside a terminal and pressed one of the stick's buttons.

Lutt prayed L.H. was using the right button and was relieved to hear machinery grinding behind the wall.

"I'm getting old and my vision's pretty bad," L.H. said. "Every system in my body seems to be failing and even my best robodocs aren't much help. I've sure been hoping you'd come around before now."

The sympathy ploy, Lutt thought. *He hasn't used that for quite a while.*

"You have Morey," Lutt said. "And I know there are other capable people in the company."

"Not family." L.H. spoke as a wall panel slid aside, exposing the steps of a motionless escalator leading upward to the secret rooms in the peak of the tower. Each step was marked on its vertical face:

PREPARE TO DIE

SURVIVAL ODDS NIL

Father's peculiar warning to unauthorized intruders should any get this far.

When Lutt remained silent, L.H. said: "You're potentially more capable, son. I sensed that when you were born. That's why I gave you my own first name. Doesn't that weigh on you?"

"It weighs on me."

L. H. waved his lefthand stick in a circle and the escalator began humming. He lurched forward and gripped a handrail, and the weight of his body set the system in motion. Lutt followed two steps behind, speaking as he went.

"Have you noticed, Father, how little our conversations vary? Always the same old arguments."

"Just like these escalator steps, eh? Around and around we go."

Lutt shook his head. "Let's bring recordings next time and save our energy—you with your standard lectures and me with a stock appeal for your approval and financial support."

The old man's quick laughter broke into wheezing coughs.

At the top of the escalator, they went down a narrow corridor and took a small elevator to the very peak—a small room packed with esoteric electronic gear—the Listening Post.

Atop a plastic table at the entrance lay two white envelopes, one labeled "Lutt Junior" and the other "Morey."

At a nod from L. H., Lutt stuffed his envelope into a pocket of his tunic.

"Aren't you curious about your allowance?" L. H. asked.

"I'll learn soon enough."

"So you will, so you will. Take the other one to Morey."

"Why didn't you bring him up here?"

"Wanted to talk to you privately. I'm worried about Morey. He's taken up with some bad people."

"What can I do about it?"

"You can remember he's your brother and try to steer him right!" L. H. nudged the other envelope toward Lutt, who took it in one hand.

A weighted silence descended between father and son.

Lutt felt the crinkling envelope in his tunic pocket, an allowance ostensibly generated from earnings of this most secret Hanson facility. An odd way to handle an allowance, considering the financial resources available, but this was Father's way and not to be questioned.

L. H. seemed to be waiting for something. *For me to tell him how I'm squeezing Morey? Is it possible he knows? Yes . . . it's possible.*

Lutt sent a worried glance around the Listening Post, hub of Father's most secret invention—a scrambler-compression system that could piggyback on any electronic communications, radio wavelengths or hard rays. Here was where spydots hidden in Hanson products transmitted their clandestine information, everything recorded, checked for voiceprint identification, then read and sorted automatically.

Father often referred to this place as his "bank."

"I sell some of it to law enforcement agencies through middlemen," L.H. had explained, leaving any other uses of the place to Lutt's imagination.

Lutt recalled his childhood awe at this place. Father bragged that no one could duplicate it, that no scanners except those of his own invention could detect the room or the spydots that funneled data into it. When Lutt had questioned this, the old man had said:

"I think differently from any person who's ever lived or ever will live. My equipment is exceedingly intricate. Still, I'm cautious by nature. The secret might be stolen and used against me. That's why I take certain precautions."

What those precautions were, L.H. did not share, but two transparent domes on pedestals in the room each held a folder—one marked "Lutt Junior" and the other "Morey."

Lutt's silence continued while he ruminated. At L.H.'s death, the sons were instructed to enter the Listening Post, using the coded signals hidden in the old man's canes, and each son was to remove his own folder.

"Take your own only. Touch the other one and it'll kill you."

Each tape came with connectors to be hooked to the recipient's head. The remaining family secrets would then be fed directly into the son's mind, "including the way you can pass our secrets along to your male offspring."

Egotistical male chauvinist, Lutt thought, his attention returning to the present.

When Lutt continued silent, the old man looked disappointed. He found a plastic container of nonferrous tools and began fussing with one of the microrecorders, replacing a chip and testing it. L.H. coughed as he worked.

"Would you really kill us if we revealed anything about this room?" Lutt asked.

"Like I warned you when I first told you about this place, son: Don't put it to the test."

"You're afraid Morey might be compromised by his criminal friends?"

"That's only one of my worries." L.H. stepped back and admired his work—a tiny component in a glittering wall of them, all looking similar (fingernail-sized rectangles of silver and gold) but each displaying a unique face when studied closely.

Lutt entertained many theories about how these devices worked. He often played a game with his father, attempting to discover the Listening Post's secret—doing this despite the elder's insistence that no other mind could follow the convoluted path of this creation. As L.H. finished his handiwork, Lutt asked:

"Is it a molecular transmitting system?"

A chuckle shook the old man's chest, but his face remained deadpan.

"There's invariably some unsealed place in every building where air escapes to the outside," Lutt said.

Was that a flicker of interest on the old man's face?

"Messages imprinted on atmospheric molecules—"

Lutt waited out one of L.H.'s coughing spells, then continued: "Those loaded molecules could be read outside a building once the air had escaped to—"

L.H. snorted. "What difference would it make whether your mythological molecules were inside or outside? Any receiver worth a damn wouldn't have to wait for a stupid molecule to go outside. As for that, some homes and many vehicles are airtight."

Lutt stared back at his father's unreadable eyes.

"So you wouldn't be able to eavesdrop on spydot messages from airtight—"

"Bushwah! Loaded molecules! Inside, outside!"

"Then I'm on the wrong track?"

"I didn't say that."

This was a new twist on their game and Lutt considered it. Was the old man leading him down a dead-end street? Could be. Time wasted on a useless project of this kind would amuse him.

"You haven't looked at your allowance," L.H. said.

"It'll be something under eighty thousand and I need a lot more."

"Something under eighty thousand, eh? That's still quite a bit of money for one month."

"You're putting ninety percent of my allowance into a pension plan but I need the cash now, not when I'm too old to do anything with it."

"When you're my age, you mean?"

"It's something to think about."

L.H. sighed. "How much do you need this time?"

"Six million."

"Six million! For what?"

"I've built my Spiral communications system and even my experimental ships with second-rate parts. This time I want to do it right—broadcast from war zones on another planet, demonstrate what my system can really do."

"For six million?"

"Two million would go for the news service—equipment, travel expenses and sales promotion. The rest would go into a new ship."

"Which war zone interests you?"

"Venus."

"I've seen Venus. A frightful, red-hot place. What about the war on Mars? At least it's cooler there."

Lutt was astonished. Was he to get the full amount? It was an extraordinary request, six times greater than he had ever dared ask for in the past. The old pattern would be for them to start dickering now, back and forth like street vendors on one of the have-not planets.

"Venus has more news value because it's the Legion against the Mao Guards and there's greater danger there," Lutt said. He recalled the strange, whispering suggestion that had come to him while Ryll slept: *'Come to Venus, Lutt. For the vorcamera, for love and more. Touch your past and your future.'*

"And you'd go there yourself?" L.H. asked.

"Yes." Lutt held his breath. What was the old man's decision?

"Two million now; more if it looks promising," L.H. said.

Lutt did not know what to say. This was ten times the old man's usual "two hundred thousand for special purposes." What game was L.H. playing? Lutt experienced a complex reaction, a mixture of love, admiration, envy and hatred. Two million was only a third of what he really needed!

A coughing spasm once more shook L.H. He leaned over, pressing a cane to his chest. When the spell passed, Lutt said: "Don't tell Mother where I've gone."

L.H. wiped phlegm from his mouth and nodded. The prosthetic lenses glittered with reflected light as they moved. Without another word, he led the way out of the Listening Post. No thanks expected, none given.

Through all of this familial exchange, Ryll had observed without interfering, focusing as much analytical attention as he could on the complex emotional substance, wishing he had paid more attention to classes in alien psychology.

Once in the outer corridor, Ryll ventured a probe: *Why is the mother not to be told?*

She would worry too much.

Your father agreed without argument.

Despite our differences, he knows I have to go my own way.

I fail to understand.

The old man really respects my independence and my drive.

But not your creativity?

I think so but I always have to hear it secondhand from someone else, never from him.

Ryll lapsed into private thoughts. What strange creatures, these Earthers. The family was at war within itself. No filial devotion. The father was a cold-blooded person. Kill his own offspring?

For the first time since linking flesh with the Earther, Ryll felt truly alone, cast adrift in a dangerous environment where no reassuring familiarity could be seen. Was it even possible to introduce real bonds of affection and love into such a society? Ryll was filled with doubts.

When I was young we still could be our own selves—individuals. And that's what I've always fought to be.

—Lutt Hanson, Sr.

From the penthouse atop his shop building near Seattle, Lutt saw the wreckage of his *Vortraveler* on the concrete pad ten stories below: a charred and twisted carcass. Workers scurried around it like carrion insects. The shop's early-afternoon shadow touched the far edge of the wreck, cutting across the demolished drive section in a wavy line.

Here in the privacy of his own quarters, Lutt dared speak aloud to the partner of his flesh. "So they didn't return any of your Dreen ship?"

I could identify nothing familiar.

"Zone Patrol bastards! What are they doing?"

They're watching, and the slightest mistake could land us in jail . . . permanently.

"I have to assume you're right."

Why else do you think I haven't resumed control of our body? I'm still not sure I could mimic all normal human responses.

"So you say."

I say the truth. Tell me, Lutt, why do you treat your own brother in such abominable fashion?

"Did you see how quick he forked over the first payment?"

But your father gave you so much.

"Nowhere near enough! You see that ship down there? I'm going to rebuild it and do it right. You're going to help."

How can I help? You're planning a very dangerous—

"You don't know the first thing about danger! But you'll learn if you don't tell me all the secrets of Spiral travel."

I was only a passenger on an automatic ship.

"Don't lie to me!"

Lutt slammed open the sliding window in front of him and, before Ryll could interfere, climbed out on a narrow ledge. He teetered there, one hand holding a window frame.

What're you doing?

"You think you could idmage our flesh back to life if I dived onto that wreckage?"

Ryll experienced terror and the ticklings of a memory from his schooldays—something about separating from merged flesh at a moment of death. All he said, though, was: *You wouldn't!*

For answer, Lutt released his hold on the window frame and swayed against a wind blowing along the ledge.

All I know is it takes seventy Dreen minutes by Spiral to reach Earth from Dreenor!

Lutt resumed his grip on the window frame. "I've heard of a Venusian hour but what the hell is a Dreen minute?"

Approximately 2.57 Earth minutes. Please! Let us go inside.

Lutt ducked back through the window but left it open.

Not daring to try for control of their body lest Lutt dive through the window in the struggle, Ryll focused on the opening through which Lutt stared at a distant snow-crowned mountain.

Privately, Ryll thought he would have to tell desperate lies, concealing innate knowledge of Spirals known to every Dreen.

"You see that mountain?" Lutt asked. "When you refuse to help me or answer my questions, I'll hang glide from the top."

Memories in Lutt's mind made it clear what he intended.

Don't do that! Ryll protested.

"Treacherous downdrafts up there," Lutt said. "They can drop you to the ground—much farther down than out this window."

You're insane!

"Old L.H. taught me how to get what I want. And you know my glider was designed only for my original height and weight."

But we're heavier and taller now!

"I've been warned not to use that glider if I gain five pounds. Very dangerous. This could be real sport."

Why would you take such chances?

"I enjoy danger. You read me and know that."

But you were never this crazy before the accident.

"So maybe the crash changed me. This is the new Lutt."

Ryll did not know what to do or say. The evil situation was getting worse by the minute.

When Ryll did not respond, Lutt said: "You try to take over our body and I'll jump out that window or something worse first chance I get."

Ryll experienced a surge of anger. *Ingrate! I brought you back to life. Is this the thanks I get?*

"What's that funny smell?" Lutt demanded.

Smell? Oh, that's the odor of Dreen rage.

As he revealed this, Ryll knew he had made a mistake.

"Kind of a floral perfume," Lutt said. "I'll remember it. I wish Morey gave off signals like that. Did you see how mad he was when he handed me the money?"

He looked angry enough to kill.

"Morey? Kill? He's too much of a coward."

I'm told Earthers change when pushed into a corner.

"Is it the same with Dreens?"

I have no way of knowing.

"Interesting. You know what I like about our arrangement, Ryll? It's how healthy I feel. And right now, I'm hungry."

Will you at least let me have some say in what we eat? If this gets too dull, I may become desperate.

"I'll know it when you give me that wonderful smell."

Wonderful? It's a terrible smell.

"That should tell you how different we are. There probably are lots of things I'd think are marvelous and you'd hate . . . or vice versa. Sauce for the goose could poison the gander."

Ryll's thoughts went immediately to bazeel.

"I've a great place to eat," Lutt said.

Pausing only to don a dark-blue cape, he ordered up a long Cadichev limo and drove it himself, much too fast through dense foot and vehicular traffic in the city streets.

Ryll dipped into Lutt's memories, recognizing their destination when they came to it. A red neon sign across the front of a high-rise building announced: "The House of Health."

It began to rain as they emerged and went up a short flight of steps to a security door and into a parlor dominated by red velvet and crystal. There was the nearby sound of low music and laughter mingled with clinking dishes. Smells of spiced food were heavy on the air.

A burly male attendant in antique black and white formal attire took Lutt's cape.

"Good to see you again, sir," the attendant said.

Reading Lutt's experiences here, Ryll felt repelled. What a strange combination of activities!

Some of Ryll's emotions leaked through to Lutt and he shared a gleeful thought:

It's a good business. That's undoubtedly why Morey decided to invest.

A combination restaurant, health spa and house of prostitution?

Why not? Isn't health composed of many factors?

But isn't this sort of thing illegal?

Wealthy patrons pay off the police and it runs smoothly. We call it among ourselves "The House of Delights."

The attendant gestured Lutt through a wide doorway into an anteroom dominated by a short metal tunnel lined with flashing lights and hairlike probes.

Lutt stepped into the tunnel with easy familiarity, allowing the probes to touch his head and hands. He began to read aloud from a overhead display showing "BOS +.05."

"Brain Oxygen Supply plus .05. That's the best I've ever shown."

Careful, Lutt! Can this machine detect alien cells?

It reads my chemistry. Now it's showing which organs are supplying the oxygen and other elements I need.

But they'll compare this new assessment with your previous readings.

So what? There's no 'ray attachment to the thing.

What's the purpose?

There's a vending machine at the other end where I can get "super medicine" to compensate for deficiencies. They'll also add things to the food I order.

I can see that food is not your primary interest here.

Yeah! The bordello is the best on Earth.

Lutt, please don't.

Come on! I'm going to be generous and let you pick some of the food.

A heavyset female attendant in a green jumpsuit bulging with concealed weapons helped Lutt out of the tunnel's far end.

"You see that?" Lutt crowed. "Nothing for me from the dispenser. It recommended healthy exercise upstairs!"

"You're in superior condition, sir," the attendant said. She had a gravelly voice. "Congratulations."

"Food first," Lutt said. "Nothing like one of your fine meals to tone up the gonads. I'll want a private room. Send Priscilla with the menu."

"You're not going to have Toloma, your favorite?"

"That's a definite maybe."

The private room accorded with Lutt's memory preview. Ryll took it in at a glance: mirrors all around, small glass-topped table, two spindly chairs, thick white carpet, low coved lights at the edges of the ceiling.

Why the mirrors on the ceiling? Ryll asked.

Can't you read it in my memories?

I'm afraid of what I may discover there!

The mirrors are great. Wait and see. Look at this wall panel. It pulls out and there's a bed. The table and chairs go into that slot over there.

The carpet's so thick.

Yeahhh. Sometimes you don't even bother with a bed.

You're really disgusting, Lutt!

Priscilla, entering the room behind them, interrupted this exchange.

"Oh, hello, Lutty!" she cooed.

Ryll saw a blond with narrow face and large breasts. She wore a transparent bikini and shoes with spike heels.

A pneumatique forty-four, Lutt gloated.

Lutt! Please send her away!

I thought you wanted to learn about humans firsthand.

Priscilla extended a thick folder. "Here's the menu. I just never know what you want."

At least send her away while we're eating, Ryll pleaded.

You Dreens are such prudes.

We are merely fastidious.

Lutt said: "Toddle along, Prissy."

Priscilla pouted. "Don't you want my recommendations?"

"Another time."

She flounced out, saying: "I'll send Toloma!"

Lutt opened the menu. "Hey! They must have a new source of fresh basil. They've restored pesto Genovese to the menu."

Ryll felt a surge of consternation. Basil! The Earther name for bazeel! Oh . . . how tempting, but dangerous . . . very revealing to Lutt. No Dreen could idmage-block the drug's effects.

We'll have pesto for sure, Lutt gloated. *And red wine.*

I may turn your pesto into rummungi or worsockels.

What the hell are those?

They vie with bitter peeps as Dreen favorites. But Ryll thought privately. *No matter what I do, the bazeel will remain.* The dreadful drug defied idmaging. Dreens whispered that bazeel's origins lay buried in a "scattering" that preceded even Habiba. No one appeared certain of anything about it.

Would I like them? Lutt asked.

I don't know. But aren't you curious?

Yeahh, a little, but don't mess with my pesto. I'll order something else for you. Lutt studied the menu. *Smoked eel . . . No! I hate it. Too rich.*

Dreens love rich foods and especially rich desserts.

Then maybe we should stick to my preferences.

You promised.

Sometimes I break my promises.

Is that something I should learn to do?

Maybe you've already learned it.

You Earthers are so suspicious! You have unimaginative, dull minds. Your taste in foods is the same—very dull. No imagination.

Look here, my Dreen friend, we have to get along. I'll admit I needed you after the wreck and maybe I like some of the benefits but . . .

Such as being alive?

Like being bigger and healthier. That machine downstairs doesn't lie.

We're stuck with each other for now, Lutt, but I'm going to separate us as soon as I'm able. Most of this flesh is mine!

Anytime, baby. But right now we eat pesto.

Even if I object? For the love of ampleness, can't we compromise?

How?

As a beginning, each of us could select half of this meal.

Okay. But can you separate our taste senses?

They spoke of it at school as being very difficult.

You let me know when you're ready, huh?

Ryll, tempted to utter a sigh of satisfaction, stayed completely separated from bodily control. As a major effort in dissimulation, this had not gone badly. Lutt needed help in rebuilding his *Vortraveler?* Very well, to the extent possible. Ryll recalled vaguely that the great Storyships had something to do with breaking the bonds of merged flesh. By helping Lutt build the ship, Ryll thought he might free himself in some way.

If only I can remember what they said when I wasn't paying attention.

Earther life was idmaged for symmetry according to the Dreen ideal, but also with a discordant asymmetry. The symmetry of two eyes, two arms and two legs conflicts with asymmetry: one side of the face different from the other, one arm longer, one foot larger and so on. This can only be a source of other discords as life seeks to find symmetry in the midst of asymmetry.

—The Habiba Commentary

From the bordello, with Ryll choked into dizzy remoteness by the effects of bazeel and Earther lovemaking, Lutt took their shared body back to the *Enquirer*, hiring a "House of Health" attendant to drive them.

Ryll felt that he cowered in this body, weak and unable to do anything except record vague sensations of the flesh through Lutt's responses. Those awful mirrors! And not just in the ceiling but folding out of the walls. The grunting, thrusting, sweaty performance—how utterly disgusting . . . except at the very end. What an oddly pleasant sensation.

Wrapped tightly in his cape, Lutt stretched out on the wide seat, muttering.

"Gotta wrie t'marra's edi . . . editor'l. Crissakes! I shunt be drunk on th' li'l bitta wine I had wi' dinner!"

Barely in control of consciousness, Ryll held his silence, fearing tricks his bazeel-fogged mind might play on him. Lights in buildings they passed jiggled and danced to unheard music.

Not caring what the driver might overhear, Lutt said: "Hacum we're so drunky, Ryll baby?"

When Ryll did not reply, Lutt became belligerent. "I'm talkin' t' you, baby."

The driver spoke over one shoulder: "Sir?"

"Not talkin' t' you! Talkin' to him!" Lutt pounded himself on the chest.

The driver faced forward and concealed a grin until he was sure Lutt could not see it.

"So you're gonna play dumb, huh?" Lutt demanded. He pinched their left ear. "Ouch! Tha' turts!"

"Sir, would you like me to stop someplace for a detox?" the driver asked.

"You jus' drive us t' the *Enqui . . . Enquirer*. Crise! Wha' was in tha' wine?"

At the *Enquirer*, Lutt turned the limo over to a photo-team driver with orders to park it and send the "House of Health" attendant home with a large tip.

Employees tried not to look at him as he staggered down a long hallway past antique signs that said "Composing Room," "Press Room" and "Proofreaders." Recorded sounds of a press rumbled in the building and synthetic scents of an antique newspaper plant wafted on the air.

"I like all th' ol' stuff," Lutt told Ryll. "Smell 'at? We pipe't in: prin'er's ink, dus . . . dust, newsprin', bad coffee an' sta . . . stale san'wiches."

Lutt stopped and put a palm to each side of his mouth, concentrating on clear speech.

"Stale ambience." He dropped his hands. "Tha's wha' I call it." The "it" came out with a hiccough.

He launched himself into motion and made it to his office, collecting bruises from collisions with walls and doorways.

Lutt's office appeared to Ryll like the control room of a primitive Earther spaceship. Large panels displayed pages on demand. A keyboard projected from one wall with a contour chair in front of it. The arms of the chair held buttons for the selection of mode—editing, review scanning, new material . . . Lutt slumped into the chair and ordered caffeine. When a copyboy brought it, he gulped the liquid, belched and bent over the keyboard.

Ryll, temporarily resigned to the role of observer, watched words appear on the screen and sampled Lutt's thoughts. Despite the senior Hanson's objections, Lutt obviously was determined to stir up emotions and increase the *Enquirer*'s circulation, making the business even more profitable.

The editorial called for creation of a city-county Housing Authority to promote ways of improving the lives "of those unfortunate wretches clinging to the shadows of our lives."

Now, to incite pressure for Mother to serve on the commission! Lutt gloated. *I'll do it secretly.*

Ryll soon tired of the observer role and, strength returning, reflected on the bordello experience. Toloma, Lutt's favorite, had been a surprise—at least fifty years old and with hair a garish henna-red. Lutt's memories said she had known the senior Hanson for more than thirty years. The old man had brought Lutt to her on his fifteenth birthday, saying:

"Break him in, Tolly."

What a confused and convoluted person you are, Lutt, Ryll intruded.

"Stay out of it when I'm writing editorials!" Lutt barked.

Don't say these things aloud! Someone might hear.

"Then shut up!"

Ryll lapsed into sullen remoteness.

Toloma definitely was a surprise, as was Lutt's reaction to her, telling her: "You're my best friend, Tolly."

Toloma had shown astonishment. "You don't mean that."

"Sure I do."

Ryll-observer had found it more pleasant to sample Lutt's memories and avoid the immediate fleshly involvement. Hanson Senior's attitudes shocked Ryll. The old man had told his son before the first visit to Toloma that Hanson men had to become buddies the way military companions did.

"Where's the war?" Lutt had demanded.

"It's against women, boy! Don't you see that?"

Once more, Ryll intruded on Lutt's work: *Your father's sick and it must be contagious. You've caught it, too.*

Lutt took his hands off the keyboard and leaned back into the chair. *Listen to me, you Dreen prude! Next time you interfere with my work, I'm going to run down the hall shouting: "There's a Dreen in my head!"*

You wouldn't!

How long before it gets back to the Zone Patrol? They're sure to have spies here!

Right. Now stay out of it!

Lutt returned to his writing.

A subdued Ryll returned to his private thoughts, wondering if the Dreen idmager of Earth might have been mentally ill. There was no doubt about aberration in Lutt. While making love to Toloma, Lutt had engaged in a waking dream, pretending the woman with him was his faceless "Ni-Ni."

Similarities between Lutt's waking dream and Dreen idmage projection techniques did not escape Ryll. Was there useful knowledge in this fantasy "Ni-Ni"? Who was the mysterious "other man" Ni-Ni was supposed to love? Why couldn't Lutt see her face and identify his rival? It was the stuff of nightmares. Where did insanity stop and sanity begin?

Dreen primary school warnings about merging flesh haunted Ryll. Bits of his lessons suggested separation might be achieved by adapting a Spiral ship's equipment but none of this assured success. Stories from the few who had merged and separated shared a common comment:

"The way in is the way out."

Whatever that was supposed to mean! Ryll felt ever more hopeless about his situation. Take over the body and risk being identified as a Dreen? Did he dare?

Lutt finished his editorial, unfolded a cot from a wall, stretched out and dimmed the lights, preparing to sleep.

That editorial will anger your father, Ryll intruded.

It won't make Mother happy, either. Now, let me sleep.

Ryll felt his flesh-partner drift into sleep and dreaded the dreams that might come. What an evil creature this

Lutt was. No gratitude at all about being saved. He didn't care about others, only about his own desires.

If I can separate us, he'll die. Why doesn't he suspect?

Ryll returned in memory to the deck of his Spiral ship, that first awakening after the crash and the subsequent merger of bodies. He remembered cellular intrusion into a shattered body.

The way in is the way out?

Ryll asked himself if it might be possible to idmage their body smaller than the present one, reducing it precisely by the amount of Lutt's commandeered flesh.

Ryll swiveled his eyes inward and began the idmage formula for a new human body but encountered immediate resistance. Even while asleep, Lutt projected a powerful will to live.

He is attempting to survive by preventing my idmage efforts!

As he prepared himself for a new attempt, Ryll felt Lutt awaken.

"So you didn't believe my warning?" Lutt demanded. "Okay, baby. Today, we go hang gliding."

Lutt! Don't! I was—

"I know what you were doing. And after I warned you, too."

Ryll retreated into his private consciousness, resolved to increase his idmage strength by reviewing every schoolday lesson he could recall.

Oh . . . why didn't I pay more attention?

And this hang gliding venture could be fatal!

Ryll tried to remember the lessons on how to escape from a merged body that was dying. Parts of it came through daydreams about commanding his own ship in the Spirals but there were frustrating gaps. The instructor's words mingled with Ryll's own dreaming commands to the fantasized ship.

He felt a sudden anger at Lutt.

This Earther is being cavalier with my body!

"I smell that interesting smell," Lutt whispered.

Ryll ignored this. Anger and fear had cut through some

of the frustrating memory gaps. The instructor had been talking about how to escape a combined life form at death, even though trapped in it during its life.

"You dare not act too soon or too late." The words burned into Ryll's memory.

But what was too soon or too late? Did it require regaining his own mass or shifting to another fleshly mass?

Memory provided no answer and he could feel Lutt's gloating confidence.

Privately, Ryll thought: *It's my body, damn you! Mine! You're the alien intruder.*

Certain things I know innately, but I cannot explain the source of my knowledge. I know there occurred in the seeding of this universe a Dreen who might discover a way to conceal his thoughts from me. I have no way of knowing whether this awful ability can be passed along to offspring. There could be many Dreens with secret thoughts.

—The Habiba Commentary

An evening breeze blew through tall brown grass, moving the stalks against Prosik's new body. He did not like the absence of legs but the idmaged form possessed a slithery suppleness, as had the original in the zoo where he had first observed it.

After hiding his ship, the *Kalak-III*, under a swamp, he had thought it a brilliant maneuver to sample Earther animal types at the nearest zoo and there he had found the perfect creature for creeping up unseen: *A giant snake!* It was a much better disguise than assuming Zone Patrol shape and uniform. Too many unknowns there that might give him away.

Through a wide doorway about thirty meters distant and directly ahead of him, Prosik could see into an enormous hangar where Zone Patrol technicians worked cautiously over the remnants of a Dreen Storyship. Enough wreckage remained that he identified *Patricia*, the ship designed for erasure of Earth.

Nothing remained of the drive section except random strands of once-molten metal.

Between Prosik and the open doorway lay a flat paved surface. His green-scaled snake head, its tongue darting out and back in automatic fashion, was concealed by grass and a raised lip on the concrete.

Soon it would be dark and he thought he might venture from the concealing grass for a closer look at *Patricia*. The erasure system had been built into supporting struts for the control center. Some of it might have survived the crash.

While he waited, Prosik went over the memorized erasure procedure in his mind: *first a twist of this plate and then . . .*

A great clattering sound intruded on his thoughts. It grew louder with frightening rapidity and now there was an added swishing noise. Prosik lifted his head slightly and peered toward the sound. He was in time to see an enormous automated power mower bearing down on him from the right. Before he could wriggle a tail muscle, the thing was on him. Cutting blades tore through his idmaged snake body. Pain coursed through him as the mower chewed its way across his center section, spattering blood and torn flesh through the fallen grass. He fought to maintain consciousness in what was left of his body behind the head—less than a third of the original mass. Urgency drove him, propelling the intact section across the scattered shreds of flesh, reassembling, taking what he needed where he found it, snatching up two unfortunate ground rodents when he required their mass.

When it was done, he cowered near the raised lip of the concrete and watched the mower devour another section of tall grass, thus removing the cover on which he had counted.

Did anyone see me?

He lay there along the concrete, waiting. And when the mower moved far enough away to permit distinguishing other local noises, he thought the sounds from the hangar did not change—still occasional screeches of torn metal being moved, the grinding of machinery, voices.

As he listened, he reflected on his narrow escape from destruction and thought: *This is a dreadful world. Wemply the Voyager was a traitor to all Dreendom when he created it. I will be glad when Earth is no more!*

But if I'm the one to erase this awful planet, I may be no more, too.

Prosik felt deeply sorry for himself then and longed for just a small amount of bazeel to soothe his anguish.

As evening shadows grew longer, he heard changes in the noises from the hangar and risked a look across the concrete. Yes . . . it appeared the workers were concluding their labors for the day and were preparing to leave. Tools were being stored, a guard posted. Different lights were turned on, bathing the hangar entrance in a brilliant wash of illumination through which even a small flying insect might be detected.

Prosik felt a sinking sensation. How could he traverse that lighted barrier without being discovered?

He scanned the building and then remembered his adopted form. Snakes could climb. He had seen this at the zoological gardens. He would go to the shadowed corner of the building, up a drainpipe and down along the top of a sliding door, then into the hangar at an upper corner of the doorway where guardians were not likely to look. Once more, Prosik congratulated himself on the shape he had chosen.

Eagerly, he waited for night, noting how lights went on all around the Zone Patrol compound. Small flying craft began to flit back and forth across the area and Prosik suspected they were scanning the ground with unseen rays. He would have to cross the open concrete area rapidly between such scans.

Darkness came and the bright lights at the open doorway of the hangar appeared even brighter.

Habiba, help me, Prosik prayed and slithered to a corner of the concrete apron. Waiting until one of the small flitters had passed, he sped across a shadowy expanse of the flat surface and up the drainpipe. The pipe creaked alarmingly with his weight but the snake body performed even better than he had hoped and he soon found himself atop a sliding door. Here, he used more caution and moved slowly, ever alert for indications that he had been detected.

As he had seen from the ground, the door was suspended on heavy rollers that rode atop a track. The track afforded a good avenue for him to traverse but the rollers were heavy with grease that soon coated much of his body and made it difficult to keep from slipping off. Insects attracted by the light distracted him.

Relieved when he reached the end of the door, Prosik ventured a look down into the hangar. The guard sat at a small desk in a near corner, feet up and head back, a dark handkerchief over his face. The rhythmic sounds of sleep breathing could be heard quite clearly.

Abruptly, a buzzer sounded and the guard snorted to wakefulness, glanced around and activated a control on the desk. The bright lights went off and the door beneath Prosik began sliding closed along its track, carrying him with it.

Frantically, Prosik fought to stay out of the rollers and remain on the track. A roller crunched across the tip of his tail and a piece of him dropped outside. He grabbed flying insects to replace his mass but that distracted him even further and the door pinched him into a corner as it closed.

Several minutes were required for him to disengage himself and by then a small group of humans had entered the hangar through a side door. Prosik watched them through a crack where the door overlapped the hangar wall. It was a limited view but his acute hearing brought their voices to him clearly. They walked around the Dreen ship's wreckage while the guard stood stiffly at attention nearby.

Their leader appeared: a tall, bald man, lean and with a birdlike beak of a nose.

"This is a pretty typical Dreen ship," he said. "As usual, the drive system is such a congealed mass that we have no hope of discovering anything useful from it. We have confirmed, however, that it was remarkably small."

"What does its size tell us?" one of the others asked.

"That their technology is supersophisticated," the leader said. "We're going to try disassembling the drive supports next. As you can see, the support structure is different from that on any other ship we've taken."

"Are we apt to set off a self-destruct system such as that which destroyed the drive?" another asked.

"That's always the risk," the leader said. "Most of our casualties have come that way." He turned away from the wreckage. "This is it, then. I wanted you to see the actual thing. We'll go back to the lab now and study the photos and sketches."

As the group left, the leader paused beside the guard and asked: "Any sign of intruders?"

"Nothing, sir," the guard said.

"I see we've baited the wreck," the leader said.

"That's the routine, sir."

When they were gone, Prosik waited for the guard to settle down but the man appeared nervous. He walked over to the wreckage and studied it, then looked all around at the shadows before returning to his desk and chair. Even there, he continued to look around him.

Prosik dared not move lest a sound attract the guard. Would they stay this way until daylight exposed him here clinging to the track and the edge of the door? It was a frightening thought.

Time passed and Prosik's snake body ached with inactivity.

A buzzer sounded and a red light flashed on the guard's desk. He pressed a button and a slot on the desk surface opened, presenting him with a steaming container of food.

As the guard concentrated on eating, Prosik began to hope. Earthers were notorious for being distracted by food. Indeed, the fellow appeared uninterested in his surroundings.

Slowly, thinning and elongating his body, Prosik descended between the door and the wall. At the bottom, he slithered around the edge of the doorway and hugged the base of the wall.

At last!

He was in the hangar and the guard gave no notice of the thin addition to the dark juncture of wall and floor. Even when behind the guard, Prosik dared not relax. He moved faster, however, making for the end where the wreck would conceal him.

With a patience Prosik had not suspected he possessed, he crept around the hangar, achieving finally the concealment he had sought. Even here, he dared not relax because it came to him belatedly that the wreckage also concealed the guard. What was the Earther doing over there? Prosik listened to faint buzzings and clangings from the guard station. What was their significance? And what had that Earther group leader meant by "bait" in the wreck?

The exposed space between the hangar wall and the wreckage appeared dangerously magnified by his fears. He paused to condense his snake body into its original anaconda muscularity and then, praying once more to Habiba, he slithered out onto the floor, moving as fast as he could.

At the wreck, he inserted himself into a space beneath it and lifted his head carefully until he could look across the hangar at the guard. The Earther sat with eyes half lidded, obviously far gone in digestive torpor.

Excellent!

Prosik withdrew his head and began examining the damaged ship. Yes—the drive was an unreadable meltdown as the Earther had said. But the erasure system was intact and the self-destruct safeguard remained.

Would there be time to open the system and activate the erasure sequence now?

He ventured another look at the guard and felt a surge of terror. The seat at the desk was empty and the guard was nowhere to be seen. Even as Prosik contemplated flight, he saw a door open behind the desk and the guard emerged. There was a brief glimpse of toilet facilities before the door closed. The guard returned to his seat with a satisfied grunt.

Prosik lowered his head and once more studied the supports that concealed the erasure system. Two had been badly twisted but the protective covers remained intact. Critical structures with the controls showed a few dents but the system was duplicated and allowance had been made for possible damage. Essential elements were buffered by protective shielding. Prosik swiveled his eyes inward and began the idmaging to extrude a manipulative arm. Before he could do this, he smelled a familiar odor.

Bazeel!

A small mound of the wonderful drug lay on a flat surface of the wreckage only centimeters away.

Prosik moved his head toward the bazeel and his tongue flickered out in its automatic snake fashion. The tongue withdrew with a generous dusting of bazeel on the tip. Prosik felt the familiar soothing sensation.

Ahhhhhh.

He allowed himself another taste.

A small dalliance, he told himself.

Only when he was close to complete bazeel torpor did he remember the Earther's remark about bait. A sound behind him cut across his memory. Prosik, his head wavering deliciously, turned and looked toward the sound.

Horrors!

The guard stood there with the muzzle of a long weapon pointed directly at Prosik.

"What have we here?" the guard asked.

Prosik could not move a muscle. He wanted only to sink into bazeel fog but terror would not permit this.

The menacing muzzle of the weapon moved closer.

Prosik stared at it, completely fascinated.

"A snake?" The guard's tone was clearly incredulous.

Summoning all of his energy, Prosik dropped his head behind a broken metal surface and sought a way to bury himself in the wreckage. He knew he could not move backward without tearing scales from his snake body and that effort was beyond him.

An ear-shattering explosion interrupted his frantic search and a metal surface slammed against his back. This was followed immediately by another explosion and the sizzling eruption of a self-destruct system. Molten metal seared one side of Prosik's snake body and he reacted instinctively, slithering out of the wreckage as fast as he could.

The guard lay on the floor, half his head torn away by the blast that had ignited the self-destruct system.

Without thinking it through, Prosik idmage-scanned the dead guard and cast himself into that shape, complete with torn uniform and a few bloody but lesser wounds. It was done in seconds and Prosik stood in his new form to hurl the guard's body into the inferno that had been one of the ship's erasure activating systems.

As he slumped back to the floor, there to allow himself to be discovered by the Earthers he could hear racing toward the scene of disturbance, Prosik knew he had added a new dimension to his problem. In the brief moments of his flight into this disguise, he had seen the drive supports still standing on the far side of the wreck. If they survived, he now had only one control system with which to carry out his mission but, if his disguise succeeded, he might be able to gain undisturbed access to what remained of the erasure ship.

Leaders must never set a bad example for those who follow. But the band of followers also must set a good example—both for their leaders and for their fellows. Otherwise, the social compact dissolves and society descends into chaos.

—Dreen aphorism

Lutt awoke on the cot in his office with a most memorable headache, which, on asking a few internal questions, he found was shared by Ryll, the partner of his flesh.

We will tend to share most bodily ills and good feelings, Ryll explained.

But I seldom have hangovers, Lutt complained.

Perhaps it was the combination of the foods and the drink, Ryll suggested.

There wasn't anything I hadn't eaten before . . . or drunk.

In that combination?

Well . . . we sure got around one helluva lot of pesto.

At mention of the dish that had contained the bazeel, Ryll felt an involuntary shudder go through their shared body.

You seemed to like the pesto, Lutt said. He glanced at his watch. *Keerist! I'm due at the editorial conference. Gotta order up some coffee.*

Ryll found the coffee helpful but he sensed the beginnings of suspicion in Lutt about the contents of their meal.

Lutt asked himself if certain Earther foods might have an adverse effect on Dreens and if there might be an advantage in this. A dangerous line of questioning, but Ryll felt helpless to divert it. Any such attempt would be sure to increase Lutt's suspicions.

The editorial conference definitely was not a rerun of the earlier one Ryll had watched. From his first entry into the room, Lutt displayed a new confidence and sense of his own power.

Suzanne Day, obviously aware of his hangover, had closed the shades on the eastern windows to reduce the morning light. Lutt felt grateful for this as he sat down and scanned the six faces around the long table. His head still felt misused and his eyes burned.

City editor Anaya Nelson, who had been reading through a stack of notes, looked up at him with open amusement.

"We could draw red ink right out of your eyes," she said. "You really tied one on last night."

Lutt ignored her and focused on Ade Stuart. The managing editor's electric cart was pulled up close to the conference table on Lutt's right. Stuart's softly rounded face was held in bland immobility.

"I'm tapping the special fund, Ade," Lutt said. "We're going all out on my Spiral News Service project and that's where we're getting some of the money for it."

Nelson, with her usual condescending expression, emitted a barking laugh. "So we're not out to make a profit, after all!"

Lutt looked down at the polished surface of the table while he silently counted ten, then aimed a hard glare at Nelson. She ran a hand through her golden hair and grinned at him.

"I've had it with you, Anaya," Lutt said. "If I get any more crap, we're going to my father, just the two of us, and have him tell us which of us is running this paper. Meanwhile, I expect your full cooperation in what I'm about to do."

She went pale under his glare and wet her lips with her tongue. Lutt could almost hear the thoughts racing through her head. Anaya surely knew old L.H.'s hopes for his Number-One Son. She knew the old man would back his son in a showdown.

Lutt pressed his advantage. "If I see the slightest sign that you are not cooperating, one of us will no longer work for this publication. Is that clear?"

Stuart, always the diplomat and certainly worried about his precious special fund, entered the breach. "We'll cooperate, Lutt, but what're you planning and how much of the special fund will you need?"

Lutt returned his attention to Stuart, but not before noting how much this exchange pleased Suzanne Day. The Style Section editor studied Lutt with a softly contemplative look, obviously asking herself what personal advantage she could gain.

The others, even old Mark Sorrell, who had edited the business pages "since coming off the Ark," watched Stuart. Young and old, they all knew who mediated trouble on the staff.

"I'll need all of the fund, Ade," Lutt said.

That brought them to attention.

"The best little war we have is between France and China on Venus," Lutt said and fell silent as Ryll, reading the plan in full at last, objected: *No, Lutt!*

Shut up, Ryll! I'm busy.

"What about Venus?" Stuart asked.

"I'm going there personally," Lutt said. "I'll set up at Pe-Duc or Berguun and—"

"You'll report the war yourself?" Nelson asked.

"Personally."

"Who's going with you?" Nelson asked.

"Were you thinking you might like to be part of this?"

"Perish forbid! They kill people on Venus."

"I'll use our existing staff there and hire others if I need them," Lutt said. "We'll call it the Hanson Task Force."

"All of this out of my special fund?" Stuart asked.

"Every penny. And there's more. We'll send our copy back instantaneously from the war zones by Spiral transmission."

"You call it Spiral now and not vorspiral?" Day asked.

"It sounds better," Lutt said. "We'll call the news service SNS instead of VNS."

Thanks for the small concession, Ryll intruded.

"It'll give us a time advantage, certainly," Stuart said, "but the special fund is—"

Lutt cut him off. "It'll also pay for a big kick-off party to which you will invite all of our competitors. Every one of you will be there selling access to Spiral News Service."

Stuart was shocked. "But the special fund provides—"

"It's there to help us make a profit," Lutt said, adjusting his glasses. "And when we get subscribers, our profits will replenish the fund."

"Cle–ver!" Suzanne Day said. "We sell hard or there'll be no money in the special fund."

"Get the business office to set the subscription price," Lutt said. "I want it as high as the traffic will bear."

The editors exchanged glances.

Nelson leaned forward, elbows on the table. "How heat-sensitive is your transmission equipment?"

"Good question," Stuart said. "It's at least eight hundred degrees Fahrenheit on the Venusian surface."

"Don't belabor the obvious, Ade," Lutt chided him. "My lab has been studying ways we can adapt inceram to our needs. An inceram casing will protect everything we use."

They took a few seconds to absorb this. Countless war stories and articles analyzing human occupation of Venus had made inceram a household word. Without the ceramic porosity of inceram's high-temperature insulation, the forms of life known on Earth could not survive on Venus.

"Will you just be reporting the war?" Stuart asked.

"Yes," Suzanne Day intruded. "What about terraforming efforts and the role of women on Venus?"

"I hear the Foreign Legion has the best bordello in the universe up there," Nelson said. "That'd make one helluva story with a woman's angle."

Day was not diverted. She smiled politely and continued: "The word is that your father thinks Venus has a big potential as a power source."

Nelson turned a different, heavily weighted look on the younger woman. "How the hell do you know what the old man thinks?"

"I have my sources," Day said.

Nelson nodded, accepting this. "Right. L.H. believes Venus could make a lot of money for Hanson Industries . . . once it's terraformed. He's thinking of harnessing volcanoes to augment solar power."

"We have a multiple stake in the planet," Lutt said. He sat back to let them absorb this.

Ryll took the opportunity to renew his objections. *Why will you put us in such danger?*

You don't know about real danger, Ryll baby. Anaya's right. They kill people on Venus.

Nelson returned to a previous thread, a reflexive tone in her voice. "Why Pe-Duc or Berguun?"

"The southern hemisphere is where the heavy action is."

Stuart at last indicated full acceptance of Lutt's plan. "It's also the most dramatic—the Foreign Legion fighting the Elite Mao Guards. We still get a lot of mileage out of that even without instantaneous transmission."

Nelson shrugged. "Okay. We'd better alert our bureaus on the other planets. France and China are fully mobilized along their common borders on other areas of the solar system."

"But only fighting on Venus," Stuart reminded her.

"Until one of them breaks the nuclear ban," Nelson said.

Lutt offered her an olive branch. "Anaya's right. The treaty won't stop nuclear war if one of them gets backed into a corner." He looked at Albert Li, dark and saturnine director of the editorial pages, who sat at the far end of the table, above all this, and mostly silent at conferences unless directly addressed.

"You getting this, Albert?" Lutt asked.

Li lowered his chin slightly.

"Start preparing our readers," Lutt said. "Editorialize about the fragility of treaties, recap nuclear ban efforts, make comments on other Earth colonies where France and China face each other, that sort of thing."

Li granted them another almost imperceptible nod.

The business editor finally decided to demonstrate his special expertise. Sorrell was well known as one who carefully gauged proximity to the throne by how he addressed superiors. The first-name basis was as close as you got and heretofore he had always addressed Lutt as Mister Hanson.

"You'd better know, Lutt, that getting you to Venus may cost more than the special fund can afford. National Security is about to impose new restrictions."

"What restrictions?"

"Seats to Venus are being set up on a higher priority basis: Zone Patrol agents, military advisers, presidential aides. The press comes last."

"Okay, what are they fishing for?" Lutt demanded.

"Heavier payoffs to a few top officials. It takes big backsheesh to support our democracy. The bagman is Senator Gilperton Woon on the Interplanetary Transportation Committee. He splits with three other ITC reps and one Congressman."

"Can we prove it?"

"Not likely."

"Tell you what, Mark," Lutt said, accepting the man's new self-appointed status. "Get to Woon. Tell him we're preparing an editorial attack on corruption in government, that we'll demand grand jury investigations of ITC activities."

"He may just laugh at us and we've made an enemy," Stuart objected.

"Not if Mark makes it plain we won't rock any boats if I get low-cost priority on a seat to Venus."

Sorrell nodded and said: "Let me suggest you travel under an assumed name."

"False papers?" Lutt asked.

"We can make it part of the deal with Woon."

"Good. Arrange it."

Nelson cleared her throat. "Okay. Is fun and games time over? We do have everyday ordinary news to publish. And I have a report that someone tried to blow up a Zone Patrol hangar last night."

Lutt stood and looked at Stuart. "Take over, Ade. I'll provide all of you with memos on your parts. Right now, I have to get out to the lab and set things in motion."

Without waiting to see the effect of his words, Lutt strode to the door. A trick of the room's acoustics picked up Nelson whispering to Stuart: "If last night's drinking bout is any indicator, he may be starting the Hanson *Flask* Force."

Stuart's whispered response was equally clear: "Lay off, Anaya. You can't lose in this. If he shows big profit, L.H. will accept it. If he flops, the old man will be doubly delighted."

Lutt closed the door behind him with a soft click and smiled tightly.

Once they were in the outer hallway, Ryll resumed his arguments. *Lutt, you've plenty of talented people you could send. There's no need to risk us.*

If you want a thing done right, you do it yourself.

But think of the dangers!

Yeah! I'm looking forward to that. And did you hear what Anaya said about the Foreign Legion's bordello?

This is insane!

Maybe, but it's sure gonna be fun.

Ryll lapsed into his own thoughts, wondering if he dared try to take over their body. But this new strength in Lutt frightened him and there was an added fear: *What if I tried and failed?*

They were in the elevator now and they emerged presently in the underground parking garage. Lutt strode toward the reserved limo area, ignoring the other human activity in the garage—people coming and going, vehicles leaving and entering.

Ryll, only part of his attention on their surroundings, was attracted suddenly by the sight of a characteristic Dreen aura—a faint glow of yellow—around two figures approaching them. The pair appeared normally Earther, nondescript men in ordinary business attire.

Those two Earthers approaching us are Dreens, Ryll alerted Lutt.

How do you know?

Trust me. They seem very interested in you.

They do, don't they. Why is that?

They obviously recognize this as Dreen flesh.

Before Lutt could explore this, the two men were abreast of him. Without warning, they whirled and, one on each side, grabbed Lutt's arm.

"Identify yourself!" one of them growled.

With his Dreen-amplified human muscles, Lutt hurled the men aside and started running toward the limos. The two recovered and rushed in pursuit. Lutt dodged between the vehicles and temporarily confused the pursuers. Crouching behind a limo, he peered through the windows at the two disguised Dreens.

What do they want? Lutt demanded.

I think they have been sent to capture me. They probably suspect who I am.

Shit! I would have to be locked in with a fugitive.

Lutt glanced left and right. The whole incident appeared to have attracted no attention from others in the garage. He was on his own unless he called for help.

Let me help, Ryll offered.

How?

For answer, Ryll swiveled their eyes inward and idmaged a transparent barrier around the pursuers.

The two collided with the barrier immediately but responded with their own Dreen powers, idmaging an opening in the barrier only to find that Ryll had superimposed another barrier around them . . . and another . . . and another . . .

It soon became apparent that Ryll's idmaging powers were superior to those of the pursuers and they stopped in defeat.

Ryll was elated. Those had to be two adult Dreens and he, a mere student, had bested them. He was tempted to go to them and gloat but found this an unDreenlike response. Perhaps the Earther side inflicted him with hubris. He would have to watch out for such weaknesses.

We can go now, Ryll told Lutt.

As Lutt drove them out of the garage, Ryll removed the barrier around the two Dreens, wondering at himself. Letting the two Dreens capture him might have led to freedom from Lutt. Ryll began to lament his own foolishness.

Lutt drove with characteristic gleeful abandon. *That was clever what you did back there, Ryll baby. But you said once you would like to see a war. And that's where we're going.*

The seven days in the Dreenor week are called Old Story Day, New Story Day, Journey Day, Home Day, Rest Day, Marriage Day and Birth Day. Some choose to follow this pattern in their lives but you may engage in any permitted event on any day.

—Dreen schoolbook

Incomplete though it was, the idmaged shield around Dreenor presented a wide patch of gray in the morning sky. Habiba thought it appropriate this first test of the shield should occur on Home Day, the day tradition said all Storytellers should choose for their return to Dreenor. She sat at the peak of her cupola with only Jongleur nearby—waiting to give her another message about that accursed Earth, no doubt.

On the barren plain in all directions, uncounted numbers of her subjects knelt in united idmaging effort to produce this test shield.

They must idmage more powerfully, she thought.

Habiba knew their problem. Some were shirking, giving less than their full effort. And who could blame them? The shield spelled an end to a familiar and necessary element of their lives. Everyone knew this must bring other changes. Future birthings would present problems. Gaps must be opened temporarily to admit sunlight onto the seedhouses.

But the Earther threat was real and uncontrolled.

Recent reports said Earthers already had reached the tenth planet in their system. They called it Kassina. A dark ice giant, the planet orbited beyond the one they knew as Pluto. Even without Dreen technology, Earther ships soon would reach beyond Kassina.

Jongleur had reported this with obvious fear.

"Their ships are slower than ours but with only minor modifications could reach Dreenor."

The ships would certainly arrive bearing terrible weapons.

We must raise the shield!

She looked down at the patient Jongleur. "Urge our people to the utmost effort. Warn them again about the Earther threat. Find those of us who have adapted to reliance on a chemistry more conservative of sunlight. Concentrate on demanding that they try harder. The shield must be idmaged."

"It will be done, Habiba. May I give you my report now?"

"If you must."

"We believe Ryll has been seen. It must be Ryll because all other operatives have been identified."

"Then why hasn't he been returned to Dreenor?"

"He is in the guise of Lutt Hanson, Jr., and, Habiba, he resisted our operatives. He idmaged barriers our people could not overcome."

Jongleur could not disguise his pride at such superior ability but there was a tone of fear in his voice. It pained him that his son might be a rogue.

"I am happy if your son lives, Jongleur, but what of Mugly's erasure ship? Has Prosik found it?"

"Prosik . . . yes. But there was an explosion at the ship and Prosik may be dead or a captive."

"Mugly sent only Prosik?"

"He felt that sending others might bring Earther attention to our concerns and cause them to stiffen their defenses. The Zone Patrol is certainly keeping that Hanson fellow under close watch."

"Why didn't you order Mugly to send others?"

"Habiba! That ship is Mugly's responsibility."

"But you are Chief Storyteller."

"You know how Mugly is when he's crossed. The smell of anger . . ."

"Don't let Mugly intimidate you. He must do as you instruct. I have a thought about your son and his Earther guise."

"You fear he may have merged with the Earther?"

"That would explain his behavior. You are certain the person seen is Dreen and that it is Ryll?"

"Why would any Dreen resist our operatives?"

Habiba nodded in the manner of her people, with the entire upper portion of her body. "Merging does produce bizarre responses and various mental disorders. Three who did it were suicidal."

"But it usually occurs only under the most urgent conditions."

"To survive serious injury, yes. And there *was* that collision with the erasure ship. You are right. The evidence suggests it is Ryll and he has merged with the Earther."

"Unless my son is a stowaway on a joyride somewhere and this Dreen in the guise of Lutt Hanson, Jr., is a captive who has somehow become Earther-contaminated."

"Not likely. No mature Dreen would endanger Dreenor."

"Then I must send stronger idmagers to capture him."

"No! I have decided we need our strongest to raise the shield. We can spare no more people."

"But what of Prosik and the erasure ship he seeks?"

"Use people we already have on Earth. That is an order, Jongleur."

"Yes, Habiba, but if our people free any captives, may I employ them as operatives?"

"Except for the stronger idmagers. Return those to Dreenor."

Accepting dismissal, Jongleur sped away from Habiba's exalted presence.

It were better that my son died, he thought. *A merged monster may do anything . . . anything at all!*

The list of matters I do not understand grows longer. My list may be far more complex than that of any other Dreen. I must always weigh a wider range of issues. Oh, the terrible burden of my ignorance!

—Habiba's journal

Lutt spent part of the Venus passage reviewing data about the planet and wondering if he would find Uncle Dudley there. Perhaps the investigators had missed something in their search for him. It was so easy to vanish on Venus.

The *Amita-Oho*, the ITC ship carrying him, provided a wide spectrum of Venus publications, including one titled "Survival in a Fiery Hell." He reread the first entry several times.

"The Venusian atmosphere blocks the escape of infrared radiation. This 'greenhouse effect' creates an average surface temperature above 450 degrees Centigrade. You will see the ground glow. In an atmosphere with pressure more than ninety times that of Earth, Venusian winds of only a few knots can blast the unwary visitor into oblivion.

"Inceram armor meeting UL standards compensates for heat and pressure but exceptional conditions can kill you. Of particular danger is the 'thermistone' phenomenon peculiar to the planet. This is the term for extremely high temperatures that may concentrate in small mineral pockets on the surface.

"Such pockets may appear to the eye no different from the ordinary glowing surface even though they can be so hot that inceram in contact with them can be destroyed in four minutes. The so-called 'Venusian hotfoot' is no joke. Keep moving when on the surface. Watch the readings on your heat-sensors. Travel only in groups. Never go anywhere without your medical pack, your inceram repair kit and an operating transceiver, and always carry a spare wind-deflector attachment."

Absorbing this information with Lutt, Ryll found it terrifying. Their flesh might be consumed before any idmaged barrier could be created. He suggested idmaging emergency sheets of inceram.

Lutt was excited. *Can you do that?*

Yes, but it's a complex material and will require much practice. I don't think I can do it very rapidly.

Try it at the first opportunity, but not where anyone can see us.

I should've thought about this earlier but you were so busy with your Spiral News Service and that work on your ship. Personally, I would not trust that assistant to do everything correctly.

Sam's perfect for the job.

Ryll thought of responding with an audible sniff but Lutt might suspect an attempt to take over their body and, here in space, who knew what he might try as punishment? Still, Sam R. Kand was a worrisome figure in Ryll's thoughts. Another "helper" with a peculiar name: Where did he originate?

On that final visit to the lab before departure, Kand had been more interested in the new *Vortraveler*'s hull than in the Spiral News Service equipment. It had been late afternoon of the day before the Venus trip and Kand, standing in Lutt's shadow, was a wiry, dark-skinned acolyte as he hustled them through the tour of inspection. The nostrils of his hooked nose dilated as he indicated two workers attaching the metal skin to a hatch.

"As long as there's no overheating problem in Spiral space, the plasteel will do fine. More structural strength for its weight."

"But what about the news service equipment?" Lutt wanted to know. He pointed to the workers. "Aren't those two part of the crew you had working on the transceiver housings?"

"Everything you need will be ready before your big sales party, Boss. Don't worry."

"Everything has to be first quality, Sam."

"That's why we're only this far along on the ship. Some of our parts are on back order. And the cost! If you'd come up with more money, I could bring in more men and robots, really speed things up."

Lutt, knowing he already had tapped his brother and other sources for as much as they would bear, shook his head.

"Then maybe you should delay the Venus thing," Kand suggested.

"Just go along with me, Sam. In the long run, Venus will speed up completion of this ship. Our profits are going to be big."

"If you say so, Boss. We're salvaging as much as we can off the wrecked ship. Some internal structure survived but you told me not to sacrifice quality."

"Do the best you can, Sam. And put those two men back to work on the transceivers. That's first priority for now."

Ryll had thought the exchange unsatisfactory. The assistant clearly was more interested in the ship than in the news service equipment, a mixed blessing from the Dreen point of view.

Lutt, internally seeking data from Ryll to improve the ship, had seemed to offer an opportunity that would create a way of separating them from this merged flesh. But try as he might, Ryll could not remember the lecture material he required. Daydream interference blocked his memory at every turn.

Or was it daydream blockage? Obviously, if Earthers acquired the means of reaching Dreenor, all of Dreendom was in peril. It occurred to Ryll that diverting Lutt into a concentrated effort on the news service at the expense of the ship might delay the ship until Dreens could find a solution to this accursed planet . . . something less drastic than (Habiba save us!) erasure. But Lutt saw the news service as only a temporary diversion of effort, and if it did bring great profits . . .

The Earthers were a truly formidable creation: unpredictable, greedy, readily corrupted. The Earther senator who had arranged this trip struck Ryll as dangerously typical. Senator Gilperton Woon and his cronies controlled ITC. The senator had appeared amused by Lutt's bargain-seeking efforts but there had been something hard in his eyes.

A dangerous enemy. Ade Stuart was right in his judgment of Woon. No doubt of it, but Lutt did not heed warnings about this.

And the use of faked identification papers might rebound against Lutt, although the justification sounded reasonable.

Lutt traveled under the name of Peter Andriessen, a byline he sometimes used. It could be argued that famous people needed anonymity in public. But what if the deception became the object of a criminal accusation?

Now that they were actually en route, Ryll found his mind dwelling on countless dangerous possibilities. Why did Venus attract Lutt? The planet held little of apparent value save for the geothermal potential, and this was a power source too distant from the more industrialized planets to be of immediate use. But Lutt argued on his father's side when it came to this point.

"History has a way of turning up uses for the most inhospitable places."

He cited something called "Seward's Folly" and the "Xerxic Pluto Land Purchase."

Midway through the second day in solar space, Lutt emerged from his compartment on the USS *Amita-Oho* and joined his fellow travelers in the lounge. The *Amita-Oho* was a venerable sunpellet ship with Spartan private quarters, but it had posh dining and lounge accommodations, although they were upholstered in a hideous shade of green with black trim.

Venus was visible through the forward viewscreen, a brilliant pearl growing larger by the hour as the ship approached.

The recently announced dramatic increase in price of passage to Venus had produced a logical result, Lutt thought. The ship was less than half full. He wondered if Woon and cronies had reached the point of diminishing returns. But there was no great competition for passengers. Perhaps the ITC had other motives. Lutt identified only three other media people among the passengers and two of those were from publications known to favor the present administration. Earth history was replete with examples of junket control as a potent tool of those in power.

One of these media representatives, Lorna Subiyama, presented Lutt with a problem. She knew the byline Peter Andriessen, and gave signs of recognizing Lutt. A gabby columnist from the All-Tex Syndicate, Subiyama was a power in the industry and had been known to embarrass the administration. She was an enormous woman with a bouffant blond wig framing a puffy face. Her blue eyes were a size too small for all of that flesh but they carried a penetrating stare. There she was now off to Lutt's left chattering at a bony dark woman in a jumpsuit.

Lutt took a seat where he could watch the forward screen and Subiyama immediately broke off her conversation to join him.

"It's amazing how much you look like Lutt Hanson, Jr.," she greeted him.

"The boss is somewhat smaller than I am but I hear that a lot," Lutt said.

"I've seen your byline," Subiyama said. "You write quite well for someone off in a jerkwater place like Seattle."

"I'll look you up for a letter of recommendation if I ever need it," Lutt said.

What if she identifies you? Ryll wanted to know.

It'll make a good story and help sell subscriptions to our news service.

"I'm amused by all the talk about Venusian volcanoes and the great energy potential," Subiyama said.

Oh, oh! Lutt thought. *She's been hired by the oil industry to pry into Venusian development plans!*

"The volcanoes are big," Lutt said, "and the planet itself is hot enough just on the surface."

"Hell! We got a fire department in Dallas could put the whole damn planet out in half an hour."

"Yeah! Everything in Texas is bigger and better."

"You bet, Buster! I can get in my car and drive straight ahead for three days and I'm still in Texas."

"I had a car like that once," Lutt said.

Subiyama threw back her head in a loud guffaw and slapped him on the back hard enough to bring tears to his eyes.

"Hey! I like you, Buster."

Now I've done it, Lutt thought. *I'll never get rid of her.* He closed his eyes in despair.

You wish to drive her away from us?

I don't think it can be done. She smells a story.

Even as he thought this, Lutt felt his eyes swivel inward. A damp weight settled on his lap and, once more in control of his eyes, he looked down to see a brown protoplasmic blob.

Shocked, Lutt thrust it away with a quick jerk of his arm. The blob landed in Subiyama's lap and she jumped up with a loud squeal. The blob fell to the floor and wriggled there, creeping back toward Subiyama. She fled to the bulkhead, staring at the thing in horror.

"Great balls of fire! What is that?" someone asked.

It looked to Lutt like a large mound of excrement that had suddenly come to life. It writhed and snapped toward Subiyama, leaving a sluglike film on the floor. Lutt smelled something faintly sweet.

"Keep it away from me!" Subiyama screamed.

That got rid of her, Ryll intruded.

You did that?

I idmaged it. This trip has been as excruciatingly dull as Dreenor itself. Creating a lumpy is an interesting diversion.

What the hell's a lumpy?

Every Dreen makes them occasionally . . . as amusement. They are primordial organisms. But the stupid things must draw their sustenance from the ambient air.

Why's it going for Subiyama?

I analyzed the substance of her garb, which gives off barely discernible gassy effusions. Those effusions are now the food of my lumpy.

But what do we do now? How do we explain it?

Pick it up and put it in your pocket. Say it was a joke.

The lumpy had almost reached Subiyama's feet. She stood on tiptoe, moaning and shuddering as she stared down at it.

A small crowd gathered to look on but no one touched the blob.

"Where'd it come from?" someone asked.

"It fell on that guy's lap," another said, pointing at Lutt.

Lutt stood and forced his way through the onlookers. He bent and scooped the blob into both hands. It felt like a mound of animated gelatin. He slipped it into a pocket and grinned at Subiyama.

"Gotcha!" he said. "You should see some of the other things I brought. It gets dull as hell on Venus, they told me."

"A practical joke!" someone said.

Subiyama glared at him. "Jokesters should be consigned to the nethermost hell!" she said.

Lutt shrugged and returned to his seat.

Subiyama stalked out of the lounge.

The bony dark woman Subiyama had been talking to when Lutt entered turned and smiled at Lutt, who winked.

"I could've used that thing an hour ago," the woman said. "I thought she'd never stop talking about Texas."

That sent chuckles through the lounge but no other passengers joined Lutt. He leaned back and closed his eyes, hoping this would be another signal to leave him undisturbed.

Why must you swivel our eyes to idmage? Lutt asked.

It's not absolutely necessary for all forms of idmaging but it does help concentration.

It feels weird in my brain.

Our brain, Ryll corrected him. *Would you like me to do it again while you participate? We could reconstitute our lumpy on that dark lady's head.*

Let's just eliminate the thing. It's making my pocket wet.

"Oh, all right. Go ahead and swivel our eyeballs inward.

Lutt attempted to do as instructed but could not feel movement.

Here, I'll do it, Ryll interrupted.

Lutt felt his eyes turn slowly counterclockwise. The faint glowing visible through his eyelids vanished in blackness and a tiny pinpoint of light replaced it.

Concentrate on the little light, Ryll instructed.

Lutt suddenly felt all of his brain's energy focused within the pinpoint of light, which expanded in flowing waves like the ripples from a rock dropped into a pond.

The wet blob vanished from his pocket.

Does it always take that long? Lutt asked.

I did it slowly to let you share in it. An accomplished journeyman Storyteller can do it in an eyeblink. Would you like to try it on your own? See if you can make a small inanimate object?

You think I could do it alone?

Only if I facilitate it, but this does help while away the boring trip. Now concentrate.

What'll I make?

Try for a grain of sand. Remember to concentrate on how a grain of sand looks and feels.

Again, Lutt felt his eyes swivel inward and the pinpoint of light appeared. He concentrated the way he had as a small boy whenever his governess told him to pray for something. Lutt had always prayed for things he wanted—electronic gadgets, as a rule. Once, he had prayed for the death of Henry Ivory, a twelve-year-old classmate. Both of them had been seeking the attentions of Mareeka Perino, another classmate who had matured early—a young beauty whose body had expanded into repellent fat when she reached her teens.

Lucky thing Henry didn't die or I'd have been stuck with Mareeka, Lutt thought. *Mareeka Freeka we called her.*

Stop daydreaming and concentrate!

Lutt returned his attention to the task. *It seems stupid just to make a grain of sand.*

Later, you might try forming the silica of the sand into glass, then ultimately convert it to a fiber optic strand. That is known as superimposed idmaging and possibly you can learn it.

For the better part of an hour, Lutt tried to no avail.

Ryll finally stopped the effort. *I don't think you'll ever be able to do it alone.*

Are Dreens the only ones who can idmage?

There are no reported examples of others doing it. That does not mean it's impossible, because we are taught that anything created in thought can occur in the external universe.

That doesn't sound logical.

Habiba, our Supreme Tax Collector, says, in theory, a non-Dreen may idmage under certain circumstances, a precise set of conditions apparently unknown in our universe.

Lutt felt his eyes swivel outward. He opened them and stared at the forward viewscreen. Venus was a much larger pearl. Sunlight reflected creamy yellow from its sulfuric acid clouds. One spot of orange in the cloud cover indicated a volcanic eruption.

A female flight attendant came up beside Lutt's seat to share his view of the screen.

"Mount Maxwell is erupting," she said. "Not to worry. We'll touch down on a plateau at least ten thousand klicks southeast of the volcano."

Conversation around Lutt rose to a new pitch as others looked at the screen and began to question the attendant. Lutt listened with only half his attention.

So what if Maxwell was more than fifteen kilometers high, nearly twice the height of Earth's Mount Everest?

"Just one of the many Venusian volcanoes," the attendant said. "They spew out sulfur and searing heat."

"Maybe this is what Hell's supposed to be," someone said.

"I wish France and China would settle their differences and let us get on with developing the place," another offered.

"You hear how hot it is in some of the military command centers under the surface?" someone asked, and answered his own question: "Six hundred Centigrade at least."

Hearing this, Lutt thought about the three inceram suits he had brought for himself.

"Guaranteed no more than a one-degree-Centigrade rise in skin temperature even at depth," the salesman had promised. "The best you can get. As good as the best used by the military."

Lutt wondered if he should have done some comparison shopping . . . but the salesman worked for one of old L. H.'s companies and preparing for the sales party and this trip had made urgent time demands.

I should've talked to Murphy.

Who's Murphy? Ryll asked.

Lutt paraded the story of Murphy's Law for Ryll to study, adding: *Every time I learn a lesson the hard way I say, "Well, Murphy got me again."*

An imaginary impish Irishman. That's quite amusing.

But Murphy's like a germ developing immunity to antibiotics. He rarely strikes the same way twice.

Why didn't you curse this Murphy figment after our collision?

It just didn't occur to me.

Dreens never blame their mistakes on external entities. All errors are of our own making. They originate from subconscious impetus. Your Doctor Freud touched on this.

The Murphy School of Psychology serves me better. Never make the same mistake twice.

Unless your mistake kills you.

So I hope Murphy won't ambush us. I'm going to make our first transmission from one of the military command centers.

First, hadn't we better test our inceram suits at those temperatures?

You're damn right! The way you beat Murphy is to anticipate his next move.

"Christ! Would you look at that?" one of the passengers said.

Lutt returned his attention to the screen. Definite streaks could be discerned in the acid clouds—patches of dark and light yellow punctuated by flaring balls of orange.

Passengers talked about the surface heat, the war, how long they expected to stay. Some who had been on Venus before told newcomers what to expect. Most offerings came out of the pamphlets Lutt had read.

One Venus veteran had comments about hotels.

"The two ITC hotels at the spaceport are best. You can get cheaper accommodations, but they're likely to have hairline leaks. Inside temperatures are bearable only if you're low on funds. Have to wear your armor even in bed."

"You'll get sick of living in your suit," another offered.

"Venus doesn't sound like a place to run out of money," the dark woman said.

The man who had spoken of hotels said: "Get your return ticket in advance and post it at the ITC computer bank."

"That's safest," another agreed. "No one can steal your ticket unless they can copy your retina print."

Hearing this, Lutt dwelled on another worry. He carried his return ticket in the form of a thin, hardened inceram chip in an inceram wallet. Although he had been warned about the dangers, he had chosen this because of the assumed identity. His retina prints were on file with the military for sure. But he would have to guard the ticket against thieves and murderers. A return ticket to Earth meant survival to disillusioned adventurers stranded on Venus—mercenaries, for the most part, who could not make it in either the French or Chinese armies. Mostly, they waited on Venus to die when government aid ran out.

None of the others admitted carrying inceram-chip tickets but Lutt's Dreen-amplified senses detected new signs of worry in some of the faces around him and there was definite stress in a few voices.

Lutt patted his wallet pocket and made sure the flap was double-sealed.

I probably could idmage a new ticket if we lost that one, Ryll offered.

I don't like that word "probably."

I'll practice in our room. Look! We're about to land!

Safety cocoons automatically snapped into place around the lounge passengers. Its velocity reduced, the *Amita-Oho* submerged in the acid clouds, emerging presently above the plateau called the Plain of Yornell and the massive insul-plat slab that formed the foundation of Gorontium, the sixth-largest city on Venus and stronghold of the French Foreign Legion.

Lutt recalled the pamphlet description: "The inceram slab is two hundred meters thick and cooled by freon-exchange water."

The screen displayed a murky scene of mounds and curved surfaces—the city itself rising above its slab on the haze-obscured Plain of Yornell.

Old L. H.'s insurance underwriters had briefed him on this place but none of their words had prepared him for the actuality. Their concerns had been with the statistical odds.

"No policy issued for Venus will insure against failure of the insul-plat. Such catastrophies occur."

One of Lutt's seatmates chattered on about Venusian conditions as they settled to the surface with a slight bump and waited for debarkation orders.

"Most of the water comes from offworld," the man said. "They treat it with anti-evaporation chemicals. It looks like brownish-pink piss."

The hotel expert was not to be outdone. "Wait until you see that water all around you in the canalways. Personally, I prefer moving around by skytram or, if it's only a short distance, I walk."

The dark woman wanted to know if it was safe to just walk around.

"On the public constone docks beside the canals or on the walking bridges, yes," the hotel expert said. "Stay out of the side streets and alleys unless you have an escort."

A flight attendant entered and interrupted this exchange.

"Your debarkation suits are being brought up. Get into them immediately. Help will be provided in this if you ask. You can collect the rest of your luggage in the terminal. The area down the walkway from ship to terminal is inceram-shielded. Follow the signs. Legion-censored maps of Gorontium will be issued in the luggage area. Do not attempt to enter a restricted area. Those of you being met by someone must go to the nonpassenger security area after collecting your luggage. Welcome to Venus."

Ryll, aware that he was being carried willy-nilly into extreme danger, felt an odd tug of almost pleasurable excitement. The pleasure astonished him and he realized at last some of what Lutt must feel when flirting with disaster.

Let's go look for Murphy, Lutt thought.

Our first hint that something was amiss came with a slight trembling of the insul-plat. This was followed immediately by two sharp quakes and the eruption, which, luckily, occurred about ten klicks distant. From our relatively elevated vantage, we saw everything in the red light of the lava plume. The insul-plat split and buildings, people, everything, dropped into the inferno. Steam from the broken canals quickly hid the catastrophe but we had seen enough. It was hideous.

—Eyewitness account,
the Ragol catastrophe, Venus

The room reserved for Peter Andriessen in ITC Hotel Number One (known locally by the Latin, "Uno") was designed for safety first and comfort second. There were no rugs. The low double bed carried a notice on the headboard that an inceram cocoon would enclose it in an emergency. Floor, walls and ceiling were inceram tile, furniture inceram-formed: toilet, washbasin, bedstands, chests of drawers, two chairs—all inceram. A hanger shaped like a praying mantis was provided for taking off and donning inceram body armor.

One of his father's devices told Lutt the room was dotted with spy eyes. When he called to complain, he was told with a definite note of glee the devices were mandatory, ordered by the Legion to expose Chinese agents.

Once he was out of the armor, Lutt sat on the edge of the bed to take stock of his situation.

The spare armor stood in its packing cases against one wall. His inceram luggage with its supposedly tamper-proof locks lay on the lower of two chests. The vorcameras in their inceram shipping cases formed an untidy stack in the middle of the room.

He thought the room uncomfortably warm but the desk clerk had warned him about "slightly increased temperatures—part of the current energy conservation program."

Lutt felt certain a report on him already lay on the desk of a Legion functionary, but Woon had assured him the Legion would know his true identity and media entree to press liaison would come.

Call the Enquirer*'s Gorontium bureau?* he wondered. *No, best wait for the Legion contact.*

It was midafternoon at Gorontium, only an hour after the *Amita-Oho*'s touchdown. A jitney boat had taken them from the terminal, plowing misty canal water that was vaguely pink under an orange sky. Their escort, a large Gorontian in glistening but pitted armor, introduced himself as "Mr. Toka."

Through the visor of his armor, Lutt looked on a scene tinged gray by the smoke shading of inceram glass. Mr. Toka and the other passengers seated under the curved armor glass in the boat were giant doll figures in their bulging armor.

Mr. Toka was immediately occupied at the front of the low jitney helping Lorna Subiyama adjust her suit's thermal controls. The All-Tex columnist was red-faced, panting and asking for a medic before Mr. Toka calmed her.

"Your problem is the spin valve," Mr. Toka said. He indicated the offending valve on the side of her armor. "You have left it open."

Turning to the others ranged along both sides of the boat to the rear, Mr. Toka took the opportunity for a lecture.

"The spin valves are manual regulators." Speaking loudly, his voice clipped by his suit's speaker, he pointed to the valves. "You can cool yourself to the point of hypothermia in a good suit. These valves set the desired temperature range. Note the eye-level thermal meter just inside your visor. Most of us like to stay between eighteen and twenty-three degrees Centigrade. Now, do you all know about your K-Dial?"

From briefings and lectures, Lutt knew this referred to the Karson Kooler in the flexible lining of his armor, a body comfort regulator that pushed cooler air toward the wearer's skin through thousands of tiny holes. Lutt located his K-Dial on the control panel box under his suit's chin locks. He touched the dial as he saw some of the others doing.

"Good," Mr. Toka said. "Now, every thirty days when you change your Ungian batteries, have your Atmospheric Modulator checked. The pump motors are silent so don't count on hearing them. If you have an AM failure Venus will give you a fatal hug."

When no one responded, he explained: "Atmospheric pressure will crush you." He touched the jitney's homing controls. "Okay. Let's go."

Through the entire run to the hotel, Mr. Toka kept up a tour-guide chatter.

"You see few sharp corners on the buildings. Curved surfaces are stronger. Here on Venus, a hotel may occupy the same building with a weapons factory. There are no zoning laws and there is very little city planning. Keep your maps with you at all times when you go out. If you can't read French, learn the basics immediately. Most of the signs are in French."

Lutt felt himself getting drowsy from Mr. Toka's flat voice and the incessant droning whine of the jitney's engines. He longed for his room and a bed.

Through the armor windows, he saw a city vaguely familiar from news accounts but much more immediate and reflecting the sky colors. It was "right there"—very tall buildings by Earth standards but built in stacks of large balls and wildly curving extensions. The building on his right at this moment was an inverted pyramid of silvery balls, each progressively larger as the structure climbed into the orange sky. Each ball displayed a black diamond marking. Just beyond this structure was a bright blue mobius strip carrying a bold yellow-on-red sign: D'ASSAS ANON. The strip stood on one sharp curve and reached upward, encircling other buildings like a flat serpent.

The canal curved left and brought into view another building with no visible foundation. The structure hovered over the water in defiance of gravity.

Everyone in the jitney stared at it.

"Transparent supports," Mr. Toka explained.

Lutt looked back at the building as they passed it, seeing the faint distortions of the supports.

Beyond the building, the top of the ITC spaceport was still visible against the orange sky. A glowing patch of brightness indicated the sun's location. Abruptly, a yellow bolt of lightning flashed across the sky followed by a rolling drumbeat of thunder.

"Don't worry about a rainstorm," Mr. Toka reassured them. "Any sulfuric acid that forms in the clouds evaporates before it can fall."

The jitney's engines changed cadence and then roared into reverse as it came up to a flat pier beside a geodesic dome that carried an illuminated sign: ITC X-ONE.

"Here we are," Mr. Toka announced. "Once you're through the lock and in the lobby you can unsnap your helmets. I advise you to replace body liquids as soon as possible. There's a self-service bar just inside where you can get glucose, root beer and Crocades.

Ryll, who had remained silently observant through the passage to the hotel, now intruded: *I would enjoy a chocolate sundae.*

Why not?

But the first thing to greet them in the lobby was a red-haired woman with leathery skin who went from passenger to passenger asking them to sign organ-donor cards. She had a dry, matter-of-fact voice that went with her creased skin.

"Death is rather common here," she told Lutt. "My group is nonprofit. We will see to it that your organs go to truly needy individuals."

They're mostly my organs! Ryll intruded.

"I'll pass for now," Lutt told the woman.

She pressed a card on him. "Please call us if you change your mind. Be very careful. Some groups will murder you once they have your signature. They will even forge donor cards, copying the signature from your wallet or other documents."

Lutt began to wish he had brought a contingent of Hanson Guards despite the added cost. He felt defenseless, denied weapons by Legion rules that said any visitor caught with a weapon would be considered an enemy—potential saboteur and assassin.

This was a frontier, Lutt reminded himself. And the French were tough, made extremely touchy by recent Chinese victories. The latest reports said the Mao Guard was throwing more troops into the conflict and introducing new weapons, including something identified only as a "scatter rocket."

The hotel lobby attempted a garish Louis XIV decor but there were no carpets and everything in sight displayed its inceram base. A sign above the reception desk announced that this was the HOTEL LES MARRONNIERS, but Mr. Toka had warned them to call it "Uno. That's the only name anyone will recognize."

Still, the place smelled clean after he dropped his helmet onto its neck hinges. Lutt's agents had assured him it was the best available. Legion officers had long before commandeered the premier lodgings. Reports said they brought with them the finest foods, wines and harlots in the solar system.

Lutt signed in as "Peter Andriessen, Tacoma, Washington, U.S.A., Earth," and noted the sudden interest of the clerk.

An oily little man with bloodshot eyes, the clerk looked at him like a spider assessing a fly and said: "The Legion has asked that you remain in the hotel until they contact you, sir."

"Senator Woon briefed me on what to expect," Lutt said. "I'll dine in my room."

The clerk was amused. "*Dine*, sir?"

Thinking he could rely on Ryll to provide them with a special menu, Lutt grinned back. "That's right. Let me know when my Legion liaison arrives."

There was no amusement in Lutt as he sat on the edge of his bed now and reviewed his situation. Confined to the hotel. He thought suddenly of how easy it would be for Woon to arrange the death of an inconvenient newsman.

Woon or anyone else, Ryll interposed. *And we've made an enemy of that Subiyama female. What if she has powerful friends here?*

You and your damned lumpy!

It was amusing at the time. You must admit that.

Tell me about it when we're being cooked in some convenient accident!

Should I try to create some inceram now?

With Legion agents watching? You nuts?

Then I dare not even idmage a banquet.

You got it, Ryll baby. Low profile is what we show for now.

Very well. I see the need for caution. You know, Lutt. I may be the very first Dreen to visit this planet.

Life, once freed of its creator's touch, may achieve its own destiny.

—Dreen aphorism

The first morning on Venus, no word yet from the Legion, Ryll insisted they eat breakfast in the hotel dining room.

In the confusion of many diners, I might be able to make some changes in the contents of the dishes.

Anything would be better than that swill they served us last night.

Uno's dining room turned out to be a heat-sheltered garden court with spindly inceram furniture made to look like metal.

Lutt, prepared for a more appetizing meal, was dismayed when Lorna Subiyama, oozing sweet forgiveness, sat down opposite him without invitation.

"No more of your tricks, you funny man," she greeted him. "May I call you Peter? Isn't the food here awful?"

Seeing a waiter hovering over her, Lutt decided on tact. "I've had worse."

She noticed the waiter. "Oh, there you are. Bring me another of those sweet roll things and a pot of coffee." To Lutt, she said: "The breads here are acceptable and the coffee's not bad, although the French tend to make it too bitter."

"I'll have the same," Lutt told the waiter.

"I suppose you're wondering why I'm on Venus," Subiyama said. "I know everyone's curious about it."

"I can hardly wait for you to tell me," Lutt said.

She leaned across the table confidentially. "I'm here to do a story about Captain Danjou's hand. We think it's a fake, a skillful copy."

Lutt stared at her. Danjou's hand? What the hell was she talking about? He managed a fairly noncommital "Oh?"

"You know he died heroically in Mexico in 1863," she said. "He had a wooden hand, which, since his death, has been kept in an atmospherically controlled box and brought out only for ceremonies."

"That would've been during the reign of Emperor Maximilian," Lutt offered, recalling his Mexican history.

"The year before, I believe," she corrected him. "Anyway, it's a very important Legion relic. But we think the Danjou hand here on Venus isn't the original."

"Wouldn't that be bad for Legion morale if you revealed it?" Lutt asked. "I mean—"

He broke off as their waiter returned and served them. When he left, Lutt resumed: "I mean you could get yourself in real hot water with the Legion."

"I wouldn't repeat this around a legionnaire, but word has it there are many wooden hands all over the solar system, all used to inspire the troops."

Lutt looked down at the table, realizing there must be spy devices here as well as in the rooms.

"You go ahead and stick your neck in the guillotine," Lutt said. "I happen to admire the Legion."

"Oh, everyone admires the Legion," she agreed, speaking around a mouthful of sweet roll. "But isn't it hypocritical of them if they tell each expeditionary force their particular mission is so important the captain's hand has been sent to them for the extra power and pride it brings?"

"Hasn't it occurred to you the Legion might think you're working for the Chinese?" Lutt asked.

"What a terrible thing for you to say! I purely hate those little yellow men."

"They aren't exactly yellow and I've seen some pretty big ones," Lutt said. "My advice is for you to scrap this idea. Do a piece about Legion women."

"Be a nice little woman and write about nice little woman things, is that it? You're just like all men. Well, Buster, I'm here to cover a war and I'll do it my way."

"I thought you were going to call me Peter."

"I may call you some other things. Keep your nose cool, Buster. This is one hot place."

She finished her roll, gulped a cup of coffee and left him to his breakfast.

Lutt closed his eyes and shook his head, feeling the abrupt inward swivel of his eyes and their return to normal.

I've put some fresh fruit in the roll, Ryll told him.

When he opened his eyes, Lutt saw the roll apparently unchanged but there was, indeed, fresh fruit in it—juicy peaches.

I have a suggestion about our body, Ryll intruded.

My body! It's been mine for thirty-five years. You've only been around a few days.

You never pay attention, Lutt. The very fact that you don't need real glasses should tell you this is not in fact your original body.

What's your suggestion?

The only practical solution seems to be for us to split up the control each day. You do what you wish until midafternoon and then I take over.

You ever hear about possession being nine points of the law? I'm in possession of this body.

But it's mostly composed of my flesh! I was being generous offering you a split. Are you forgetting I saved your life? Without me, you'd have nothing.

I warned you what I'd do if you tried to take over.

I might survive you anyway. The instant this body became unusable, I could idmage my own Dreen body or select a more favorable human with whom to cohabitate.

I'd like to see you try that on the surface of Venus without inceram armor.

The way I read your will to live tells me you're bluffing, Lutt.

Shall we step outside right now and test it?

They won't let you through the lock without armor!

You told me in the ZP cell Dreens can be casualties. If this body dies, it dies. And there's a lot of you in this body. So see if I'm bluffing.

But you have a strong will to live and aquire tremendous personal power.

It seems we understand each other a little better. You'd like to escape this sharing and I'd prefer to be on my own. We both want the same thing.

Ryll remained out of contact for a time, thinking privately that his predicament worsened daily. What would the Legion do if it discovered a Dreen here? Exposure on Venus might be far worse than capture by the Zone Patrol.

Tell me when you're ready to separate us, Lutt thought.

At the first opportunity. Meanwhile, we have another problem. This body is still growing as I warned you it would. Haven't you noticed a little tightness in your clothes?

I've been eating a bit more than usual but . . .

Only a few centimeters' growth per week, Lutt, but it adds up.

My God! That would make my inceram armor worthless!

Don't panic.

But without armor . . . Why didn't you speak up during the fittings?

I didn't think it necessary.

You fool! Inceram armor has no growth tolerance. Which is why children born on Venus are shipped offworld immediately in special incubators. Venus has regulations against births. Birth control is mandatory!

So now maybe we can bargain.

Bargain? What do you mean?

I am capable of re-idmaging the armor to larger dimensions and I doubt anyone would notice the change.

"Are you all right, sir?" It was the waiter and Lutt looked up to see the man staring at him.

"The food and that Texas bore didn't agree with me," Lutt said.

"Better food is available, sir . . . at a price, of course."

Get rid of him, Ryll insisted.

"I'll talk to you about it later," Lutt said. "Have to consult my bankers."

The waiter's grin was not pleasant but he went away without further comment.

Lutt returned to his argument with Ryll. *So you can adjust the armor for my growth.*

Our growth. Yes. Do we split up control of the day or do I let nature take its course?

The last time I let you have a hand in events I had the worst hangover of my life.

The food didn't agree with my Dreen flesh.

The minute he revealed this, Ryll knew he had made another mistake.

We didn't eat anything strange. The pesto was the best I've ever tasted and you seemed to enjoy it at the time.

I've enjoyed many things that disagreed with me.

What'd happen if I ordered a pesto dinner right now? You heard that waiter. Better food is available.

Ryll remained out of contact for almost a minute.

No comment? Lutt asked. And he thought: *Something in the pesto. What? The pasta was ordinary enough. The seasoning? Could he have an aversion to basil?*

Ryll felt powerless to interfere with these thoughts. He knew he had waited too long to divert Lutt from this course. Anything he introduced now might only add to Lutt's suspicions. Perhaps the bazeel could be removed from . . . but Lutt would be sure to notice.

Let's try for another hangover tonight, Lutt insisted.

I'm trying to be reasonable with you, Lutt. Dreens always try to be reasonable. Think over my day-sharing proposal and we'll discuss it later.

Sure we will. After we recover from our hangover.

Every defense minister in the solar system knows the economic realities. While robots can function well in some combat situations, human troops have become easier and cheaper to replace. Under public pressure to preserve human life, democracies use some robotroops, but the Chinese are under no such restrictions. Their severe overpopulation makes the decision purely economic. Because we cannot match them soldier for soldier, we must rely on superior strategy.

—From officers' manual,
French Foreign Legion,
NSC translation

When there was no contact from the Legion by the second afternoon, Lutt decided to take matters into his own hands. First, he called the *Enquirer* bureau and, instead of the Roy Humperman listed as the company employee here, got a woman who identified herself as "Roweena Humperman, Roy's widow."

"Humperman's dead?"

She seemed casual about it. "Poor Roy got it three days ago covering that Chinese attack at Pe-Duc. French deflector rays broke down and there were no survivors. Who'd you say you were?"

"Peter Andriessen."

"Oh, yes. I've seen your byline in the files. Well, I hope you last longer than Roy. He only had eleven months. One thing you can say about dying on Venus: No body to bury."

"I'm not here to replace Roy. I'm on a special project."

Briefly, he explained about vorcameras and instantaneous transmissions, and his present predicament.

"And they've confined you to the hotel? Let me see what I can do about that. There's a French officer who has the hots for me and he may be able to spring you. In return, I'd like you to do what you can to have me hired as Roy's permanent replacement."

"Get me out of here and you've got the job."

"Just like that? You must have some clout with the Hansons. Hey! Is the Little Boss really the great ladies' man everyone says?"

"The stories are all true," Lutt growled, resenting her reference to "Little Boss." *Someday, I'll be Big Boss, honey. My bod's still growing and I'll have my own base soon enough.*

"I bet I could teach him a thing or two. Well, you stay right there, Peter honey, and I'll get back to you. When I say tonight's the night, my Frenchy may come and get you himself."

Roweena called back in just under ten minutes.

"Wowee, Peter honey! I thought I'd have to get a stick and beat him off at the door. Now, here's the drill. You have to go through the payoff channels. At Uno, that's the concierge. Be dumb and ask him for a directory of military offices. He'll just send you to the Tribunal office for this jurisdiction, but you act dumb and butter him good, you hear?"

"How much?"

"Five hundred francs should do it. I'll meet you at the Tribunal with my Frenchy in tow."

The concierge was an immense specimen with dyed black hair slicked back from a central part like beetle wings, a great hooked nose and a remarkably bulging stomach that made it impossible for him to look down and see his own feet. Lutt wondered how the man dressed himself, and certainly fitting him to inceram armor would be a serious problem. He presented a figure of profound dignity beside a tiny desk in the lobby, dispensing advice in English with a thick French accent.

"I am sorry, Monsieur Andriessen," he said in response to Lutt's question, "but there is no such directory." He peered at Lutt dispassionately from tiny eyes recessed in fat cheeks, adding: "In truth, there are no directories whatsoever in all of the Legion territories."

"I know I need a pass to visit the battlefront and I've been told to confine myself to this hotel. How do I take care of that?"

"The battlefront?" The concierge was horrified. "Ahhh, you brave correspondents! You throw yourselves into deadly peril and for what? That people may read of such things over their breakfasts."

Lutt spoke dryly. "The news is big business." He rubbed the fingers of his right hand together. "Profits."

"But why do you not cover the war as other newsmen do? Every afternoon at five o'clock, the Legion shows pictures and briefs the correspondents. It is called 'The Five O'Clock Follies.' You can write your stories from the security of your own room."

"I'm a photojournalist and have to send pictures."

"Ahhh! The bravest of the brave. I should have known just by looking at you. But, monsieur, you can hire photographers here very reasonably. I have a cousin who—"

He broke off as Lutt removed a prepared roll of bills from his pocket and began counting off five hundred francs.

"Monsieur, one as rich and brave as yourself should preserve himself. Ask me about restaurants or quaint little shops where one can purchase gifts for his lady love." He glanced around at the others awaiting his services. "She is with you?"

"No. This isn't a pleasure trip." Lutt held the five hundred francs loosely in one hand. "How do I leave the hotel? I don't wish to violate regulations."

"There are so many regulations, monsieur." The concierge's chins quivered with indignation as he spoke. "We all violate regulations on occasion. Unwittingly, of course. It is always a question of which regulations the Legion wishes to enforce."

"How do you know those regulations?"

The concierge's shoulders heaved in an immense Gallic shrug. "No one has ever been able to determine this. I would recommend you begin at Number 1205 triple B, Ruecan D'Monsard. That is the Tribunal office for this jurisdiction."

"But won't I be violating regulations if I leave the hotel?"

A broad smile creased the concierge's face as he extracted the bills from Lutt's hand and pocketed them. "Oh, that, monsieur. It is already arranged."

His armor secure, the map chip in its slot for projection against his faceplate, Lutt went through the lobby lock and entered the furnace world. His meters showed the exterior temperature shooting up but all he heard was a faint clicking and he felt the cooled KK air against his skin.

The doorman wanted to provide a guide but the map showed the Tribunal only half a kilometer distant. Lutt thought he could walk it. He paused only to ask about the increased redness in the atmosphere.

"They are diverting a lava blow to the south. The plume provides a lovely color, not so?"

"Oh, yes. Lovely."

The map directed him across an elevated conveyor to the opposite side of the canal and up an escalator to another dock level. He threaded his way through armored pedestrians, noting the occasional faceplate directed squarely at him, but faces were not visible.

Our progress is, perhaps, clumsy enough to betray the recent arrival, Ryll suggested.

That's okay. Here we are at the Tribunal.

No, this is 1205B. I distinctly heard him say triple B.

Lutt consulted the map. *Yeah. It's a bit farther along.*

This time he wound up at 1205BB and noted that he had picked up a trio of followers in patched and pitted armor.

I don't like the look of those three, Ryll warned. *It occurs to me that our armor must look very new. That, too, would be a mark of the newcomer.*

What would you suggest I do about it?

I note that you are versed in ways of self-defense. Dreen-augmented muscles can account for at least two of those brigands . . . if they are brigands. Let us be wary.

Once more, Lutt consulted the map. Yes, the Tribunal was down this narrow side alley. He turned in at the alley and saw the three followers turn behind him, closing the distance between them quickly. One of them had some sort of tube device in one armored hand.

That must be a weapon! Ryll cautioned.

Lutt turned and faced the trio but before he could even assume a posture of defense, a door beside him snapped open. Five armored figures darted out. Lutt had only time to note the Legion crests on their helmets and arms, then the five were around the three followers. It was over in seconds. The three were pinned against a wall, the weapon removed, metallic bindings were thrown around them and two of the legionnaries led them away.

One of the three remaining legionnaires faced Lutt and saluted. "Sergeant McCauley at your service, Monsieur Andriessen. Colonel Paul has ordered us to escort you to the Tribunal."

"Good. Those guys were really after me, eh?" Lutt started to turn down the alley the way he had been going.

An armored hand restrained him. "Not that way, monsieur. The dispenser at Uno gave you a rigged map. It was intended that you fall into this trap. There will be punishments."

"The concierge?"

"Oh, no, monsieur. He is the one who alerted us."

"Good God! It's really dangerous here, isn't it!"

"Until you learn our ways, monsieur. This way, please."

The Tribunal was around two more curving corners. It proved to be a bulging dome with a Legion squad guarding the entrance lock. Lutt and his escort were passed through without ceremony.

Inside an immense inceram-tiled lobby, Lutt was confronted by a scene of confusion. Lines of armored people, their helmets thrown back onto the hinges, ranged across the floor and clustered along a counter that extended from one side of the lobby to the other. A babble of voices—shouts and cries—filled the place.

Without lifting his own helmet, Sergeant McCauley helped Lutt fold back his helmet and said, "Down this side, monsieur. Colonel Paul awaits you."

Lutt was led around the left side of the room, noting the resentment-filled looks from people he passed. There was a rich smell of sweaty humanity and inadequate waste recycling in the room. They went through a wide double door into a hallway and then into a large round office where an unarmored man and woman stood facing each other. They turned toward Lutt as he entered.

Sergeant McCauley saluted and said, "Monsieur Andriessen, *Mon Colonel!*" and closed the door as he left.

Lutt was struck first by the disparity in the sizes of the couple. The woman was tiny, a full-figured pocket Venus with dark auburn hair and gamin features. Smile creases etched the corners of her mouth and she aimed a piercing stare at Lutt from large green eyes.

Colonel Paul was tall and slender, a blond, blue-eyed Nordic wih sharply chiseled features. He stepped forward and clapped a hand on Lutt's armored shoulder.

"Delighted to be of service, dear fellow." The accent was faintly British. "Paul Carlson at your service." He turned toward his companion. "And this is the lovely Roweena."

"I've just gone through Roy's coded dispatches about you," she greeted him. "Why the hell didn't you tell me who you really were?"

"On an open phone line?" Lutt asked.

"It'll be all over Gorontium by tomorrow, anyway," she said. "Especially about your prowess with the ladies. So I have the job?"

"You have it . . ." Lutt glanced at the colonel who had stepped back two paces. "If . . ."

"Everything will be arranged, dear fellow," the colonel said. "What do we call you? Surely not Monsieur Andriessen?"

"My friends call me Lutt."

"And we will be friends," the colonel said.

Humperman grinned. "I've never been friends with the boss before, but Roy always did bring me luck."

"You don't seem very sad about him," Lutt said.

"Roy was my fifth. My fourth was a Legion sergeant who bought it from a Chinese scatter missile the same way Roy did, I think. That's life on Venus, Lutt."

"And death," the colonel added. "Meanwhile, we must be merry. Is it true you wish to transmit from Legion headquarters?"

"The underground headquarters, yes."

"That may take some arranging."

"It'd be easier to get into a battle zone," Roweena said.

"I myself go to the front next week," the colonel said. "You could accompany me."

Ryll, observing, was horrified. *Don't do it, Lutt!*

Stay out of this or I will!

To the colonel, Lutt said: "I want this first vorcamera transmission to be something very dramatic, preferably in your headquarters during a battle."

"And who will have access to the transmission?"

"Our subscribers on Earth."

"And the Chinese would become aware of this?"

"I'm sure of it, in time."

"The Chinese are devious," the colonel said. "You must not reveal the location of your broadcast. It is in your own interest, as well. The Chinese use antipersonnel weapons our ray defenses find difficult to stop. We have some robotroops, of course, but the Chinese have none."

Roweena chimed in: "The Legion is mostly gallant, brave men fighting for Legion and Country."

"You must have Legion cameramen," Lutt said. "Could one of them run the camera while Roweena and I do the interviews? That way we could ensure nothing sensitive is transmitted."

Roweena was suddenly excited. "You want me on camera?"

"You're the new bureau chief," Lutt said.

"Will video pick this up?" the colonel asked.

"Not immediately, but they're sure to want in on it later."

"How many of these special cameras do you have?"

"Three."

"Are they difficult to use?"

"They might be dangerous on a battlefield. They're rigged to self-destruct if anyone tampers with them."

"I was about to suggest we send one of your cameras to the front. But these new Chinese missiles often go out of control, killing more of their own troops than ours. And there are so many more of the enemy. It is clear they do not mind killing everyone on a battlefield as long as our boys get it, too."

"Is that any way to fight a war?" Roweena asked.

"Are there rules?" Lutt asked.

"Very few in this war," the colonel said. "Well, I will see what I can do for you. The sergeant will escort you back to your hotel and make the arrests. There will be heads chopped."

"I didn't know you still used the guillotine," Lutt said.

"It was a figure of speech, dear fellow. Actually, we throw them armorless into the nearest lava cauldron. Quick, and there's no mess to clean up afterward."

Roweena linked arms with the colonel and smiled at Lutt. "Thanks for the job, boss, but Paul and I have other business to attend to right now."

The colonel grinned down at her. "Oh, indeed, we do." He turned the grin toward Lutt. "I will send a Legion PTV for you when we get your clearance. The usual passes and things will be sent to Uno or arranged there. I advise you to wait at the hotel."

"What's a PTV?" Lutt asked.

"Personal Transport Vehicle. They're pilotless and coded to follow an ion track. You will be reasonably safe. I'm sure you understand we cannot provide you with an escort everywhere."

When they were safely back in their room, Ryll almost exploded with indignation. *Reasonably safe! I can't practice providing us with replacement inceram. I can't even make us something decent to eat unless we're down in that restaurant and then only if you order something in which I can conceal—*

Will you shut up? I have to call the Enquirer *and see how they're doing. You re-idmage my armor while I'm doing that.*

Our armor!

Oh, yes. We are a growing boy, aren't we. And tonight, we'll have a really good meal. I'm sure that nice waiter can provide us with a superb rendition of pesto Genovese.

Ryll subsided into shielded and sullen reflection. Bazeel! This evil Earther was going to observe the effect on Dreen flesh for sure. This called for desperate countermeasures. But was it possible to take over their shared flesh? And even so, could a Dreen simulate Earther behavior under these circumstances?

There was this dumb ol' Okie drivin' across Texas and it took him three months 'cause ever' time he saw one of those "Clean Restrooms Ahead" signs he stopped and he cleaned the restrooms.

—Story told by Lorna Subiyama

Jongleur teetered on the edge of a fretful frenzy, rocking back and forth—left feet, right feet, left feet . . . Habiba sat on the saddle of command at the peak of her cone directly above him. Dreenor's morning sun, dimmed by an incomplete shield, gave her dark skin an olive cast.

What was Habiba doing? Reconstituting the Earth-erasure project and now—so much effort into the shield while other matters suffered. The shield idmaging had improved, though, and Habiba's prediction of "success soon" gave heart to some.

Not to Jongleur.

"That's enough for now," Habiba said. "Give them a rest and we'll try it again this afternoon." The cone immediately brightened. "Well, what is it, Jongleur? The new ship again?"

"The replacement erasure ship progresses according to plan, Habiba. Mugly says it will be ready soon."

Jongleur noted with a twinge of regret that he no longer had difficulty referring to erasure. Earth's problems did that to one. Surely Habiba did not intend to order the erasure, though. This must be a project to occupy Mugly and keep him out of trouble. Or was it?

"It's the overnight report from Earth, Habiba. Are you sure you cannot assign some superior idmagers to—"

"I told you not to bother me with that until the shield is perfected, Jongleur. Give me the report."

"Prosik has managed to send a message through one of our operatives. The first erasure ship was, indeed, damaged and—"

"I thought as much. Where is Prosik? Is the ship unable to complete its mission?"

"Habiba!"

"I have thought long and hard about my former objections to the erasure of Earth, Jongleur. Difficult problems may require difficult answers."

"*Former* objections?"

"Well . . . almost former. I would sooner achieve a peaceful solution. Tell me, what of Prosik and the ship?"

"One activation system and the erasure mechanisms survive but the Earthers continue to dismantle the ship. They are almost certain to set off the self-destruct sequence."

"Prosik is unable to recapture the ship?"

"Unfortunately, Prosik is on his way to Venus."

"To that hellish place? For what reason? Did you not send orders that he—"

"Habiba, please let me explain."

"Very well, but I am displeased."

"An Earther destroyed one of the ship's activation systems and, in the explosion, was killed. Prosik assumed that one's guise but . . . but . . ."

"Well?"

Smelling the faint effluvia of Habiba's anger, Jongleur spoke hastily.

"The guise Prosik assumed was that of the Zone Patrol guard responsible for protecting the wreckage of the ship. He was blamed for the explosion and is being sent to Venus as punishment."

"Then have him escape and assume another guise."

"That would surely arouse suspicion, Habiba. No ordinary Earther escapes from Zone Patrol incarceration. Even our own Dreen captives find it virtually impossible, although they are guarded much more severely."

"Of what possible use is it to have Prosik on Venus?"

"You recall we speculated about my son and . . ."
"The merger with that Hanson creature, yes."
"Hanson is on Venus."
"Jongleur, are you still trying to rescue your son?"
"I have issued no such orders, Habiba. But Hanson does know part of the secret of the Spirals. We must learn what he is doing."
"Earth! Oh, if only this problem were behind us. How can Prosik get word to us from Venus?"
"Hanson plans to transmit news broadcasts via the Spirals. We, of course, can listen to those and—"
"Prosik does not sound bright enough to gain access to this equipment. I'm sorry, Jongleur, but my fears guide my tongue. I know you are doing your best."
"That is all any of us can do, Habiba."
"We do what we must, yes. That is always the way of it. Well, get on with it. I will want to know immediately when the new erasure ship is completed."
"They will work on it until the next shield effort, Habiba. I am following your orders to have the best idmagers drop their other works and join the shield effort when you command it. Are you sure we require the erasure ship?"
"In the past, we have left too much to chance. We no longer can afford such luxury."
As he left the sanctum, Jongleur thought sadly that Habiba was coming to sound more and more like Mugly. Oh, what a desperate state of affairs this awful Earth had produced!

We do not deal with a situation such as yours in this department, monsieur.

—Typical response of the
French bureaucracy on Venus

Lutt awoke the next morning with another severe hangover and ideas about the effects of pesto Genovese on Dreen flesh.

Was it the herbs, the basil, Ryll baby?

Ryll remained uncommunicative in a painful near-stupor. The bazeel effect felt more intense than it had before and he wondered if he were forming an addiction.

A vidcom call intruded on their wake-up agony. It was the concierge with word that the Legion was sending a PTV for Monsieur Andriessen. The concierge sounded impressed.

The PTV was a snub-nosed, short-winged little rocket with a cargo pod tucked under its belly that swallowed his equipment. It carried another armored passenger of impressive dimensions whose every movement joggled the PTV. They were strapped in securely and on their way across a glowing, pitted landscape before Lutt made identification through the thick faceplate.

"Lorna Subiyama?"

"Y'all act surprised. This thing's goin' to the front, isn't it?"

She displayed a black inceram chip with PASS inscribed on it in English. "This allows me three days of action, Buster."

"Do they know what kind of story you intend to . . ."

"Oh, that! They think I'm doin' some glamour stuff for Sleep-A-

Vision, Dallas. You know, brain-contact news for busy execs." Her voice took on an advertising jingle tone: "News in color while y'all dream. Let your neurons learn and scheme."

"And you're going to the front?"

"They gotta drop one passenger first. That you, Buster?"

"I have some high-level interviews to do."

"No shit! How'd you do that?"

"Influence. How'd you get that pass?"

"It wasn't easy."

"Did they send you to the Tribunal?"

"Along with seventy-'leven other poor slobs. Then to a dump on Ruecan D'Arnee where they sent me to a little office in Place Beaumair and on and on . . . I've seen petty bureaucrats but these French make a fine art of juggling the buck."

"You got your pass, though," Lutt said, adjusting his suit's outside spin valve because he had begun feeling too warm.

"They never sent me to the same office twice and that made me believe I was making progress. No direct answers, of course. Always, 'We send inquiries such as yours to this address.' And they'd hand me a little card or slip of paper."

He felt the suit's cooling mechanism at work and spoke with a sense of relief. "But how'd you get through the red tape?"

"Green influence. Moola. Yankee dolla."

"Venus is no place to be locked up in a military brig."

"Never fear. But I was damn near ready to give it up for the day. Then I thought I'd try one more of their stupid offices. Remember that building with no visible foundation?"

"The one we saw on the way in, yes. What about it?"

"Dusty little hole was up near the top o' that un. Had a woman in it. Crazy! She was wearin' custom inceram armor made to look like a cowgirl's duds—Western boots, helmet like a Stetson . . . I mean it was *all* there. And she had those shifty color-changin' contacts in her eyes, green one instant, blue the next. Ah tell y' it was somethin'."

"Sounds different from the others."

"You better believe it, Buster. Right there on her bazoom she had a big yeller rose. Texas, Buster. Texas! I just reached over and kissed that rose."

"And you paid her off?"

"Shit, no! But us Texans know each other. She just kinda grinned and asked me if they'd been chasin' my ass all 'cross town. And I said my feet felt like they'd been roped and branded and she said she was gonna quit for the day and why didn't we have a drink somewhere?"

"But how'd that get your pass?"

"I tell you, Buster, mos' Texans do their bess work with a drink in front of 'em. Sue Ellen, thass mah new frien', she took me t' this cute li'l bar down near the spacedocks and she tol' me all 'bout the Triple Ells."

"What in hell are the Triple Ells?"

"Low-Level Legionnaires. They have a mos' peculiar code of honor. Won' ask for a bribe. But if y'all freely volunteer a few hunnerd francs . . . I mean, how you think someone like Sue Ellen kin buy that fancy armor?"

"So you bought your pass."

"Three days at the front—eighteen hundred francs. Sue Ellen set it up for me and we didn't even have to leave that bar. Got myself a nice lay out of it, too. Big ol' horny Legion sergeant with stripes tatooed up his ass."

Ryll intruded with an observation: *Could they be sending her to the front to be killed?*

"You have any trouble on the streets?" Lutt asked.

"Not much. A few con artists tried to hustle me but I stayed out of alleys and I always made sure there were lots of strays in my herd. Never get yourself into a tight spot with only a few pedestrians on Venus."

"You heard about the Chinese scatter rockets?"

"One of 'em is s'posed to take out six hunnerd square meters. I mean, Buster, that's worse'n oil-field nitro."

"That's what you're going to find at the front."

The Legion may not like it if you warn her, Ryll cautioned.

"I'm just going to dip in and dip out so I can say I've been there," Subiyama said. "War correspondent, y'all hear? Then I'll cover the five o'clock follies like the rest of my drinkin' buddies. Say! Any chance you can ring me in on these interviews of yours?"

"No way! I don't want any part of that story about the captain's hand."

"Chicken, huh?"

"You go ahead and make your nightmares for busy execs. Venus isn't exactly a hotbed of good news and pretty dreams."

Subiyama guffawed, then: "Venus a hotbed! That's sirloin choice, Buster. I tell you that was one hot bed I had last night. May have set a record. Fourteen times in eight hours. One real horny stud, my sergeant. Almost like he'd just discovered Texas sex."

Disgusting! Ryll intruded.

Wish I liked fat women, Lutt countered. *This one might be fun.*

Fun!

"This PTV is sure one fast piece of machinery," Subiyama said, peering out the armor glass on her side.

Lutt looked out his side. The PTV hugged the broiling surface to avoid detection by the Chinese. The Uno concierge had told him not to worry about this.

"They are guided by a mag-pull system, monsieur."

Lutt had no idea what a mag-pull system might be but it was taking the PTV along a deep canyon of flowing red lava at the moment. Presently, they climbed over a high mountain range and through a pass. The peaks displayed a pale blue color, relatively cool at altitude but no doubt still plenty hot.

The pass disgorged them onto a high golden plateau.

"How you coverin' your stories?" Subiyama asked. "Don't see any equipment." She lifted a dark inceram box from beside her. "Got me a new inceram-shielded electronic clipboard. This 'ere sucker records, takes notes, ever'thin'."

"My cameras are in the cargo pod," Lutt said.

"You ever meet old L.H. himself?" she asked.

"Oh, yeah."

"That ol' whore chaser! My mamma tells me about the time once down in Wes' Texas, she and a couple of friends with nothin' to do were in this bar. In comes this big guy with a loud voice and says nobody else pays for the rest of the night. It was him, all right. He left with one of Mamma's friends."

I'm not all that different from Father, Lutt thought.

You are a driven breed, Ryll told him.

I guess we are. Father'd never admit we're alike. I have trouble doing it myself.

But it's true. Like father, like son.

Is it that way with Dreens, too?

Parents always seek to impart only the best.

Who decides what's best?

Better pay attention. She's talking to you.

"I said I think we're gettin' there," Subiyama said. "This thing's slowed down considerable."

Lutt stared ahead at a glowing yellow streak surrounded by the inevitable orange of Venus's heat-baked atmosphere. The PTV banked sharply to the right and, far across the plateau, Lutt saw explosive flashes of brilliant green and purple.

"That sure looks like artillery fire," Subiyama said. "Hear that?"

As though her words had created the sounds, Lutt heard the distant thump and higher-pitched pop-a-tat of explosives.

"If that's the front, it doesn't look all that far away," Subiyama said.

The PTV banked right and the surface shaded into the dark brown of a rift valley, appearing cooler and more solid, as though the planet were creating illusions to make them unwary. Inceram gray bunkers were visible along each side of a flat, blackened area that glowed yellow at its edges. The concierge had said the yellow was a signal of mag-pull guidance.

Lutt began to wonder about mag-pull technology. It might be French for one of the conventional ion-track systems but that yellow glow suggested something different. Would it be worthwhile prying into the way it worked? It might be a military secret. Curiosity would only raise hackles. Perhaps a few private questions, though, to Roweena Humperman?

The PTV came in fast to the landing strip and sat down with a skidding thump that drew long drag marks along the surface. As soon as it stopped, a red light flashed on the ceiling and a speaker emitted a barking order:

"Everyone out! On the double!"

The cockpit cover slammed back and steps dropped to both sides. Lutt clambered down and found the cargo pod open. He grabbed up his equipment and trotted around the PTV to find Subiyama already racing toward an opening in the rift wall where an armed legionnaire stood beckoning them and shouting:

"Under cover! Quick!"

His words were punctuated by a brilliant flash off to the left and a thumping roar that made Lutt stumble.

A klaxon behind Lutt began blaring: "Braaak! Braaak! Braaak!"

He raced after Subiyama past the beckoning legionnaire and into a dimly lighted tunnel. The exterior-reading meter below Lutt's faceplate immediately displayed a sharp rise in temperature, but the armor compensated and he felt none of the outside heat.

The tunnel curved sharply right and then left, opening into a larger staging area where humanoid Legion robots in khaki, blue, white and red inceram stood in long rows.

Human legionnaires fanned out through the robots, running along the lines, checking, adjusting.

Subiyama stopped in front of a legionnaire whose armor bore corporal's stripes.

"What's going on?" she demanded. "Is this the front?"

"No, ma'am," the corporal said in a heavy Tennessee accent made tinny by his suit's speakers. "This here's jus' a li'l' ol' Chink probe. They do that now an' then t' keep us on our toes."

"Whooee!" Subiyama said. "Got us a boy from down home."

"Glad t' make y'r 'quaintance, ma'am," the corporal said.

Lutt stopped beside Subiyama. "I'm supposed to meet Colonel Paul Carlson. And my assistant, Roweena Humperman."

"I 'spec' the colonel will be along presently, suh," the corporal said. "You jus' wait here where it's safe."

The robots began marching out of the staging area in long powerful strides, something slowly methodical about the movement but covering remarkable distance in a short time.

"Sue Ellen sure was full of the Legion," Subiyama said. "Every man in the ranks is a finely tuned athlete, she said."

"They're supposed to be exquisitely conditioned," Lutt agreed, speaking for the corporal's benefit. "Capable of competing in almost any Olympic event."

"Won't let us compete," the corporal volunteered. "Ruskies got us barred as professionals. They're fine ones to talk!"

"Kilo for kilo, these are the premiere troops and military technicians in the solar system," Subiyama said. "My sergeant last night sure lived up to his billing."

"Just got a flash on you, sir," the corporal said. "You Lutt Hanson, Jr.?"

"I knew it!' Subiyama crowed.

"That's me," Lutt said.

"I'm to escort you down into the command bunker, suh," the corporal said. "You really the Hanson of all them companies and the money?"

"He's one of 'em!" Subiyama said.

"Sure don't unnerstand why you're risking your skin up here, suh," the corporal said. "This way, please."

"What about me?" Subiyama demanded.

"She's supposed to go on to the front," Lutt said.

"Don't think that's possible right now," the corporal said. "The Chinks kinda plowed up our landing strip. Why don't you just tag along with us, ma'am, and somebody down below will know what to do about you."

"You see how it is when you live a clean life?" Subiyama asked. "You get laid regular and good stories fall into your lap."

Is there native dust on Venus or is it only the substance of God's design?

—Sermon topic,
Venusian archdiocese,
Episcopal Church

Roweena Humperman, in remodeled armor, the cut-down lines visible at waist and hips, met them inside the Command Center heatlock with her helmet thrown back and a stiff smile on her lips.

"Colonel Paul is in a little hot water for this, Lutt. Who's this with you?"

As they tipped back their helmets and inhaled air cleaned of armor-recycling odors, Lutt introduced Lorna Subiyama.

"Ain't this the damndest piece of luck?" Subiyama asked.

"We'll see. They're talking about not letting us out of here. Come along. Paul's down this way."

She took one of the camera packs from Lutt and led them through another heatlock where Legion guards examined their passes, then out into another passage lined with glittering red rock of ruby stone darkness and intensity. The floor was large tiles of the same material grouted in white. Stone benches of the red stone were spaced along the walls near red stone vases holding thick-leaved tropical plants. Walls and ceiling were polished smooth to reflect shadowy images of everything within them.

The decor of this place is no accident, Lutt thought.

What do you mean? Ryll wanted to know.

These dark reflections, there's something ghostlike about them. This is intended to be the nether world with shapes of dead legionnaire heroes all around.

I find the place morbid.

As they went deeper into the command complex, the echoes of voices and footsteps became more attention-demanding—some distant and small, others immediate and loud.

Very clever design, Lutt thought and was forced to explain the correlation between architecture and psychology he had learned while redesigning the Enquirer Building.

Abruptly, running footsteps sounded behind them. A Legion corporal in secured armor passed them, turned and held a hand for them to stop.

"You the newsies? Yes, I see you are. General says there's some action topside right now. Give you all the drama you want. This way."

Humperman was first to seal her helmet but not before turning a demanding look on Lutt, eyes burning, nostrils flared.

She thinks we're being sent up to be killed, Ryll interpreted.

There was no time to object. The corporal herded them down a side passage and into an elevator. He waited outside, one hand on the door control.

"This will let you out on Level One C. You'll find a ramp that leads up. Take it to a set of double doors. Show your passes there and follow directions to the surface."

"The surface?" Humperman demanded, voice stricken.

"Wow!" Subiyama said. "One minute we're headed to see the brass, the next minute it's straight into the war."

"Where's Colonel Paul?" Lutt asked.

The corporal spoke as he sealed the door. "Busy fightin' a war, monsieur. This is a full-scale attack. Stay behind the deflectors topside if you can. Very bad there."

Lutt, feeling the adrenaline surge of excitement, silenced Ryll's objections with logic.

If you want us to survive, strengthen me any way you can.

I will idmage a Dreen body or other appropriate guise if you suffer fatal damage, Ryll warned, knowing the threat was false.

Whatever you say, Ryll baby. Now shut up and let me work.

Ordering Humperman to watch what he did, Lutt unsealed the

camera he carried and instructed her in preparing the camera she had taken from him.

"Those are sure strange-looking cameras," Subiyama said.

Sensing a possible subscriber, Lutt gave her a brief explanation.

Excitement thickened Subiyama's accent. "Instantaneous? Y'all mean lak rat naow?"

Lutt was saved from further explanation by the elevator stopping and the door opening. They emerged at the foot of the ramp the corporal had described but it was filled with robotroops and human attendants.

No one asked for passes. The robotroops marched up and out. Lutt followed with his camera humming.

As the vorcameras were activated, Ryll felt a strong tug in his mind, the primal connection all Dreens experienced with the Creative Spirals—a link with all his people who had ever been and ever would be. The sensation increased his discomfort and sense of his own frailty. If things went wrong here, his connection with Dreendom would be broken.

Oh, do be careful, Lutt, Ryll thought.

Lutt ignored this, too intent on watching the action. Humperman on his left, camera at her shoulder the way he had instructed, was capturing her own view of things, carrying on a running commentary to explain her pictures. Subiyama walked beside her, talking into the electronic clipboard. Lutt heard only part of Subiyama's recording.

". . . and on my right is Lutt Hanson, Jr., the scion of the Hanson empire, proving to the universe that he's a working newsman."

Good copy! Lutt thought. *I hope it gets through.*

He saw the green light at the corner of his image focus telling him he was transmitting and being received. Then they were out onto level high ground with a shattered inceram parapet directly ahead. Wounded and dying Legion troops and broken robots lay all around. The replacements marched through and over the casualties. Lutt crouched and recorded. He saw Humperman bend over and dash to the left, there to aim her camera over the broken parapet. Subiyama crouched beside him, still recording into her more primitive device.

". . . with heavy casualties here at the Legion Command Center but the brave defenders are mounting a counterattack."

Lutt heard the loud static pops of deflector rays but the system was invisible except for occasional bursts of purple light.

Subiyama focused on the same phenomenon, recording: "The much-touted French deflector-ray system appears to have been breached but is working once more. I can see the laser hits overhead and in front of me. They look like purple flowers."

Lutt turned with his camera at nearby motion and saw a squad of six-legged robomedics emerge from the command complex. They began ministering to the wounded and dying, removing some of the casualties on inceram stretchers.

Lutt followed this action with his camera, adding his own commentary as he shot.

"The Chinese attack on this French stronghold appears to have inflicted heavy casualties. You can see the Legion artillery on the high ground beyond us beginning to return the fire. We can assume the Chinese also are taking heavy losses."

He aimed the camera as he spoke, watching through the lens as the guns belched black and silver clouds. The ground trembled with the explosions and his armor's mike system attenuated the sound automatically to protect his ears.

From her position crouched by the shattered parapet, Humperman called back to him: "Air attack nine o'clock."

Lutt saw her turn and aim her camera. He did the same, seeing a dark swarm of aircraft in the middle distance. Bursts of purple light appeared in the swarm as the Legion artillery found the range.

"Let's get off of here!" Subiyama shouted. "This place is a target."

She led the way at a crouching run whose speed surprised Lutt. He followed, keeping his camera more or less turned toward the attackers while he explained what was happening.

Once beyond the parapet, he found himself on brittle brown Venusian stone that crunched underfoot. This shaded into a slippery red sandlike surface much softer than an Earth beach. It slowed him dramatically.

Recalling the Venus survival pamphlet, Lutt thought: *Keep moving! The Venusian hotfoot is no joke.*

Ryll, observing all of this, could not refrain from comment. *You don't even feel the tragedy! You just see it all through your cold, emotionless newsman's eyes.*

That's the way it is, Ryll baby. Now stop distracting me unless you want us killed. This is the war you wanted to see.

I no longer want to see it. Let's go back inside.

And leave a great story? You are nuts! Now shut up!

Subiyama leading and Humperman right behind, they passed a staging area for casualties. Opaque inceram cocoons covered most of the wounded but a few cocoons had transparent insets that showed men wrapped in bloody blankets.

Lutt paused for a few closeups through the transparent insets. None of the legionnaires or robomedics took offense at this activity. They appeared familiar with news coverage and even pointed to areas where the attackers were being shot down.

Humperman ran up beside him and shouted: "Are you sure they're getting all of this back on Earth?"

"As long as that green light shows in your image screen."

"Can they talk to us through this thing?"

"When we're in transceive mode. I'll show you later."

Ryll, observing the air attackers approaching, feeling the vorcamera Spirals as possibly his last link with all that was Dreen, experienced mounting terror. Some of this began to bleed through into Lutt's awareness.

Please, Lutt, Ryll begged. *Let us go somewhere safe.*

You told me your life was dull. I'm doing you a favor, Ryll. And at no little expense.

I've changed my mind!

Too late, Ryll baby!

When it became apparent there would be no deflecting Lutt from this course, Ryll subsided into Dreen analysis and probing of the Earther. To Ryll's surprise, he learned that Lutt on rare occasions showed compassion for others. For Ryll, however, Lutt felt no such emotion. Ryll was an alien irritant, as unworthy of consideration as a brute animal.

Through all of this, Lutt kept his attention mostly on the viewfinder screen of his vorcamera. He was an observer detached from the misery and carnage, without even thoughts of personal danger.

Ryll found this an extremely odd form of concentration. In its exclusion of exterior distractions, it was sharper in intensity than Dreen idmaging.

Abruptly a searing pain tore from Lutt's lower back to the base of his skull, cutting through flesh and vital organs. Ryll, sharing the agony, knew an explosive had penetrated the armor.

Somewhere, a female voice shouted: "Hanson's been hit!"

Lutt felt the jerk and vibration of his armor's emergency system as it pushed replacement inceram emulsion and cool medicinal foam across the damage area.

Numb, his consciousness fading, Lutt felt himself falling. Bright yellow and orange colors flashed across his vision. He saw his vorcamera dropping in slow motion, still transmitting to Earth. He had a brief thought of every news medium in the solar system replaying those images, reporting in every language. A deafening roar filled his ears. He sensed black oblivion.

You're dying, Earther! Ryll told him. *Why didn't you listen to me?*

"I'm not!" Lutt screamed.

I think you are. You're obviously weaker and can't hold me off any longer. I'm going to cast you out and assume full control. Goodbye and good riddance!

No . . . don't. I'll make a sharing arrangement . . . anything. You saved us once. I know you can do it again.

Ryll, already busy repairing the damaged flesh, wondered privately if he really could rid himself of Hanson. There was a way of escaping from dying flesh without another merger. He knew that much, but lack of attention in class denied him the necessary information.

Ryll lamented his own pride and foolishness, his juvenile ideas about what a gifted student might accomplish. He knew this wound had destroyed flesh and he began to speculate on whether he would have to use flesh from a dead or dying legionnaire.

This raised another question: Could three personalities occupy this body? Ryll assumed it was possible.

Using Lutt's fear and weakness as leverage, Ryll began to insinuate himself into control of their body—first the eyes, then the major motor systems. He lay flat on the hot surface, wondering if the inceram was about to be breached by a Venusian hot spot. Humperman came into view, bending over him to read the exterior repeaters of his suit meters.

"You conscious?" she asked.

"Yes." The voice was weak, but Ryll thought it a fair approximation of Lutt's tones, especially in view of the injury.

"Don't worry. Medics are coming," Humperman said. "I got the whole thing on camera. I was aimed right at you when the thing hit. Looked like an explosive fragment from a scatter rocket."

"Where . . . Subiyama?" he managed.

"She ran back inside to see if there was a way to file her story. Christ! Here come some more rockets!" Humperman threw herself flat beside him.

Ryll, now fully in control of his body, felt the ground jump beneath him. An almost continuous flare of laser contacts painted the air purple all around him. He could see the jeweled purple reflections in Humperman's faceplate. She did not move.

"Medics on the way?" he asked. "That what you said?"

There was no response.

Ryll managed to tilt his head slightly, aiming the faceplate along Humperman's armored body. The armor below her waist vanished into a steaming puddle of blood. Sickened, desperate, Ryll wondered how he could gain access to what remained of her and use the flesh to restore the Hanson body. Any armor open to Venus would let in the searing heat already consuming Humperman.

Oh, why did I ever put the idea of seeing a war into Lutt's head?

Another explosion shook the ground.

Lutt surprised him then by intruding with a sharp thought: *So you took over, did you? Think you can keep control when I interfere?*

I'm trying to save us, you fool!

I see Humperman bought it. Where are the damned medics?

There's been a scatter rocket attack. May be no survivors.

Those damn Chink bastards! Look! Her vorcamera's still transmitting.

For all I know, so is the one you were using.

What a story!

Is that all you can think about?

I can also think you didn't get rid of me. Can't do it, can you?

I have not yet tried.

I wonder what the French would do with a captive Dreen?

Please cooperate, Ryll pleaded. *We can't oppose one another and live*. He focused on Humperman's body. *Do you want that to happen to us?*

Lutt found it unpleasant looking through eyes controlled by another, but he could not shut out any part of the scene. As Humperman's exposed flesh burned away, bright yellow and orange flames tore through what remained of her armor, filling it with light. Her face and head were the last to go, visible through her faceplate to the hideous end. At last, even the charred fragments melted into the planet.

It doesn't look like the medics are coming, Lutt observed. *So that's the way we'll die.*

She said they were on the way!

They've soldiers to care for. We're just expendable civilians.

They wouldn't just leave us here!

The Legion does what it must. That's one of their mottoes.

Ryll felt the medical foam and inceram repair system tight against skin. It remained cool in the armor but he wondered how long that would last.

I'm not dying while someone else controls my body, Lutt thought. He began inserting his own commands into their shared nervous system. The body twitched and twisted.

And I will not die in any but Dreen shape! Ryll insisted.

Overriding Lutt's efforts, he swiveled his eyes inward and began idmaging the familiar Dreen body he had known since emerging from the seedhouse.

Only a primitive white blob appeared on the Earther chest but it was too much for the armor. The front of the armor split and the searing touch of Venus consumed the blob. Inceram foam immediately flowed across the breach but Ryll, overcome by the blast furnace heat, emitted a primal Dreen scream and sensed Lutt joining him in a dark pit. The pit became unconsciousness as both fainted.

You better damn well believe I'm a war correspondent! I've been right in the middle of blood and dying and it wasn't fun!

—From an interview with
Lorna Subiyama

"It was your son, Ryll," Habiba said. "A primal Dreen scream that came to me across the Spirals."

She faced Jongleur in the original Dreenor home preserved beneath her cone. The mud-brown walls usually felt reassuring when she dealt with unpleasant matters, but not this evening.

"Is he . . . is he . . ."

Jongleur could not complete the question.

"I cannot say for sure, Jongleur. There was great pain and confusion . . . as though an Earther also were sending me his message of agony.

"That awful merging!"

"I fear that is the case."

"But you located him on Venus?"

"There is no doubt of it. The circumstantial evidence, the reports from our operatives on Earth, the great pain I sensed. It was fire, Jongleur. I fear he was being consumed by fire."

"Oh . . . my poor misguided son," Jongleur moaned.

"The sad example of his life must be used to educate the young," Habiba said. "In that way, Ryll's mistakes will not be a total waste."

"Yes . . . yes, of course."

Jongleur found this small compensation for the emotional pain caused by Habiba's information but it helped that she would make the effort to soothe him. *Blessed Habiba!*

"Tomorrow, we must gather the forces of our best idmagers and complete the shield," Habiba said. "It must sound cruel, dear Jongleur, but nothing is more important. As for other matters, they must be set aside. The shield must be made."

"And the replacement erasure ship?"

"Mugly tells me the improvements are taking more time than originally estimated. But whatever happens, Ryll's fate cannot be the fate of all Dreendom."

"Then you really think he is . . . he is . . ."

"It appears most likely, Jongleur. And that might be best for him. You know the fate of those who have merged."

"Madness and . . ."

"Unpredictable behavior!"

It suddenly struck Jongleur as strange that Habiba should equate madness with unpredictability. Could she, indeed, predict the behavior of all sane Dreens? He found this repulsive. Was nothing private? Was nothing totally and uniquely his own? But, of course, in the Thoughtcon, Habiba shared any data she cared to read. Thus . . . thus, he must be part of Habiba's thoughts. And she . . . could she control Dreen actions in Thoughtcon?

Jongleur's recent concentration on Earther matters made him see this in a different light. Was it wrong to suppress all individuality? Or was that another mad thought?

"What are you thinking, Jongleur?" Habiba demanded.

For the first time in his life, Jongleur contemplated the concealment of his thoughts from Blessed Habiba.

"I am thinking how to strengthen tomorrow's shield idmaging," he lied.

Immediately, Jongleur felt icy cold. What were the consequences of misleading Habiba? But this was such a small lie. And he did want to strengthen the effort on the shield.

"Dear Jongleur," Habiba said. "You are always so supportive of my every desire. With you helping, I know we cannot fail."

From the outside, the ship looks kinda fancy but that hummer is big! Big as a Legion warship and just as well protected. I mean, the Legion wants its whores but it doesn't want them hurt.

—Eyewitness description,
Legion bordello, Venus

Lutt felt himself floating in and out of consciousness, remembering a dream. A big soft creature with four legs peered at him in the dream and berated him for being secretive.

He felt no pain but there was this curious feeling of being separated from his body and then uniting with it, a sensation repeated several times.

Is this what it's like to die?

There was movement. He sensed it vaguely but could not see it. Was it more of the weird dream?

A woman's voice cut across these thoughts.

"Quick! He's bleeding badly!"

Where am I?

Abruptly, he remembered. *Surface of Venus, hurt by a Chink rocket. Ryll! Am I rid of that Dreen bastard?*

No response from Ryll.

He felt himself being lifted and pain returned. He sensed armor pressed tight against his skin.

Blurred vision, pink with ruddy orange light behind it, revealed three . . . maybe four creatures in podlike armor lifting him. *The medics?*

Their suits were gray inceram with no insignia.

The damn Chinks?

A helmet came close to his faceplate and he saw a woman's face behind the armor glass—definitely female, a mixture of Oriental and Caucasian features. She appeared concerned. She and the others were putting him on a gray gurney suspended from some sort of flying ship directly above them. He strained to identify the ship through uncooperative eyes.

Massive. It filled the orange sky. Streaks of color along its length. Chartreuse. He saw white and blue neo-Victorian decorations around portholes, hatches and vents.

What the hell is that thing? Chink? Legion hospital?

Lutt found his voice. "Wha' kinda ship? Looks like a flying bordello."

A female voice from somewhere behind him said: "Smart boy. Let's see if we can restore him enough to get a little life out of him."

A high-pitched feminine laugh greeted this.

Lutt tried to turn and see who laughed but an inceram pod clamped shut over his gurney and he was left in gloomy green isolation with the sensation of swinging on the end of a cable.

Something in the enclosing pod emitted a burring sound and he felt the soothing departure of both pain and consciousness. They were using sonosthetic! Maybe it was a hospital.

Lutt awoke strapped in a bed. Green ceiling and some red surface below that. Medical connections to his body. He felt softly cocooned. A hospital room. He saw his clear-lens glasses on a side table, still unbroken.

I should dump those things, he thought. *Haven't needed them since I got Ryll's eyesight.*

There were sounds—human activity, voices nearby, rumbling of engines and an echoing series of thumps. Explosions?

Someone moved into his range of vision. He glimpsed svelte black clothing that clung to a slender, sensuous body.

The lovely face he had seen behind an armor glass helmet bent over him. One of his rescuers. Did the Legion use female medics?

She had brown eyes, a definite epicanthic fold to them. Skin dark and smooth. Tiny black beauty mark on the right side of her full-lipped mouth. Nose turned up slightly. A Caucasian nose.

"You feel better?" A softly lilting voice. Her lips opened to reveal small teeth, evenly spaced.

She reached out a long-fingered hand and touched his arm. Electric sensation of warmth.

"Where?" he managed.

"You are in our infirmary. Do you hurt?"

"Sore as hell." He turned slightly and grimaced. "My back hurts."

"Don't try to sit up. Our doctors used red-laser acupuncture two days ago to facilitate cellular regeneration in your back wound."

"Two days?"

He glanced around, seeing the room more clearly. Red walls, fuzzy surface and tiny yellow flowers printed in it. Brass lamps. Furnishings dark and ornate. Everything bolted down. An oval port on his left showed him a distant Venusian landscape with a low mountain range coming into view.

"You have been here three days," she said. "Your ID says Peter Andriessen but I have seen a rebroadcast from Earth that says you are Lutt Hanson, Jr. Which?"

"Lutt."

"My goodness! We have a famous visitor!"

"What is this ship?"

"This is the Legion's flying bordello. We go where we are needed."

Keerist! A flying whorehouse!

He stared up at his rescuer. "Are you . . ."

"I am called the Virgin Chanteuse. I sing for the boys but I do not perform on my back."

"You're one of the group that went down to the surface and rescued me, aren't you?"

"That is another service we perform when the need arises."

"How bad . . . was I hurt?"

"Our doctors say you are remarkably lucky. Surface burns and contusions, no serious internal injuries."

So my Dreen got in a few repair licks before he vanished.

"My back?"

"The injury missed your spine."

She smiled and dimples formed beside her mouth.

"Thirsty," he said.

There was a sensuous grace to her as she moved to a wall spigot and drew a cup of water. He smelled carnation perfume when she helped him drink.

"So you sing," he said when she removed the empty cup.

"I also wait on tables, make my own clothes and supervise the ship's seamstresses."

"And help with the wounded."

"I am with you partly because I speak your language well. And we were curious. Why would a Hanson risk his life here?"

"Business."

"But it is so dangerous."

"Then why are you here?"

"We were poor and . . ." She shrugged. "But you, you really came here on business?"

"Right."

"When we suspected you might really be a Hanson, one of our girls said, 'If a Hanson jumps out a tenth-story window, you must follow him. Profit is to be made there.' "

"Is this flying bordello profitable?"

She tittered. "The better girls are no longer poor. Never call them whores. They are love specialists. These are the women of the Legion, the toughest and most deserving troops in God's creation."

"How did you . . . I mean, what . . ." He broke off, wondering if his desire for this woman was visible in his eyes.

"My father and three brothers were legionnaires, all killed in battle against those damnable Mao Guards. But a woman cannot serve the Legion except . . ." She glanced around. "Besides, I am Catholic and I have a care for my soul."

"You're certainly beautiful enough."

"So I am told frequently, but . . ." Again, that gentle shrug. "I promised my father and elder brother I would not sell my body."

"The virgin singer," he said.

"It sets me apart," she said. "The Madame says it is good for business, something they can dream about but cannot have."

"What's your real name?" he asked.

"I am Nishi D'Amato." Her eyes flashed a definite hazel as she smiled at him. "But I must go now. Others need me."

The clinging black garment rippled over her back and buttocks as she left the room.

Nishi. Is she the Ni-Ni of my dreams? Was I drawn to Venus to be with her?

That is a very mystical idea, Lutt. Your Venus on Venus!

So the damned Dreen was still here!

We still share this flesh, Lutt. A lucky thing for you I was here to effect idmaged repairs of our body. It does not appear the doctors discovered our secret.

Maybe not.

When we were dying, you made promises about sharing our body. I think it's time we—

Forget it, sucker. I can promise anything when I'm in trouble.

But you promised!

I warned you once I may not keep my promises.

Lutt, this is something I will remember. And next time . . .

Shit! You didn't help because you wanted to save me. You were saving yourself just like anybody would.

I will separate us at the first opportunity. This is my promise, Lutt. We Dreens keep our promises.

Lotsa luck, Ryll baby. I don't think you can do it.

It never really gets dark on Venus. This is a war fought in murderous orange. Night becomes a nostalgic memory and everything around you captures the look of Hell.

—Lorna Subiyama,
a story from Venus

Prosik stared out an armored window of his Venusian barracks and pondered the malignant fate that had brought him to this place. The landscape glowed with a fiery ferocity and he shuddered at the things he had learned about the planet. Agony and quick incineration could well prevent any idmaged attempt to save himself if his inceram armor malfunctioned.

The barracks he shared with nine other Zone Patrol men presented an almost unused appearance after their breakfast in quarters—ten lockers, ten bunks, racks with spare armor—everything inceram gray. The others already had gone to their assignments. None had known the Earther Prosik mimicked, a guard sergeant named Lew Doughty. All said this was punishment duty and sympathized when he told them about the damage to the Dreen ship for which he had been blamed.

"I guarded some Dreens once," one said. "Make you wanta puke. We oughta blow 'em all away."

Venus duty centered on the United States Consulate and Sergeant Doughty was scheduled to stand guard in two hours. In the interim, he studied a manual titled "How to Stay Alive on Venus." It was not reassuring.

Prosik's defense in his Zone Patrol guise was to play dumb and resentful, a pose he did not find difficult. He also drew on every Earther story he could remember but he knew the other men already thought him clumsy. Prosik had heard one whisper to a companion:

"Give you odds this one doesn't last ten days."

Prosik thumbed through the survival manual, more and more dismayed as he read:

> Use the buddy system and never go alone into the city. You could be killed for your armor or your organs.
>
> Gorontium is Legion territory. Never get into an argument or a fight with a legionnaire. You can't win.
>
> Stay away from the Legion bordello! Even if you manage to get inside you will never emerge alive.
>
> Eat and drink only Zone Patrol fare. Addictive substances and other dangerous additives have been found in bars and restaurants here.
>
> Ask no personal questions of new acquaintances. They will take you for a spy and that can get you killed.
>
> Remember the Four *C*'s at all times: Courtesy, Caution, Coolness, and Courage. Be suspicious of everyone and everything except your Zone Patrol buddies.
>
> Check your armor after every servicing and before using it each day. Always run a function check in the exit lock. You cannot survive outside without working armor.

Habiba protect me! Prosik thought.

He suddenly found the familiar prayer meaningless. Had it prevented this state of affairs? No! Had it ever brought him anything he truly wanted? Never!

Prosik longed for a frond of bazeel and time to enjoy it.

Bazeel, my only friend.

"Sergeant Doughty!"

It was the speaker above the exit lock at the end of the barracks.

"Yo!" He had heard the others respond that way.

"Your duty assignment has been moved up. You are due at the consulate in twenty minutes."

"But I haven't checked my armor or—"

"You're replacing a casualty. Get moving!"

Prosik threw "How to Stay Alive" onto his bunk and began getting into his armor. That, at least, was familiar from the drills on the transport that had brought him to this hellish place.

And how do I find the time and conditions to seek out the Earther, Hanson, and that awful Ryll who got me into this fix? How does Mugly expect me to do that? He must know the difficulties. Curse them all!

Earthers place great store in their tools and other toys. Weapons particularly are attractive to them even though experience has demonstrated that weapons are just as perilous to the users as to anyone thought of as enemy.

—*The Habiba Commentary*

Nishi brought Lutt's dinner on the evening of his first day of consciousness and informed him the flying bordello had just settled to its home berth at Gorontium. He could see the outlines of buildings bathed in lambent orange out the armored port of his infirmary room.

Lutt thought Nishi looked radiant in a white singlesuit of clinging cut. He took a deep breath to put aside lustful thoughts and concentrated on her almond eyes.

"What happened to my equipment, my cameras?" he asked as she put the tray on his bedside table and fluffed his pillows.

"They are stored in a nearby room. Nothing seems to have been damaged."

"How do you know?"

"I looked. Are those cameras valuable?"

"Quite valuable."

"I thought so. I put them under our house seal to protect them for you."

"Why are you taking such good care of me?

"I have read about you and looked up your history."

"And you're curious."

"That, too. But I am also practical. You are very rich and you are not married."

Lutt found himself utterly charmed by her candor. No beating around the bush. He was a rich catch and she would not lie about it.

"And you could probably bring yourself to find me physically attractive?" he asked.

She placed his glasses on his face. "Oh, that is the easiest part. You are very brave and you have the intellectual look I admire. If I ever give myself to a man it will be to someone like you."

"And you would like to be very rich?"

"Oh, yes!"

Lutt, now amused as well as charmed, entered into the spirit of her straightforward honesty. "Do you think you could be a rich man's wife? What would you do?"

"I would watch his diet and his health. I am a very, very good chef. And I would help him entertain important people."

"But rich men hire cooks, and what do you know about how important people are entertained?"

"Hired chefs need supervision, and as to important people, you might be surprised at the names I could reveal, people who have visited us here."

"I might at that. But isn't the entertainment here pretty simple? I mean . . ."

"Oh, sex is only part of it. We are taught here how to discover what people really want. I am very good at that, too."

"So you know what I want?"

"You want me but there is more. You are a man who wants great power."

Lutt was startled by her perception.

"You are surprised," she said. "There is also something very strange about you, Monsieur Hanson. Something in your eyes."

He suddenly felt cautious. "What about my eyes?"

She studied them—large, olive. "You see deep. Perhaps it's because you have been close to death, but . . . no. There is something else. You look at things in a different way from anyone I have ever known."

"Maybe I do."

"Tell me how your cameras work."

The change of subject startled him. "Why?"

"I am an amateur photographer. Perhaps I could help a rich man there, too."

"How?"

"Who knows what things might be valuable if they are photographed?"

"Like what?"

"Like the inside of this bordello?"

Once more, he was startled.

"You have heard stories about this place?" she asked.

"A few. Is it against rules to shoot in here?"

"It is a private enterprise of D'Assas Anon. Nothing is impossible if the Madame allows." Nishi sat on his bed and took his left hand in both of her hands. "Tell me of your valuable cameras."

Why not? he asked himself. *It'd involve us in something together.*

Lutt found he wanted nothing more than to be involved with this charming woman . . . so beautiful, so young . . .

"How old are you?" he asked.

"I am twenty-three. Will you teach me the cameras?"

"Bring one of them," he said.

She slid off the bed, left the room and returned quickly with one of the cameras in its inceram case.

Lutt pushed himself up in the bed, took the camera in his lap and began explaining it.

Nishi was a quick study and her questions were pointed.

"And if anyone tries to dismantle the camera to learn its secrets, it will explode?" she asked.

"It will self-destruct."

"Who in the Legion knows about your cameras?"

"Colonel Paul and . . . and that's all I know about."

"He is dead. He tried to recover Madame Humperman's body."

"I . . . I didn't know."

"These Spirals where your signals go, where are they?" she asked.

"Everywhere, anywhere. I don't know."

"Then why do you call them Spirals?"

He knew he could not tell her about the *Vortraveler* and the Dreens but he had to say something. Lamely, he said: "Because there's a funny twisting sensation when you use the camera." That, at least, was the truth.

"And the transmission is truly instantaneous?"

"Almost."

"Do you think anyone will ever see your Spirals?"

"I hope so."

"Can you also send messages without pictures?"

"Of course."

"And no one without such a camera can intercept them?"

"Of course not."

"The Legion might find this very valuable, Monsieur Hanson."

Lutt was suddenly conscious he might be dealing with a Legion espionage agent. And spy devices could be focused on him here. Venus, after all, was a complex and dangerous place.

"How valuable?" he asked.

"So valuable that I have made sure you are in a room without spy eyes. For a businessman, Monsieur Hanson, you seem very innocent of the possibilities of your invention."

Stung, he said: "And you seem very sharp for a twenty-three-year-old virgin singer in a Legion whorehouse."

"My father always said it was my bourgeoisie ancestry. I think you need me, Monsieur Hanson."

It was the truth and he knew it. "I think maybe I do." He reached out and patted her buttocks.

Nishi twisted away. Her face flashed rage, then calmed. "Not just yet, monsieur."

"I wish you'd call me Lutt."

"Very well, but do not think that a sign you can take liberties with my body . . . Lutt."

"Don't you want me to take liberties?"

She stared at him for a moment, then: "I think I have been too forward. I would be pleased to be rich but you must think perhaps I am teasing you."

Lutt felt a surge of lust. "I have a chance with you?"

"Perhaps. But first there is the business of your cameras."

"What about them?"

"I will transmit pictures to your people on Earth and tell them where you are. I will say I am working for you. It is well your people know your situation."

"Why?"

"The Legion can be ruthless, Lutt. But they also can see a position of strength where they must bargain."

"And right now I'm their prisoner, more or less."

"Oh, no! You are a guest of an independent contractor. And the contractor is also interested in making a profit. This is a business, Lutt. Never forget that."

"You're saying the people who run this . . . this business will want their cut off the top."

She raised her shoulders in a Gallic shrug. "I think we can keep them from being too greedy. They will not kill the goose of the golden eggs." She reached down and squeezed his cheek. "And you, I think, are the big goose."

"Am I *your* goose?"

"I think maybe you are, but we do not make the nest just yet." A smile danced at the corners of her mouth.

"Give me a kiss to seal our bargain."

"What bargain?"

"That you're working for me."

"But you have not said it."

"Okay! I've hired you for the *Enquirer*. You're a full-fledged field rep."

"And what is my pay?"

"What does this place pay you?"

"Three hundred new francs a month and I keep half my tips. In a good month I make a thousand of your dollars."

"Your starting salary with the *Enquirer* is five thousand."

"That is too much. I do not intend to earn it in your bed. No! You will pay two thousand plus expenses and give me five percent of whatever I get you from the Legion. Agreed?"

Charmed more than ever by her candor, Lutt nodded. "Agreed."

"Now, we must talk about the camera," she said.

"I've told you how to run it."

"Yes, but if it were not a camera, just a transceiver, could it be made smaller?"

"Y–yes, it could."

"Then I will send a message telling your people to make such a device for the Legion. They would pay very much. Who should I tell?"

Lutt was amused by her cupidity, but asked himself: *Why not?*

"Have the *Enquirer* relay orders to Sam at my shop," he said and pointed to the camera on his lap. "Use this. Tell them now. And if there's any question you can put me on to confirm it."

"Is this how a wife helps her rich husband?" she asked.

Lutt broke into laughter. "So you *are* after my money."

"Remember my bourgeoisie ancestors. I wish the proposal, not the proposition."

"Nishi, honey, you may get just that."

"When?"

Suddenly cautious, but still amused, Lutt said: "I'm just like you, Nishi. When it comes to my body, I say when."

"Very good!" she said. "Now you learn to bargain. I will teach you of this. I can see you do not know it well." She turned to the camera and slowly but methodically activated it, giving the call signal for Earth station response, then focusing on Lutt.

Lutt put his dinner tray aside as Ade Stuart came on the response cell. "Lutt? Is that really you, Lutt?"

"It's really me, Ade."

"Where the hell are you? We thought you were dead."

"I'm in the infirmary of the Legion bordello on Venus. They rescued me."

"In the . . . oh, for Crissakes! I swear, Lutt, if you fell into a shithouse it would turn out to be a gold mine. Who's running the camera?"

"A new employee, Nishi D'Amato. Put her on the payroll at two thousand a month plus expenses. How did the sales party go?"

"A smash hit! Christ! Those pictures of the battle. We got one hundred percent acceptance from every rep at the party. We hit every front page in every major paper in the country and they're clamoring for us overseas."

"Has L.H. been in touch?"

"Just to ask for a copy of the sales report. Hey, look. How badly are you hurt?"

"I'll be up and walking in a day or so." He reached for the camera and turned it toward Nishi. "This is Nishi D'Amato. She has some orders for you to relay for us. Get word to Sam at the shop immediately."

Nishi flashed a dimpled smile and then turned serious. "First, you will get the word to the French ambassador in Washington and to the government in Paris through your own ambassador there that Monsieur Hanson is here and under the protection of D'Assas Anon, the owners of our ship."

"You want me to say exactly where he is?"

"But of course."

"Do as she says," Lutt said.

"Okay. But your mother may think this is even worse than believing you dead. I mean, she took it pretty hard, Lutt, but . . ."

"Just do it, Ade."

"Monsieur Hanson's life may depend on it," Nishi said. "It must be done at once."

"At once. Got it. What else?"

In a brisk tone, wasting no words, Nishi gave him the message for Sam R. Kand.

"Just a communicator?" Stuart asked.

"As small as is practical," she said. "And when it is done, he must send the devices to Monsieur Hanson in care of D'Assas Anon. And they must be protected against tampering."

"Self-destruct system," Stuart said. "Anything else? When do we get more copy from you?"

"Nishi will send you some stuff soon. An exclusive from inside this bordello."

"Porn?"

Lutt looked at Nishi and shook his head.

"It will be a feature story," she said. "An interview with Madame and some of the other women. Pictures of the women in their leisure moments, meeting clients, dressing, eating, chatting and discussing their experiences. Perhaps some of the legionnaires will consent to speak to me."

"Life in a Legion bordello!" Stuart said. "Great! When can we expect it? The subscribers are pressing us."

"Today," she said. "Now, we must not waste more time. Tell the ambassadors at once." She deactivated the camera and placed it on the floor beside the bed. "There. That is the first step."

"And what's next?"

"I have been thinking about us. It is the custom of my people to require a marriage contract."

"Are you proposing to me?"

"Is that not my right?"
"Sure, but what if we're not compatible?"
"Not com— Oh, you tricky man. Is this a proposition?"
"I think we should conduct a test."
She shook her head from side to side. "I am not one of the professionals, Lutt, but I have studied them at work."
"You . . . you watched?"
"When they said I could and when they did it in public. You will not find me a poor student. We will be compatible."
Lutt grabbed her hand and pulled her toward him. "But shouldn't I have that kiss to seal our bargain?"
"Just the kiss, nothing more. Do not presume too much. There are men of the Legion aboard. If I shout for help, they may come and injure you severely."
"And we wouldn't want that," he said, pulling her closer. His arms went around her and he pressed his lips to her cheek, then to her mouth. When he cupped a hand over her breast, she pushed him away and pulled back.
"Now, now, Lutt!"
He wanted to force himself on her. Would she call for help? Kill the goose? As he was resolving to test it, Ryll intruded.
That's enough, Lutt!
Oh, for Crissakes! You still with me?
We are with each other. I have been observing and thinking. You are doing a very dangerous thing. For whom does this woman work?
For me! You heard us!
Indeed. I heard it all.
She's just playing hard to get.
If she is playing anything, she is playing you, and she is doing it superbly.
She wants to be my wife. You heard her.
I heard her, yes. But what we heard is not necessarily true. Do you think such a beautiful woman does not have a lover?
She said she was a virgin.
Yes, I heard her say it. And she also has a head for profit, but she did not accept your first generous offer.
Her percentage on any deal we strike with the Legion could make her very rich!

But she has no contract. Do you not always require contracts? Did she not speak of a marriage contract? She plays a very strange game, Lutt. You should be more suspicious.

"Lutt, why are you looking at me that way?" Nishi asked, freeing herself from his arms and standing beside the bed.

"What way?"

"I cannot describe it. Sometimes, your eyes frighten me. It's as though a stranger looked out of them."

"It's a head injury I got in a crash," he said. "Sometimes it hurts."

"Are you schizo?"

"Not really. I'm just a little remote at times. It's not dangerous."

She took a deep breath. "Do you take medicine?"

"Sometimes. Hey, look. We're in a crazy place on a weird ship in an oddball war for control of a nearly useless planet. Who wouldn't go a little weird here sometimes?"

"You call this a crazy place but it is the only place I have known for five years. It is not crazy if you know how to survive here."

"You weren't fully grown when you came here?"

"My body was fully grown but not my mind. I have learned much here. Other places seem crazy when I hear about them."

"I think we need each other, Ni-Ni."

She gasped. "What did you call me?"

"Ni-Ni."

"Only my father and brothers have ever called me that! How did you know?"

"It . . . it seemed right to call you Ni-Ni."

Her expression softened. "I like it when you call me that. You may call me Ni-Ni when we make love."

"And when will that be?"

She patted his hand and drew back quickly when he tried to grab her. "Soon. Do not be impatient. First, we must have the proper contract."

See? Ryll demanded.

She's just being cautious. A good business head. This is the woman for me, Ryll. This is my Ni-Ni.

She probably has other lovers! Many men who do disgusting things with her!

I don't think so. She would enjoy having money but I know it goes deeper. This is Ni-Ni. I've found her!

Many of the lesser planets created by our great Storytellers experience sewer and garbage problems. Dreenor is more fortunate. Wastes are idmaged into delectables. You will perfect this procedure in your present class. Adults should not be expected to clean up after you all of your life.

—Proctor's presentation,
Dreen elementary school

Prosik arrived at the consulate as a crew was removing what remained of the man he replaced. The removal crew did not have to exert themselves. Some shards of inceram armor and a few ashes were all that remained of the late guard.

The consulate was a domed building that sat by itself on a raised black inceram platform above the Gorontium base. It looked like half a giant eggshell on an overdone slice of toast. A large U.S. flag and a golden eagle, all in colored inceram, were worked into the front of the building above the entry lock.

The fatality turned out to be the man who had wanted to bet that Prosik would not last ten days.

"A sniper from somewhere up the canal got him," a fellow guard explained. "Some kinda rocket. I think there was trouble over a woman and it may've been the other guy. Don't mess with another man's woman on Venus."

Prosik shuddered and took up his station inside the lock. Two of them had the duty here, checking passes.

Prosik recalled his fellow guard's name from the introductions that morning: Hollis Weatherbee, a slender redhead with burn-scarred face.

"Your name's Doughty, Lew Doughty, right?" Weatherbee asked in the first lull.

Prosik nodded.

"You wanta buddy up? We look out for each other? I'll teach you the ropes well as I can. You keep an eye on my back."

Prosik glanced out the lock where the last of the casualty was being swept off the black inceram.

"Hicks never wanted to buddy," Weatherbee said. "Afraid what people might say, I think. Don't get me wrong, Doughty. I prefer women."

Prosik did not really understand this conversation but he nodded positively.

"What about it?" Weatherbee asked. "If I can keep you alive long enough for you to learn the ropes, we could make a good team."

"Yes, I will buddy with you," Prosik said. "Why was Hicks outside?"

"I dunno. He left his station without saying. I think someone beckoned him out. A woman, most likely. They probably set him up. What about you? You go for women?"

"Not ones who lure me to destruction," Prosik said.

"You know, you got a funny way of talking but you make sense. I think we're gonna get along fine, buddy. Look sharp now. That's the consul himself coming in."

Prosik drew himself up to attention as an armored figure came through the lock and marched past them without acknowledging their salute or lifting his helmet. When he was out of earshot, Weatherbee said: "Snooty bastard. Didn't even ask about Hicks."

The words were a long time coming to focus in Prosik's mind. He was suddenly distracted by a familiar sensation—the twisting awareness that always accompanied access to the Spirals. Someone was opening the pathways of infinity and it had to be nearby. Was it a Storyship? Prosik thought not. The sensation was definite but weak. It had to be that damned Earther and his crude instrumentation!

"What is in this locality?" he asked Weatherbee.

"Not much that concerns us. We keep a clear field of fire all around. But if you go over to that port behind you and look to the right you can see the Legion's flying whorehouse. It came in a few hours ago. Better believe the manual on that place, Lew. That is pure poison."

"Poison?"

"Legionnaires don't let many outsiders in there. One of our guys saved a Legion captain's life a few years back. Got two whole days in there as a reward. He came out ga-ga. Said he'd never go into another whorehouse long as he lived. Pure spoiled by this one. Said it was better'n that one on the boat off LA. And I always thought that one was the best. Man! I'd sure like to get me in that Legion cathouse just once."

Prosik nodded as though he understood. The Spiral sensation ended. Was it in the Legion place? Cathouse?

From his Earther studies, Prosik knew something of their sexual habits but most of the idiom escaped him. What could cats have to do with that place? He did not dare ask, though. Danger lay in showing too much ignorance. That much he understood well.

The arousal of prurient interest by this thinly disguised pornography must be recognized by the courts as meeting the legal definition of obscenity. Nothing about this display can be categorized as news.

—From a brief seeking an injunction against the *Seattle Enquirer*

Lorna Subiyama inspected the exterior of the Legion's flying bordello with a jaundiced expression, then looked at the armored figure of her companion and guide, Sue Ellen Pratt. Sue Ellen's cowgirl armor reflected dancing orange light from the clouds that attenuated the tiny spark of the noonday sun.

"That's it?" Subiyama asked.

"Pretty fancy, eh?" Sue Ellen said.

"I've seen fancier in Lubbock. You ever been inside?"

"I'm jus' a civilian employee of the Legion, honey. They don' let us in there 'les we wanna go t' work. B'lieve me, I've thought about it. Those gals make *bowcoo* bucks."

"What stopped you?"

"I see all the Legion schlong I want without tyin' m'self to that routine. An' what th' hell, honey? You see one schlong, you seen 'em all."

"I wish I knew for sure he was in there."

"Lissen, honey, he's in there. My Legion pals wouldn't lie to li'l ol' Sue Ellen 'bout that."

"He's gotta come out sometime."

"Mebbe. Depends on what he's doin' in there."

"You know anything at all about this Lutt Hanson, Jr.? His daddy was capital H Horny but I hear he's worse. What I'd like to know is how he got in there."

"Mebbe he rescued a legionnaire. Been a few like that."

"The stories didn't say. Made him out as some kinda hero, though. 'In the best tradition of journalism,' my ass!"

"We can't jus' stan' aroun' out here an' gawk, honey."

"Anyplace we can keep an eye on this flying cathouse and not be like two chickens in the middle of the road?"

"Well, they's one li'l ol' place in the U.S. Consulate lobby where you can see the ship an' its main lock. Mebbe if we was t' cozy up t' the guards they'd let us stay there awhile."

"Let's give it a try. My editors are kicking ass to get this story, especially after all the *Enquirer's* battle pix and that big spread about life in a Legion bordello. Shit! I gotta admit it. That Hanson bastard is good."

"Good as you, honey?"

"Man don't live who's good as me, Sue Ellen. I can drink and screw and write and fight with the best of 'em and leave 'em all in my dust."

Osey came running into my room and said, "So much for your meddling! He's found a woman in that Legion cathouse."

—Memoirs of the Raj Dood

On his fifth morning in the bordello, the doctors said Lutt could get into a robe and accompany Nishi to breakfast in a dining room. Lutt thought the doctors and other attendants were treating him oddly, not quite deferential but certainly with a courtesy that went beyond professional demands.

Nishi, though, still kept her distance and Lutt found himself ever more enamored. Was this because she would not get into his bed? he wondered.

"I am your negotiator," she said. "The Legion wishes another demonstration of your communicator. I am determining how that may be conducted. We must control the circumstances."

"Shouldn't I be the one talking to them?"

He asked this as they sat down at a table near the dining room entrance. Nishi, in the red dress accented by blue and white trim that was standard with Food Service employees, pursed her lips, then: "I think not."

Lutt glanced around the sparsely occupied room—three women in black gowns at a corner table, two women in red at a table near the center, and one stocky legionnaire nearby in full battle regalia, helmet thrown back. The legionnaire picked slowly at a plate of chicken and rice.

"Why shouldn't I talk to them?" Lutt asked.

"Important people do not waste time on preliminaries. You notice how well they treat you? D'Assas Anon has ordered that you are a most honored guest. Do not stare at that man."

She touched Lutt's arm to divert him from studying the lone legionnaire.

"They do not like to be stared at by strangers," she said. "You notice how he looks at the small woman in black over there?"

"I . . . uh . . ."

"You did *not* notice. She is available and he wants her. He may even do it in here."

Lutt rubbed the pulsing vein on his temple. "In the dining room?"

"Wherever he wishes. That one woman or all three."

"He'd have to take off his armor."

"They would help. Sometimes, when the desire comes over a legionnaire, he will knock over the table, the chairs, anything that stands in his way."

"Doesn't anyone object?"

"Oh,no! They are showmen. Such behavior is for the benefit of other legionnaires. This one most likely will not do that. He is alone. I do not think he would do it for you."

"He isn't looking at you, is he?"

"He looked at me but they all know I am not available. He wonders about you and me, though."

The legionnaire began to eat with angry movements, shoving large morsels of food into his mouth and gulping them. Presently, he put down his fork and beckoned the smaller of the women in black, a platinum blond with darker eyebrows and gamin features. She responded immediately but with slow, deliberate movements and strolled to the legionnaire's side. He grabbed her arm and jerked her down until her head was close to his. There he said something to her fiercely. She glanced at Lutt and shook her head. The legionnaire thrust a hand into her hair and shook her head angrily.

"*Oui!*" the woman said, "*Oui!*"

"What's he doing?" Lutt whispered.

"Perhaps he has told her to give herself to you."

"No!" And Lutt thought: *Can this be me? Would I really turn her down?*

The legionnaire released the woman and she went to the food service counter where she spoke to one of the attendants.

"Lutt," Nishi whispered, "I must warn you. He has ordered something for you. Whatever it is you must eat it."

"Why?"

"I think he is testing you."

"What the hell could he order for me?"

"I think it is fugu."

"What's fugu?"

"You don't know? I assumed everyone knew. The samurai warriors of Japan originated the custom. Fugu is Japanese for the blowfish or pufferfish. We hire licensed Japanese fugu chefs."

"Why would he order a delicacy for me?"

"Fugu can be very poisonous if the chef makes a mistake. The poison is in the liver, the ovaries and intestines. The fish must be cleaned and cooked precisely or it will poison you."

The platinum blond woman accepted a plate from an attendant at the food service counter and brought it to Lutt's table. She slapped it in front of Lutt and flounced away without speaking. It was a dark blue plate containing a single small fillet of gray meat adorned with a sprig of green onion.

Lutt felt a surge of excitement as he looked at it. The feeling was familiar. He had felt the same while hang gliding, while defying death in many ways.

Don't eat it, Lutt! Ryll objected.

That legionnaire will kill me if I don't.

No! He may think you a coward but he will not—

Stay out of this!

This is insane!

Hell no! This is really living!

Lutt took his fork and broke off a large bite of the fugu. Ryll tried to interfere but Lutt forced it, breaking Ryll's will with the admonition: *You want them to discover a Dreen?*

If it kills you, I will idmage my way into another body! Ryll boasted. Privately, he thought: *How could I do it? How? Why oh why didn't I pay closer attention in class? Wait a minute! Yes, maybe. Just maybe . . .*

So you have an out and I don't. Now shut up!

Lutt put the bite of fugu in his mouth and chewed it. Bland. He took a bite of the onion, another bite of fugu.

Nishi stared at Lutt with a look of fascination.

"Have you ever seen anyone die of this?" Lutt asked.

"No, but there have been six deaths in our dining rooms. The chefs committed hara-kiri and the new chefs have not yet had any fatalities."

"How soon do you know if it's poison?"

"It strikes quickly, I'm told. Convulsions and paralysis. Legionnaires consider fugu a test of courage, one more obstacle to overcome. I think you have not been poisoned."

"Why didn't you try to stop me?"

"I would have killed that legionnaire if the fugu took you from me."

Lutt stared at her, sensing a deep thread of fanatical determination in her. What kind of woman was this?

Abruptly, Nishi stood and took the plate from him. It still contained about half the serving. She carried the plate to the legionnaire and slammed it onto the table in front of him. He looked up, startled.

"This is safe for you to eat," she said. "Eat it. And remember this: By the memory of my sainted father and brothers, if this fugu had been poison I would have found a way to kill you!"

The legionnaire's face darkened. He started to reach for her and thought better of it.

Nishi pivoted on one heel and returned to her chair. The legionnaire abruptly pushed himself back and left the room.

"Lucky for him he did not touch me," Nishi said. "My friends would have torn his body apart. Better to die in battle."

"I'm still hungry," Lutt said.

"It would be a gesture to order more fugu," Nishi said. "Do you wish to do that?"

"I found it bland," he said.

It was delicious! Ryll objected so impulsively he surprised himself. *I have been thinking about this. Order more. I think I can save us if it is poison.*

You think?

Idmage interference with complex proteins is not beyond my capabilities! And he thought privately: *Am I really saying this? Have I been contaminated with an Earther's foolish pride?*

Okay, Ryll baby. But this time we flavor it my way.

Reading in his thoughts what Lutt intended, Ryll sent a frantic objection: *No! I hate that stuff!*

Lutt grinned and said: "Nishi, see if your chefs can fix me more fugu but this time with a pesto sauce on the side."

"Pesto?"

"It is a sauce with fresh basil, parmesan cheese, olive oil, garlic and pine nuts. Delicious with fish."

"Fresh basil. I don't know if we have that."

Ryll held himself in cautious mental isolation while Nishi went to the food service counter. Everyone in the room heard her order fugu but the rest of the conversation was in a lower voice. Ryll strained to hear it, torn by deeply ambivalent feelings. A little bazeel would be welcome, more would be dangerous. Lutt was becoming more and more suspicious of its reaction on Dreen flesh.

She returned presently and shook her head. "I am sorry. No fresh basil. The chef will make you a sauce with tarragon."

"Can they get me some basil?" Lutt asked.

"Why is it so important?"

"I must have some!"

"Ahhh, you are the perfectionist even with foods. I, too, am a chef and I should have known. I will speak once more to the chef."

When she left the table, Ryll intruded out of desperation. *I can change your precious pesto into something more to my liking.*

What do you have against it, Ryll baby?

You don't let me choose anything I like!

I'll trade you a strawberry sundae for the pesto.

It's not a fair exchange.

It's the basil, isn't it, Ryll?

I find your sauce repugnant.

Nishi returned to her chair. "He thinks you are a crazy Yankee but he will try. There's been an inexplicable run on basil. None has been shipped here in almost a year, so it's not in any of the ordinary channels. But on the black market, who knows?"

Presently, a signal from the food service area sent Nishi once more away from the table. She returned with another blue plate containing a fugu filet and a side dish of green sauce.

He ate it quickly, noting how Nishi and the others in the room watched him. Again, there were no signs of poisoning. When he was finished, Lutt sat back.

"You're not eating, Nishi."

"I eat with the staff at different hours. Now, you will go back to your room. They do not want you fatigued."

"I know something that'd restore my energy."

"But we have no marriage contract, my sweet goose."

"Will you at least stay with me?"

"Of course. That is what I am supposed to do until the Legion calls me back to the bargaining. They are very interested. Madame says D'Assas Anon will sit in as an observer. They guarantee your safety and your presence."

"What does that mean?"

"No one will harm you but they promise you will be at the final bargaining sessions. Come. It is time to go back to your room."

"Is it still free of spy eyes?"

"I think so."

"Where's my armor?"

"It is being repaired, but the contents of your inner pockets are with your cameras under house seal."

"Bring the stuff from my pockets. I've a device there to tell if we're being spied on."

In the corridor outside the dining room, Lutt turned toward his quarters and was immediately brought up short as the legionnaire who had ordered the fugu stepped out of a side passage. A tall brute with mean eyes, the man still wore his armor.

"So you would dally with our Virgin Chanteuse?" he growled.

"Go away if you know what's good for you," Nishi said.

The man ignored her. "You hide behind the skirts of a woman, eh?" He lunged at Lutt.

The special training imposed by Hanson Security dominated Lutt's reactions, aided by Dreen-amplified muscles and responses. Without thinking, he twisted to one side, leveraged the lunging legionnaire by the man's own momentum and sent him careening down the hallway into a wall at the end. The legionnaire fell and came up shaking his head. With a bellow, he charged at Lutt, who once more twisted aside and sent the man headlong into the wall at the other end of the hallway.

Dazed, the legionnaire struggled to his feet, but before he could renew the assault, a door near him opened and a Legion officer emerged. The officer, a stocky, dark-haired man with an aquiline nose and large brown eyes, wore only his trousers. He looked appreciatively at Nishi.

"What occurs here, my little dove?" the officer asked.

Nishi pointed at the dazed legionnaire. "That one offended me, General, and my protector has punished him." She clutched Lutt's left arm.

The legionnaire had recovered sufficiently to prepare himself for another attack. The officer stepped forward squarely in front of the angry man. "You! Is it true you have offended our Virgin Chanteuse?"

For the first time, the legionnaire recognized the newcomer. "*Mon General!* I . . . I . . ."

"I asked you a question, scum!"

From a side hall, four men in red uniforms, carrying stunsticks, came into view. They stopped at sight of the general.

Lutt noted the D'AA insignia on the uniforms and glanced at Nishi. She raised a finger for Lutt to be silent and wait.

The angry legionnaire pointed at Lutt. "That *merde* has been dallying with her!"

The general looked at Lutt.

"This is my employer and protector," Nishi said, pressing against Lutt's side.

"I recognize you, monsieur," the general said. "Lutt Hanson, Jr., no? I am here to speak for the Legion about your Spiral device." He looked at the D'Assas Anon guards. "No need for you, gentlemen. The Legion takes care of its own, including its own scum." He returned his attention to the hapless legionnaire. "You have not answered my question. Do you disobey orders?"

"*Mon General*, I . . . I meant no offense to anyone except the Yankee *merde!*"

The general flicked a glance across Lutt. "And you, monsieur?"

"I protect myself when attacked, General."

"Did you punish him?"

"I slammed him into that wall down there and when that wasn't enough, I slammed him into the wall where you see him now."

"Slammed?"

"It is true," Nishi said.

"But this is one of our legionnaires in full armor," the general said. He studied Lutt with new curiosity.

"Would you like me to demonstrate?" Lutt asked.

"Hmmmm." The general focused on the legionnaire.

"With the general's permission," the legionnaire said, "I will separate this *merde* from his limbs."

"I think not," the general said. "Are you drunk?"

"No, *Mon General!*"

"Monsieur Hanson has behaved with admirable restraint by not killing you. I take the word of Ma'amselle D'Amato on this. But I have no such restraints. Further trouble from you and I will have you staked out on the plain. Understood, scum?"

"*Oui, Mon General.*" The words were forced from the man but there was no doubt of his fear.

To the D'Assas Anon guards, the general said: "Eject him. He is denied the privileges for six months."

When guards and prisoner were gone, the general gave a short bow to Lutt. "My apologies, monsieur. You have the word of General Claude Speely DeCazeville that we mean you no harm . . . unless, of course, you *are* dallying with our little dove."

"He has asked for my hand in marriage!" Nishi said.

"Indeed! And what have you said, ma'amselle?"

"My response awaits the negotiation of a marriage contract."

"Very wise!" The general grinned at Lutt. "If all goes well with you, monsieur, you will be the envy of the entire Legion. Now . . ." The general glanced back at the door from which he had emerged. ". . . other matters require my attention. I think we will see each other again."

When they were back in Lutt's room, Lutt grabbed Nishi's shoulders. "What was all of that?"

"General Claude is here to meet with you but if I had not spoken at once about your intentions toward me, it could have become quite serious. He remembers my father and brothers. The Legion is very protective of its own."

"Didn't sound like it when he was talking to that trooper. What'd he mean he'd stake the man out on the plain?"

"That? They pin a man in a hot place with inceram stakes. Eventually, the armor breaks down and fire consumes him."

"Good God! That's taking care of their own!"

"They can be very severe in punishment. That poor man will suffer much because he cannot return here for six months."

"No doubt."

"But you were so brave and strong! I feared for you. And that legionnaire in full armor was like a child in your hands."

Our hands! Ryll intruded. *Remember that.*

Nishi pressed herself against Lutt, her head in the crook of his neck. "You are not only rich but strong! Oh, I am so lucky!"

Lutt held her tightly and bent for a kiss but she turned her head away. "No! I might be very weak."

"Good!"

"No!" She struggled in his arms. "Please do not make me call for help."

"Would you really?"

"I think so. You do not want to test it and neither do I. Besides, we have other matters to discuss." She freed herself and stepped back.

"Our marriage contract?"

"That can wait. First, we must decide what to do about the press."

"What the hell does the press have to do with us?"

"There is one called Subiyama who was with you at the battle and now knows you are in here. In a way, it is funny. She hired the Zone Patrol squad at the U.S. Consulate to spy on our ship. She wishes to know when you emerge and where you will go."

"She hired the whole squad? How do you know?"

"We know everything the Zeeps do."

"Zeeps?"

"Zone Patrol, ZP, Zeeps. This Subiyama is a fat lady but very sexed. She is, how you say, shacked up with one of the Zeeps. Do you wish her removed or . . ."

"Let it go for now. She could be useful."

"Ahhh, my protector is very sly. Perhaps you will bargain better than I thought. I must be careful. But you will sleep now, sweet Lutt, and I will guard that you are not disturbed."

She tucked him into bed and dodged his groping hands under the pretext of hanging up his robe.

"You must not touch unless I say," she said.

"You're pretty good at avoiding it."

"I have had much practice, Lutt."

"What about the stuff from my armor's pockets?"

"I will get that later. Now, you will sleep. It is the doctor's order and it is my order."

Better do what she says, Ryll cautioned. *You'll need all of your wits about you when it comes to the bargaining. And I can sense your fatigue.*

Don't you mean our fatigue?

I, too, am low on energy, but our flesh is not yet fully healed and I must idmage more repairs.

Well, do it while I'm alseep. It makes me sick when you turn my eyes inward.

Nishi brought a chair to the foot of the bed and composed herself there with her feet tucked under her.

"Sleep, sweet Lutt," she whispered.

Sweet Lutt, he thought. It was a pleasant thought and it helped him drift into slumber.

Ryll waited until the mental rhythms told him Lutt was deeply asleep and then, fighting the induced urge to join him in slumber, swiveled his eyes inward.

It was a complex idmaging problem with timing and placement that required a nicety of application. Presently, a small slip of paper drifted from the air above Nishi onto her lap. She picked it up and looked at the message there.

"Do nothing to awaken Lutt. Our lives depend on it. This message is from the one who shares his body. Eat this paper if you wish to learn more."

She looked at the sleeping figure and then with a pensive expression, chewed and swallowed the note.

Ryll materialized another note above her. She caught it before it reached her lap.

"How do you do that?" she whispered.

Having anticipated the question, Ryll already had provided the answer on the new message. "I have the power to create such things. That should prove the truth of what I tell you. And I tell you not to get him the basil. It would be very dangerous. Eat this message and I will provide another."

Obediently, Nishi ate the second note and looked up at the place where the messages originated. Presently, another note materialized there and, wide-eyed, she watched it drift to her lap before picking it up and reading it.

"My name is Ryll and Lutt has stolen my body. Lutt's body was severely damaged in an accident. He seeks to gain complete control of this body with the basil, which is a drug to me. But the basil will make him ineffective, too, because this is mostly my flesh. Now, eat this message, too."

She ate the note and whispered: "What do you want of me?"

The next note was a time materializing. Ryll found the effort drew more energy than anticipated. "Deny him the basil and I will get you to Earth with much money. Eat this note."

"But I want the marriage to this man!" she whispered after swallowing the paper.

Ryll drew on fading energies to answer: "That can be managed, but his mother is sure to raise objections and she could prove difficult. Trust me. Do not trust Lutt. He wishes only to use your body and gratify his disgusting lust. I share his mind and know this. Now, eat this note."

Slowly, Nishi masticated the paper and swallowed it.

When no other message was forthcoming, she bent close to the sleeping figure. "How do I know this is true? Tell me!"

But Ryll, too, drained of energy, had joined his fleshmate in slumber. Deep snores shook the recumbent figure.

Chinese population controls of the last century contributed to this crisis. With more than forty percent of their people over age sixty-five and millions of one-child families, it was inevitable the new generation would throw off restrictions and compete in the breeding arena. They were only temporarily delayed by a ratio of 3.4 males to every female, an imbalance due mostly to earlier female infanticide. They met this by drastic measures such as outlawing abortions, economic benefits for live births, forced female immigration from neighbor countries, a law permitting divorce on grounds of infertility, and Assignation Bureaus to spread pornography and promote casual liaisons.

—"The Liebensraum Crisis,"
NSC analysis

Lorna Subiyama stared at Lew Doughty with delight and amazement. "I'm your first? You mean it?"

They sat in the murphy bed of quarters obtained for Subiyama by Sue Ellen Pratt. It was a cramped apartment by Earth standards but Sue Ellen had assured her it was in a Security Area whose inviolability was guaranteed by the Legion.

Subiyama had no doubt that Sue Ellen was taking a kickback on the rental but that was part of the game here. And the two small rooms did include a tiny kitchen and an adequate dry bath. The bed, though, could only be described as "intimate."

She and the sergeant she knew as Lew Doughty had arrived almost three hours earlier after his afternoon shift, their arms loaded with inceram containers of black-market produce. Subiyama prided herself on her culinary abilities and frequently said, "People who don't like to eat aren't any good in bed, either."

Her new lover had definite tastes in food. He demanded she cook him something with basil. He pronounced it strangely, calling it "bazeel," but there was no doubt what he meant. The basil sauce she made for the outrageously expensive caribou steaks evoked an odd reaction. He actually "slurped" it up, washing it down with an American chablis of doubtful provenance, and showing increasing signs of inebriation.

His reactions in bed she found equally amazing. He obviously admired her ample, darkly tanned flesh and, in the throes of sex, called her his "blessed Habiba." He also shouted several times, invoking "the Great Bazeel." His unbridled enjoyment inspired Subiyama to experiment, attempting with some success several sexual variations about which she had only read or heard reports.

It was when they both lay exhausted that he produced his ultimate shocker. "I have never done that before. I always thought it would be disgusting but it is sublimely enjoyable, especially after the bazeel."

At first, Subiyama refused to believe him. "How could you live this long, especially in the ZP, and still be a virgin?"

"It is shameful," he said and actually blushed.

Beginning to believe, she asked: "How could you hide it?"

He looked down at his sheet-covered lap. "One can pretend many things if one knows the culture."

Subiyama found this a quite erudite response, especially convincing when he looked at her with calflike eyes and asked: "You will keep my secret?"

"Honey lamb, it's *our* secret! Hey! I never had a virgin before. You're a first for me, too. Wow! The things I am going to teach you!"

"You will be kind?"

"As gentle as I can be." She smothered him with kisses and felt his body tremble with renewed excitement. "You learn fast, sweetie pie. What we're going to do now is called 'the Australian Crawl.' "

"Afterward, could we have more bazeel?"

"Anything your little heart desires, sweetie. You know? I like this. Sex hasn't been this much fun since my first orgy back in Dallas."

The proliferation of cult movements in the latter half of the twenty-first century set the stage for the technological refinements and sophistication in the present runaway spread of such groups as the Raj Dood following on Venus. That such blind manifestations display the corruption and hypocrisy found in earlier cultish power centers did not surprise your investigators.

—"Cults and Cultists," an
article in *Psychology Today*

Nishi awakened Lutt with a cup of bitter coffee. She had brought a net bag containing the contents of his armor's pockets, and she had an odd expression on her face.

She waited until he drained the cup, then: "Who is Ryll?"

The cup fell from his hand and shattered on the floor. Lutt sat up in bed.

"Where did you hear that name?"

"Never mind! You say we will make the marriage and all the time you know your mother will not give us her blessing!"

"She doesn't live my life!" Lutt snapped.

"I do not have the proper pedigree, is that it?"

"She sure as hell will know where you worked on Venus but that has nothing to do with—"

"I still have my honor!"

Lutt sent a probing thought to Ryll: *Where'd she learn about you?*

The Dreen did not reply.

You sneaky alien! You told her, didn't you?

Ryll remained isolated from him.

"I can see it is all true," Nishi moaned.

I don't know how you did it, but I'll get you for this! Lutt raged.

"You are two people in one body," Nishi said. "That is what I have seen in your eyes."

"This is my body and this is me!" Lutt said.

"And you can make notes that drop out of the air," Nishi sneered.

So that's how you did it!

Nishi began to cry. "If you made a gun for me right now I would shoot you with it!" she sobbed.

Ryll found this shocking. Make a gun? He felt competent to idmage almost any manufactured product, provided he had raw materials and imprint. It was a higher form of Dreen creativity for which schooling and talents had prepared him but . . . a weapon? If he idmaged a weapon, he would be the first Dreen to do such a thing and he did not relish the distinction.

You've really done it this time, Lutt accused. *We need her to survive and you've made her our enemy.*

Ryll was shocked out of isolation. *Why do we need her?*

One wrong word from her and we're dead!

You're dead. I could survive.

Staked out on the plain?

They wouldn't!

Shall we test it? Let's say I rape her and see what happens.

No! Wait!

For what?

She wants marriage. Promise her marriage.

Lutt thought about this. Married to his Ni-Ni? Wasn't that what every dream encounter told him he most desired? But the mystical oddity of such a union filled him with fear. *How could I dream about her before I even knew she existed?*

Perhaps it's a glitch in the original idmage of Earth, Ryll offered.

Glitch?

An anomaly in the idmaged plan.

I don't like it.

You mean you really wouldn't like being married to her?

Lutt stared at Nishi. She had stopped crying but she looked at him with an odd expression of fear and something else. Hope?

"Ni-Ni, my sweet," Lutt said, "we need each other. You want to go back to Earth as—"

"I do not need anyone! I survive quite well on my own!"

"And you would not like to be the rich wife of a rich man?"

She put a finger to her chin and her expression definitely was one of calculation. "So you remember my ancestry."

"And I want you."

"Want! You never speak of love! It is always want!"

"Isn't love just wanting?"

"It is more . . . much more."

"I've never even considered marrying another woman."

"And you truly wish the marriage with me?"

"Yes, dammit!"

An enchanting smile dimpled her cheeks. "Then I will ask General Claude to negotiate the marriage contract for me after we make the arrangement to lease him your invention."

"Is that a yes? We'll be married?"

"Provided I get a satisfactory contract and you explain to me about this person Ryll."

"First a small precaution," Lutt said. He took his father's spy detector from the net bag and scanned the room. The device flushed out a spy dot on the bed's headboard. Lutt pried the thing out, examined it and destroyed it.

"A listening device only," he said. "Whose?"

"The Legion or D'Assas Anon," she said. "No one else could possibly do it."

"Just on the possibility that I've missed more of these things, I'm going to delay telling you about Ryll," he said.

"But you promise?"

"I promise."

She should know how empty your promises are, Ryll sneered.

Shut up, you Dreen sneak! I've saved our bacon for now but I'm not forgetting about you! Maybe we'll make an inceram hang glider and ride the winds of Venus!

"Lutt, there is another matter," Nishi said.

"What now?"

"The fugu chefs wish me to do a story about them and—"

"Do it. You'll be a regular reporter yet. Maybe General Claude would grant you an interview. And you might do a piece on the grunts fresh from the field."

"You make me work for my pay? That is good. But there is a matter I hesitate to mention because it is delicate."

"Delicate? How?"

"My guru knows you are here."

"Your *guru?*" Lutt began to laugh.

"Do not make the joke of it. He is the most important guru on Venus, the Raj Dood. Many legionnaires go to him for advice. My own father swore by him."

"And got killed anyway."

"Because he did not take the Raj Dood's advice!"

"How does this dude know I'm here?"

"I told him and he ordered me to tell you it is very important he meet you and talk to you. Very important. He said that several times."

"What the hell could a nutty guru want with me except my money and influence?"

"He is not like that! He is very spiritual and never asks for donations. He has but one goal in life, to help the needy."

"Sure he does."

"He was very worried about me, that I might be attacked in here by a drunken legionnaire. He gave me a magical incantation for escape and told me to use it if I am in distress. And now he has told me to say the magic words when I am with you."

"And then he gave you a little doll to stick pins in."

"No, Lutt! The Raj Dood is no ordinary man. He has power, so much that he fears no one, not even the Legion. I knew if I told you this you would think it silly!"

Lutt grinned at her. "Are you distressed with me?"

"I am very distressed!"

"Then say your magic words but if they don't work you have to get into bed with me. Okay?"

She stamped a foot. "Sometimes, men are just awful!"

"Let's hear the guru's magical incantation."

"Very well! But I will never get into your bed unless we have the marriage contract and the proper ceremony! I think you are not to be trusted, Lutt Hanson, Jr.!"

"What's supposed to happen when you use this incantation?"

"You will see!" She pressed her lips into a grim line and closed her eyes. In a low voice, she said, "Om Mani Come To Me My Melancholy Baby Padme Sayonara Hummmm Slide Down My Cellar Door."

As she uttered the final word a brilliant flash of red light filled the room, forcing Lutt to close his eyes. He felt himself falling and was brought up short sprawled on a hard surface. He opened his eyes and found himself on a transparent floor inside a metallic cylinder that stretched upward as far as he could see. There was no sign of Nishi, the infirmary room, his bed . . . everything gone. He was alone in his infirmary pajamas.

That was a Spiral phenomenon! Ryll interjected.

Not really alone, am I!

Slowly, Lutt sat up and looked down at the transparent floor. The cylinder also stretched downward into infinity.

Lutt's stomach lurched and he tasted bile in the back of his throat. The transparent floor felt suddenly insubstantial. There were no sounds here except those of his own movements, no smells except the acridity of his own fears.

What do you mean it was a Spiral phenomenon? Lutt asked.

Before Ryll could respond, a disembodied male voice, deeply resonant, intruded. "This is the Raj Dood."

"For Crissakes, where am I?" Lutt got to his feet.

"You knew me as your Uncle Dudley," the voice said.

"Uncle Dudley? You're this Raj dude?"

"Think of me only as the Raj Dood. Look at the floor."

Lutt looked down and again tasted bile.

"That floor is your will to live," the voice said. "If you lose the will to live, the floor will disappear."

"Come on, Uncle Dudley! No more jokes!"

"This is no joke!"

"Is that what you've been doing since you disappeared twenty-five years ago?"

"I have never disappeared. I have penetrated the secret of spiritual ascendancy. Observe!"

Static crackled at Lutt's side and Nishi materialized there holding Lutt's net bag. She stumbled and dropped the bag. It fell through the floor and soon vanished from sight.

"That bag has no will to live," the voice said. "Hello, Nishi, my dear. The floor under you is Lutt's will to live and yours now, too. It is all that supports you within infinity."

"What are you doing, my guru?" she whispered.

"I am testing Lutt, my dear. I have a message for him."

"Look here, Uncle Dudley," Lutt said. "This is no way to treat your own nephew."

"Lutt!" Nishi said. "What are you saying?"

"That's my mother's elder brother. He used to work with my father but they had a falling out and—"

"No falling out, Lutt," the voice said. "I merely achieved enlightenment and your father remained in darkness."

"Yeah? Well, I heard it was a question of something you two invented together. Is this place—"

"You display ignorance and a lack of proper respect," the voice said. "Be serene and listen to my message."

"I don't know what the hell you're up to, Uncle Dudley, but say what you have to say."

"Your father himself has given me this message for you. He wishes me to warn you your brother has conspired with Senator Woon to have you killed on Venus."

"Morey? Conspiring to do murder?"

I warned you about pushing him too far! Ryll intruded.

"I'm frightened," Nishi whispered.

"My brother's nothing to be afraid of," Lutt said. "He's a stumblebum who can't get out of his own way."

"I think the floor is getting soft under us," Nishi whispered.

"Nuts! Uncle Dudley? You still there?"

A clipped, mechanical voice responded. "The Raj Dood has been called away on urgent business. This is his answering service."

Nishi clutched Lutt's arm. "The floor is definitely softer!"

"Whoever the hell you are," Lutt flared, "we came here because this Raj dude said Nishi could use his stupid words for escape."

"The escape clause, yes," the mechanical voice said. "Ahhh, I see. There was a message he agreed to give you personally. Have you received the message?"

"I received his damn message!"

"Under the circumstances, perhaps it is better you await his return in the waiting room. I am sorry he left no instructions but his departure was quite abrupt."

"Lutt!" Nishi gasped.

He looked down and saw her feet sinking into the floor.

"Hey!" Lutt shouted. "Get us out of here! Send us back to the ship where we came from!"

"I am, indeed, sorry," the mechanical voice said. "But I have only limited powers and there is the injunction of the escape clause. I can only send you to the Raj Dood's waiting room."

The Chinese on Venus want their enemies to believe they use only mindless masses and can conquer by sheer numbers and rocket inundations. This skillful propaganda is designed to undermine Legion morale. Anyone promoting this viewpoint must be considered an enemy of France, subject to the most stringent retaliation.

—Claude Speely DeCazeville,
general commanding, Ninth Legion

"I have good news and bad news," Mugly said.

He confronted Jongleur in the lowest anteroom of Habiba's cone, a space she had set aside for him because of new demands on their time. It was a tiny, west-facing, dark space made even darker by the filter effect of their new planetary shield, which reduced the afternoon sunlight by at least half.

Through the single window behind Mugly, Jongleur could see the sun—a dim speck in a dull sky.

"Let's hear it," Jongleur said.

"But I was hoping to tell Habiba herself."

"She has ordered me to hear all messages and relay only the most important. Habiba contemplates the shield and its effect on Dreenor."

"I hear the flaps allowing sunlight to fall on seedhouses are working very well," Mugly said.

"Is that your good news?"

"That is no part of my news. It was merely a comment."

"Mugly, you are wasting my time. What is your news?"
"Which do you want first, the good or the bad?"
"In whatever order you care to give it."
"The bad news has several components. First, we have no contact with Prosik on Venus, although there are distinct signs that Hanson employs his crude Spiral technology there."
Mugly cleared his throat portentously. "Second, Earthers continue to probe *Patricia* for her secrets. They appear jubilant about their latest efforts although we do not know what they have achieved."
"You consider that news I dare convey to Habiba?"
"Why not?"
"Do you think she might order the immediate dispatch of the new erasure ship?"
Mugly shrugged. "You should know better than I. That brings me to the good news. The new ship should be ready within the week. We are putting in the finishing touches right now. Those new idmagers she sent me are superb."
Jongleur groaned. "You call that good news?"
"You are a poor loser, Jongleur," Mugly said.
"How dare you speak so lightly of this?"
"Jongleur! I apologize. I know your son is still there in that accursed solar system but we must think of all Dreendom."
"Which is what I wish you would do. Earth is driving us insane! I sense disaster in whatever we do. Habiba . . . Blessed Habiba . . . Mugly, she is changed."
"Changed? In what way?"
"It is hard to describe. She sits silently much more than ever before. And she is short with me. She has never been short with me before. And Mugly, I have heard her curse you."
Mugly was aghast. "Curse . . . me?"
"And Wemply the Voyager who idmaged Earth. She curses him, too. I have heard her curse both of you in the same breath."
"Jongleur, I must speak to her!"
"No! She forbids it."
"Forbids . . . but do we not have a Thoughtcon to—"
"She forbids the Thoughtcon, too. I fear for her, Mugly. She looks and sounds so sad."
"But the shield is working. We are protected. We have time to do whatever we—"

"Time? Is that not the very problem, Mugly? Have Dreens ever before been concerned with time? We possessed infinity. Now, what do we have? We have a dark sky and people who cower beneath it wondering how long it will endure. We have petitions from Dreens asking *when* Habiba will make her decision about Earth. When, Mugly! We mark time until her next pronouncement. All of us are concerned with time. We who had infinity now concern ourselves with bits and pieces of time. Earth has cursed us. Damn them and their finite impudence!"

When I contemplate the infinite, I see the vitality of Time. Our Spirals, infinitely engaged, cannot touch all being and all substance. Those require Time. If we ignore Time and accept infinity as our holy and unquestioned right, then we are less than we might be. Is that not the lesson of Earth?

—Habiba's journal

They arrived with a roar of static and a flash of red light in Raj Dood's waiting room. The place struck Lutt as surprisingly ordinary until he looked at the window wall on his left. This gave him an angled view onto the metallic tube where he had arrived from the infirmary.

Has it occurred to you to question your uncle about how he does this? Ryll asked.

Do you know?

As I said, it's obviously a form of Spiral technology.

That cylinder doesn't look like a Spiral.

But I can feel the tingle of Spiral contact when we move at your uncle's command.

Keerist! Is that what he and Father fought over so many years ago?

I have no way of answering such a question. However, I would very much like to see his control center and observe the way it works.

"Lutt?" Nishi tugged at Lutt's arm.

"What is it?"

"Is Raj Dood really your uncle?"

"That's what he said."

"How does he do this?"

"It's magic and we're the poor natives who're supposed to shit green when he demonstrates his powers."

"How can you treat this so . . . so . . ."

"I knew the old bastard. Look at this room—the chairs, that sofa, that table and those magazines." He lifted a magazine and waved it at her. "*The Weekend Golfer.* And there—a copy of *Modern Psychiatry!*"

"But that!" She pointed to the view into the cylinder.

"Yeah, that's something else."

"Where is the answering service person?" she asked. "There's no one here but us."

"I am not a person. I am a device." The mechanical voice came from nowhere and everywhere around them. "What is it you wish of me?"

"Can the Legion or anyone else hear what we say here?" she asked.

"The Raj Dood does not permit eavesdropping."

"Lutt, while we wait, tell me about this Ryll person."

Why not? Lutt thought. And he said, "He's a Dreen who got into my body after I had an accident with my new spaceship."

"Got into your body?"

"Yeah. He sneaked in while I was unconscious."

I did not sneak! I saved your life!

But you didn't give me any choice!

Ryll lapsed into sullen isolation, shocked by the truth in Lutt's response. Would Lutt have chosen to die? He really was not asked.

"Can he talk?" Nishi asked. "I want to talk to him."

"Of course I can talk!" The voice was a shuddery falsetto as Ryll took advantage of Lutt's surprise and assumed control.

"Stop—that!" Lutt objected, but it was a voice that cracked and wavered. Face contorted and body twisted, Lutt and Ryll fought for control.

"I don't . . . care . . . who . . . sees . . . this!" Ryll said. "I . . . will . . . talk to her!"

Lutt subsided into dismayed passivity. He sensed both anger and urgency in Ryll. And there was that floral odor.

"Earth and the solar system may be erased while this fool plays his petty power games," Ryll said. And he explained quickly about the erasure ship, *Patricia.*

"How can all of this—" Nishi waved her arms "—be something you made?"

"I did not make it. Wemply the Voyager made it."

"That's crazy!"

"I, too, suspect Wemply of derangement."

She shook her head, seeing they were talking at cross purposes. Another thought struck her. "But . . . but this ship, you said it was wrecked in the collision with Lutt's ship."

"They can always make another."

Are you finished? Lutt demanded. *You've frightened her.*

I'm gratified that someone shares my fears.

Why haven't you been ragging me about this?

I considered we had time but on mature reflection, I have begun to wonder.

Mature? You?

Stressful situations are known to mature one. It is odd how this does not apply to you, Lutt.

Go ahead! Insult me. But I'm in here with you and I know you're a tricky liar.

I have been utterly candid with you under extremely trying circumstances and where the advantages of fabrication have been quite substantial.

Nishi had been staring at the window wall while she chewed her lower lip. She spoke without turning. "Ryll, you say you merged to save your lives. Can you be separated?"

"It is possible but I'm not sure I have the proper facilities."

"And the Zone Patrol will imprison you if they learn you are a Dreen in human guise?"

Now see what you've done! Lutt raged. *She can make me do whatever she wants by threatening to throw me to the ZP.*

A gamble I thought worth taking. She desires a rich husband and you can make her promise of silence a provision of your marriage contract, cutting her off entirely if she speaks.

Say! You're turning into quite a bargainer.

I am learning by observation. Look! Something is happening out there.

A throng of people occupied a cylindrical area visible through the window wall. In their midst stood a tall figure Lutt recognized.

Uncle Dudley!

Time had been kind to his mother's ne'er-do-well brother. The man's angular features bore a benign expression. Skin smooth, blond hair caught in a gray sweatband and draping across his shoulders. His blue eyes twinkled. But that costume! Uncle Dudley wore a white robe emblazoned in red and blue letters: "Raj Dood . . . Raj Dood . . ." He strode through the throng as imploring hands reached out toward him, but no one touched him.

In the excitement of the moment, Lutt groped tentatively for control and Ryll allowed it.

He is your uncle. Best you deal with him. But find out how that cylinder works.

The window wall abruptly distorted the view and the scene wavered as though seen through water. But Uncle Dudley remained clear.

Spirit Glass! Lutt thought.

Uncle Dudley marched through the glass into the waiting room. The throng followed, distortion vanishing as they entered. The area around Lutt and Nishi became jammed with sweaty, pleading people. They pressed Lutt and Nishi into a corner with the Raj Dood.

The guru silenced the babble with a great shout: "Eczema!" He put a finger to his cheek. "Or is it Eureka?"

Noticing Lutt and Nishi, he said, "Forgive my abrupt departure but Osceola required my presence. Now, where were we? Oh, yes. Morey and Woon, the conspiracy."

Without waiting for a response, he turned and looked across the people crowding the waiting room.

"I have places to go, places to be."

"Raj Dood be praised!" the people shouted.

"Those two are deserters," Nishi whispered in Lutt's ear. She pointed at two men in Legion uniforms. "I have seen posters with their pictures." She abruptly turned her attention to three Chinese in Mao Guard uniforms. "Heaven preserve us. Those are the enemy!"

Lutt, too, studied the throng as they pressed closer to the Raj Dood. He noted a woman with a crying baby, a quartet of singing drunks whose accents sounded Irish, a woman in the uniform of a spacetruck driver, two women in gowns that bore the tiny D'AA mark identifying them as D'Assas Anon employees, a Sephardic Jew, a fat man wearing swimming trunks . . . Motley was the only word for this group.

As the guru looked at them, the people once more began to submit their pleas. Lutt had trouble distinguishing separate requests.

"If you could only . . . I am afraid that my . . . When will . . . You said my husband . . . Where is . . . "

"*Silencio!*" Raj Dood shouted.

In the abrupt silence, he lamented: "I am too kind. It's time to change my magic words."

"I don't see how they could've prevented a rapist from attacking Nishi," Lutt said. "By the time she spoke those words it'd all have been over." He touched the guru's arm as he spoke.

"You touched me!" Raj Dood gasped. His face twisted in dismay. "Never touch a holy man!"

"Why not?" Lutt asked.

"It's a rule, that's all," the guru said. He touched his sweatband.

Lutt noted now that the band appeared to be metal. It was scratched and dented.

"You are right about the length of the incantation," the guru said. "I will make the new one shorter." He clasped his hands in front of his robed stomach and stared pensively at Lutt.

"Uncle Dudley, I'd like to know how that cylinder works," Lutt said.

"You will address me as Raj Dood," the guru said. "The cylinder, as you call it, does not *work*. It just is."

"Is that what you and Father fought about?"

"The past is only the past," the guru said. "Observe."

Without knowing how it happened, Lutt saw visions from his past, a parade of scenes, images from a quarter century ago when Uncle Dudley visited. Most of the visions involved dinners at the long refectory table in the Hansons' main house above a lake, sessions where Uncle Dudley tried to explain his ideas to L.H. Sometimes there were arguments, and once L.H. left the table without finishing his meal. The visions ended with Uncle Dudley departing and Lutt realized he was seeing the last visit. Uncle Dudley never returned.

"I asked why you never returned," Lutt said. "One of the help said you and Father had a fight."

"Reliable help is difficult to find," Uncle Dudley said. "Now, be still while I decide what is best. We cannot permit a fratricide. Morey must be frustrated. As for Woon, it is time we tested his will to live."

Lutt found himself impressed. Uncle Dudley displayed a profound sense of dignity.

But what does he know of the Spirals? Ryll demanded.

"Ryll must not disturb my meditations," the guru said.

He eavesdropped on my conversation with Nishi!

"I did not eavesdrop. It is not necessary. I always know what I need to know. Be still, Ryll. Your predicament is not my immediate concern."

A hush fell over the room as the guru closed his eyes and bowed his head. Presently, he looked at Nishi.

"Yes, marriage would be best." He looked at Lutt. "One of you must always dominate your body but with cooperation from the partner. To thwart Morey, you go to Earth immediately."

"I have unfinished business here," Lutt protested.

"You cannot have a dancing foot and a praying knee on the same leg," the guru said. "Benign monarchy is best."

What's he talking about? Lutt wondered.

He's telling us to be tolerant of each other. He reminds me of Habiba.

"Physical and ethereal are not truly separate," the guru said. He waved an arm and the throng vanished from the waiting room, leaving only Lutt and Nishi with him.

"I wish you'd explain how you do that," Lutt said.

"You would try to understand and that would prevent your understanding," the guru said. "Think of it as magic." Once more he looked at Nishi. "You love the part of him that did not knuckle under to his father. That is fortunate."

"Uncle Dudley," Lutt said, "I have to know about these whispers that come out of nowhere and the people with bizarre names who appear so mysteriously to—"

"Do you love Nishi?" the guru interrupted.

"Yes, but—"

"In your own way, I see, you do."

Nishi felt a rush of warmth. Lutt admitted he loved her! This made her feel responsible to him. "How can we leave when our negotiations with the Legion are incomplete?" she asked.

"Others can conclude your business with the Legion," the guru said. "Will you marry her, Lutt?"

"My legal department will draw up a marriage contract," Lutt said. "You'll get a negotiator's percentage."

"Never try to snow a guru," the Raj Dood said. "Nishi, guard Ryll's interests. I fear he may never return to Dreenor. Now, off you go. Osceola awaits."

"Wait!" Lutt objected. "I have to ask you about vorspirals and—"

"The essence never waits!" the Raj Dood shouted, adding in a lower tone, "Of course, all that about essence is bullshit but I teach it anyway. Now, indeed, you go to Earth."

Woon is on the Moon.

—Raj Dood incantation

"I tell you it's like you set fire to an anthill!"

Prosik's buddy, Hollis Weatherbee, his helmet thrown back, stood in the living room–bedroom of Subiyama's Gorontium quarters. The red-headed Zone Patrolman frowned at Prosik, who stood in green shorts near Subiyama's shoulder. Subiyama towered over him like a Sumo wrestler in an immense pink robe with a golden belt.

"You were right to come immediately with this," she said. "What time is it?"

"A quarter to seven. We got a couple hours yet before our morning shift but Harper called me at the barracks and asked should we tell you? I went and had a look. It's a madhouse. So, like I said, I called this friend."

"Go through it again," Subiyama said. "Exactly what did you see?"

"People running around, shouting. The big French general himself stood outside the lock of that flying cathouse telling people to go this way and that way. I heard Hanson's name called but there was no sign of him unless they gave him Legion armor."

"So then you called this friend of yours in the Legion?"

"Well, he's kind of a friend. My sister back on Earth is married to the guy who smuggled this guy out of Marseilles and got him the false papers so he could join the Legion. She wrote me about him and . . . well, we've had a few drinks together."

"And what did he say?"

"He says this Hanson sneaked off the ship in his bare feet and pajamas with a dame, someone they call 'the Virgin Chanteuse,' if you can imagine a virgin in a cathouse."

"That sneaky son-of-a-bitch!"

"They're watching the spaceports but, shit! With all the Hanson loot behind him, that bastard could be anywhere."

"You think Hanson's really taken French leave?"

"Yeah, I think so. My friend was real excited. Said the Legion would fry Hanson's ass for running off with this woman. She's some kinda pet or something."

"What chance would he have getting off Venus?"

"Hell, lady! You can buy anything here."

Weatherbee leaned to one side to address Prosik. "Lew, I got a message for you from the captain. He wants to see you right away."

"Did he say why?"

"No, but the duty sergeant says it's about your re-up. He says your papers were late arriving and you're ten days past your re-enlistment date. It's just routine."

"Wait a minute," Subiyama said. "Does this mean you're no longer tied to the ZP, Lew honey?"

Weatherbee grinned. "Lady, on Venus they got you because they got your ass. He re-ups or they lose the voucher for his return transport. That's why they sent him to Venus. This is punishment duty!"

"But if he has a return ticket?" she asked.

"Then they confiscate his armor. That's ZP property."

"How much does a good suit of armor cost?" she asked.

"Thirty, forty thousand. It all depends."

She smiled softly at Prosik. "Lew honey, why don't you just send word to this captain he can stick his re-up where the moon don't shine?"

Prosik was startled. "But what would I . . ."

"Honey, my family made it in oil when we still had it. I can stake you." She pinched his bottom. "For a price."

"Where would I go?" Prosik asked.

"We, honey! We would go back to Earth. I got me a hunch that slick bastard of a Hanson is headed home to collect on his little promotion scheme. He came up here for one thing—to sell his news service. The word is he did that and big. Now, it's time to go put his Stetson under the jackpot."

"But what would I do?"

"You would keep me happy, honey, and . . . well, I been thinking. You like that funny herb so much, I was wondering why we didn't set up housekeeping on some land I got near Austin? You could raise all the basil you wanted. Must be a market for it somewhere."

Prosik stared at her, hardly daring believe his good fortune. "Raise our own bazeel?"

"Basil, bazeel, whatever you wanta call it, honey."

Prosik closed his eyes and wondered if he dared attempt his own limited idmaging—some little gift, something to show his gratitude. But it would raise unanswerable questions. This sweet Earther must never learn his Dreen origins.

"What about it?" she prompted.

"Anything you say, my sweet Habiba," he said.

"That's the way to talk, honey!"

Weatherbee smirked at Prosik. "Of all the damn fool luck! I don't know what you got, Lew, but it must be something. You know, I may get my keister in a sling but I'm gonna enjoy carrying this message to the captain. That little pissant is gonna shit green."

Prosik slipped an arm around Subiyama and caressed her bottom lightly. She grinned at him.

This could be a good life, Prosik thought. Some way would have to be found, of course, to sabotage the erasure ship and alert the Zone Patrol if any new ships arrived. Anonymous letters? Perhaps.

To Weatherbee, Subiyama said, "You're all still on the payroll. See if you can confirm whether Hanson's skipped. I'll get on to my Earth contacts. He shows up down there, we'll know."

Oh, see Ola! Oh, see Ola! Oh, see Ola!

—Morning aerobics chant,
Spirit Glass factory

I wonder if your Uncle Dudley has found a way to idmage? Ryll asked. *That might explain this phenomenon.*

Lutt did not bother answering. He felt too euphoric but without a physical rush. From the waiting room to the cylinder it had been but one step through that odd Spirit Glass. Nishi's sweaty hand in his, he looked back to see the Spirit Glass, but something at the end of the cylinder above the window demanded his attention.

Venus! No doubt of what he saw up there—the hot red of the volcanoes seen without any cloud cover, the spouting fire of Chinese rockets. He and Nishi hovered in the cylinder, no floor under them, no wind, nothing substantial except for that silvery cylinder enclosing them. He began to doubt the enclosing wall itself was substantial.

"Look!" Nishi tugged his hand and pointed downward.

Lutt looked down. At the other end of the cylinder the gnarled blue marble of Earth grew larger with alarming rapidity. Now, he could see browns and greens in the landscape. Other bits of color came into view with details of the surface—chasms, mountains, buildings. An airplane drew its contrail above the land. He saw an ocean, then a familiar outline of harbors and inlets . . . a city.

"He's sending us to Seattle," Lutt said.

"Is that your destination of choice?" It was a husky voice from behind them. Lutt and Nishi twisted themselves into a tangle as they tried to turn. When they had it sorted out, they still clasped hands but at arms' length and faced a darkly withered crone of a woman in a long dress printed with flowers and plants in brilliant greens, yellows, reds and oranges.

All of them were suspended in the cylinder with the tall buildings of Seattle just under them.

"Well, what you staring at?" the woman demanded.

Lutt tried to swallow in a dry throat. This was a very familiar face. His feeling of euphoria vanished.

"Who are you?" Nishi whispered.

"Osceola! In the flesh! Who else?" She grinned at Lutt. "If it weren't for that damn Dood, I'd drop you into the nearest nasty jungle. I like having a Hanson in my clutches."

She raised one gnarled hand and clenched it into a fist, twisting it in front of him.

"I've . . . I've never hurt you," Lutt protested.

"Innocence is no defense!" she snarled, but she lowered her fist. "Well, where do you wanta go?"

"My private office at the *Enquirer?*"

She looked at Nishi. "You, too, dearie?"

"Yes," Nishi whispered. "I will go with Lutt."

"Women in love seldom show good sense," Osceola said.

"How do you do this?" Lutt asked. "We were on Venus and . . ."

"You Hansons never ask the right questions," Osceola said. "And y' never know when to just shut up and watch! That's one thing I gotta hand your Uncle Dudley. Knows how to use his senses. Sometimes I wonder if he ain't really Seminole."

She waved her right hand and a tennis ball appeared in it. She squeezed the ball and it sprouted a lily that dissolved into a rattlesnake that became a cane. "Magic," she said. "That's how we do it."

It's some kind of idmaging! I know it! Ryll intruded.

Lutt felt his eyelids close and the eyes swiveled inward. When they swiveled back and opened, Osceola held a dripping length of sea kelp and there was a startled expression on her face.

"If you knew how to do this all along, why you wasting my time?" she demanded, glaring at Lutt. "Or was it you?" She shifted her glare to Nishi. "Or is it that damn Dood with his little jokes? You around somewhere, Dood? You having your little laugh? I catch you, by gawd, you're not getting in my bed again!"

Nishi squeezed Lutt's hand. "It was Ryll, wasn't it?" she asked.

"What in the name of ten thousand white devils does a rill have to do with this?" Osceola asked.

"I did it," Lutt said. "But I cannot do the things you and Uncle Dudley do."

Liar! Ryll accused. *How dare you take credit for my prank?*

You wanta explain to her who you are?

When Ryll did not respond, Lutt said, "I apologize, Osceola. I'm just a beginner."

"Pretty good for a beginner," she said, shaking kelp and seawater off her hand. "You still wanta go to your office?"

"If you please?"

You're being very polite, Ryll intruded.

This dame could dump us into a volcano if she wants!

She does appear to be a superior adept. It's very odd. I have been told other beings may find a way to idmage, but this is a combination of artistic talents I did not suspect. She does not even require a Storyship and, if that was a Spiral we came through, it was a most peculiar Spiral.

Lutt did not reply.

"Mother of God, help us!" Nishi pleaded.

Ryll found himself in possession of his merged flesh, his attention focused outward, concentrating with a power he had never suspected he possessed. The city lay close beneath, but still no wind touched him. He felt Nishi's hand gripping his painfully. There were people on the streets, a zoo . . . insects. He realized he could see the smallest living particles, things no Dreen or Earther ever saw with naked eyes.

Abruptly, it was over. He and Nishi stood in Lutt's private office at the *Enquirer*. Ryll had the odd sensation that his flesh had been disassembled and reassembled. The ability to see minutiae had vanished. The office odors were as he remembered—ink, coffee, stale dust, rancid food—the synthetic aromas Lutt had caused to be sprayed here for his own peculiar reasons.

It suddenly occurred to Ryll that smells were an area of idmaging he had never truly explored.

What a delightful idea! If I ever idmage a world, it will be a place of marvelous aromas, a place difficult to describe even in an assimilated story.

"You okay, Lutt?"

Ade Stuart in his electric cart sat in the doorway.

Ryll felt cold. He clutched Nishi's hand. There was no internal sign of Lutt. What was he doing? *Are you there, Lutt?*

No response.

"I'm . . . I'm okay," Ryll said, trying to emulate Lutt's voice.

Nishi looked at him with a questioning expression. His voice sounded different.

"You're the one did that story on the Venus bordello," Stuart said, looking at Nishi. "A great job! You people sure made a fast transit. Did the military bring you back?"

"We . . . ah, had a special service," Ryll said.

"You sure as hell must have. But I'm glad you're back. Big story breaking. Zone Patrol found an alien in a high-security area the day after you left for Venus. They couldn't keep a lid on it. Rumors all over the place. They caught him. He got away. Who knows? We're on it with a full team."

"We left the vorcameras on the ship!" Nishi suddenly wailed. "The Legion will find out how they work and never pay!"

"The cameras are here," Stuart said. "Just arrived by special messenger with a note: 'Courtesy of the Raj Dood.' Isn't that the crazy guru on Venus? You get a story on him, too?"

"No . . . story on him," Ryll said.

"How come you're in pajamas?" Stuart asked.

"We had to leave rather abruptly," Ryll said.

"Copyboy!" Stuart bellowed.

A slender young man in a black singlesuit came up behind Stuart. "Sir?"

"Get Mr. Hanson's clothes out of the closet over there." Stuart pointed to a door in the corner of the office.

The copyboy squeezed past Stuart and went to the closet. "Any particular things you want, sir?" he asked, looking at Ryll.

"Anything, anything," Ryll said. He looked at Nishi.

"You sound very strange, Lutt," she said. "Did you get a chill during the . . . I mean, when we came?"

"I am fine," Ryll said.

"Where'll I put these, sir?" the copyboy asked. He held a pair of red trousers, a black shirt and white tie, a black jacket and white shoes with white socks, plus organdy boxer shorts.

"There." Ryll pointed to a desk.

"You going to wear that outfit?" Stuart asked. "You'll look like a Mafia hit man in a B movie."

"It's fine, fine," Ryll said.

"You do not sound well, Lutt," Nishi said. She put a hand to his forehead. "You are perspiring."

"I am all right," Ryll said. *Lutt? Where are you, Lutt?*

"Spiral News Service is a smashing success," Stuart said. "We're making new sales every day. The special fund is healthy again."

"That's fine," Ryll said, staring at the colorful pile of clothes.

"What you want us to do about the alien story?"

"Just carry on as you were."

"Will you do one thing for me, Lutt?" Stuart asked. "Tell me how you got in here without any of us seeing you arrive?"

"It's . . . it's a family secret," Ryll said.

"I'm sorry, Lutt, but I had a weird idea. You see, the rumor is this alien came on some kind of ship that may be similar to the ship you're working on with Sam. The stories say it has something to do with . . . well, they say, 'Spirals.' I couldn't help but make the association with our news service."

"Yes, yes, of course," Ryll said. He wished Stuart would leave or shut up. What had happened to Lutt?

"My weird idea," Stuart said. He pointed to a large gray box with a glowing orange screen standing against the wall to Ryll's left. "I came along here because I heard that vordata receiver chattering . . . and there you two were. I thought, Jesus H. Christ, is he *traveling* by this spiral thing, too?"

"That *is* a weird idea," Ryll said. He looked at the orange screen. Flesh disassembled and reassembled? Did Osceola and Uncle Dudley transmit people as well as pictures?

Lutt! Where are you, Lutt?

Still no sign of his fleshmate. Ryll suddenly felt bereft. How could he simulate Lutt's behavior and carry on without the damned Earther? Already, Nishi was suspicious. Could he fake an illness?

"Were you transmitted on that machine?" Stuart asked.

Perhaps we were, Ryll thought. *Did it separate us?* He did not dare allow himself to hope.

Abruptly, Ryll freed his hand from Nishi's, thrust himself past Stuart and bolted down the hall. Stuart's voice floated after him: "Your clothes, Lutt! You're not dressed!"

What was it Raj Dood had said about an essence? It occurred to Ryll that Lutt might have been delayed in transmission and at this very instant might be trying to find their body.

I must get as far away from that vordata thing as I can!

Slipping and skidding in his bare feet, Ryll dashed in his pajamas down a hallway to a door marked EXIT and pushed through. He found himself on concrete steps and went down two and three at a time, counting the landings marked on doorways he passed. At the first floor, he slammed open a heavy door and burst into the lobby. It was cold tile and chilled his feet. A mirror wall confirmed that he still looked like Lutt but he had lost his glasses. The mirror showed him something else that dismayed him.

Lutt's mother strode toward him across the lobby. Ryll turned from the mirror and saw that she recognized him. She stopped. Phoenicia Hanson's mouth dropped open in shock. A look of horror came over her face. Her mouth contorted, sharpening the creases at the corners.

Only one thing to do, Ryll thought. If he spoke to Lutt's mother, she might suspect he was not her son. She had heard the story of the body invasion. He dashed past her.

"You!" she screeched as Ryll ran past. "What terrible thing have you been doing? Those pictures from Venus were base! I've never been so humiliated! What are you doing, Lutt?"

He ignored her and plunged through swinging doors to the sidewalk. There, he slowed to a smooth, jogging stride. People looked at him strangely but joggers were a familiar sight. A man called out, "Hey! Tough guy! Love your PJs. Is barefoot the new way to jog?"

Shit! Where have you taken us? It was Lutt, a frantic thought in Ryll's awareness. *Where we going? Why are you running?*

Ryll came to a stop and leaned against a lamp post. He felt ill, both dismayed and relieved.

That damn Osceola! She still doing things to us?

Ryll held his thoughts to himself, trying to maintain bodily control, but Lutt was pressing. Ryll felt muscles tremble and jerk.

That bitch! She sent me through Hell! I been inside a volcano.

An insect eaten by a bird. I was some kinda fish chewed up by a shark! And even worse! And all the time, I could hear her laughing. Damn chicken cackle! Where the hell are we, Ryll?

On the street near the Enquirer.

Where's my Nishi?

In your office, the last I saw her.

Why're we still in pajamas?

No time to change.

I'm taking over, Ryll! Let go of our body or I'll make sure we do something the ZP is sure to hear about.

Your mother's in the Enquirer *lobby and she's angry.*

Ryll allowed him a memory glimpse of the encounter.

Why'd you run like that? Lutt asked.

It seemed a good idea at the time. I, too, dislike that Osceola creature.

She do something to you, too?

I do not wish to discuss it.

Neither do I. Now, get outa the way, Ryll baby. I'm taking over!

With a definite feeling of relief, Ryll relaxed his hold on their flesh and felt Lutt assume control. Ryll found himself astonished at how welcome it was resuming the observer role. *Am I becoming a voyeur?*

People stood all around him on the sidewalk, some passing, some standing to gawk.

A woman said, "He does not look well."

A man said, "Hey! That's Lutt Hanson, Jr. You sick, pal?"

Lutt looked to his right. The *Enquirer* was two blocks away and across the street. He recalled the Lowtown incident and the young woman spitting on Phoenicia's hand.

I'm out here without Hanson Guards! And these people know who I am. Not good.

The man who had asked about his health stepped one pace closer. "You need help, Mister Hanson? Your foot's bleeding. Why are you barefoot?"

"It was a bet and I won," Lutt said.

"Those crazy Hansons!" one of the gawkers said. Laughter greeted this, but it was a friendly outburst.

"Excuse me," Lutt said. He pushed his way through the throng. They yielded easily.

Someone asked, "How much did you win?"

"Puh-lenty!" Lutt said.

"Way to go!" a man shouted.

More laughter. There appeared to be no enemies here, but Lutt walked back to the *Enquirer* at a brisk pace. He did not breathe easily until he was in the lobby and saw a squad of Hanson Guards trotting toward him.

"We were just coming to look for you, sir," one said as they closed in around him. "You shouldn't leave without us."

There was no sign of his mother in the lobby.

"Have you seen my mother?" Lutt asked.

"She went out, sir," a guard said. "But she wants to see you pronto. Where do you wish to go, sir?"

"Back to my office for some clothes and then we'll go to the Hanson compound. Does anyone know where my brother is?"

"Mister Morey is out of town, sir," a guard said. "An errand for your father."

Sent him someplace to keep him away from me, I'll bet, Lutt thought.

But your brother has criminal companions, Ryll reminded him. *Would they not do his bidding? And where is this Woon?*

I'll have to find out.

You live a very dangerous life, Lutt, but I am beginning to see its attractions.

Upsy daisy, downsy daisy!
Kicksy daisy, stampsy daisy!
Picksy daisy, stripsy daisy!
Tearsy daisy, killsy daisy!

—Children's chant from the
childhood of Lutt Hanson, Jr.

The noonday sun hot and brilliant behind her, Lorna Subiyama paused in the opening of the French doors from her pool patio near Austin, Texas. In a custom-made pink swimming suit that gave the illusion of enormous nudity, she ignored the wet trail she left as she moved into the room's shadows.

Prosik, wearing a lemon-yellow jumpsuit, stood at a table near the center of the room leafing through a stack of papers.

"Carmelita said you wanted to see me muy pronto, honey," she said. "What you want, I hope?"

"Oh." Prosik looked up from his papers. "Your office called. Hanson's been seen in Seattle. There's a message. They said to tell you right away." He pointed to a vidcom screen built into the wall on his left.

She gave his bottom a hard slap, leaving a wet handprint as she passed him. "How you coming on the garden plan, sweetie?"

"We plant tomorrow. The marketing people arrive next week for planning and they want to hire a lab."

"Why they want to do that?" She stopped at the communicator and touched its keys.

"They want a better way to ship bazeel fresh. If we can get it as far away as New York undamaged, profits will be very big."

She leaned close to the vidcom screen, reading as she spoke. "You got a good business head, Lew honey. Wouldn't be a bit surprised if we made a killing in your bazeel."

"I learn from you, my sweet Habiba. It was edifying when you made a profit from resale of my armor after our return."

"Paying for our honeymoon, isn't it?" She glanced back at him. "Mister Lew Subiyama! Man, I thought that clerk would freak out when you told him you'd take my name. And that preacher!"

"It is an odd custom for the man's name to dominate," he said.

"My great-grandmother was Choctaw and she used to say the same thing. Said it was a wise child knew his own father but you sure know your mother. Said white folks were crazy. A woman's name disappears like sugar in the water. You got any Indian blood, honey?"

"I do not think so. Was it an important message?"

"Hanson's been seen in Seattle. The bastard was running down a street in his pajamas. Honeymoon's over, Lew. It's back to work. Turn the planting over to Heysoos. He's a good major-domo. Put the marketing people on the back burner. We're going to Seattle."

"Yes, my sweet Habiba."

She strode to his side, swung him around and enveloped him in a gigantic hug.

"I still can't believe my luck, honey," she said. "You really love me. You don't want me to diet, you just . . ."

"Do not change, sweet Habiba! I love all of you."

"That's what I mean. Say! You've never explained why you call me sweet Habiba. It sounds Arabic."

"It is a thing of my infancy, a mother figure."

"And I thought you were Irish."

"Is this world not called a melting pot?"

She hugged him tightly. "That it is, sweetie. Have you thought about us having kids?"

His voice was muffled against her bosom. "I often think of little else. Us sitting by the seedhouse—" He broke off, recalling the reproductive system employed by Earthers.

She pushed him away slightly. "Sitting by the what?"

He caressed her abdomen. "The seedhouse where our infant would grow."

A great bellowing laugh shook her. "You got gardening on the brain, honey! I love it. Now hurry up. We gotta get packed. There's a big story in that Hanson bastard and we're gonna get it."

Idmaging is not a singular process. Complexities encompass many variations—one procedure for life forms, another for inanimate objects, another for correcting mistakes. Variations must be infinite. In an infinite universe, one does not impose limits on infinity.

—Habiba's journal

Nishi gasped as Lutt led her into his house in the Hanson compound outside Seattle.

The house, one of five set among tall silver firs around a lake, was cool and shadowy on a hot afternoon. The senior Hansons' home was just visible on a cantilevered platform over the water on the opposite side of the lake. Like Lutt's home, it was built of a Hanson proprietary material, Fabriwood, that mimicked natural wood but never needed painting and was impervious to insects and rot. The seniors' home appeared to be a series of bleached silver blocks stacked together, but Lutt's dark-brown home drew on Japanese tradition and sat almost concealed in trees and bushes. Morey's home, to the east, copied that of his parents. The other two residences, occupied by guards and aides, lay completely hidden in the trees.

"It is so beautiful," Nishi said. She looked at Lutt beside her in his red, black and white clothes.

The foyer where Lutt and Nishi stood was lined with potted bamboo and led to steps that went down into a lower living area furnished in wicker.

"I'm glad you like it," Lutt said. "I had a cute little Jap guy design and build it."

"I do not like that way of referring to him," Nishi said. "I have Japanese ancestors as well as French."

"Japanese, Jap—what's the difference, long as you know what I mean?"

"Sometimes, we mean more than we think." She went down into the living area. "Perhaps I should not have come here."

"Why not?"

"You will try to take liberties."

"And you don't have legionnaires to protect you here?"

"Oh, I think I have a protector. Ryll, would you protect me?"

You try to hurt her and I'll cause trouble, Ryll intruded.

What the hell could you do?

I think I can prevent the flow of blood to a . . . certain . . . inflatable part of our body.

You wouldn't!

Nishi has been charged by your uncle with protecting me. I, in turn, will protect her.

You son of a bitch!

I am the son of Dreens. That is distinctly different.

"Why do you not respond, Ryll?" Nishi asked.

Grasping for voice control, Ryll spoke in a weak falsetto: "I can protect you. I have warned him."

Lutt wrenched back control of their voice and shouted: "Someday, I'll get you, Ryll! You just see if I don't! And when I do, baby . . ."

"You see?" Nishi asked. "I will never be far from my protector."

Sullenly, Lutt said, "There's a guest room up the stairs on the right. I'll have the housekeeper bring you some clothes."

"You have clothes for your women guests?"

"We have a lot of things here."

"And so many servants."

"You saw the dogs and guards when we came in? Nobody gets past the boundary fences or leaves unless they belong. Just you remember that."

"That is not a very loving thing to say, Lutt."

"I'm getting tired of your cat-and-mouse game."

"You are accustomed to getting what you want when you want. Yes. I see that."

"Osceola said you love me. Is it true?"

"I begin to wonder if it is you I love or if I have seen Ryll in you and, perhaps, love him."

"Shit!"

Nishi spoke in a soft voice. "My guru says you love me in your own way, Lutt. What is that way?"

Lutt glared at her in angry silence. *Yeah! I love her. She's my Ni-Ni. But what kind of hell must I go through to get her?*

Perhaps you will be required to change, Ryll offered.

In a pig's ass! She's the one who's going to change.

Would you still love her then?

The question shocked Lutt.

Before he could respond, there was a pounding on the front door.

"Lutt! You're in there, Lutt! I know you're in there!"

It was L.H.'s familiar angry bellow.

Lutt stepped to a wall, slid a concealed panel aside and pushed a button. They heard the front door open.

L.H. lurched into their presence on his canes. His prosthetic eyes probed for them like insect antennae. He stopped short and stared at Nishi.

"What have we here?"

"This is Nishi D'Amato," Lutt said.

"We are to be married," Nishi said and then wondered why she offered this information.

L.H. eyed her up and down. "Are you really?"

"Yes." Lutt's voice was unmistakably sullen.

"This is a pretty sexy lady you got here, boy," L.H. said. "You already tried her out?"

"That's none of your business," Lutt said.

"Playing hard to get, is she?" He turned his attention to Lutt. "I tell you something that *is* my business. You put your own locks on this place. I warned you not to do that."

"This is my home! I'll lock it any damn way I want."

"And it's my compound, boy!"

"You going to kick me out?"

"Boy, why do you rile me so? You could boss the whole shebang if you ever come around to it."

"And be another one of your slaveys?"

"I'm not gonna fight you about it now, but you change those locks or I will."

"And make it easier for Morey to get in here, too?"

"So you got my warning. How is old Dudley?"

"He looks fine."

"Stupid son-of-a-bitch! Always worried about what our inventions would do to people. I always said, 'Long as they make a profit, who cares?' "

"You see, Lutt?" Nishi asked. "I told you the Raj Dood is a good man."

Lutt ignored her. "You've seen the profit sheet on my Spiral News Service, Father. What do you say now?"

"Peanuts. Enjoyed the story about the Legion whorehouse, though."

"Nishi did that story," Lutt said and grinned at her maliciously.

"Did you now?" L.H. looked at her with new interest. "You one of the girls?"

"I am still a virgin," she said.

"Christ on a crutch! What you got here, boy?"

Lutt glared back at him silently.

L.H. nodded as though coming to a private decision. "So you got my message about Morey. What you doing about it?"

"Looking out for myself."

"What'd you do to rile him so?"

"I got him to invest in my projects. Where'd you send him?"

"Sent him to Uranus. Some new hydrogen mining claims. He's doing it on commission. Be back soon. But you can rest easy, son. I broke the Morey-Woon connection and let the Legion take care of Woon's hit men on Venus. Now! I want you and Morey in my office together when he returns." He shifted his attention back to Nishi. "Who were your folks?"

She stared at his prosthetic eyes as she told him.

"Legion. That's a problem. Phoenicia will raise hell."

"Because Hansons only marry quality?" Lutt asked, his voice deceptively soft.

L.H. responded with a barking laugh that broke into a fit of coughing.

Trying to suck me in with sympathy again, Lutt thought.

When the coughing spell passed, L.H. said, "Didn't I teach you how to treat women? Maybe you're not as much like me as I thought. Morey, now . . ." He left it there.

Piqued, Lutt asked, "You ever take him to the House of Delights?"

"Naw. I left his sex education to his mother. I think she showed him a book."

Once more, L.H. turned his attention to Nishi. He reached into a pocket and removed a gold pin emblazoned with the Hanson crest. "I gave this to Lutt's mother when he was born. When she read that Venus whorehouse story, she threw it at me and dented it. Was going to get it fixed but now I think not." He thrust it into Lutt's hand. "Here! If you marry this lady, give it to her when she produces a son."

Lutt accepted the pin, wondering what game the old man was playing now.

Nishi, her face red, flared, "I will produce nothing for this family unless I have the marriage contract!"

"A contract, now!" L.H. seemed delighted. "You looking for the pot of gold, honey?"

"It is the way of my family! And they were all heroes of the Legion!"

"Thinka that now!" L.H. swung his prosthetic eyes toward Lutt. "You have anything to say about this, boy?"

"Nishi saved my life on Venus. I owe her something."

"Then pay her off and get rid of her!"

Lutt thrust the Hanson pin into his pocket. "No, we're going to be married."

"You are the most obtuse, knuckle-headed Hanson ever born! This is a gold digger after our money! Saved your life? She was saving it for herself!"

"She didn't know who I was when she saved me!"

"So she's a do-gooder! We don't need any of those in our family!"

The old man's obstinate attitude only made Lutt more angry. "You're not going to change my mind! We're going to be married!"

L.H. swung his eyes toward Nishi. "So you want a contract? Tell you what. You negotiate your contract with Phoenicia."

Casualties were heavy, but names are being withheld pending notification of the next of kin. Witnesses say the explosion took out the entire northwest corner of the ZP base. Presumably, the blast and subsequent fire also destroyed the mysterious alien spaceship reportedly being studied there. ZP sources would neither confirm nor deny this but National Security censorship has been sought to suppress these accounts and the NSC has refused to rule on this "blanket of silence," reportedly acting on the President's orders.

—From an *Enquirer* story

"Something's going on in this burg and it's sure as hell more than meets the eye," Subiyama said.

She sat at a portable vidcom in the office by her Seattle hotel bedroom, leaning forward to look directly into the eyes of the man on the screen.

"We sent you up there to stay on top of this story," the man said. "How soon can you file a follow-up on the explosion?"

"Don't press me, Jake! We're onto some hot leads and you'll get 'em soon as we confirm."

"We? You hiring help up there without asking for—"

"Lew's helping me."

"That Zone Patrol swabby you're shacked up with?"

"Shacked up, hell! We're married."

"This story's too big for amateur—"

"Don't you get your bowels in an uproar, Jake! Lew's the one got us the inside account of what's going on at that base. He is one damn fine leg man. You forgetting he was in the ZP?"

"We need more now! They're beating the shit out of us!"

She sat back and tugged at her lower lip, then: "Okay. I was going to hold this until Lew gets back with more, but you're going to have to credit 'unidentified sources.' Got that?"

"Shall I turn you over to rewrite?"

"No! You handle it and don't put my byline on it. I don't want Hanson Guards looking for my hide."

"What've you got?"

"Lew says there's a story at the base that Lutt Hanson, Jr., was involved in a crash with this alien spaceship. The ZP rescued him and held him incommunicado while they grilled him. When they released him, they exacted a promise he would not reveal anything about the alien ship."

"Wow!"

"I'm not through. Hanson's ship, the one that collided with the alien, was an experimental thing that's supposed to be faster than a roadrunner with a burning match up its ass. His copilot in the crash reportedly was killed. We're still trying to confirm that and get the guy's name."

"Heysoos Creesto!"

"There's more. They're now saying at the base that the blast occurred when investigators touched off a self-destruct system in the alien ship."

"You were sitting on this?"

"That last was going to be my new lead."

"Any luck on an interview with Junior?"

"Don't hold your breath waiting for it. He's gone to ground at that Hanson compound with all the guards and fences and dogs. He isn't even talking to his own paper."

"You holding back anything else?"

"A little but it's too hot to use without confirmation. Lew's doin' okay, isn't he, Jake? For an amateur, I mean?"

"Give me a peek at what you're holding."

"No! You might use it. You got your story. Go with it."

"What about the woman he took out of that Legion bordello?"

"There's a report she's with him at the compound but don't you dare use that."

"What was she called? The Virgin Chanteuse?"

"I'm warning you not to use it. You check with Legal. This doll can draw on the Legion war chest to sue us or worse. Up on Venus you hear stories about how the Legion takes care of people it doesn't like. Very, very bad news."

"When you expecting word from your Zeep leg man?"

"My *husband* should be here in about an hour. Now, you get off my back or I'll find a news service that appreciates me."

We never promised you fair!
We never promised you fun!
We only promised you blood
While gettin' the job done!

—ZP marching chant

Phoenicia Hanson marched into Lutt's living room like a conquering general about to survey captives. She noted Nishi seated on a wicker couch with Lutt standing behind her and waved a hand at Lutt.

"Leave us."

"Mother, I—"

"You've done enough to disgrace our family. Now, I will handle this. Have you seen a doctor?"

"What?" The non sequitur startled him.

"I am quite aware your aberrated behavior is due to your accident and your delusion about having another personality in your body. Simple schizophrenia brought on by unfortunate trauma. Have you seen a doctor?"

"Yeah," he lied. "I've been thoroughly scanned."

"And what did the doctor say?"

"Nothing wrong with me."

"We will get other doctors. Now! Leave me with this . . ." She looked down at Nishi as though discovering something slimy under a rock, " . . . this person."

"This person is my fiancée, Mother. She is—"

"We will discuss that later."

Nishi got to her feet, face pale, mouth drawn into a tight line. "Yes, Lutt darling, leave us. Your mother and I have things to discuss."

Lutt looked at his mother, at Nishi, and again at his mother. Nishi, he recalled, was a self-avowed expert at learning what people really wanted. She must know Phoenicia wanted the family rid of this intruder from Venus. But were there other things his mother wanted more? Interesting to find out.

"Okay," he said. "You two fight it out. I have to see Sam and inspect the progress on my new ship." He kissed Nishi's cheek. "See you later, sweetheart." It amused him to note the hostile glitter in his mother's eyes at this demonstration of affection.

When the door closed behind Lutt, Nishi smiled sweetly and said, "Please sit down." She gestured to a chair, lady of the manor being gracious to a guest.

"What I have to say, I can say standing up."

"Very well."

"How much?"

"I don't understand."

"How much money do you want? What, as my husband often says, is the payoff?"

"We are here to discuss a marriage settlement, a contract to protect me in a marriage to your son."

"You'll marry Lutt over my dead body!"

"I surely hope not. That might distress Lutt."

"You don't really care about his distress!"

"I care about Lutt very much. I will be a good wife to him. I am exactly the kind of wife he needs."

"You?"

"Really, *Madame* Hanson, you do not understand my situation at all."

"You lived in a . . . in a . . ." Phoenicia could not bring herself to say the word.

"Oh, yes. But I am *virga intacta*, a virgin who can prove her virginity."

"That's *your* story!"

"And I have other stories. While I was an employee of D'Assas

Anon, I heard many stories. I'm sure you would find some of them interesting."

"The only thing about you that interests me is what it will cost to be rid of you!"

"But these are stories about Lutt and your husband. The girls in such an establishment will talk, you know? Some of them get around and they bring their stories with them."

Phoenicia's face paled. "What are you saying?"

"I'm saying, were I to approach a publisher of your more lurid books, I would have an interesting story to tell, one full of many verifiable accounts about Lutt and your husband."

Phoenicia groped behind her for a chair and slumped into it. She looked up at Nishi as though suddenly discovering a poisonous snake.

"What you really want most, madame," Nishi said, "is your good name and the admiration of your friends. As Lutt's wife—"

"Never," Phoenicia gasped.

"As I was saying, madame, I will guarantee your good name and the admiration of your friends. They will think me a heroine to have maintained my honor under such difficult conditions."

"What . . . what could you . . ."

"I will find the sob sister, someone like this woman, Subiyama, who writes such interesting stories about your son's accident and these events of the Zone Patrol and the Legion."

"Subiyama? My husband says she's a bloodsucking leech!"

"Even a leech may be valuable. And I will unfold such a beautiful story for her—how I sang for my living instead of earning my keep on my back."

Phoenicia shuddered.

Nishi sank onto the wicker couch, bringing her eyes level with Phoenicia's. "We will have a medical person confirm that I am *virga intacta*. Most daring of us, don't you think?"

"Surely you are not serious?"

"Quite serious, madame. It will be a marvelous story—how I rescued Lutt from the battle where the rockets were exploding and how I nursed him back to health while he hovered between life and death."

"You didn't."

"But I did. And legionnaires will speak of my heroism and my devotion. They called me 'the Virgin Chanteuse,' you know."

"They did?"

"And I will tell how Lutt and I fell in love there in the infirmary."

"But what about those awful pictures from the . . . from the . . ." Phoenicia still could not say the word.

"Think of the dangers I braved to reveal the terrible life those women live. Think of how that will add to my heroism, that I managed to escape such a life with my honor intact."

"You . . . you really can prove this?"

"You may choose the doctors to examine me, madame."

"I . . . I wish you would not call me that."

"Call you what?"

"Madame."

"Then what should I call you?"

"Mrs. Hanson will do for now."

"But I, too, will be Mrs. Hanson."

Phoenicia stared at her, then: "Provided your story is true, you may call me Phoenicia. But please do not do so in public until I have confirmed your story."

"Very well, Phoenicia. And now we must discuss my marriage contract."

"But what more . . ."

"Your son has led a most profligate life. I'm sure you know this. He loves me but what guarantees do I have that he will not return to his old ways once we are married?"

Phoenicia put a hand over her eyes, then lowered it to look confidentially at Nishi. "The Hanson men are such a trial."

"I'm sure we will be a great help to each other, you and I," Nishi said. "But, of course, I must have an independent income commensurate with my new station."

Phoenicia sighed. "Yes. That's what I got."

"You did?"

"My father insisted."

"Ahhh, what a wise man."

"He had L.H. investigated but would not reveal what he discovered."

"Some things are better left unsaid."

"You are so right, my dear. But you have no father, do you?"

"I am an orphan. My father and brothers died on Venus. It was they who made me swear on my mother's name that I would maintain my honor."

"Ohhh, you poor dear. Don't fail to tell this when you reveal how you saved Lutt's life."

"Trust me . . . Phoenicia. With you to coach me, how can I fail?"

We have Earthers to thank for insights into this phenomenon they call unconscious behavior. Before Wemply's creation, such a concept was never applied to Dreens. Now, we are forced to admit the possibility that some of our actions are designed for ends we have not foreseen.

—Habiba's journal

"Mugly has just informed me that the new erasure ship is completed and ready for use," Jongleur said. He spoke formally, forcing the words, aware that Habiba saw his distress.

A great shudder trembled through Habiba. She was a dim figure in the gray gloaming atop her Cone of Control saddle. Once, this had been her favorite time of day, when shadows lengthened and she could relax and admire the Dreenor landscape. But now, everything was gray and diffuse under the shield.

"Does Mugly still volunteer to take the ship himself?"

"He does."

"Has there been any word from Prosik?"

"He was last reported on Venus but there is nothing new. We must presume he perished on that awful planet."

"Another brave soul lost to us."

"And what of the brave souls who are captives of the Zone Patrol?" Jongleur asked. "What of our operatives on Earth?"

"What would you have me do about them?"

"At the very least, we must warn those who are still free to leave."

"How would we do this?"
"Surely, Habiba, you must have some plan for them."
"I depend on my aides for such matters!"
Jongleur thought he heard something near hysteria in Habiba's voice and drew back one pace, almost falling off the spiral ramp where he sat during Thoughtcon.
"Habiba, I did not know . . . I mean, I thought you . . ."
"Must I think of everything?"
"I would require time to consider various alternatives," Jongleur said.
"Time! Time! That's all anyone talks about anymore!"
"Please, Habiba! I beg you. This has been so upsetting to me. And now I worry about our poor captives and about our operatives. Are they to be sacrificed?"
"Ahhhh, Jongleur, forgive me. Of course you are right. We must do something about our fellow Dreens on Earth. They did not volunteer to be sacrificed. They deserve more from us."
"There must be something we can do," Jongleur said. "Should I ask for volunteers to go warn them and for others to try to free the captives?"
"Every time we've done this, we've lost more people," Habiba moaned. "Those terrible Earthers!"
"Perhaps we have not chosen the right disguise for those we send," Jongleur said. "Perhaps . . ." He fell silent and fanned the air with one ear flap while thinking.
"You have thought of something," Habiba said.
"I truly don't know, Habiba."
"Out with it, Jongleur! What has occurred to you?"
"Well . . . while scanning the available data about Venus I found accounts of that curious military group known as the Foreign Legion."
"Yes, yes. I know. They do many violent things."
"And they are much feared, Habiba."
She spoke dispassionately: "That's the natural evolution of how Earth was idmaged."
"Even the Zone Patrol fears them. They tell their people on Venus they cannot win in a conflict with the Legion."
"I fail to see the significance of this."
"Habiba, this Lutt Hanson, Jr., has aroused the ire of the Legion

by removing a female from their midst. Perhaps we should send a force in legionnaire guise to deal with this matter."

"What matter, Jongleur? You are not making sense."

"The matter of the stolen woman, Habiba."

"But wouldn't such a subterfuge be exposed immediately?"

"Not if we confuse them by making it appear legionnaires have taken this matter into their own hands."

"You really think you can do this?"

"Habiba, I think our past failures may have resulted from too much secrecy. They expect us to sneak into their midst. But if we march in openly in the guise of the Legion . . ."

"You may have something there, Jongleur. I will delay the erasure while you put your plan in motion."

All volunteers for this mission to Seattle will receive double pay and double time-in-service allotment. I remind you, this is for the honor of the Legion and to protect one of our own! But we also are eager to acquire this new device Mademoiselle D'Amato demonstrated.

—General Claude Speely DeCazeville,
Private Order Number 50112

Late in the afternoon, after exploring only part of Lutt's house, Nishi sat in a semidaze at the dining room table sipping a cup of tea provided by the automatic kitchen.

It was difficult to accept the wealth she saw. Nishi felt almost guilty. Here she sat at a table of exotic dark wood, her chair a softly cushioned affair that supported her arms. The dark blue kimono she wore was silky against her skin.

She had bathed in a whirlpool bath, showered in a "sensurround" that washed her body in perfumed waters. She had dusted herself with sweet powders and squirted flowery scents onto her skin, then dressed in the kimono left on her bed by someone.

Nishi had not seen the servant's arrival or departure. Perhaps it had been one of the little robots programmed by the housekeeper.

She finished her tea, inhaling the cloying scent of jasmine, and returned to the automated kitchen. Glass-fronted cupboards and walls revealed kitchenware, preserved foods, blinking lights and the conveyors of the automatic chef. There were signs and labels all around.

One sign above a red button said "Key Lock for Personal Cooking."

She pushed the button and a mechanical voice from the ceiling asked: "Do you wish only to choose the spices or is an entire recipe to be ordered?"

"Spices," she said.

Two glass-fronted panels on her left came alight with bright yellow illumination from under the shelves. Nishi bent close to study the labels. "Cayenne . . . Cumin . . . Date Sugar . . . Dobinoi . . . Elm (sweet) . . . Fenugreek . . ." She skipped ahead: "Lemon Essence . . . Marjoram . . . Paprika . . ." All alphabetical. Abruptly, she scanned back to the upper shelves. "Basil!"

There was the spice Ryll so feared. She removed the container, took off the lid and sniffed. Familiar pungency greeted her nostrils. She recalled her father had enjoyed basil in a dish he often ordered. "Wop food," he had called it. Her Japanese mother had threatened to pour it on his head.

A tear slid down Nishi's cheek.

Swallowing past a lump in her throat, she dumped the spice into the sink, washed it down the drain and threw away the container. Looking at the ceiling voder, she said: "Basil is never again to be used in this household."

"Provide a key name for the order, please."

"By orders of the household chatelaine!"

"So ordered."

She depressed the red button and the lights over the spices went dark.

As she stood there wondering if this were enough to protect Ryll, the front door buzzer sounded and a wall screen on her right came alive to show a tall man outside the door.

"Lutt? You home, Lutt?" the man asked.

"Who is it, please?" Nishi asked.

"You must be new! I'm Lutt's brother, Morey."

"Lutt is not home."

"Who're you?" Morey asked.

"I am Lutt's fiancée. We are to be married."

"The whore from Venus? He says he's gonna marry you? That's great, dearie. He often promises that." Morey slipped an envelope from his pocket and dropped it into a slot beside the door. "Tell him I brought what he ordered. And if you're not real busy, how'd you like to invite me in for a little entertainment?"

"I will give him your message," Nishi said. "And you might tell your mother what you called me."

"She's the one told me about you, dearie."

"Your mother and I have made our own agreement, Morey. After you've spoken to her, I will expect your apology."

A worried frown creased Morey's forehead. "Agreement? She didn't say anything about an—"

"Your information may be a little out of date," Nishi said. "Don't return unless it's to apologize."

She left the kitchen and encountered the housekeeper loitering in the passage to the service area. A gray-haired older woman with vaguely Oriental features, the housekeeper had a knowing gleam in her eyes.

"What is your name?" Nishi asked.

"Mrs. Ebey."

"Do you often listen to conversations in this house, Mrs. Ebey?" Nishi asked.

A smile twitched the corners of Mrs. Ebey's mouth. "It's the only way to survive here."

"Then you heard my conversation with Lutt's brother?"

"Him? Trash! Master Lutt never lets him in the house."

"And what did you think of my exchange with his mother?"

"Watch out for her. She's trickier than she looks."

"Are you siding with me, Mrs. Ebey?"

"For the time being. You're pretty good in the clinches. Are you really a virgin?"

"I am."

"You may be the first one ever to cross our threshold."

"Is there a way to secure the door to my room and prevent Lutt from entering?"

"I'll see to it. You want a palm lock, an eye print or a five-slot key?"

"What do you recommend?"

"Key. It can't be picked and if there's only one, he can't duplicate it. He can break in, of course, but that'd take hours. This house is built solid."

"Thank you, Mrs. Ebey. I will not forget your help."

"That's what I'm counting on. You should know Master Lutt may be a little late getting home. There's a big party at the main house. He's to be diverted at the gate."

"Diverted?"

"They'll escort Master Lutt to this party."

"What's important about the party?"

"The old lady's parading another eligible female past him. She's still hoping to beat you some way. Do you really have a lot of whoring stories about Lutt and old L.H.?"

"More than enough."

"That's rich. Everybody knows it, of course, but proving it's another matter."

"I have proof."

"More power to you, honey! I hope you soak 'em good. Will you be needing anything else?"

"Not for now."

Mrs. Ebey went down the hall and turned a corner. The clicking of her heels remained audible for a time and vanished with the sound of a door closing.

Nishi stared at the empty hall, thinking about her new situation. In a way, some of the elements here were not much different from those found on Venus. You had to remain on guard all the time, probing for hidden motives, listening to tones of voices, aware of places where you might be ambushed. Venus had been a good training ground for survival in the Hanson family.

Our intelligence reports from Venus make it clear the Legion is taking increased interest in Lutt Hanson, Junior. I recommend a 24-hour watch on him and we should get an agent into that shop of his adjoining the family compound.

—Major Paula Captain,
ZP Security memo

For the first time in Dreen memory, Habiba appealed directly to her people, bypassing the Elite and showing herself to everyone as she flew over Dreenor in her cupola. The ranked spiral of Elites below her provided only the motive power, and Habiba straddled her saddle in regal immensity as she viewed the Taxables massed on the plains in accordance with her orders.

The noonday sun that was filtered by the defensive shield provided dull shadows, and the landscape appeared faintly repellent to Habiba. But she put down such thoughts, fearing they might filter through to her trance-bound Elites.

Using an amplifier in the base of the cupola, Habiba exhorted her people: "Be brave and patient! Trust in my love. The idmage shield guards us well. I work for the betterment of all and a return to the good old days of superb storytelling."

The people looked up with adoration and responded with a great moan of submission.

"Dreenor must be kept inviolate for Dreens," she said. "The unbroken succession of our days will be restored."

Over and over, she repeated this as she flew.

When she returned her cupola to its position at the Cone of Control, Habiba dismissed all but Mugly and sat silently while the Elites filed out. She wondered if her words had restored calm or added to unrest. Jongleur had suggested this appeal after noting the spreading signs of distress among the people.

"It's the gray sky as much as anything," he said.

She watched Jongleur leave her presence at the end of the procession and saw him turn a worried look in Mugly's direction. Jongleur obeyed her command, though, and left with the others. One could always depend on Jongleur's steadfast devotion.

When only she and Mugly remained, Habiba looked over his head at the Sea of All Things, noting the reflections in the slick surface—gray and oily—a doubled landscape of volcanic cinder walls. The dimness of the light suited the scene.

Mugly cleared his throat, then: "Blessed Habiba, I am overjoyed that you have at last consented to see me."

"It was imperative we talk, Mugly. You of all my Taxables are most likely to do something I have not anticipated."

"Habiba!"

"Don't deny it. I am aware you conceal some of your thoughts from me in a method I do not care to know."

Mugly, his secret thoughts blocked away from his awareness for what he had anticipated would be a Thoughtcon, felt deep shock at her words. The injustice of Habiba's accusation struck him bitterly.

Before he could respond, Habiba said, "It has come to my attention that you have been saying the idmage shield is not enough protection from Earthers."

Because this was among the thoughts he had concealed from himself, Mugly could only gape at her stern countenance. He felt he had been dropped suddenly into an insane situation. Did Habiba mistake him for someone else? Was this truly Habiba?

"If the shield is not enough, Mugly, what else could we possibly do?" she asked.

This was a strange sort of test, Mugly decided. Was she throwing him onto his ultimate resources? *The shield not enough?* What else could they do?

"All of us wonder how we could defend ourselves should the Earthers attack," he said.

"And how do you suggest we do this, Mugly?"

"That must be left to you, Blessed Habiba."

"Just as the first erasure ship was left to me?"

Mugly found this a strange question. He imagined Habiba herself had ordered that ship in some odd way. Was this the method she employed? He remembered no previous such testing, though. Had she commanded him to forget?

"I will obey you in anything, Blessed Habiba," he said.

"No, you won't! Jongleur obeys me, you do not."

"Habiba," he whispered.

"Out with it!" she commanded. "What would you do to make us invulnerable?"

"Idmage defensive weapons?" he asked.

"I thought that was in your mind!"

Now he was angry. "It was not in my mind until you asked, but drastic times perhaps call for drastic measures."

"That's a wishy-washy answer, Mugly," she accused.

Mugly took a deep breath, smelling the awful odor of his own anger.

"Since you insist," he said, "let us discuss the question of defensive weaponry."

"So you are advocating it, at last!"

"I'm not advocating it! *You* raised the question!"

"It's a bitter day when you place such a false accusation on your own Habiba," she said.

"False accusation? But you've been—"

"Enough! I warn you, Mugly, you are not above censure."

"Habiba, I am trying to serve you as best I can, and the question of defensive weapons—"

"Will be dropped immediately! If we create weapons, the possibility of a pre-emptive attack against Earth will dominate every thought. This would lead inevitably to the destruction of all we hold dear. Even the most high-minded could not prevent the march of annihilation that would overtake our universe. I will not tolerate the existence of weapons on Dreenor!"

Mugly trembled, aghast at the thought that had suddenly occurred to him.

"But isn't the erasure ship a weapon?" he whispered.

Habiba stared at him in stunned silence. Mugly was right. The awful thing already had happened. She began to shudder uncontrollably.

"Habiba, I'm sorry," Mugly said.

Her voice was an ugly husking appropriate to the gray gloominess of this day. "It is too late for sorrow, Mugly."

While crediting the Raj Dood with saving him, Woon invoked "national security reasons" in refusing to give details of the famed Venusian guru's heroic exploit. Woon said he was held the entire time on the Moon in a tiny cell without any human contact. The abduction, he accused, "was an act of violence by hideous alien creatures too awful for me to describe."

—From the *Seattle Enquirer*

Lutt had never seen his mother more obvious in her attempts to control him. In some ways, she was worse than Father, he thought.

She had chosen the "underwater room" of the main house for her gathering and, at nightfall, the lake lights had been turned on beyond the armor glass to illuminate exotic fish swimming there. A Titicaca shark swerved past the glass as Lutt, wearing a dark maroon tuxedo, entered. He thought the shark appropriate. A room full of sharks would certainly attract their brethren.

Phoenicia met him at the foot of the stairs with a young woman in tow.

"Lutt, darling, here's Eola VanDyke come all the way from Spokane just to be with us tonight."

He glanced at Eola VanDyke's tabloid-familiar features—hard eyes to go with sharp bones and a frame of highlighted blond hair. She was packaged in a ball gown of silvery fabric that lifted her breasts to unbelievable points. He stared deliberately at her cleavage and grinned.

"Eola VanDyke," he said, taking her hand. "May I call you VD?"

"Lutt!" Phoenicia gasped.

Eola's features darkened with a rush of blood but she managed a faint laugh.

He released her hand and turned his attention to the hard babble of voices in the room, seeing two bankers and their wives, Morey already drunk, several of Phoenicia's older female friends and their husbands, Eola's parents, standing by the underlake window and trying not to watch the meeting at the foot of the stairs. And, of course, a sprinkling of Hanson Guards decked out in Louis XIV livery to serve the drinks and hors d'oeuvres.

"Where's Father?" Lutt asked.

"Your father is not feeling well and retired early. I worry so about him, Lutt. He is so anxious for you to assume your proper position in The Company."

"The Company," Lutt said, looking at Eola. "That's what we call our many holdings. But you already knew that, didn't you?"

"There are so many stories about you," she said, "one does not know which to believe." Only a slight trembling in her voice betrayed her anger.

"Very good!" he said. "Believe them all, especially the worst ones."

"You're being simply awful," Phoenicia complained.

"Just being myself, Mother." He nodded toward Eola's parents and winked. "I think your mother's trying to get your attention, Eola," he said. "And I need a drink."

Eola excused herself and, when she had gone, Phoenicia flared at him. "Why do you test my patience this way? You're one of the most eligible bachelors in the world. Even the rival media report your encounters with young women and Eola is a sweet girl."

"I'm engaged to a sweet girl, Mother."

"You really should take more time to consider that liaison," Phoenicia said. "You know I'm thinking only of you, dear, when I say you should marry into a better family. And Eola—"

"Is duller than dull, Mother. It's the dullness of being born rich and letting your brain atrophy." He captured a drink off a tray. "Shouldn't I go look in on Father?"

"He said he did not want to be disturbed."

"Did he send for the doctor this time?"

"You know he never tells me." She brushed a speck off his lapel. "I'm glad you took time to change into this tuxedo. You're really quite handsome when—"

"Mother, stop it. Your guards insisted and I didn't feel like making an issue of it. However—" he pulled up one pants leg to reveal bright orange and yellow plaid socks "—I did keep my socks on."

Tittering laughter revealed that others had seen his display.

Phoenicia paled and started to say something but thought better of it.

In a loud voice heard clearly throughout the room, Lutt said, "I'm going to find Father and drag him back here."

In a low voice, Phoenicia said, "Lutt, he distinctly said he was not to be disturbed."

Ignoring her, Lutt said, "If I bring Father back, that'll restore me in my mother's good graces. We can't have a party without the old man himself."

Phoenicia threw up her hands. "You're incorrigible!"

Lutt gave her a pecking kiss on the cheek and, carrying his untasted drink, went back up the stairs. *Where would L.H. be? In his study, most likely.*

He found the study door slightly ajar and pushed it quietly. L.H.'s high-backed chair was turned away from the door, the top of his head visible above the back. The old man's prosthetic eyes lay on the desk behind him.

"I thought I'd find you here," Lutt said.

There was no response.

Lutt put his drink on the desk and went around it to look down at L.H. The senior Hanson sat leaning back into a corner of the chair with his eyes closed.

Lutt, he is not breathing, Ryll intruded.

Lutt put a hand to L.H.'s cheek. The skin was cold. He lifted an eyelid and saw emptiness there.

So this is how it happens, Lutt thought. He found a chair and sat in it facing the body. L.H. looked more peaceful than Lutt had ever before seen him.

"We never did have that real man-to-man talk," Lutt said. He glanced around the room, seeing the eclectic collection of L.H.'s memorabilia.

Lutt stared at a dented red and white hard hat hanging on the wall beyond the body. "I always thought this room suited you better than that damned office in the MX complex. Remember how you used to let me play with that hard hat from your days as a space docker?"

Lutt, he is dead, Ryll objected. *He cannot hear you.*

You don't know that.

This is macabre!

So leave me alone! He was my father for better or worse.

I do believe you're actually feeling grief.

Maybe I am.

Lutt's attention went to the prosthetic eyes on the desk and he slowly became aware that they were weighting a sheet of paper with something written on it. He leaned over and captured the paper, reading in his father's familiar scrawl:

"I know this is the end, Lutt, and I hope you get this. It's all yours now. I can't—" Whatever his father could not do was lost in a trailing line of ink.

"So it's all mine, is it?"

Lutt stared at the paper, feeling the upswelling of blind rage. "You think that's a big joke, don't you, Father?"

He glared at the peaceful face. "You're laughing! I know you are!"

Lutt waved the piece of paper. "Okay, but I'll have the last laugh! With this in my hand, I'm going to rule the roost! You see if I don't!"

"Lutt! Please don't raise your voice that way. We can hear you all the way down to the party."

It was Phoenicia standing in the open doorway.

Lutt folded the paper containing his father's last words and put it in his breast pocket. He felt icy calm.

"He's really done it this time, Mother. He's really done it."

She tried to grab his arm as he brushed past her but he shook himself free.

"Where are you going?" she demanded.

"To my house where I can get out of this monkey suit and then to his office. That's where I'm supposed to go now."

You have all seen these old John Wayne movies and I want you to use them as a pattern. Each of you must be strong and silent in your Legion guise. Silence will protect you. Strength will make you feared.

—Jongleur's instructions
to his Dreen volunteers

Nishi heard Lutt come slamming into the house and she retreated to her room where she locked the door, clutching the key in one sweaty hand. A window beside her showed lights still bright at the main house and an odd underwater glow from the lake directly in front of it.

The noises of Lutt moving around the house had a savage sound, doors slamming, shouts for Mrs. Ebey, curses. She heard him pounding up the stairs finally and the doorknob turned. A fist slammed against the door.

"Nishi!"

She forced herself to speak calmly. "What is it, Lutt?"

"Open this door!"

"I will not do that, Lutt."

"Come on, Ni-Ni! My old man's just died and I need to talk to you."

"Your father is dead?"

"It just happened. Come on, Ni-Ni! We have to talk."

"I am very sorry about your father, Lutt, but we can talk through the door."

"Open the door or I'll get Mrs. Ebey to do it."

"I have the only key, Lutt."

The door rattled and there was quiet for a moment, then: "This is stupid, Ni-Ni! Open the door."

"I will not do that, Lutt."

"If you don't, I'm going to eat some basil and put Ryll out of action!"

"That may be difficult for you to do, Lutt."

"Just open the damn door!"

She remained silent, staring at the dark panel. Would it withstand him, as Mrs. Ebey said, if he tried to break it down?

"I just want to talk to you."

"Are we not talking, Lutt? What is it you wish to say?"

"I need you, Ni-Ni."

"I'm aware of that."

"This is a helluva way to show you love me. Didn't you hear me say my father just died?"

"I grieve with you, Lutt, but I will not open this door."

"I've got to go to his office."

"Was that what you wished to tell me?"

"No, dammit! You've got me all confused. I love you and now my mother's trying to marry me off to a society idiot!"

"But your mother and I have an agreement. She says she will approve of me."

"That's typical! Well, she's just been pushing this Eola VanDyke on me."

"What's an Eola VanDyke?"

"That's the mindless twit she wants me to marry!"

"Are *we* not engaged to marry, Lutt?"

"Sure we are. Now, open the door."

"You may enter my bedroom only when we are married."

"Damn you, Ni-Ni! Open this door or you'll be sorry!"

"Good night, Lutt. I will say a novena for your father."

"Say your damn novena! And I hope it satisfies you!"

She heard him slamming down the stairs. The outer door banged but she did not unlock her door.

A stair tread squeaked. *Lutt returning?* Something scratched at her door. "You all right, honey?"

It was Mrs. Ebey.

"I am well, Mrs. Ebey."

"Did I hear him say the old man's dead?"

"That is what he said."

"Whatta ya know? I'm rich!"

"Mrs. Ebey? What is this you say?"

"I'm in his will, honey! A few months in his bed and now I'm rich."

There was the sound of Mrs. Ebey clattering down the stairs.

Nishi went to the window and stared at the lights in the main house. There no longer was the underwater glow from the lake but the house was even more brilliantly illuminated and she could see movement at windows.

What an extraordinary family, she thought.

Buy one hundred pounds of dried basil. Break it into one-pound packages. Put five of them in my office. Send five more to my shop with orders that Sam hold them. Put a package in each of our limos and send the balance to my house.

—Lutt Hanson, Jr., VODG memo
to *Enquirer* comptroller

This may be my one chance for a heroic gesture, Luhan thought. He had smarted for years under Mugly's control, aware the elder Dreen held him in low esteem, knowing he would never attain a position in the Elites because of his deformity, the extruded arm that refused to shape itself to Dreen normality.

But Luhan's Earther guise displayed no deformities. Clad in jungle camouflage, he crouched with five similarly garbed Dreen companions beside a woodland road near Seattle, waiting for the darkness that would come in about an hour.

Exotic smells of the place assailed his nostrils—wet duff from a recent rain, pine needles, Earther-modified excitement hormones from his companions.

The road beside them led down into a shallow swale, over a forested ridge and along the rear fence of the Hanson compound.

Luhan's orders were deceptively simple: "Get your team in there and capture Hanson himself. At all times, remember you are dealing with a merged Dreen-Earther."

A *disgusting idea!* Luhan thought.

In accordance with Jongleur's instructions, the six Dreen volunteers for this mission presented a familial resemblance. All had assumed craggy Earther guise, lean, muscular bodies, sharp features, lush brown hair, penetrating eyes, grim mouths that seldom opened. The speech patterns they had practiced were terse—mostly melodramatic shouts and cries such as:

"For the Legion! Death to the enemy! Never surrender! Heathen swine! I spit on your grave!"

As a contingency, they had memorized responses sure to bring admiration and strike fear into opponents. Luhan especially liked "Legionnaires don't cry." And he wondered if he would ever have the opportunity to say "I'll die before I talk!"

The films and lectures from which he and his companions had gathered these mots filled Luhan with a gung-ho attitude. A derring-do abandon had replaced Dreen conservatism.

"We've never met these Earthers with the force they deserve," he muttered. "Letting our people be captured by that damn Zone Patrol! How could we send such weaklings?"

Deni-Ra, crouched beside him, asked, "What'd you say, podner?"

Of Mugly's aides who had volunteered for this sortie, Deni-Ra struck Luhan as the poorest choice. She might appear male now but she was still female. Battle was the wrong place for a woman. The Legion never hid behind skirts!

"Be dark soon," Luhan said. "Then we'll show these scumguts what we're made of."

"Ah guess that's why we're here," Deni-Ra drawled.

It galled Luhan that Deni-Ra's accent was nearest those copied for this mission. There was no doubt she had the tones and emphases correctly memorized. He had only to close his eyes and listen to her; The figures they had seen on the screen came alive.

"You jes' follow my orders an' ever'thing'll be fine," he said.

"Wall, Ah'm proud to do jes' that," Deni-Ra said.

"To the last man if necessary," Luhan muttered.

"They ain' gonna see mah back," Deni-Ra said.

"Stop that!" Luhan snapped.

"Stop what, podner?"

"Showing off!"

"Jes' practicin'," Deni-Ra said, but she fell silent.

Luhan looked over her head at the others. Good men, all of them. The best. Whatever happened here tonight, the enemy would know the Dreens had sent their best. If only Mugly had allowed him to reject Deni-Ra. Luhan felt responsible for her. She complicated the mission.

"Deni-Ra," Luhan whispered, "you stay to the rear and if things get tight, you get yourself out of here. You get back to Dreenor and tell them we did our best."

"Ah guess Ah'll have t' cross that bridge if'n Ah sees it," she said. "Now, don't you worry none, podner. Ah'm not afeard of these here scumguts."

"I told you to stop that!" Luhan rasped. "Jongleur put me in charge. You're to obey my orders!"

"Gotta prepare mahself in case Ah'm captured," Deni-Ra protested.

"You just obey orders and you won't be captured."

Deni-Ra lapsed into sullen silence.

Luhan glanced at his watch. He felt a tightness in his stomach. It'd be dark enough soon. Just down this road and over that ridge. He wished Jongleur had permitted weapons.

A rocket launcher, at least. Or even knives. The Legion was famous for its infighting with knives.

But no! Jongleur had permitted only wire cutters and pry bars for breaching the fence.

"You may defend yourselves if attacked, but only with your hands and your superior Dreen responses and muscles."

What good were hands against real weapons?

Earthers had all the advantages except for Dreen tradition and the esprit de corps copied from the Legion.

Night fell and he heard movement in front of him, people stirring, the clank of metal against metal. Damn them! They were supposed to wait for his orders! He thought of barking a command for them to be quiet, but that would not be strong and silent.

"It's dark," Deni-Ra whispered. "Shouldn't we be moving out?"

"I was just about to give the order," Luhan said. He raised a hand and gestured forward, then realized no one could see this in the darkness.

"For the honor of the Legion!" he said. "Let's go. Stay close until we hit the fence."

"You tell 'em, Sarge," Deni-Ra said. "Oopsah!"

This last came as she tripped over Luhan and sent them both sprawling.

"I ordered you to stay to the rear!" he rasped, extricating himself.

Once more, he headed down the dark road, but he heard movement ahead of him.

"Wait up!" he husked and collided with a figure stopped in front of him. "Join hands until we get to the fence," he whispered.

"*Oui,*" the figure touching him said.

Should we be speaking French? Luhan wondered. *No! We must not let the enemy know our origins!*

"Speak English!" he ordered. "They must not learn we are the Legion."

"He's right," someone on his left said. "Remember what the general said. Death before dishonor!"

The general? Luhan wondered. And whose voice was that? It did not sound at all familiar.

The hand he held felt roughly calloused and something metallic bumped against Luhan's side. *The wire cutters?*

"There's the fence," someone ahead of Luhan said. "Stay down while we set the charge."

Set the charge? Luhan felt utterly confused. *I am supposed to be giving the orders!*

But there was the fence below him visible in the faint glow of bioluminescence built into the top strands of barbed wire.

Someone thrust Luhan strongly in the shoulders, forcing him to lie flat. "Sarge says to stay down!"

Luhan looked around him as his eyes adjusted to the gloomy illumination from the fence below them. There were far too many figures, many more than his little Dreen contingent. What was happening?

A monstrous explosion cut these thoughts short.

"For the Legion!" It was a concerted shout, hoarse and exultant.

Luhan found himself hauled upright and thrust forward in a wild charge through a wide gap blown in the fence.

Are the fumes from this boiling pot not the headiest stuff you've ever inhaled? Look at them jumping around after L.H.'s money and power!

—Raj Dood to Osceola

Lutt sat on the steps in his father's office, reading the one page he had found beneath the dome in the Listening Post.

Bright light from the MX complex poured in the window behind him. It was night up on the surface but his father had seldom let it get dark in here.

"Final Words." That's what it said at the top of the page, written in the old man's cramped script, but Lutt doubted he would ever encounter the absolute "Final Words" from his father. The old man had made sure of that on this page.

Lutt still felt himself coming down from the emotional high of braving the booby-trapped pathway into the sanctum. But the controls on the cane he had found leaning against the wall beside the office door had performed without exploding, thanks to his observations of how L.H. had used them. Doors opened, the escalator carried him up without incident, and the dome opened to his identification—producing his father's hand-written page.

"You know you've always been my favorite, Lutt, and your brother is a devious, deadly type who will not balk at any crime to achieve his ends. That, however, is what Hanson Industries needs to survive. Your problem has been an internal fight, a constant rebelling against what I know is best for you."

He thought Morey more devious than you? Ryll asked. *You sure fooled him!*

Lutt ignored the interruption and went on reading: "I have discussed this with your mother. She will support Morey's bid to control The Company. And maybe he will win out.

"You'll take over only if you beat Morey at his own game. That would make you the best director The Company has ever had. If you fail, Morey will do well enough and it will go to the next generation. Maybe I can count on you to produce a proper heir.

"I don't know what happened in your accident, but it hid you from the Listening Post. Yes, I've spied on you and Morey. Since you're reading this, it means you were first into the Post. Morey's instructions were to destroy this note by a method I explained. I do not give you that privilege. But the Listening Post is all yours and yours alone. That's your advantage."

What's he mean? Lutt wondered. *His other note said it was all mine now.* Confused, Lutt continued to read:

"Your mother will have my will read immediately. You won't be able to break it so don't waste your time. My advice to you: Be tough and don't trust women."

Lutt folded the paper and put it into his breast pocket with the other "Final Words" from his father.

What had L.H. meant by "all" and would those scrawled words found beside his body change the old man's estimation about whether his will could be broken? Nearness of death was said to make the mind perform in odd ways.

Why would he think you might want to break the will? Ryll asked.

I'm afraid I'll find out soon enough. And that note beside his body wasn't signed, dammit.

Lutt looked up at the passage to the Listening Post—still open, still available to him.

Well, I know a thing or two about booby-traps!

Once more, Lutt braved the lonely pathway to his father's sanctum and, when he emerged this time, he was smiling. Let Morey try to get in there now! Lutt sealed the doors to the escalator and turned to survey the office.

There was Morey! He stood in the entry doorway, obviously stopped by his fears.

"You'd be wise not to come any farther!" Lutt called. "I found the key to safe passage but I've changed it and added some of my own touches. You wouldn't survive three steps in here."

"This is my office now!" Morey raged. "Mother told me what Father wants. She knows what's in his will!"

"This office belongs to whoever can take it and hold it!" Lutt shouted. "Come on in if you think you can do that!"

"But Father left something for me in the Listening Post!"

"So come and get it!"

"Mother and I aren't going to provide any more money for your silly projects!" Morey said.

"The Listening Post will pay for what I need," Lutt said.

But he felt a sinking sensation. Morey wouldn't make such a boast if he felt unable to carry it out.

"And you're not going to marry that whore from Venus!" Morey said. "That's not what Mother wants."

"And Mother still gets everything she wants?"

"That's what Father's will says!"

"I still have enough on you to send you to prison!" Lutt shouted.

"Mother says she'll cut you off without a penny if you fight us!"

"Then maybe we'd better compromise," Lutt said.

"Never! You're out, Lutt! Mother and I are running things now!"

"I think you better leave before I get angry," Lutt said. "You plotted to kill me on Venus. If I ever needed an excuse to get rid of you, that's good enough!"

"Lutt, I'm coming in there if I have to get Hanson Guards to make it safe for me."

"You might survive three steps. Our guards would not make it two steps and they know it! But you're welcome to try."

Lutt touched a control on his father's cane and the office door in front of Morey began to close, pushing Morey out. Before it closed, Lutt shouted: "You're the one who's out, Morey!"

As the door clicked shut, Morey squeaked: "I'll get you for this, Lutt! See if I don't!"

Lutt, still carrying his father's cane, skirted the steps and went to the window looking down on the MX complex and its bustling activities—trains coming and going, cargoes being loaded and unloaded, people . . . busy people. From the window, he went to the computer console and the readouts indicating The Company's activities across the solar system. Here was L.H.'s control center. *Do I dare try to use it?*

Would I survive touching Father's computers? They're sure to be booby-trapped. Could there be a clue in the Listening Post? But that'd be booby-trapped, too.

As he considered this, Lutt noted a flashing orange light below a small screen at the lower right of the big board. The screen showed a familiar face in a familiar uniform.

Major Captain of the Zone Patrol!

Without thinking, Lutt punched the key for audio, then drew in a sharp breath at his daring. But nothing exploded.

Major Captain's voice was now audible, however, and she obviously saw him through a lens here in Father's office.

"There you are, Hanson! Where are you?"

"That's none of your business. Why are you calling me?"

"I was calling your father!"

"My father's dead and I'm running things now!"

"Shit! Did they kill him, too?"

"They? What're you talking about?"

"Where are you, Hanson?"

"Never mind that. What's going on? Why were you calling my father?"

"Don't you know?"

"If I knew, I wouldn't ask."

"There's been a commando attack on your family compound. We think it was the Foreign Legion. They killed at least twenty of your guards and hit your house. How did your father die?"

"Why don't you ask his doctor? Whatta you mean commandos hit my house?"

"They broke in and spirited someone away."

Nishi!

"Who did they take?" he demanded.

"We don't know but we've sent in a full platoon to investigate."

"If it's really the Legion, you better send a battalion."

"Very funny, Hanson! Have you done something to bring the Legion down on you? Who would they take from your house?"

"They may have kidnaped my fiancée."

"That woman you brought from Venus?"

When Lutt did not respond, she asked: "And while we're on that, how'd you come back to Earth? You're not on any transport manifest."

"We walked," he said. "What're conditions at the family compound?"

"There's a hole in your fence and your house needs some new doors. You might think of hiring better guards, too. Now, answer my question about how you returned. Don't make me drag you in here for another interrogation."

"Osceola brought me back through her looking glass," Lutt said.

"I'll have the truth out of you, Hanson! Sooner or later. Don't make me do it the hard way."

"But you enjoy doing it the hard way," he said, and he broke the connection.

What do I do now? If they've taken Nishi . . . Serves her right for putting me off! But if they've taken her . . .

He experienced a lost and empty sensation.

Damn her! Ryll? What do I do now?

You're asking my advice?

I'd ask the devil himself if I thought it would help!

I compute it must be the Legion and they have taken Nishi.

But why?

You already know. You're just not facing it. The Legion takes care of its own.

That hogwash!

But also, thanks to Nishi, the Legion may have a deep desire for your crude Spiral device.

You think she really sold them on it?

It is possible they believe an absolutely secure secret communications system would give them an advantage over the Chinese.

That was her pitch, all right. So what do I do?

If Morey's threats are to be believed, you are not in a position to do anything.

I'll offer to bargain with them. Sam can be pulled off the work on my new Vortraveler *and we'll make more of those . . .*

First, hadn't you better hear your father's will?

But Nishi's . . .

The Legion will not harm her. Besides, she won't satisfy your animal lusts unless you marry her.

Damn her! Yeah, you're right about the will. I have to find out what the old man did. First things first.

The Company has shut off all funds for the Vortraveler *and we've used up our draw on money paid for subscriptions to your Spiral News Service. Ade Stuart says your special fund is empty. Our suppliers won't deliver unless we pay cash. What now?*

—Sam R. Kand, note to
Lutt Hanson, Jr.

Habiba swayed back and forth on the saddle in her cupola, back and forth, back and forth. Shield-filtered morning sunlight cast gray shadows across her immense body as she moved.

I should never have convened a Thoughtcon.

With the second erasure ship common knowledge, she saw many signs of storytelling sickness. Dreen skin was smoothing. *They lie to each other!* Earth's erasure would create an epidemic.

But what else could I do? How could I calm the Elite?

Below her, the Elite sat in trance but their debate went on mentally. Their distress filtered up to Habiba and required all of her powers to deflect. But it was grossly familiar.

If we permit one weapon, we should make more.

No! That is not the Dreen way!

The Earther threat must be removed.

Our shield will protect us.

For how long?

It had been inevitable that Mugly's insight would spread throughout Dreenor.

Habiba felt the most profound dismay of her life that she had created this condition—as much by inaction as by action.

How could I have overlooked the fact that an erasure ship is a weapon?

Certainly, Jongleur had seen this. He had shown no surprise whatsoever when apprised of Mugly's observation.

"Of course it's a weapon! What else could it be?"

For the first time since those almost mindless days when she had cultivated the childseed and prepared Dreenor for its happy population, Habiba began to question her own origins and the inner purposes of her life.

Why had she thought Dreenor and Dreens infinite?

When she consulted her innermost feelings, she still thought of infinity as the domain of Dreens. A calm acceptance of this permeated her. But what of Dreenor? What was the special significance of ampleness? And why did bazeel remain a fearful mystery? These were the core of her dismay.

The Elite stirred restlessly below her, all of them on the edge of emergence from Thoughtcon trance. And they would awaken with no answers to their distress.

What am I to do? How can I help them?

Platitudes and calls for devotion to their Supreme Tax Collector no longer produced the desired results. Even Jongleur responded almost with a sneer when she appealed to his love and reliability.

"Love doesn't work the way it once did. I must think about it every time now."

Habiba felt she had been precipitated onto a slideway with no escape. Down, down, down she sped and all of Dreenor with her. The inevitability of this shocked her. She could think of no alternative to any of her decisions or actions. She had done what was right and acceptable.

Was it what the Earthers called "kismet"? Fate?

From the moment Wemply idmaged the first elements of Earth, all of the present circumstances were predictable—by hindsight. What had blinded foresight?

The only answer that came to her was unacceptable.

Dreens, too, obey hidden laws.

It was becoming more and more difficult to keep the Elite in trance. She relaxed her grip on them slightly and they began to awaken—Jongleur first, Mugly . . . then a wave of watchful alertness spread throughout the spiral ranks.

Habiba held her thoughts to herself. What could she say to them? They awaited a grand pronouncement. It was what they had come to expect from ordinary Thoughtcons and this time, under these pressures, the expectation was amplified to explosive dimensions.

"Our love of Dreenor has blinded us to our destiny," she said. "We will not make other weapons. Of what use would they be except to subvert our basic nature?"

"Then we will send the erasure ship?" Mugly asked.

She heard the indrawn breath as they awaited her response.

"If it becomes necessary," she said.

"Is it not necessary right now?" That came from far down in the ranks, a place that seldom originated spontaneous argument.

"Only I can determine if it is necessary," Habiba said. And that, she knew, was an elemental truth.

"Why do we delay?" Mugly asked.

"If we precipitate violence, the consequences will be cataclysmic to us," she said. Again, she felt elemental truth emerge from her mouth.

"Failure to act could be just as cataclysmic," Mugly objected.

"You have heard my decision!" she snapped. "I will accept no more objections. You may leave—all of you."

They obeyed, but she sensed the reluctance and knew the Thoughtcon had been a mistake. It had only increased their distress.

From her secret hideaway on the Med, guarded by fanatical troopers of the French Foreign Legion, Nishi D'Amato spoke of her hard life on Venus and the fairy-tale beginnings of her relationship with Lutt Hanson, Jr.

—Lorna Subiyama's exclusive
interview with N. D'Amato

"Good riddance!" Phoenicia said. "Someday, you'll be thankful she ran out on you."

Why does she think Nishi ran away? Ryll asked.

Lutt ignored the mental interruption. Still reeling from the just-completed early-morning reading of the will, he stood in the hall outside the attorney's office and glared at his mother. Always at her best in the morning, she showed no signs of fading today. She and Morey had it all. The will made his father's "all" an empty promise! And she dared suggest Nishi had run out!

"She did not run out on me! She was kidnaped!"

"They think you'll pay ransom? Where would you get the money?"

Morey emerged from the office, folding a sheet of paper.

"They'll get the court order right away," Morey told Phoenicia.

"We will stand for no obstructions from you, Lutt," Phoenicia said. "How dare you forbid Morey access to his own father's office, especially now!"

Lutt smiled at Morey. "I didn't forbid it."

"You slammed the door on me!" Morey said.

"But I invited you inside."

Morey pointed a finger at Lutt and looked at Phoenicia. "He told me he rigged the office to kill me if I entered!"

"Now, Morey," Lutt said, relishing this small victory after the major defeat of L.H.'s will. "Our own father set those traps. You know? I think he's still testing us the way he did when we were boys. If you survive, you win."

"You got through to the . . . to the you know," Morey accused.

"What's this 'you know'?" Phoenicia demanded.

"Father made us swear a solemn oath we'd never reveal it," Lutt said. "I'm glad to see Morey still respects that oath."

"I'll talk to you later, Morey," Phoenicia said.

Lutt studied his mother with new appreciation. Now that she held the reins, there was no softness in her. Father had often bragged about her strength. But this was another Phoenicia, a whip-cracker.

She smiled her new hard smile at Lutt. "We must work together now that your father is gone. Surely you appreciate that."

"Morey told me there'd be no compromises," Lutt said. "I'm out and you two are in."

"That was a bit harsh, Morey," she said.

"But you told me . . . and the will says I'm chairman of the Hanson Industries board."

"A very bad choice," Lutt said. "Especially when you're under the thumb of organized criminals."

"That's a lie!" Morey raged.

Earthers lie with such facility, Ryll commented.

Stay out of this! I'll fight my own fight!

"No criminal organization can stand up to the Hanson Guards," Phoenicia said. "I don't care what Morey's done. That's the past. His father's will says he takes over and that's the responsibility you always refused."

She looked from Lutt to Morey and back, noting Lutt was now as tall as Morey.

"Are you wearing elevator shoes?" she asked.

Lutt lifted a plain black oxford for her to see. But his mind was on the unsigned message beside his father's body. No other person knew about it yet. He doubted its value. An attorney would have to be found, one Phoenicia and Morey did not own.

Morey favored Lutt with a malicious grin. "If you try to make out I'm a criminal, we'll have you declared insane. There's your wild babbling about an alien in your body, you know."

"You heard the will," Phoenicia said. "You have the deed to your house, your Spiral News Service and your newspaper, that's it."

"And we control the purse strings!" Morey gloated.

But I control the Listening Post, Lutt thought.

"Don't try to break the will," Phoenicia said. "I warn you not to say your father was incompetent. We are prepared to deal with that."

"I told you I'd get you!" Morey said.

Phoenicia waved a hand at him. "That's enough, Morey. You may be chairman of the board, but your father left me in actual control."

Morey subsided into glum silence.

"I am prepared to be generous with you, Lutt," Phoenicia said. "And there is the question of what you're going to do with your life now that you have no effective part in The Company."

"Oh? You have things all planned out for me, do you?"

"Don't take that tone with me!" she snapped. "Listen to what I have to say. You may find my ideas pleasing . . . unless you try to thwart me."

"He's going to fight us," Morey said. "I've always been able to read that expression on his face."

"I warned you once to be still!" Phoenicia said. She turned a bleak smile toward Lutt. "When you were a child you said you'd like to be president of the solar system. There is no such thing but there is the United States Presidency."

"What the devil are you suggesting?" Lutt demanded.

"You have one newspaper and this news service thing. With more papers plus cable and satellite television, the ownership concealed in our various companies, you could be President."

"No one's going to allow a monopoly of the media!" Morey objected.

"We'll spread the ownership," Phoenicia said. "Now, I've told you twice to stay out of this. You just walk down the hall there and wait for me at the elevators."

"But Mother!"

"Now." She waited until he was out of earshot, then: "Morey needs a firm hand guiding him."

"He plotted to have me murdered," Lutt said. "If you give him too firm a hand, are you sure he's not above taking the step from fratricide to matricide?"

"I suspected you might try to poison my mind against Morey. I will not allow that. But I will underwrite all that's required to make you President. You'll have a blank check."

Lutt considered this with new interest. Blank check? How could she know what he did with all of the money?

"You have big plans," Lutt said. "And, of course, if I win, you think you'll control the Presidency."

"Not just the Presidency," Phoenicia said. "My advisers are thinking bigger than that . . . much bigger."

"What advisers?"

"Your campaign will be managed by Gilperton Woon."

"Crissakes, Mother! Morey plotted with him to have me murdered!"

"Stop trying to poison my mind against your brother."

She's worse than your father, Ryll offered.

Lutt remained silent and Phoenicia said, "Woon has an excellent plan. You will be the underdog and we will play up your sympathy for the needy. He especially admired your editorial proposing better housing for the poor."

"Father didn't like that editorial. He thought a city housing commission would cost us plenty."

"Your father did not share my political ambitions. I'm afraid he never thought much beyond immediate profits."

"You'd sacrifice immediate profits to gain power?"

"The Presidency can be very profitable if it's managed correctly. Woon has worked out a winning platform and, once you're in office, we—"

"I can see it now," Lutt said. "Vote for Lutt Hanson, Jr. Happiness and a warm puppy for everyone!"

"Joke about it only in private. Woon has the right idea to touch the populist nerve. Your campaign will be based on the slogan, 'For the People: Warmth and a Full Stomach.' "

"Isn't that what I said?"

"I warn you, Lutt. Joke only in private."

"But of course, Mother."

"The housing issue is ideal because you've already stated your position publicly," she said. "It will be consistent for you then to propose better municipal railways, higher welfare payments, lower utility bills, that sort of thing."

"You'll be promoting voter registration in the Lowtowns next," Lutt said.

"Woon will do that behind the scenes while you, in the limelight, will urge a stronger national defense and the jobs that go with it."

"So I'm to run for the Presidency, with Woon and the American Independence party calling the shots."

"Oh, no! Woon will sabotage the AIP by making it appear to be the puppet of the wealthy and privileged few. At the same time, with his secret guidance, you will bring back the Grand Old Party as the champion of the poor."

"Mother, you are incredible!"

"I knew you'd go along with my ambitions for you."

"No, Mother, I'm not going to make a fool of myself, even for you. There's no way you can convince people the Hansons are the champions of the poor."

"You underestimate me, Lutt."

"Wrong, Mother. I'll never do that again."

The hard gleam remained in her eyes but she spoke softly. "In some ways, Lutt, you're brighter than Morey. I'm going to trust your intelligence. We have the perfect issue to guarantee you will be President."

"Empty the head and fill the gut, bread and circuses and a good lay every Saturday."

"You are worst when you're uncouth! Be still and pay attention! No one else knows it, but we captured one of the attackers at our compound and we have that attacker hidden away under guard."

"You captured a commando of the Foreign Legion?"

"A commando, but not of the Legion. Disguised as a legionnaire but actually an alien, an invader from space."

Did they capture a Dreen agent? Ryll asked. *Find out!*

Stop distracting me. I have to learn what she's plotting. She's more devious than L.H.!

"How the hell does a captured alien guarantee my election?" he asked.

"The alien will be produced at the proper moment. He is involved in a plot to destroy Earth and admits it. He will say so publicly. There is a terrible ship out there in space prepared to *erase* us! You will be elected on a platform to repel this invasion and, of course, provide many defense jobs in the process."

It's a Dreen! Ryll intruded. *Has to be.*

"I've changed my mind, Mother," Lutt said. "I'm going along with you, but not for the reasons you think."

"Just as long as your reasons don't confuse matters, Son."

"This is a real threat, Mother. I have my own reasons to believe those aliens intend to do away with us. I'll run on a platform of meeting the threat, but it's not going to be treated as a phony issue."

"Of course not! Sincerity wins votes. But if the alien we captured is any example, they're bumbling incompetents. We'll have no trouble defeating them."

"I want to meet this alien right now."

It has to be a Dreen, Ryll intruded. *I will talk to him.*

You will be silent unless I permit you to speak!

"It's a good idea for you to meet the alien," Phoenicia said, "but first we install Morey at The Company's offices."

"Later, Mother. Father left the place full of death traps."

"You survived them!"

"I'm brighter than Morey, remember?"

"You'll have to instruct him in how to use the office."

"If it suits me. But that's my only hole card, Mother. I'm not going to give it up unless I see an advantage."

"Your father said you'd be a hard bargainer. That's good, but don't carry it too far with me. You're my son, but The Company must be preserved. How do you know the alien threat is real?"

She's trying to catch you with a quick change of subject! Ryll warned. *Don't tell her about me!*

When Lutt didn't answer, she said, "It's that crazy talk about an alien in your body! There's something in that!"

Tell her about the collision with my ship, Ryll said. *That was the first erasure ship. Say you learned its secret.*

You're learning how to lie pretty well, Ryll.

I have excellent teachers! Besides, what I'm suggesting is the truth!

But not the whole truth.

I'm beginning to see that truth is the best form of lying.

"Are you really Lutt?" Phoenicia asked. "You've been so strange since your accident. And you're taller."

"I'm your son, Mother. The accident goosed my hormones."

She shuddered. "At least tell me how you know these Dreens are a real threat."

Lutt followed Ryll's suggestion and, when he finished his recital, she nodded sagely. "Why did you keep it secret?"

"I thought there were advantages. I even discussed it with Father," he lied.

"Strange. He never told me."

"You know how secretive Father was. But just look at how much he increased our holdings in defense industries during these last months."

"Of course! And it all fits into my plans. Our profits will be very big!"

"So let's see the alien. I'll tell you then how I'll go along with your political ambitions for me."

"Very well. I'll call Gil Woon and we'll—"

"No! Just the two of us, the guards and the alien. Not even Morey. I want to know how much the alien will help us."

Grand Old Party (GOP), formerly Republican party. A near-defunct political entity with one seat in the Senate and two in the House during the current session. The GOP has not offered a Presidential candidate in eighty years, has not elected a governor in fifty.

—Driesen's *Political Digest*
(Thirty-seventh Edition)

Nishi stood in the portico of her prison villa admiring the evening sunglow on the Mediterranean's green waters. She heard Lorna at work upstairs and Lew in the kitchen helping the chef. He was good in that role, Nishi thought, but his basil-heavy dishes would have to be corrected. And he had no tolerance for liquor. She had seen him in a drunken stupor too often. Lorna seemed not to mind: a tolerant mother with a wayward child.

The abduction Nishi had found bizarre, almost amusing. During the flight over the Pole, she had told squad leader O'Hara she had gone voluntarily with Lutt and planned to marry him. This had surprised O'Hara and he'd complained about "a broken contract"—the Spiral communicator Lutt had promised to provide the Legion.

"I must get further instructions," O'Hara had said.

A Legion guard, Nishi saw, was coming up the stone path from the jetty with a dumpy woman in a long black dress. *A new servant?* The Legion was most accommodating to her needs. But their questions about the Spiral communicator told Nishi she had a strong bargaining chip. Excellent! Nishi's father had taught her to bargain from a position of power.

They need me. When Subiyama has told enough of our story we will call on the Hansons and get what the Legion requires. I must remember my family's duty to the Legion.

Nishi heaved a deep sigh. She felt oddly relieved to be at a distance from the Hanson family. *I need time to examine my feelings. I miss Lutt but still . . .*

The Legion guard and the woman made the final turn before climbing to the villa's terrazzo porch. The woman looked up and Nishi recognized her.

Mrs. Ebey? Have the Hansons sent an emissary?

The guard was Captain O'Hara, a dashing fellow with wavy black hair and great self-esteem. He fancied himself irresistible, but Nishi had been forced to fend him off only once. O'Hara was Legion to the core. He stopped a pace away from the foot of the steps leading up to Nishi and restrained Mrs. Ebey.

"This one says she has valuable information she will reveal only to you, mademoiselle," O'Hara said.

"It's quite all right, Captain," Nishi said. "Mrs. Ebey is known to me."

"She has no weapons," O'Hara said.

"What would I be doing with weapons?" Mrs. Ebey protested.

"You may leave us alone, Captain," Nishi said.

O'Hara left them but only after favoring Nishi with a lingering look of admiration.

When he was gone, Nishi asked: "Well, what do the Hansons want of me?"

"To the devil with the Hansons and everything they desire!" Mrs. Ebey said.

"I don't understand," Nishi said. "When I last saw you, didn't you say you were rich because of L.H.'s death?"

"Lies! All lies! Not a word of me in his will!"

"Then why are you here? What is the information fit only for my ears?"

"The Hansons fired me, but some of the guards and servants still talk to me, Miss Nishi. The Hansons have big plans. They'll marry off Master Lutt to some brainless socialite and run him for President of the United States! That's what I've learned!"

"In the name of all the saints, how could they expect to elect Lutt?"

"It's true they'll try, and they have a captive they say will make it sure for him."

"A captive? What captive?"

"They say it's one of the Legion who abducted you."

"But the Legion lost no one. I'm told there was confusion, perhaps a few volunteer intruders on the mission, but all of the original cadre came out safely."

"I don't know about that, Miss Nishi."

"Besides, they did not abduct me. They thought of it as a rescue. We're discussing their mistake. But I'm sure they lost no one in the operation."

"It's only rumors about the captive but there's no doubt they'll run Master Lutt for President and the wedding is a certainty. Madame Phoenicia herself was heard to say it."

"Why do you bring this information to me, Mrs. Ebey?"

"I was hoping you'd give me employment, Miss Nishi. I've used the last of my little savings to come here and I'm destitute."

"How do I know you're not a Hanson spy?" Nishi asked.

"Them! I spit on them! L.H. and his big promises!"

"I believe I'll risk it," Nishi said.

"It's no risk, Miss Nishi. Just give the word and I'd kill any Hanson for you."

Nishi shuddered at the venom in the old woman's voice but showed none of this when responding.

"Go tell Captain O'Hara you're to be put on the payroll as my personal maid. If he asks what information you brought, tell him. Say, if Lutt actually runs for political office, our damaging information is even more valuable."

"I hope you ruin them all, miss. That I do."

Your Portable Speech Analyzer analyzes crowd reactions and your speech content, telling you which points are most effective and providing on-the-spot warning if you begin to lose control of your audience. Most important, your PSA gives you an immediate corrective summary with which to hold your audience.

—Instruction manual,
Political Equipment Company,
PSA Model 80147

Lutt studied the caged captive. Definitely human in appearance, rugged features . . . a bit on the John Wayne side.

The cage sat under a bank of floodlights in the center of a large secret sub-basement of the Hanson compound's main house. Rows of spy eyes looked down on it from ceiling and walls. Deadly weapons protruded from holes near the spy eyes. Weapons and spy devices, Phoenicia said, were constantly manned by Hanson Guards.

Lutt and his mother had come directly from the attorney's offices. It was still early in the day.

Phoenicia stood to one side, most of her attention on Lutt and with only an occasional frightened glance at the creature in the cage.

The captive, Lutt noted, was studying him with undisguised intensity.

Definitely Dreen and he sees my Dreen aura, Ryll informed Lutt. *He knows who I am.*

I can't see any aura.

Of course not. You're an Earther, not a Dreen.

Glancing at his mother, Lutt said, "Your captive doesn't look alien. Won't people say it's a phony thing we've dreamed up to get votes?"

She shuddered. "Wait until it shows you its real shape."

Lutt addressed the captive. "What's your name?"

The captive frowned and spoke in a gruff voice. "Well, Ah tell y', Pilgrim, y' kin call me Deni-Ra. Ah'm still decidin' what t' call yew."

"What do you mean?"

"Ah reckon you're a merged monster. Don' know if'n Ah should call y' Ryll or what?"

"What's it talking about?" Phoenicia demanded.

"I'm trying to find out," Lutt said.

Careful! Ryll warned. *She's very suspicious of you. We could wind up in a Zone Patrol prison.*

I know! Be quiet unless you have something useful.

"My name's Lutt Hanson, Jr.," Lutt said. "You can call me Mr. Hanson."

"Reckon that's as good a handle as any. A monster's a monster, no matter what y' call it."

"So you think humans are monsters?"

Deni-Ra glanced at Phoenicia, at the weapons protruding from walls and ceiling, then back at Lutt. "You're a yellow monster, Mr. Hanson."

"We'll show you who the cowards are when it comes to a real fight," Lutt said.

"Ain' gonna be no fight. Jes' gonna erase y'all. Same as if y' never was a'tall."

"Why is it speaking with that odd accent?" Phoenicia asked.

"Ah tell y', ma'am, we'uns figger y' best learn what you're up aginst. No sense beatin' 'roun' the corral 'bout it."

"I'm told you're willing to state publicly that you're an alien sent here against Earth," Lutt said.

"Yup."

"Why would you do that?"

"Ah tell y', Pilgrim, even a four-flushin' scumguts deserves a warnin' 'fore y' draw down on 'im."

"Tell me, Deni-Ra, why would anyone believe you?" Lutt asked.

"Reckon y' needs a little somethin' t' make the claim jumpers know this is it," Deni-Ra said. "Naow, y' jes' watch close like."

As Lutt stared into the cage, the figure of the captive melted into a mound of pulsing protoplasm and reshaped into a squat figure with four legs, a bulbous head with pendulous ear flaps and glaring pink eyes. The horn-tool extrusion on the face lifted to reveal a wide mouth.

A very poor job of idmaging but adequate, Ryll informed him. *I could do it much better. By the blessed snout of Habiba! That's a female Dreen!*

Deni-Ra's mouth opened and the familiar gruff voice emerged. "Naow y' know, Pilgrim. Yew been dealin' from th' bottom o' th' deck. Time to pay up."

Lutt continued to examine the odd figure. The Dreen looked much as Ryll had described himself and Lutt could not see anything to distinguish Deni-Ra's sex. Because Phoenicia was present, Lutt decided to put Ryll's inside information in the form of a question.

"Are you male or female?" Lutt asked.

"Don' make no difference, Pilgrim. Yew are out-gunned."

The heavy Western accent coming from the Dreen suddenly struck Lutt as ridiculous. He grinned.

"You don't look very dangerous to me, Deni-Ra. I mean, there you are, a captive in our cage. Your threats are kind of laughable."

"Yew'll stop laughin' when our top gun arrives."

"Why should we believe you?"

"Zone Patrol kin tell y' that, Pilgrim. They lost some o' their top hands tryin' t' pry inta one o' our ships."

Ask her if they have made a new erasure ship, Ryll intruded.

"Have you made a new ship to attack us?" Lutt asked.

"Yup. Ol' Habiba herse'f give th' order."

Phoenicia moved up beside Lutt. "Have you seen and heard enough, Lutt? Isn't it an ugly thing?"

"Actually, it's kind of ridiculous," Lutt said. "Look at those stupid arms and those funny hands."

"Yew better be keerful," Deni-Ra said. "Ah'll take jes' so much o' y'r pizen 'fore Ah come out there an' poun' a little sense inta y'."

Lutt began to chuckle. "Look at it, Mother! This thing will get laughs, nothing else!"

Don't provoke her, Lutt, Ryll warned. *This is an adult Dreen, very dangerous.*

"Reckon Ah have to show y'," Deni-Ra said mournfully.

Once more, she melted into a mound of protoplasm but when she reformed it was into a glistening green and black cobra. The head lifted and poised itself level with Lutt's eyes. The snake mouth opened and again, the gruff voice emerged.

"Yew think this yere hoosegow'll hold me if'n Ah wants out?"

Phoenicia back-stepped to the wall but Lutt held his ground.

"Lutt, be careful," Phoenicia said.

"You'd be blasted to bits before you got two centimeters out of that cage," he said.

"An' Ah'd jes' reform mahse'f," the snake said. "Yew'd run outa ammo 'fore Ah'd run outa bodies."

"Then why are you still a captive?" Lutt demanded.

"Someone's gotta tell yew nesters yore fences are a'comin' down," Deni-Ra said.

Eighty-second amendment to the U.S. Constitution: abolishes the Vice-Presidency, creates an elective chairman of the Senate and installs the runner-up candidate as Chief Executive should incumbent die of natural causes. The amendment's so-called "assassination barrier" provides for an election should an incumbent die by violence, thus removing a motive for the loser to kill the winner. It was argued that the Vice-President was a ceremonial figure and the office attracted few candidates of high caliber.

—*A History of the United States and Its Colonies*, Sidmon Sons Publishers, New York and Jupiter

"Osey, what's your interest in all of this?" Raj Dood demanded. "You're worse than I am when it comes to Hansons."

He and Osceola lay stretched out on string hammocks in the mangrove shade of Osceola's swampside porch at Gum City, Florida, wasting away a hot afternoon.

The house behind them was mostly weathered boards with gaping cracks between them and the post-and-pole porch looked as though it would blow away in a strong wind.

There had been an alert earlier when a tropical depression out in the Atlantic turned into a storm but the disturbance was drifting northward toward the Carolina coast.

"Oh, you know how it is, Dood," she said. "Sometimes I toy

with the idea of moving in on their holdings and leaving them squeezed dry like a dead lizard too long in the sun."

"Damn it, Osey, you'd be just as bad as them. Why the hell you think I quit old L.H. like that?"

"You're right, Dood. But daydreams are kinda fun."

"That's true, all right. Wonder what's happening to that storm? I was hoping it'd hit us and blow this shack away. You got anything valuable in there?"

"My Spirit Glass collection but we can replace that easy enough. You're acting kind of restless. What's fermenting in that head of yours?"

"I was thinking I might like to bring in one of those Dreen pets, those little yellow Soothers that talk straight into your mind."

She sat up and swung her legs over the edge of the hammock. "You're cooking up something, you old bastard."

He grinned up at the porch ceiling where a spider was spinning its web between two pole rafters. "Well, there's Nishi off there all alone with—"

"She's not alone!" Osceola said.

"But who can she trust? Not that Mrs. Ebey. That one would do in her own mother for profit."

"She's not spying for the Hansons, though."

"Because they haven't offered to hire her."

"Not likely they will, her off there in the Med with Nishi and those legionnaires," Osceola said.

"Nishi's doing all right," Raj Dood said. "That's why I backed out of negotiations with the Legion. Besides, I kinda like the Chinese. They're not as pushy as the damn French."

Osceola squinted. "But she's like a royal prisoner."

"That's her strength, Osey. The Legion wants Lutt's communicator and she's their key."

"If only she weren't halfway in love," Osceola said.

"Have you thought what might happen if the Zone Patrol learns the Legion's real purpose?"

Osceola pursed her lips. "You never know about Hansons. They might bring the ZP to the bargaining table."

"Phoenicia wouldn't hesitate a minute if she saw a chance for profit. She always was a skittish thing. And she's not above doing her own dirty work."

"Look here, Dood. You taking a hand in this?"

"Not really. Thought I might toss a monkey wrench into the works now and then, but you know how it is. Weather's too hot for doing much else but think."

"You think too much."

"Mebbe so. But I been thinking about Dreens, too. This thing could get out of hand, Osey. Dreens are idiot-savants. Don't know what they're doing half the time. Only idmage in three dimensions. And that one squatting in Lutt's body is just a kid."

"Pretty smart kid, you ask me."

"Seems to be learning, but what're you going to get with Lutt and his tribe as teachers?"

"I see what you mean. We better keep an eye on this and see if we can balance things should the need occur."

"You're a mother hen, Osey."

"And you're my main rooster, you old bastard. Sometimes, I wonder what would have happened if the wrong person had made your discovery."

"L.H. would've been dictator of the universe, at least. He went pretty far on his power trip with the little he was able to pick up from my notes. Look at what he did with it: that damn Listening Post!"

"Strikes me as odd the Dreens haven't had that problem," Osceola said.

"It's not their nature."

"I wish we could sneak onto their home ground and study them," she said.

"They'd know they were being spied on and that'd be like pouring gas on an anthill. We can't risk it."

"I'd still like to meet that Habiba," Osceola said. "Every Dreen we've seen seems to think she's God."

"Tax collectors always think they're God. Now leave me be for a bit. I want to conjure up one of those furry yellow things."

Politics has never been a science. It is an art form. Only those who are not gifted with imagination can think of politics as a science, and their "laws" always break down when the need for creativity arises. In fact, this is the friction point between all science and all creativity.

—*The Art of Politics,*
By Sil Amil, Seminole Publications

Senator Gilperton Woon arrived an hour late for his conference with Lutt, entering Lutt's office at the *Enquirer* ten minutes before noon with a brisk but harried air.

Having been warned by his staff researchers, Lutt sat at his desk eating a lunch of canard a l'orange and fresh haricots. One of Woon's standard ploys, the researchers said, was to arrive this way and prolong the conversation to keep his host hungry, Woon having eaten a full meal just before the meeting.

The senator, a gray-maned, rotund figure with hard little pig eyes and fat cheeks, burped gently at sight of Lutt's lunch, then: "I did not know this was to be a luncheon meeting." His voice was deep and mellifluous.

Lutt waved to a chair on the other side of the desk and waited until Woon was seated. "It's *not* a luncheon meeting. I hope you enjoyed your meal at Roselini's. Their pheasant is particularly good."

"Are you having me spied on, son?" Woon asked.

"A famous man such as yourself is always recognized, sir, wherever he goes," Lutt said. He pushed the remains of his lunch aside and waited for a copyboy to remove it. When the door closed and only the two of them remained in the office, Lutt said, "Let's stop playing games. We've an election to win."

Woon folded his hands over his ample stomach. "And what would you say is our most immediate problem there, son?"

"Number one, you stop calling me 'son.' I'm Lutt Hanson, candidate for President. Number two, how to deal with Phoenicia. She could be a real problem if we don't put a lid on her."

"Well, well . . . Mr. Hanson. Your mother told me you were a very sharp character. Glad to see she was right."

"Know what she's doing right now?" Lutt asked.

"She said she had important business to attend to and could not be at this conference."

"She and my brother are setting up new corporate headquarters for the family's holdings."

"Oh? She told me they'll make a shrine out of L.H.'s old offices. That right?"

"That will look good in print," Lutt said.

"Anything I should know about this? Anything that might backfire?"

"I'll tell you on a need-to-know basis," Lutt said. "Now, there's one thing I need to know. How far did you get in your plan to have me murdered on Venus?"

Woon's little eyes blinked hard. He paled slightly. "Mr. Hanson, I have to know how you learned about that."

"My father told me." Lutt smiled gently and embellished his statement with a lie. "He also told me other things he learned about you."

"Shit in a gumboot!" Woon said. "Get one Hanson off my back and another one climbs right up there to take his place!"

So Woon is one of those Father manipulated through the Listening Post, Lutt thought. *Full details of the plot against me must be up there in the sanctum someplace.*

"I just want you to know who's running things here," Lutt said. "My mother was never privy to Father's private sources."

"That's what he always told me but he never said a word about you."

"It's part of my inheritance," Lutt said. "Did you see the Hanson Guards all over this building when you came in?"

"How could I miss 'em? They wanted to do a body search on me until I called your mother. She apologized but said the guards were here at her orders. What's going on?"

"A minor disagreement in the family about who controls what."

"Didn't look very minor to me. Must be fifty guards I had to pass through, and all of 'em armed to the teeth."

"We'll chalk it up to terrorist threats if the need arises," Lutt said. "You can think of it as a show of strength by my mother. She's demonstrating to me who gives orders to the Hanson Guards."

"And she controls the purse strings?"

"I have other sources."

"And expensive tastes. What's this project out at your shop?"

"An invention that will make us plenty."

"How soon?"

Lutt's desktop communicator buzzed to interrupt his reply. A switchboard attendant said, "Sorry, Mr. Hanson, but it's your mother on line three."

Lutt opened the line. "Yes, Mother?"

Phoenicia's finishing-school lilt came through the speaker with only slight clipping. "There was nothing in your father's will about your shop, Lutt. I've put it under special guard to keep it safe."

Lutt scowled. "And to keep me out?"

"Now, Son. You and your man, Kand, can go back as soon as you've been briefed on the new security measures."

"So you kicked Sam out, too. I see."

"The discoveries at your shop were made on Company time with Company funds, Lutt, all while you were an employee of Hanson Industries."

Lutt suppressed a surge of anger. His mother was a wily bitch! Never mind what Father's will said, she was going to block him at every turn until she had her way!

"I understand, Mother," he said. "But Father's will says the *Enquirer* and Spiral News Service are mine. Are you contesting that?"

"Oh, no! But this odd spaceship is something else, is it not?"

"It works on the same principle as the communicators," Lutt said.

"What's this about a spaceship?" Woon asked.

"Who's that with you?" Phoenicia asked.

Lutt clicked the telekey and saw his mother's face on the desk screen. She, at the same time, saw the occupants of Lutt's office.

"Oh, it's you, Senator," Phoenicia said. "Yes, your meeting with Lutt over his campaign."

"Good afternoon, madame," Woon said. "So sorry you could not join us."

That unctuous tone, Ryll offered. *Is he wooing your mother?*

He could be. We'd better watch that.

"I hope you can make my son behave," Phoenicia said.

"And, madame, I hope we are not about to have a dramatic battle in court over your son's inheritance. That would be a rather foolish form of political suicide."

Phoenicia put a hand over her mouth.

Lutt looked at the senator. Did this mean the wily old politician had chosen to back him? A mixture of fear and political savvy could have dictated such a decision. Time to test it.

"I'm afraid I'd withdraw my candidacy if that happened," Lutt said.

"A wise decision," Woon said.

"I will not be blocked in my administration of Hanson Industries!" Phoenicia said.

"Minor matters can always be dealt with by compromise," the senator said. "May I offer my services as arbiter?"

"There's no reason for us to oppose each other," she said.

Lutt heard conciliation in her tone.

I do not understand your mother's motives, Ryll intruded.

She's ambivalent. Motherly pride wants me President. But she also sees me as a pawn in her economic schemes.

You Earthers are truly weird.

"I'm sure I can work out a satisfactory agreement for all concerned," Woon said.

"That's fine with me," Lutt said. "Mother?"

"What is it you really want, son?" she asked.

"I've always gone my own way. Father understood. It's time you understood. I need some free rein."

"I've already given you considerable free rein—a blank check for your political ambitions, my assurance you—"

"*Your* political ambitions, Mother."

"Our political ambitions?" she offered.

"If we keep our heads, all of us will profit greatly," Woon said.

"Exactly!" Phoenicia said.

"You and the senator should discuss this," Lutt said. "But your meetings had better be secret."

"Very well," Phoenicia sighed.

Lutt had heard that sigh before, a tiny victory sign.

She gave him a lilting "Goodbye!" that only confirmed his suspicion and she broke the connection.

When the screen went blank, Lutt turned a hard stare on Woon. Time to run his bluff. "Senator," Lutt said, holding a poker face, "at the first sign you're selling me down the river, I'll ruin you. I have all the ammo I need."

"Mr. Hanson, I'm your man just as I was your father's man. You're very much his son and I can live with that."

"Stay away from Morey. He's thin metal in the family's armor, not to be trusted. I know everything he does and there's nothing he can do to prevent that."

"No more than I can, I presume. That's some spy system you have, Mr. Hanson."

"The very best. Now, whatever you concede to Mother has to be empty. We run this campaign, you and I. Understood?"

"Understood. What bargaining chips do I have?"

"She wants me to be President. She also should fear what I might reveal about Hanson Industries operations. If she makes me go hunting for income, I know where to sell what I know."

Woon pursed his lips and blew out silently, then, "She wants you to marry this Spokane socialite, Eola VanDyke. How do you feel about that?"

Lutt leaned back. *Marry Eola?* He thought of Nishi off there half the globe away. Not one word from her. Another bitch! His father had been right. Never trust women!

"If that's the bargaining chip we need to bring her around, use it," he said.

"What about L.H.'s old offices in the MX complex?"

"They belong to me. No compromise. She'd remodel the place into something Father would never have entered."

"She seemed pretty upset about something you're doing there," Woon said. "I couldn't make out just what it was."

"I'm keeping her and my brother out of there."

Woon's lips vibrated with a slight humming sound. "And what if she cuts off the purse strings?"

"We have other resources, depend on it. The contributions and contributors might surprise you."

Woon heaved his bulk out of the chair. "I thought so." He looked down at Lutt. "You know, Mr. Hanson, you're a lot bigger than I remembered. You still growing?"

"My accident. I'm sure you read about it. I was immersed in a chemical that reset my growth hormones. Nothing to worry about. I'm in great physical shape."

"I saw your last report from the House of Delights," Woon said, and he smiled.

"I'm not the only one with information sources, eh?" Lutt asked. "I'd better make sure that one is plugged."

"That's why I told you, Mr. Hanson. And rest easy. Your growth is a good thing. In all the history of United States Presidential elections, the tallest man invariably wins."

There is reason to believe your mother may have changed your father's medication without his knowing. I don't know whether you would want to use this, but a case could be made that she hastened his end.

—Investigator's report,
eyes-only, for L.H., Jr.

Nishi, wearing a blue terrycloth robe, paced back and forth in the moon-shadowed darkness of the villa's living room, not knowing what had brought her to this wakeful vigil. She wore no watch, but she knew it must be past midnight. When she passed a window, she could see a brilliant path of silvery moonglow on the sea and shadows of potted palms along the balustrade—long black witch-shapes on the terrazzo of the porch.

Lorna Subiyama's snores were a distant rumble and Nishi could both hear and feel the surf rolling against the rocks below the villa. The floor trembled with an ancient heartbeat.

What do we do now that Lorna's articles have run their course? What do you want to do?

The question lay poised in her awareness and she wondered at its source. Her mind was playing tricks on her tonight, she thought.

What do I want to do?

That is question.

She put a knuckle into her mouth and chewed it.

Something stirred in the corner of the room.

One of the housekeeper's cats, Nishi thought.

Not cat. Wire thing hurt.

Nishi gasped and stopped pacing to stare at the corner where she had heard the sound. Abruptly, she strode to the doorway and flicked a light switch. Pale glowing from wall sconces lighted the room and she saw a furry yellow shape in the corner tangled in the cord from a floorlamp. She could see no head, tail or paws but shape and color suggested a cat curled into a protective ball.

Wire thing hurt.

There it was! A definite thought projected into her mind!

The creature began struggling against its restraints and a tuft of fur twisted in a pinched coil of knotted wire.

Hurt!

With instinctive sympathy, Nishi rushed to the corner and loosened the knot, carefully pulling back the wire and freeing the creature. She still saw no head, tail or paws.

"What are you?" she asked, stroking the silky fur.

Dreen friend.

Dreen? Ryll was Dreen. She recalled Ryll's notes falling from the air to her lap. *You're a gift from Ryll!*

Ryll, Ryll, Ryll. Ryll Dreen. Dreen friend.

Nishi sat on the floor and scooped the furry ball into her lap. It had a slightly musty odor, not unpleasant. A low rumble came from somewhere within it. She felt it breathe deeply but saw no head, mouth or feet. The thing felt soft and warm. It pulsated against her hands.

The musty odor triggered old memories. She sat caught in her past—her mother's face peering through bars of a crib, then leaning close to kiss her goodnight, tucking a bottle and favorite Donald Duck rubber car into the blankets. Nishi had not thought of the toy car for years. It had been light blue with Donald Duck in a matching blue sailor suit molded into the driver's seat and much too large for the car.

Whatever happened to that toy?

Not know.

The thing in her lap was talking to her, putting thoughts directly into her mind. She knew it, recognized the alien oddity of the situation, and still could not prevent the upwelling nostalgia that brought tears to her eyes.

I'm crying over a lost toy.

Nishi make many sads.

The thing in her lap was right. The tears were for many things gone from her life and never to return—friends, father and brothers lost in the war . . . her mother, dead less than a year following that awful day when a Legion captain saluted her and delivered "our sympathy for your tragic loss."

Nishi felt tears roll down her cheeks, dropping onto the furry creature in her lap. She used a corner of her robe to dry the thing's fur, noting thin black streaks in the yellow. It rolled in her hands and positioned the black streaks against her lap, appearing entirely yellow now.

The black streaks are your underside.

Downside upside not matter.

What shall I call you?

Nishi like yellow?

Oh, yes. You're my yellow thing.

Yellow Thing.

Yellow Thing, she thought. *Odd name for an odd creature.* She experienced a sudden surge of gratitude toward Ryll. *He must have known I was lonely. Oh, where are you, Ryll? Where has Lutt taken you?*

She looked down at the creature in her lap and dried her eyes. Foolish to sit here crying over what could not be changed.

Yellow Thing, she thought. *YT. I will call you Wytee.*

Cradling Wytee in her arms, Nishi returned to her bedroom where she placed her new pet on the bed while she prepared to remove her robe.

Man in window!

It was a sharply intrusive thought. She paused with her robe still on her shoulders and looked at the deep embrasure of her bedroom window. Captain O'Hara sat in the shadows of the window ledge, a cigarette in his mouth, a knowing smile on his face.

"Saw your light and thought you might be lonely," he said.

He swiveled on his buttocks and slid off the ledge into the bedroom. She saw he was wearing only a thin white robe.

Nishi spoke in her coldest voice: "Get out of here or I will scream. I'm a virgin and I intend to stay that way!"

He moved toward her, slowly and steadily. "No, I don't think you'll scream. It's time a real man tested your claim to virginity."

Not touch her!

Nishi felt the solid impact of Wytee's thought and O'Hara apparently also experienced it. He stopped short.

"Get out of here!" Nishi ordered.

You leave or hurt head bad! It was an ominous warning from Wytee.

O'Hara recoiled two steps. He glanced at the thing on the bed, then at Nishi. "How are you doing that?"

"Just leave quietly or it will go very bad for you," she said.

Want head hurt?

O'Hara squeezed his eyes tightly closed and pressed both palms against his temples.

"Stop that!" he moaned.

"Leave and don't come back unless I invite you," she said. She pointed to the bedroom doorway.

O'Hara opened his eyes and scurried past her out of the bedroom.

When the door closed behind him, Nishi sat down beside Wytee and stroked its yellow fur. "You're more than just a pet," she said.

Nishi friend. Bad man want lustful breeding Nishi. Nishi want lustful breeding Lutt.

I do, but I must not give him that power over me . . . not yet.

Her thoughts about Lutt became wistful. Would he marry that socialite? *He really needs me. He has no friends except me.*

It occurred to her that Lutt Hanson, Jr., was the most complex man she had ever met—a loner driven by compulsions. He didn't want friends. No time for them. It took energy to maintain friendships. Friends were trouble. Yet he really wanted her—wanted the intimate companionship, the love, the friendship. Could he ever bring himself to the necessary understanding of his own desires? And what influence could Ryll have on the man who shared his flesh?

Lutt was a man of two lives, not only because of Ryll, but also in the ambivalence of his own compulsions.

Sleepily, Nishi extinguished the lights and crawled under the blankets. Wytee squirmed close against her neck.

Nishi sleep. Wytee not let bad thing come.

It was a comforting thought. She fell asleep while stroking Wytee's silky pelt and awakened at dawn to feel the warm presence against her cheek, hearing the gentle rumble of its contentment. She stretched and yawned. It had been her most restful sleep since arriving at the villa.

"Thank you, Wytee."

Lady friend come.

A knock at the bedroom door was followed by Subiyama's low voice: "You awake, Nishi?"

"What is it, Lorna?"

Subiyama entered, a great mound of pink bathrobe with her hair wound into a red towel turban. "We've struck pay dirt, honey. Message through the Legion from my office. Phoenicia Hanson herself wants to see you."

"See me?"

"A confab, honey. Wanta bet she'll try to buy you off?"

Nishi sat up in bed and groped for her robe, slipping it over her shoulders.

"She tried that once and got the answer she deserved."

The bed sagged as Subiyama sat on the foot of it. "Sure, honey, but think of this as good copy. Lutt's mother tries to buy you off—as seen and reported by yours truly."

"I don't think she'll try to buy me off again. It's something different this time. And devious. You can count on it."

"One way to find out, honey. Shall I tell your Legion buddies to send her along?"

"Why not?" Nishi rolled out of bed and slipped her arms into the robe. "Where's Mrs. Ebey?"

"Makin' us some coffee." Subiyama looked at the furry yellow ball on Nishi's pillow. "A man's a lot more fun to sleep with than a cat, honey. And that Captain O'Hara sure has the hots for you."

"But I do not want him."

"You still think you can land Hanson, eh? Well, why not? A billionaire probably has more staying power than a damn Legion captain." She turned and went out the door. "See you later, honey. Think maybe I'll give Lew's staying power another test."

When she was gone, Wytee stirred, then: *Big lady want lustful breeding Dreen.*

"She's no Dreen, Wytee. She's a human just like me."

Big lady human want lustful breeding Dreen, Wytee insisted.

Nishi chuckled. "I think she's lustful for a human, too."

Big lady want lustful breed many humans. Big lady make lustful thinks bad man O'Hara.

"I'm sure you're right, Wytee. Lorna's what we call very oversexed."

Mrs. Ebey appeared in the doorway with a steaming cup of coffee. "Who're you talking to, Miss Nishi?"

"Talking to myself, Mrs. Ebey. Put the coffee on my nightstand."

"You want me to lay out your clothes?"

"I'll take care of it. You get your breakfast and I'll talk to you later about Phoenicia Hanson. I want you to tell me everything you know about her."

"Any special reason?"

"She's coming here to see me."

"Lorna's stories got under her skin! Take her for all you can, Miss Nishi. Millions!"

"We'll see, Mrs. Ebey. Run along now."

When she was gone, Wytee stirred on the bed. *Ebey lady make bad thinks Phoenicia. Ebey lady make many thinks money. Why Ebey lady make thinks money?*

Hearing someone in the hallway, Nishi composed her reply in a silent thought: *Mrs. Ebey is getting old and afraid. She has no one to care for her.*

Ebey lady think Phoenicia Hanson very bad person.

She probably is a very bad person.

Wytee not let bad persons hurt Nishi. Wytee friend Nishi.

Nishi scooped up the furry yellow ball and hugged it. *I know you're my friend. Are you hungry, Wytee? What do you eat?*

Wytee eat little air things. Take deep breath eat. Not worry. Wytee never hungry.

The engagement of Ms. Eola VanDyke to Lutt Hanson, Jr., was announced in Spokane today by her parents, Mr. and Mrs. Percival S. VanDyke. No wedding date has been set, but informed sources said the nuptials may occur in the White House, depending on the outcome of Mr. Hanson's bid for the Presidency.

—From the *Spokane Breeze*

Lutt, his shirt open to the navel, sat facing the closed door of his father's office in the MX complex. Excessive activity brought on by Phoenicia's orders made it hot in the complex this evening, almost as hot as at the *Enquirer*. Following his editorial policy on conservation, the newspaper's air conditioning had been shut off. Uncomfortable in his *Enquirer* office, sweat coursing down his chest and under his belt, Lutt had fled to the complex, using the argument that he and Woon could meet secretly here.

Woon waxed lyric about the hothouse effect in the *Enquirer* and had ordered pictures showing Lutt at work under those steamy conditions.

"Poll results show sixty-one percent in favor of your 'consistent agreement with the needs of the people,' " Woon said.

Screw the people, Lutt thought.

But the campaign was going well. Even Morey agreed. Whether on Phoenicia's orders or to mend his own fences, Morey no longer made snide remarks about "my brother, the President."

Just let me get control of the Justice Department, Morey. I'll show you how justice is administered under my orders!

The call Lutt cherished had come from Major Captain. She had reached him at the *Enquirer* the day his candidacy became public and, seeing Lutt as a possible commander in chief, she had been brisk and businesslike.

"In light of your new status, Mr. Hanson, I would like to offer, on my general's behalf, any facilities you may need from the Zone Patrol Regional Command. Of course, we will coordinate with the Secret Service for your protection and, should you require any further use of our facilities, please feel free to call us."

Lutt thought he had used great restraint not asking her if she wanted to bring him in for interrogation. She must also have nurtured thoughts about their previous meetings, because she said, "If I have caused any offense in the past, please blame zealous obedience to my oath of allegiance."

"Should I win this election, Major Captain, you may be sure the ZP will be the first to benefit."

He had thought that reply quite statesmanlike and Woon had praised it.

"You're beginning to sound like a President, by God! Now let's whip a few asses over there and get you a proper official entourage."

The immediate result was three ZP squads—one in the *Enquirer*, one at the family compound and one mobile to accompany him on campaign trips. Hanson Guards and his mother objected but Lutt had been all sweetness in response.

"It's their duty to guard me. You can't be suggesting I ask these brave people to forsake their duty."

Lutt found it amusing to see guards and ZP tripping over one another, each trying to be first and each spying on him. The ZP, Lutt supposed, reported to Woon. Guards reported to Mother.

And I report only to Father's Listening Post.

Lutt looked around him at the office, all of it much as he had found it the night of his father's death. He thought he had uncovered most of the traps but the Listening Post upstairs still daunted him. There was a pattern to the traps, Lutt thought, but he could not put it into words. Still, there was satisfaction in the fact neither Morey nor his mother dared join him here, even though Hanson

Guards waited outside right now with his mobile ZP squad. The guards flatly refused to enter L.H.'s premises.

I believe I'm beginning to think like the old man. And that may be just the fatal mistake he expected.

The main computers still pulsed and reported from the tentacles of Hanson Industries, even though Phoenicia and Morey had tried to cut this office's connections to The Company. But Lutt dared not put his own orders on line. When his mother complained to Woon, the senator played a delaying game, asking for more time.

From the first, Lutt had used this office as a retreat, leaving the impression with Morey and Woon that he was following their every move from here, just as his father had. They would test him, though. And the sham could be exposed.

Damn! Lutt thought as he looked up at the entrance to the escalator and the Listening Post.

Ryll, silent observer to most of Lutt's recent activities, saw the direction of his fleshmate's thoughts and protested.

No, Lutt! It's too dangerous!

If I can't use the Listening Post, I'm done for. I'll be another of Phoenicia's puppets . . . or even worse, Woon's puppet.

Lutt lifted himself from the chair and felt it shift beneath him. Instinctively, he dove to the floor. A barrage of darts hissed across him, spraying the area he had just vacated. He watched them slam into an armor glass window and shatter. Broken pieces of darts fell to the floor. A servobot sped from a nearby wall slot and scooped up the pieces.

Would it have scooped up the pieces of me, too?

Your father was a wild animal! Ryll protested. *Stay out of his Listening Post.*

Not on your life, Ryll baby. It's him or me now. No dead man's going to defeat me!

Taking his father's control cane, Lutt crossed the narrow lane to the escalator and set it running. Up the steps with their grisly warning he went, attention on the walls around him, the landing, the narrow passage to the Post itself.

The old man could have set other traps like that chair, that didn't go off the first time.

Lutt, please go back, Ryll pleaded.

Just as dangerous to go back as to go ahead. May be even more dangerous to go back without solving this place. Stop distracting me. That itself could kill us.

Lutt paused outside the Listening Post and examined the door jamb. No apparent traps in it, but there had been nothing to reveal the chair's secret, either.

He touched a key on the cane and stepped aside, but the door opened without incident. Slowly, leaning on the cane the way his father had, Lutt crossed the threshold.

Here it was, the innermost key to his father's soul. And the dome holding the "Final Words" for Morey remained intact, the folder visible inside.

Lutt stared at the wall modules, their oddly configured graphics and LEDs all around him. He recalled his father working on a module during that last visit here. Yes, there was the unit. Lutt remembered counting up from the floor and out from the nearest corner to mark the thing's placement.

Why did I do that?

Had it been something about his father's actions that day? Was there a clue in what his father had done? *Maybe he was trying to show me something, testing me to see if I would notice.*

Lutt looked at the transparent dome where his "Final Words" had reposed. The dome lay tipped back on its hinges and, for the first time, Lutt noted an almost microscopic red wire under the seal. He leaned close and inspected it, following it around and down the supporting stand. Into a grout line of the tiled floor it went, across the floor, up the modular wall and . . . yes, into the unit his father had removed and replaced.

Was the red wire what it seemed to be?

Lutt pondered this.

The Listening Post is now yours, all yours and yours alone.

His father's "Final Words."

No, Lutt! Ryll pleaded as he read the thought forming in Lutt's mind. *Your father was devious and treacherous!*

He was also dying and he knew it.

You can't trust him! It's too much of a gamble.

Lutt did not reply. He put a hand on the module his father had replaced. With one swift pull, he removed the unit from the wall and looked at it. Reversible! He rotated the module and plugged it back into the wall.

"Up here, Lutt."

His father's voice! Lutt looked up. The ceiling had become a screen and there was his father seated at the main computers in the outer office.

"Pretty good recording, eh?" the seated figure asked. "Answer if you want but I'm not really here for one of our old conversations. Those were pretty boring, anyway."

The figure looked directly down at him from the screen, the prosthetic eyes like antennae protruding from his head.

"That took guts to trust me, but I presume you saw the red wire and recognized it as one of my simple go-no-go breaker links. You still couldn't be certain, though." Laughter shook the figure in the screen.

"You old bastard!" Lutt said. "You're dead and still playing your games with me!"

"No sense cussing me out," the recorded figure said. "Oh, I know you pretty well, Son. I've studied you a long time. You won't let Morey or your mother into these offices but they've tried to disconnect my control and communications systems. Typical."

Again, laughter shook the figure in the screen.

"What game are you playing this time?" Lutt muttered.

"The only one who can break these connections is probably your Uncle Dudley," L.H. said. "I don't think he'd do that, but you shouldn't count on it. Dud always was unpredictable."

A fit of coughing interrupted the recital. When it passed, the old man pointed down at Lutt. "This Post is yours, Son, but it's not going to do you a damn bit of good 'less you use it the way it oughta be used. You gotta be ruthless!"

"Still testing me," Lutt whispered.

"The Listening Post's controls are beneath where I put my Final Words for you," L.H. said. "Once you got my note, all the little traps except the one under my final note to Morey were disarmed. He's the only one can get his words but you'll never let him do that. You'll worry about what I said to him, though. And you'll cuss me every time you think about it. That's a sharp spine I've stuck in your side so's you'll never forget my advice. Be as ruthless as I was, Son. That's the way to win."

Again, coughing interrupted the old voice. L.H. spoke weakly when he resumed but Lutt did not trust the appearance.

"I think your mother's done something to my medicine. No matter. I could not've lasted much longer, anyway. But she always was impatient. That's why I married her. Never liked her fancy ways but she's tough. I thought she'd give me tough children."

A bony old hand came up and waved at Lutt. "Bye, bye, Lutt. I'm gone for good now. Think you can live up to my expectations?"

The ceiling screen went blank.

Lutt touched the stand where his note had been. Cold. He pressed the flat surface. Nothing. The red wire? He slipped a fingernail under it and pulled. The stand opened like a shell and there lay a familiar array of CRT screen and keyboard, another screen and vidcom under them. Lutt's fingers danced over the search circuit keys, spelling out Morey's name, voice only.

Morey's faceless voice came from the speaker under the CRT: "I tell you, Gil, I think he's bluffing. I don't think he can spy on us at all."

"You may be right, but what if you're wrong?" *Woon.*

A recording or something happening right now?

Lutt lifted the vidcom handset and keyed Morey's name. Lights blinked on the walls as the Listening Post circuits searched out his brother's location. A buzzing sounded.

"Wonder who that is?" Morey asked. There was a click. "I thought I said we were not to be interrupted!"

"I'll interrupt you any time I want," Lutt said.

There was a gasp from the speaker. "Where are you? I'm getting no picture."

"This is the picture I want you to get, Morey," Lutt said, "I'm not bluffing. Woon! Get your ass in gear and stay away from my brother or I'll blow you out of the water! Got that?"

"Yes, sir, Mr. Hanson."

Lutt pitched his voice in a low, soothing tone. "Morey, would you see to it that Mother causes me as little trouble as possible? That way, you can continue enjoying your life. Oh! Just in case you get violent, everything I know about you will become public if I'm not around to prevent it. Everything!"

Lutt broke the connection and started to replace the handset but paused at another thought. Was it possible? He keyed Phoenicia's name. Nothing happened. What had his father called her in private? A pet name was out of character. He might have used a code name. L.H. had thought of her as tough. Lutt keyed "Tough." Still nothing. Fancy? No response to that, either. Lutt sat back and wracked his memory. "Never trust women," was too long. *Woman?* Lutt tried it and heard his mother's voice.

"Lutt will come around when I squeeze him hard enough."

A recording?

Did he dare reveal he could spy on her? Who was she talking to and where were they? At home?

He keyed the main-house number on the handset and there was his mother's study visible on the screen with Phoenicia seated behind her ornate antique desk. Her companion was not visible.

"Oh, there you are, Mother," he said. "Who's with you?"

"How nice of you to call, Lutt," Phoenicia said. "Are you calling from a safe vidcom?"

"Nobody taps Father's offices."

"So that's where you are. I must discuss that with you. It seems to me that Morey—"

"Morey stays out of my campaign and out of these offices!"

"I don't like that tone, Lutt."

"Morey's been meeting with Gil and I don't have any idea who knows it." He touched the query key on the handset and the screen spelled out a name and title of Phoenicia's companion: "Barbara Morrison, Senator Woon's administrative assistant."

"I'm calling you, Mother, because I'm told you are meeting Barbara Morrison, Gil's administrative assistant. Is that who's with you?"

Phoenicia's tone dripped ice. "Why are you interested in my meeting Barbara?"

"Our connection with Woon must be kept secret until we're ready to announce it!"

"I'm quite capable of conducting clandestine meetings!"

"But I learned about it!"

"How?" Her tone was imperative.

"I will not tell you."

"You're as bad as your father!"

"I could be worse. What are you and Barbara discussing?"

"She says your campaign is going very well. Are you really refusing to debate your opponents?"

"I am."

"Is that wise?"

"There won't be any need for debate when we spring Deni-Ra."

"But debates would give you such a splendid opportunity to show your statesmanlike character."

"Who says?"

"I will not be questioned like this!"

"I mean to win this election, Mother. You're meeting with Ms. Morrison; that could cause problems."

Phoenicia spoke coldly. "For your information, we have been discussing that very question."

"That's interesting. What have you decided?"

"The senator must announce his support of your candidacy soon. He will bring many AIP supporters with him. The American Independence party will object, of course, but the strategy of our campaign must take into account the votes Senator Woon controls."

"Ms. Morrison?"

The screen blurred, then showed both women in profile. *That's a fancy touch,* Lutt thought. Ms. Morrison was a brunette with pinched face and half-glasses that added to her look of sexless office functionary.

She faced the lens. "Yes?"

"One moment," Lutt said. He keyed her name on the spy circuits and asked for a summary. Across the upper screen paraded a brief account—birthplace, schooling, advancements, then: "AIP agent in office of Senator Gilperton Woon. Reports regularly to AIP Council."

He looked up into her eyes. "It has come to my attention, Ms. Morrison, that you are an AIP spy in Gil's office."

She gasped.

"Lutt, what are you talking about?" Phoenicia demanded.

"Be patient, Mother."

Lutt keyed the spy circuits for "damaging information," and read the new data with growing elation.

"Your little house in Virginia and what you do there are all known to me, Ms. Morrison," Lutt said. "I also know about your deal with the French ambassador. It's dangerous to play both sides of the street, didn't you know that?"

She had a palm on each cheek and was glaring at Lutt with a stricken expression.

"Now, here's what you'll do, Ms. Morrison," Lutt said. "You will tell the AIP Council Gil has had a change of heart. He intends to betray me. You can do that, can't you?"

She nodded without taking her hands from her cheeks.

"You will say the stories about an alien captive have proved untrue. There is no such captive. Got that?"

Again, she nodded.

"And you will report to me daily for instructions on what to tell the AIP Council and the French ambassador. Understood?"

Her voice was barely a whisper. "Yes."

"Now, leave my mother's house and make sure you're not seen."

"Just a minute!" Phoenicia objected.

Barbara Morrison wavered.

"Get out!" Lutt ordered.

The administrative assistant fled.

Lutt looked at his mother. "Your political naivete has almost ruined my campaign, Mother. She was going to set me up at a debate, make me look ridiculous."

"Lutt . . . I swear I didn't know."

"Of course you didn't know! So from now on you make no political decisions at all without consulting me!"

She bridled. "I do have some intelligence, Lutt. And I am still your mother."

"But you're not my campaign director."

"Yes, Lutt."

Lutt recalled hearing her use that precise tone with his father. It did not fool him.

"You'll regret it if you cross me," Lutt said.

"Are you threatening me?"

"I see I've made myself clear."

"But I'm your mother!"

"So act like one!"

"I can't believe I'm hearing this."

"There's another thing, Mother. I want you to increase the budget for Sam Kand at my shop."

Her back stiffened. "That's a financial matter. Morey and I have decided—"

"Undecide, Mother. Your fancy friends would really enjoy hearing about how you almost messed up my political future."

"You'd destroy your campaign just to hurt me?"

"Don't test it, Mother. I don't want these petty things distracting me when it comes time to revitalize the GOP."

He broke the connection and looked up at the ceiling.

"Was that ruthless enough for you, Father?"

Mme. Hanson will be taken to the island from Marseilles in a sealed helicopter, unable to see out. Be certain she is not armed. She will be guarded at all times en route. If the meetings with Mademoiselle D'Amato are private, all conversations between the two must be recorded secretly.

—Special Order OE'B Number 30,
French Foreign Legion

Nishi remained at the window for several minutes after the messenger's departure. Lunch sat heavily on her stomach.

So Phoenicia was arriving within the hour.

Was it wrong to say Lorna could not be at my meeting with Phoenicia?

A sound behind her brought her around. Servobots were cleaning, dusting and arranging the reception room. One of the 'bots, Wytee informed her, was a spy device.

Once more, she faced the sea. A sharp wind rippled the waters. It was a cold late fall day. She had not expected it to be chilly on the Mediterranean. Nishi shivered.

Or is it just apprehension about this meeting?

Wytee, on a settee nearby, rippled its yellow fur. *Nishi not worry. Wytee help.*

I know you'll help, Wytee. I just can't understand why Phoenicia would come in person.

Soon learn.

She looked fondly at her pet. *No . . . much more than a pet.* Since Wytee's arrival, life had become smoother and more interesting. The creature reported not only the thoughts of her personal associates, but also those of anyone who came within range. What would Phoenicia Hanson's thoughts reveal?

The entire Hanson family is unpredictable, she decided. *Why didn't Lutt come? Is he angry because of Lorna's stories? But he hasn't even tried to send word and it's been three months! Of course, there's his political campaign. But all those stories about his plans to marry Eola VanDyke. Surely he won't go through with it.*

Nishi not worry!

She felt a wash of soothing sympathy from Wytee and tried to relax.

Lutt, my man of two worlds—Dreen and human, private and political. Why is he seeking such exalted office?

Nishi learn soon, Wytee offered.

And what is happening to poor Ryll?

Ryll Dreen. Dreen friend, Wytee responded.

From her window she could see two of the Legion's gun batteries—turreted gray mounds with long barrels protruding—all framed against a background of evergreens.

Weapons everywhere. Even Lorna had brought a weapon, an antique she called "my equalizer." The Legion thought it a joke.

Nishi sighed. The ninety-day wonder of Lorna's articles had passed and the publishers clamored for new revelations. They even wanted a book. Lorna spoke of very large offers.

"They'll pay millions, honey!"

Phoenicia comes because she fears a book's revelations. What will she do if I say Lutt breaches the promise to me?

That had been Lorna's idea, one eagerly taken up by Mrs. Ebey. Trust Mrs. Ebey to focus on the money.

Well, why not? What else do I have? And my life is my own concern! Lutt certainly appears to have no worries about me!

Nishi fussbudget, Wytee quipped.

Wytee had dredged the term from someone's mind and used it now whenever she needed joking out of her apprehensions.

Nishi smiled, then frowned. The mystery of Wytee did not concern her deeply but she occasionally wondered if the creature might be having a secret influence on her. There were oddities. Everyone thought Wytee was a cat. Even O'Hara had come to that idea and apologized to her "for unseemly behavior," blaming "too much of the drink." But no one investigated her pet. Did Wytee prevent curiosity?

Wytee Nishi friend, Wytee offered.

She felt a soothing wash of the creature's concern and shook her head. Worries did her no good. Her gaze went to the horizon. Was that faraway dot the chopper bringing Phoenicia Hanson? The dot grew larger with alarming rapidity and resolved into a Legion copter. She heard the engine and rotors. *Is it the one?* Sometimes, other choppers came, some with officials to tell her about conditions on Venus and urge actions to gain Lutt's communicators.

Because of Wytee, she knew it was not just communicators the Legion desired.

They sought bigger game. The Legion wanted Lutt's Spiral technology with its space-travel advantages.

But three months now and she was losing patience with both Legion and Lutt. And where was Raj Dood's promised help?

I should never have pledged my honor not to escape!

The Legion's regional prefect was almost reason enough to defy her code of honor. An oily fat man with a black toupee, he spoke only in unctuous tones. "We must not arouse the curiosity of the enemy. You are a woman wronged and have a natural interest in this man Hanson."

The prefect's lack of candor angered her. "Do the Chinese not see reports of Monsieur Hanson's news service?" she asked.

"Naturally! But they show no dangerous curiosity."

And the prefect said not one word about the wires she had sent to Lutt, all of them unanswered! What more should she do? Go crawling to Lutt on her knees? Not even for the Legion!

She wanted no more of the prefect's platitudes. "The Yankees always try to get the most out of us," he said. "Squeeze these Hansons, little one. Our agents say the stories of Madame Subiyama bring the perspiration to his brow."

So the Legion used blackmail instead of money! Where was the honor in that? It was inexcusable, even if things were bad in Paris and very bad on Venus. And was it honorable for them to play this game while their "little one" rotted in a stupid villa?

I have done enough, she thought. *I no longer am content to be a prisoner, even of the Legion.*

The arriving helicopter swung wide over the villa and came down on the small field north of her where, according to local stories, the Roman Emperor Trajan once had practiced his horsemanship.

It gave her an odd link with history, Nishi thought. She and Lorna used the place for target practice with the antique pistol that had belonged to Subiyama's grandfather. Although the Legion thought the ancient gun amusing and not very dangerous, they made Subiyama take it out only under supervision.

Nishi watched a woman in a well-fitted gray suit emerge from the chopper and dodge under the rotors. The woman glanced at the villa and Nishi recognized Phoenicia Hanson. An officer accompanying her held her arm and brought her to a stop outside the danger zone. They conversed there, the words unintelligible in the chopper's noise. The officer gesticulated and said something vehement but Phoenicia shook her head.

Nishi! It was Wytee with something urgent.

What is it, Wytee?

Phoenicia lady brings poison thing to kill you!

Nishi shot a glance at Wytee, then out the window where Phoenicia still argued with the Legion officer.

Are you sure?

Wytee sure.

But how could she do it and not be caught?

Poison take three days. Make no noise. You not feel poison thing. Guard men not find.

Damn her!

Abruptly, Nishi dashed out of the room, up the stairs and into Lorna's quarters. Subiyama, in a billowing magenta housecoat, sat reading a book on her bed. Nishi was not fooled by this apparent agreement with her orders to stay away from Phoenicia. Subiyama intended to sneak downstairs and spy on the meeting the minute Nishi was involved in the reception room.

"You changed your mind," Subiyama said. "You want me there when the Hanson dame talks to you."

"No. Where is your weapon?"

"My weap— You mean Grampaw's hawgleg?"

"The gun we shoot!"

"Why'n hell you want that thing? You gonna have a shootout with Old Lady Hanson?"

Nishi held out a hand. "Give me the revolver, please."

"Okay, honey. But this better be good copy." Subiyama fished under her mattress and brought out the antique pistol, a stainless steel .357 magnum with fitted grips.

Nishi grabbed it from her.

"Now you be careful with that thing!" Subiyama warned. "Remember it has a hair trigger."

The revolver felt heavy and deadly in Nishi's hand and she almost rejected it. *But I must protect myself!* "It is ready for shooting?" she asked.

"It's fully loaded. Now tell me what's going on!"

"Come down. You may listen outside the door."

Subiyama picked up a small recording camera and heaved her bulk out of the bed. "I knew you'd change your mind!"

Without pausing to see if Subiyama followed, Nishi dashed out of the room and down the stairs. In the reception room, she pulled a small table from against the wall, placed a chair behind it and seated herself with a revolver hidden in her lap. The door from the porch stood open in front of her and she could hear footsteps growing louder there. Wytee remained a curled-up ball of yellow on the nearby settee.

Poison thing in purse handle, Wytee informed her. *Nishi want Wytee hurt bad lady head?*

Don't frighten her off! We must learn what's in her mind.

Wytee tell Nishi.

Phoenicia, clutching a purse to match her gray suit, entered the open door and paused for her eyes to adjust to the room's shadows. An older officer Nishi had seen several times with the prefect came in beside Phoenicia and also stopped. He squinted at Nishi.

"Oh, there you are, mademoiselle."

"Leave us," Nishi ordered.

"I will be nearby if you call, mademoiselle," he said and bowed before leaving.

"The nerve of those people!" Phoenicia said. "They made me come alone! Wouldn't even let me bring my secretary." She moved into the room, turning the purse slightly until the handle was almost aligned with Nishi.

Warning! Wytee said. *Bad lady waits man be away.*

Nishi cocked the revolver and brought it up, pointing it at Phoenicia. "If you turn that device any more in my direction, I will kill you," she said.

Phoenicia froze. They stared at each other, weighing the situation, Nishi alert for movement of the purse, Phoenicia seeking anything she might turn to advantage. Nishi noted the hardness in Phoenicia's pale blue eyes, the set and practiced strength of the woman's face. Nishi's lips felt dry but she refused to moisten them lest that reveal her fear.

Phoenicia did not try to deny her intentions. "How did you know?" she asked.

"I have my sources," Nishi said. "Drop the purse."

Phoenicia opened her hands and the purse clattered to the floor. The impact fired the dart mechanism. There was not even a hiss, but a faint "click" sounded as a projectile hit a wooden "Weeping Virgin" statue beside the door to the library.

"Now what?" Phoenicia asked.

"I am thinking," Nishi said. "You know, do you not, the Legion still employs the guillotine for offenses against the state?"

Phoenicia paled. "You can't be serious!"

"I think my Lutt would be well rid of you," Nishi said.

"Don't you realize who I am?" Phoenicia demanded, but she rubbed her neck.

Bad lady think cut off head, Wytee offered.

Why did she think she had to kill me?

Wytee transmitted a flood of information that almost made Nishi dizzy.

Lutt son want lustful breeding Nishi. Lutt son want . . . want . . . Bad lady want Lutt son make lustful breeding Eola lady . . . want Lutt son President. What means President? Oh! Subiyama make bad story Lutt son. Maybe make Lutt son not President.

Was that enough for her to want me dead?

Bad lady want hurt Lutt son. Want Lutt son afraid.

Phoenicia shifted her weight to her left foot and Nishi, fearing there might be another weapon, raised the revolver slightly.

"Make no sudden movements," Nishi said. "This weapon has

the triggered hair." Nishi chewed her lower lip, knowing she had said it incorrectly. It always happened when she went beyond her nervous tolerances.

No more poison things, Wytee said.

"There must be something you want enough that we can bargain," Phoenicia said.

"Your son?"

"You surprise me, Miss D'Amato."

"You do not surprise me, Phoenicia."

Phoenicia's lips went thin at the familiarity but she said nothing.

Bad lady worry Lutt son too much drunk, Wytee said. *Bad lady blame Nishi.*

"Do you think it's my fault Lutt has been drinking so much lately?" Nishi asked.

"You're part of it. There's also the recent death of his father."

"And I'm interfering with your plans."

"My son must learn mature behavior," Phoenicia said. "He must follow the path I have laid out for him."

"And marry this Eola VanDyke?"

"He must marry within his social class. I'm sure you can understand that. You French are perfectly aware of social necessities."

Bad lady think Nishi want much money, Wytee offered.

"You still think you can buy me off," Nishi said.

"Everyone has a price," Phoenicia said.

"It would've been so much cheaper to kill me, is that not so?" Nishi asked.

"I'm a businesswoman, Miss D'Amato."

"And you think in centimes and francs. And I am a whore who can be paid for her troubles. You could return to Lutt and tell him you bought me off."

"For his own good!"

"A mother-dominated, shattered little boy unable to live his own life! I don't think I want such a man."

"Then what do you want?"

"I want the secret of Lutt's Spiral communications system and one of his spaceships fully operational."

"You want what?"

"You heard correctly. In a few minutes, I will summon my Legion protectors. They would come anyway because I'm sure they listen to all conversations in this villa. They will study your purse and the mechanism in it."

"You think they'll really bring a charge against *me?*" Phoenicia asked, but there was little force in her voice.

"They will hold you for an offense against the state. Your son will be told the price of your life. Do you think he will pay?"

Phoenicia rubbed her neck and spoke in a weak voice. "Don't be melodramatic, young woman."

Bad lady think Lutt son not save her, Wytee said.

"You doubt your son," Nishi said. "He may not come to your rescue as the Legion came for me?"

"They won't dare hold the mother of the next President!"

"But if I make it impossible for him to be elected?" Nishi asked. "As the mother of a loser, how would you then be different from any other criminal assassin?"

Phoenicia opened her mouth and closed it without a sound.

Bad lady think many hurts Nishi, Wytee offered. *Nishi not safe. Bad lady do many thinks Lutt son. You want bad lady thinks?*

Tell me, Nishi ordered.

Obviously, conversation had brought an outpouring of Phoenicia's thoughts about Lutt. Wytee, with limited vocabulary, was almost at a loss conveying them to Nishi.

Bad lady make hates dead father. Now make hates Lutt son. He make hurts her. Maybe he cause head cut off. Lutt son tell bad lady she not do politics. He make lustful breeding many womans. He not tell truths. Lutt son make hurts Morey brother. Lutt son bad man.

Enough! Nishi ordered.

She took a deep, shuddering breath. She had suspected the extent of evil Lutt had absorbed from his awful family but there was no doubting it in the face of Wytee's revelations. "I know Lutt," she said. "His threats are to be believed."

A red flush spread from Phoenicia's neck to her face.

Nishi pointed the revolver to the right and touched the trigger. The roar of the shot filled the room and the bullet smashed into the stucco wall, dropping plaster onto the tiles.

The officer who had brought Phoenicia was in the room before

Nishi could count two. He was followed immediately by a squad of her regular guards under Captain O'Hara.

Phoenicia cowered with both hands over her mouth.

Nishi gestured with the revolver. "There's the purse with the device she intended to kill me. The poison dart went into the statue of the Virgin over there. I wish to see the regional prefect."

"As soon as he can be brought, mademoiselle," O'Hara said. He took a firm grip on Phoenicia's right arm. "You were very astute, Mademoiselle D'Amato, to take advantage of the situation. I'm sure we will get everything we require now."

"I'm *not* sure of it," Nishi said. "Lutt may let you kill her if you don't handle this correctly."

Subiyama lumbered up beside Nishi holding the tiny camera. She gave a low whistle. "Got it all, honey. You thinking what I'm thinking?"

"Lutt will never lose if he can prevent it," Nishi said. "We must make no mistakes about what he will do to win."

And she wondered how much pressure she could put on him. Reveal that a Dreen shared his body? No. That would put Ryll in jeopardy. She knew she could not do that. Especially since the Raj Dood had charged her with protecting the Dreen. But Lutt need not know her reservations.

Ryll Dreen, Wytee offered. *Help Dreen.*

"If you have the queen bee you have him," Subiyama said.

Nishi sighed. So even Subiyama did not understand Lutt.

"His mother a common assassin?" Subiyama crowed. "Oh, no. He can't let that come out. It would kill his election."

"He must be made to see the full picture," Nishi said. "Where's Mrs. Ebey? I wish her to carry an ultimatum to my former fiancé."

"You're giving up on him?" Subiyama asked.

"I do not wish to ally myself with such a family," Nishi said. "It is unfortunate because I would have made a perfect wife for the poor man."

It is with extreme regret that I sever my long relationship with the American Independence Party. At the same time, I consider myself fortunate and I must say I am proud to declare my support for Lutt Hanson, Jr., and the platform of the Grand Old Party. Recent developments have left me no choice. The AIP, once the strong guardian of human rights, has become a callous tool of the rich. We are fortunate that the GOP is here to pick up the sacred torch.

—Gilperton Woon,
formal announcement

I won't let you threaten Dreenor, Ryll insisted. *If your warlike stance were only a political trick, I'd tolerate it, but when you suggest mounting an attack on my sacred homeland . . .*

Drop it, you Dreen idiot! I'll fight the French or the Dreens. I'll do any damn thing I want and you can't stop me.

Lutt stood near the windows of his father's old offices in the MX complex, a wet wad of basil in his left hand. He hated the idea of chewing and swallowing the basil and had been nerving himself for it all morning. The herb always made him feel almost drunk. But the just-concluded session with the French ambassador tipped the scales toward basil.

This is my lunch, Ryll baby, he gloated, hefting the herb.

Ryll contemplated the bazeel with loathing and longing. How pleasant to drift in a bazeel haze, no worries, no arguments with his fleshmate. But Lutt tolerated the dreadful drug, even though he became belligerent and his mind lost its sharp edge. He stumbled a great deal, too. But there could be no doubt who ruled their body when it was saturated with bazeel.

You need me alert and able to advise you, Ryll argued as Lutt lifted the bazeel toward their mouth.

Advise me about what, Ryll baby?

Lutt bit off a mouthful of the herb and swallowed.

You make many mistakes, Ryll pleaded.

Like what?

The ZP plays its own game when it keeps your secret about Deni-Ra. It was an error allowing your brother to arrange this. And your decision to abandon your mother is wrong!

Mother made her own bed! And Morey—I wanta scare the shit outa him! Already, there was a slight blurring of Lutt's mind but elation drove him. *You know what'll scare him most? The idea of me as President!*

But the ZP and Deni-Ra are dangerous, I tell you! Ryll felt his mind blurring faster than Lutt's.

Morey can't plot anything with anybody 'thout me knowing. My Listening Post catches everything. Besides, Deni-Ra's guards will tell me what they talk about.

Woon's coming and he'll think you're drunk!

So what?

Desperate, Ryll tried once more what no other Dreen had ever done: to idmage-block the bazeel. As usual, he failed.

Lutt, sensing the attempt and Ryll's fading mental strength, began to laugh.

The laughter enraged Ryll. He felt himself withdrawing into bazeel ecstasy. Through a drug-induced mist, he saw Woon enter the office and come up the stairs to Lutt's level.

My level!

It was a useless thought. In a bazeel hallucination, the senator appeared to expand like a balloon and contract into a miniature figure.

Ryll thought this funny and tried to share the joke. Lutt ignored the intrusion and took a seat near the windows where he concentrated on the visitor.

Their conversation came to Ryll filtered with bazeel distortions—sometimes low, then echoing, now loud, remote, near, clear, fuzzed . . . but Ryll was unable to block it out and retreat into private thoughts.

"The AIP is offering that whore, Toloma, big bucks to speak out against you. Is it true you had a fight with her?"

Woon. First loud and then whispering.

"I got drunk and had a crying jag. The bitch had the nerve to say I was supposed to be balling, not bawling."

That was Lutt. Ryll wished he could giggle.

"What?" *Woon again.*

Lutt spelled it for the senator, who seemed to shout:

"Toloma says you were crying about someone named Ni-Ni. The word in the back alleys is you told her you didn't take advice from a whore."

"So what if I did? Where does she get off telling me I'd been coming to the wrong place all these years if I was looking for a prom date?"

"You have to be more careful, Lutt. It's going to cost us plenty buying her off. Are you drunk right now?"

"Hell, no!"

"You're head's shaking kind of strangely, fella."

"I'm not your fella, Woon! I'm your candidate for President!"

"Dammit, you've been drinking and it's barely noon."

"What I drink and when is none of your business!"

"Just as long as you don't appear in public this way."

Lutt leaned forward belligerently. "Are you trying to tell me what to do?"

"I am your campaign manager, Lutt."

"You're my figurehead, Woon. That's what you are."

A surge of rage distorted the senator's fat cheeks and vanished immediately. He smiled.

"I'll try to remember that . . . Mr. Hanson."

"Well, what'd you wanta see me about?"

"That guru on Venus, the Raj Dood, called me out of the blue this morning. He wanted to talk about some agreement you're supposed to be making with the French Foreign Legion. What the hell are you doing with the Legion?"

"Yeah, Uncle Dudley did say something about carrying on with the negotiations. Tell 'im to stuff it."

"Uncle Dudley? You mean the Raj Dood is—"

"—my mother's brother."

"Jesus H. Willy! If that ever gets out! Can you keep a lid on him? Does he want money for . . ."

"Uncle Dood doesn't seem to care about money. I think he and old Osceola are a nesting pair."

"The Spirit Glass lady? That Osceola?"

"None other."

Woon found a chair and sank into it. Lutt was amused that Woon chose a chair L.H. once had booby-trapped to goose whoever sat in it. *Shoulda left it the way Father had it.*

"Do you have any other little surprises for me?" Woon asked.

"Yeah! It may be all over the media soon anyway. The French ambassador's been here. He says my dear old mama tried to assassinate Nishi D'Amato. The ambassador called Nishi the Legion's mascot and said this is a crime against the state."

Lutt drew a finger across his throat.

"Oh, my God!" Woon gasped.

"There's a bright side," Lutt said. "We won't have Mama to kick around anymore."

"You can joke about it?"

"Why not? Think of the mileage we'll get outa this. We deny the charges. My mother would never do such a thing! They chop her and we go into mourning. The sympathy vote would give me a landslide victory."

"Your own mother? You're not serious!"

"Is there anything wrong with my analysis?"

"I don't give a damn about your fucking analysis!"

"Hey! Aren't you a campaign manager?"

"Okay! Then you better know this is the kind of thing that can backfire and ruin us. The opposition would suggest you might use the Presidency to revenge yourself on the French."

"Yeah, I might."

"Have you gone mad?"

"I'm gonna win this election, Woon. And when I do, I'll show you a thing or three about using power."

"Will the French bargain with us to cool this thing?" Woon asked.

"They say my former housekeeper . . . Remember Mrs. Ebey? They say she's coming with a message from Nishi. I *may* bargain with her if Nishi is willing to put out for me."

"Put . . . out?"

"Crissakes! Don't you speak English?"

"I'm afraid I do. Are you suggesting you would bargain for your mother's life if this Nishi will jump into bed with you?"

"You got it!"

Wide-eyed, Woon stared at Lutt as though seeing a stranger. When the senator spoke, it was in a low, growling voice. "Any idea what the French want?"

"Sure! They want my Spiral communicators and my spaceship. They'll trade Mother for those little concessions."

"Give them what they want."

"If they give me what I want."

"I've cut a few corners in my life," Woon said, "but you make me look like a Sunday-school teacher by comparison." He grabbed both arms of his chair and levered himself to his feet. "I'll talk to this Mrs. Ebey. And I believe I'd better see your Raj Dood."

"You do that. And ask his advice." Lutt pictured his voice in a parody of Woon's booming tones. "I hear Dood gives great fucking advice."

I wish Wemply the Voyager had lived. I'd like to send him searching for the bottom of the Sea of All Things.

—Mutterings of Habiba

I am not the Habiba of old nor will I ever be again.

The thought drifted through Habiba's mind and was gone.

She stared out of her cupola at the gray morning shadows of her beloved Dreenor. Amplified vision revealed a crowd of her most responsible Taxables lurching along a pathway near the horizon, all obviously far gone on bazeel. She did not have the heart to reprimand them nor prohibit the drug. It was being grown quite openly now in many homes.

Jongleur had just departed after delivering an account of Deni-Ra's captivity.

"Mugly says Deni-Ra may be a Latent," Jongleur said.

Latents, capable of wildly unpredictable idmaging, were a periodic problem among Dreens, but they had always been managed with Soother therapy.

It did not seem possible in the present circumstances that they could get a Soother to Deni-Ra.

Of late, Habiba had entertained the suspicion that Wemply might have been a Latent. That would explain many things, but the suspicion came far too late.

"We will waste no more of our people on that accursed planet," Habiba ordered.

"Does that mean you will *not* send the erasure ship?" Jongleur quavered.

"It means only what I say it means!"

Jongleur, recoiling as a wave of Habiba's rage-scent swept over him, fled into the morning without her dismissal.

"Send Mugly!" she bellowed after him.

Mugly appeared presently but stood at the base of the cupola's spiral ramp. Did he think distance protected him from her probing stare?

"If I ordered an immediate Thoughtcon, what would I learn from you?" she asked.

Mugly, with no time to idmage a memory block, looked around him in fear and trembling. No other Elites shared the cupola. He had never heard of a Thoughtcon with a single Elite. Was that possible?

"I know what I would find," Habiba said.

Did my idmaged memory block fail?

"I have never needed a Thoughtcon to read the hearts of my Taxables," Habiba said. "You have conspired against me, Mugly!"

"Blessed Habiba! I have always acted only for the good of Dreenor."

"Don't give me that Blessed Habiba crap! You're the most prideful Dreen I've ever known. You planned from the first to be the captain of that erasure ship!"

Mugly drew himself up stiffly on all four legs. "I am willing to sacrifice myself for the good of my people."

"They are not *your* people. And what do you know about the good of Dreendom? You have infected us all with an illness for which there may be no cure!"

"Habiba!"

"Erase Earth and the consequences will be catastrophic!" she said. "The accursed planet and its life forms are woven all through our legends and lore. Before I put a ban on it, Earth was our most frequently visited Storyteller scene!"

"The more reason to remove it, Habiba."

"You don't listen to me! Without Earth, Dreen abilities will be crippled. Storytellers will fear the consequences of every idmage. 'Am I creating another Earth?' they will ask. And our universe will explode in a burst of Storyteller frustration!"

"But the flaw of Earth is known to us. Free Will and its evolution have—"

"Pride, that is the flaw! The same pride that drives you, Mugly, drove Wemply to that insane creation."

"Surely, Habiba, this cannot be as bad as—"

"Your pride drives you now to question even me!" Habiba accused. "I have a cure for that, Mugly. We will hold a Thoughtcon immediately. It will place *you* on trial. You are the shame of Dreendom. Your evil will be known to all!"

Mugly's horn-tool nose quivered. Abruptly, he lurched into motion and began climbing the ramp.

Habiba watched him approach, curious at his behavior. She had not asked him to come closer. What was he doing?

Two paces below Habiba, Mugly paused. The odor of his rage was unmistakable. She saw his eyes swivel inward for idmaging. A length of the ramp vanished to supply idmaging material and a long staff appeared in his hands. When his eyes swiveled outward, he lunged at her with the staff.

A spear!

She recognized it from stories of Earther violence. The smell of anesthetic poison on the blade chilled her. Mugly intended murder!

Habiba jerked aside as the spear gashed her left arm. She reacted in pain and dismay. *I need a defensive weapon!*

From the depths of her survival instincts, and with superior idmaging, she sealed her wound and created a weapon. A tommy gun materialized in her hands as Mugly drew back for another thrust. Without conscious volition, Habiba squeezed the trigger. A chattering roar deafened her as bullets drew a line of yellow holes across Mugly's chest. The impacts threw him off the ramp and he fell far down to the floor with a sodden "thump."

Feeling coldly remote, she leaned over to stare down at him. Was he conscious? Could he idmage repairs to his damaged flesh? But the fall had rendered him unconscious. She saw his yellow blood oozing onto the floor. He lay there unmoving as life drained from him.

Habiba felt the moment of Mugly's death and a dreadful stillness permeated her, draining her maternal spirit. The skin tightened across her forehead, removing Storyteller wrinkles.

She looked down at the tommy gun in her hands and grined it out of existence with a shudder of revulsion.

What have I done?

She tried to rationalize the awful occurrence.

Mugly would have killed me. I defended myself for the good of all Dreens.

That carried the suspicious ring of Mugly's arguments.

Am I the most prideful Dreen?

It was a shattering thought. Could Mugly have been right about Earth? No! Her arguments about the consequences had skirted something far deeper in her awareness. Somewhere within her lay the certainty that Dreenor would end if they erased Earth.

Premeditated annihilation of all that life? I cannot bring myself to order it.

But I killed Mugly.

Slowly, she descended the ramp and stood over Mugly's body. It looked pitiful. A wave of anguish swept through her. She picked up the body, pausing to grine away the evidences of disaster on the floor. Once again, deadly stillness drained her. The ancient familiarity of the feeling set her trembling.

My Taxables must not learn what I have done.

Carrying Mugly, she descended a private passage to the red mudbrick dwelling, her first home on Dreenor. There, she idmaged a deep hole in the floor and buried Mugly. When the floor was restored, she squatted and contemplated her problem.

I am but one person. I cannot hold all creation together by myself.

But what is the difference between defending myself from Mugly and defending Dreendom by erasing Earth?

Consequences.

The consequences of defensive actions always had to be weighed. Mugly was gone and his absence certainly would involve her in elaborately fanciful storytelling fabrications.

But am I not the Supreme Storyteller?

This thought vibrated an odd chord of memory deep within her. She could not quite place it. But someone once had called her that.

"You are the Supreme Storyteller. The task is yours."

She could almost hear the voice. It was someone she could not identify. Someone who no longer existed.

How could there be someone such as that? Did she not know every Dreen?

She squatted there, trembling with the things hidden in her, unaware for several heartbeats that Jongleur had returned and stood in the doorway from the lower hall.

"Habiba?" he ventured. "What was that loud noise? Many heard it but . . ."

"I did not summon you," she said.

"Love brings me, Habiba. What is wrong?"

Thus the fabrication begins, she thought and said: "I have had to send Mugly on a difficult mission."

"Mugly? I did not see him leave. What mission, Habiba? Not the erasure ship!"

"A mission even more difficult than that," she said.

Medical records available to us show Candidate Hanson has grown several centimeters taller and gained at least seven kilos of weight in the past few months. How does he explain this? Does he suffer a dangerous hormone imbalance? The public deserves a full clarification of this oddity.

—An opposition news release

"Ladies and gentlemen, in two days we will elect the next President of the United States."

The announcer, Utley Trask, a familiar, benign, gray-haired figure chosen especially for this moment, paused and smiled as cheers, whistles and shouts erupted from the crowd packing the floor of the convention hall below him.

Lutt, seated to Trask's left with Eola VanDyke *Hanson* at his side, thought they had done pretty well filling the hall at 9:00 A.M. He glanced at Eola, seeing the glitter of her new wedding ring. She produced her finishing-school smile for the cheering people. Although he had purposely avoided subduing Ryll with basil, Lutt felt a surge of belligerence.

Eola for show, Ni-Ni for bed!

No response yet from the French but he felt confident. The Legion still kept the Phoenicia story under wraps. *A sure sign they won't refuse my demands.*

Utley Trask raised both hands to restrain the crowd. The calls and cheering slowly subsided.

Lutt glanced into the platform wings to his right. A wheeled cage containing Deni-Ra in human guise waited there.

In a few minutes we cinch the election! Lutt thought. *Fear and the promise of jobs will do the trick. I'll win by a landslide.*

"The moment has come to show you why Lutt Hanson, Jr., is the only man for this most sensitive position in our universe," Trask said. "But first, one of the most pleasant moments of my life."

He grinned at Eola, then returned his attention to the crowd.

"A wonderful surprise, folks. Early this morning, in a quiet ceremony at his home, Lutt Hanson, Jr., and Eola VanDyke were joined in the holy bonds of matrimony!"

A deafening roar boomed through the hall. Calls and shouts continued for five minutes. When they subsided, the announcer grinned and waved at Lutt.

"Ladies and gentlemen, the next President of the United States—Lutt Hanson, Jr.!"

Lutt took his position at the microphones, glancing at the ranks of cameras aimed down at him, at the crowd, then at the Portable Speech Analyzer in the palm of his left hand. He aimed a practiced smile at Eola and swung it back toward the floor of the hall. Presently, he raised both arms.

The uproar quieted quickly. They had been prepared for a momentous announcement—stories leaked about "a world-shaking revelation." Expectation could be seen in the uplifted faces. Even the media people sat poised behind the glass of their booths, knowing he would not have built them up for anything but a big story.

What was this "alien menace" hinted at in stories being leaked from Hanson headquarters?

"My friends," Lutt said, "we all know the time has come for us to revitalize this great nation. My opponents have led us into a desperate situation. Food prices have doubled in the past year. Unemployment is on the rise."

He paused and assumed a grim expression before continuing to read the prepared speech projected onto the transparent screen in front of the lectern.

"How can we be uncaring when so many Americans live dreary lives in shanty homes?"

That was for the masses of voters Woon's people had registered in the Lowtowns.

"Yes!" he shouted. "We need food for the poor. Yes! We need jobs for people my opponents ignore, people who want only to stand proud in the knowledge they support themselves."

Lutt slid the PSA into its wrist sheath and placed a hand along each side of the lectern. He gripped the wood until his knuckles went white, a gesture he had learned from Woon.

"But there is something even more menacing my opponents have ignored . . . even though they are well aware of it!"

He looked up at the ranked lenses. The opposition was out there monitoring every word, every movement.

"I face you today with dogged determination, with a deep conviction based on Dedication, Intelligence and Ethics. Those initials spell DIE. And we all will surely *die* if my message is ignored!"

He gestured for the waiting Hanson Guards and Zone Patrol troopers to wheel out Deni-Ra's cage.

The cage trundled onto the stage with a calculated squeaking of wheels. The crowd stirred. Strobe lights flared. Cameras turned toward this new development. Whispers sent a susurration through the hall.

"Who the hell's he got in the cage?"

"Looks like a leftover John Wayne stand-in."

"Shut up and listen!"

The guards stopped the cage two paces to Lutt's right and stood there with weapons ready.

Deni-Ra clutched the bars and glared truculently at the crowd.

Lutt pointed at the caged Dreen. "Creatures such as this walk among us!" he shouted. "You might never give one of them a second glance! They look just as human as any of us! But they are not! They are alien! They intend to destroy us!"

On cue, Deni-Ra's human guise slumped into a mound of protoplasm and reformed in Dreen shape. Two six-fingered hands rattled the bars, rocking the cage back and forth.

A concerted gasp lifted from the crowd. The guards pointed their weapons at the Dreen and one of them said: "Stop that or we shoot!"

Deni-Ra slouched back on all four feet. "Shoot if you must, you scumgut swine!" she bellowed. "But you nesters are agonna git yours! You're on Dreen land! One day soon, you'll have till sundown to git off!"

Still pointing at Deni-Ra, Lutt shouted: "Your so-called leaders have left us defenseless in the face of this menace! I am calling for an end to that head-in-the-sand stupidity! We must build weapons and warships for space! We must attack and destroy these aliens on their own ground!"

Lutt lowered his head and swept his gaze across the crowd. "My opponents whisper behind my back that I am making a secret accord with potential enemies—the French. That is a lie! Do any of you think the French Foreign Legion will fail to fight beside our brave Zone Patrol once this menace is seen?"

A cheer roared through the hall and subsided in gasps.

Lutt glanced at Deni-Ra. As rehearsed, the Dreen had shape-shifted into a cobra and threatened to slip through the bars. The guards prodded Deni-Ra back into captivity.

"All of Earth must rally behind us in the face of this threat!" Lutt shouted. "We must convert factories and build new ones! The technology to destroy these aliens is known! Yes! It is a product of my own invention! I am prepared for this terrible task! Are you?"

The roaring, stamping response told Lutt all he needed to know. A glance at the PSA confirmed it. He had them. Fear of an alien threat meant jobs in a new weapons industry. All could see it. And his people had leaked enough stories about Lutt's *Vortraveler*. "An invention from the fertile mind of Lutt Hanson, Jr."

If the French want into the act, okay. But only on my terms!

Ryll had heard and seen enough. His Earther lessons coalesced into a demand for action.

Lutt baby, Ryll intruded.

Shut up, Dreen!

No way, Lutt baby. What happens to the election if your Zone Patrol guards see you exposed as a Dreen?

You wouldn't dare!

If I have to go to prison, too, so be it, Lutt baby.

Stop calling me that!

Calling you what?

Baby!

But I learned it from you. And this is showdown time, Lutt baby. Even if I can't retake control of our body—which is an unresolved issue—I certainly can raise questions to which the ZP has answers. Got it?

You mean it?

Think about it—no Ni-Ni, no Presidency, nothing but a prison for the creature who posed as Lutt Hanson, Jr. You'll be part of the alien menace you've been at such pains to announce.

What do you want, Ryll?

I told you I wouldn't permit you to attack Dreenor.

Okay, no attack.

But you don't mean it.

I promise.

And I see through your empty promise.

What do I have to do?

You already know. Turn over control of our body to me on my demand and no more bazeel unless I ask for it.

Never!

Never is an awful long time, Lutt. Especially if we're in a ZP prison.

Can we share control of my body?

Our body.

Okay! Our body.

That's what I've proposed all along. And if you agree, you'd better remember I can read every thought in your head.

The convention hall clamor was diminishing. Lutt's shoulders slumped. The Portable Speech Analyzer immediately prompted him: "Straighten up. Look firm and sincere."

He obeyed.

In his private thoughts, Ryll observed this and came to a determination. *I will rule this Earther!* And now he knew how to do it. It was a basic truth he had come to recognize through observation of Lutt. *Let a person desire something enough and you can rule the person through that desire.*

Lutt wanted power. He lusted after it more than he lusted after any woman.

Nishi must never be bound to this Earther, Ryll thought. *I will protect her.*

In this position, the blade gun appears to be an ordinary short-bladed pocket knife. Give the handle a half turn as shown, press the raised decoration (number three on the diagram) and the blade shoots where it is aimed—deadly within eight meters. The BG's automatic re-arm instantly puts another projectile in place for seven more shots. Poison- or anesthetic-injector blades are available. Blades, sold in cartons of 24, and the knife handle are high-impact plastic. They will not trip a metal detector.

—A brochure privately
circulated to officials

Nishi paced across her suite at the Madison Hotel in Washington, D.C., admiring the antique French decor and the sepia engravings of Napoleonic Paris. Even the vidcom was concealed in a graceful vase. Draperies hid the streets and muted the morning sunlight. She could almost imagine she had been moved back in time to those less frenetic days pictured on the walls.

Wytee was a ball of yellow fur on an Empire chair, its thought-spying range defensively reduced because of *Many bad thinks here*.

So much evil in this nation's capital overwhelmed Wytee's native naivete, Nishi reasoned.

Mrs. Ebey was next door. Lorna and Lew Subiyama occupied connecting rooms and her prefect protector with Legion guards in mufti had adjoining quarters beyond the Subiyamas.

She glanced at her watch. Lutt should arrive in a few minutes.

President Lutt Hanson, Jr.

It was odd to think of him that way but she had watched media coverage of his inauguration and acceptance speech, had seen him display a captive Dreen. And she knew the United States capital bustled with new activity—many nations seeking a share in the Human Defense League with its lucrative weapons contracts.

Human Defense League. It was a clever label. Her prefect was here because of that organization.

"We must share the burden."

He want share profits, Wytee had translated. *He want Nishi boss Lutt President.*

Is that why I'm here? Nishi wondered. *Bait? A bargaining chip?*

But the French had Phoenicia and that still-unannounced charge of an offense against the state. They could execute her.

Why does Lutt insist I come here? He has a wife.

Lutt President want lustful breeding Nishi, Wytee said.

Lorna and Lew Subiyama slipped in the connecting door. Lew looked fearful, his gaze downcast. He kept glancing at Wytee as though afraid Nishi's pet would attack him.

"Not here yet?" Lorna asked. "Heysoos! The frigging President of the United States coming to you instead of you going to him! You got some hold on that bastard's balls, honey."

"The prefect insisted we keep to the hotel," Nishi said. "Here, we have our own security."

Prefect man make spy things, Wytee offered.

"Those business suits on your legionnaires didn't fool that White House arranger one second," Lorna said. "But I was surprised he caved in so fast."

"I have a diplomatic passport," Nishi said.

"Yeah, honey, but this is still the President. I'll bet he wants inta your panties. Should we leave you two alone?"

"I have already explained my position!" Nishi said.

"But a gal's got a right to change her mind," Lorna said. "Let me know if we should hightail it outa here."

A soft rap sounded on the hall door. It opened to reveal Captain O'Hara in a Harris tweed suit. "Your guest is coming up the elevator, mademoiselle," he said. "Secret Service men are here and we have cleared the hallway."

"Very good, monsieur," Nishi said.

"Lew, go hold the door," Lorna ordered.

Lew scuttled to obey and took the door handle from O'Hara, who went out of view. His voice could be heard. "A man at each elevator. Be polite but firm."

"Isn't it cute the way Lew does everything I want?" Lorna asked.

There was no time for an answer. An abrupt flurry of sounds in the hall signaled the arrival of the president. Lutt, accompanied by two Secret Service men, swept past Lew and stopped three paces from Nishi. He looked her up and down.

"Everybody but Nishi out," Lutt said.

"But, sir!" a Secret Service man protested.

Lutt hooked a thumb over his shoulder. "Out!" He glanced at the Subiyamas. "You, too."

"Have fun," Lorna said. She took Lew's arm and left with the Secret Service men.

When the door closed behind them, Lutt asked, "How about this, Ni-Ni? President Hanson!"

"And how is your First Lady?" Nishi asked.

"Forget her, Ni-Ni. She's for show and to please Mother."

"You wish to discuss your mother's situation now?"

"Hell, Ni-Ni! Didn't that fat French bastard clue you to what's going on?"

"I do not understand, Mister President."

"Come on, Ni-Ni! Take off your clothes and let's get with it!" He began unbuttoning his suit coat.

"None of that!" she said, backing away from him. *Wytee? Help me, Wytee!*

Wytee help.

Lutt suddenly moaned and put both hands to his head. "Jesus! What's happening?" He staggered to his left. "You doing this, Ryll, you son-of-a-bitch?"

"I will speak to Ryll," Nishi said.

As he had done fruitlessly several times in the past week, Ryll demanded control of their body.

You made a solemn promise, Lutt, and I know you meant it. If you go back on your word, I will carry out my threat!

To hell with you!

I see it all now! Ryll said. *You have learned to play at being sincere! You really mean to attack Dreenor!*

Lutt twisted his head and groaned. "You lying Dreen son-of-a-bitch!"

I warned you I would not permit an attack on my people!

"You're killing me," Lutt moaned. "Please stop."

It is not I who causes you pain, Ryll offered. *It is that yellow creature on the chair.*

It's you! Just when things are going great, you mess it up!

I assure you it is the Soother. I do not know how Nishi acquired it. They are reserved for Latents and other aberrated types.

Lutt staggered to an Empire couch and collapsed onto it.

Enough, Wytee, Nishi ordered.

Lutt took a deep breath and slowly lowered his hands. Nishi saw the fight for transition to Ryll as a flickering of movement in face and eyes, the slight sagging of jaws, a brighter gleam in the eyes that faded and returned.

Ryll remained on the couch. "I am happy to find you well, Nishi," he said. "These are times to try one's soul."

"Why has he brought me here?" she asked.

Lutt tried to interfere and regain control. The shared face grimaced, lips moved, grunts issued from the mouth.

Wytee, Nishi prompted.

Once more, Lutt clutched his head.

"Okay! Okay!" Lutt gasped.

She waited for Wytee to relax the pain, then: "Ryll?"

Again, Ryll's voice issued from the familiar mouth. "He wishes only disgusting, lustful things with you, Nishi."

"I thought so!"

"The French envoy said Lutt must make his own repellent way with you. Lutt was led to believe you agreed."

"The prefect? He said nothing of this to me!" Nishi protested.

"So I surmised."

"This is awful!" Nishi said. "Has the Legion abandoned me?"

Ryll looked at Wytee. "An idea occurs to me." He returned his attention to Nishi. "Could you part with your Soother?"

"My what?"

Ryll pointed at Wytee. "Your Soother."

"Wytee? What could you want with Wytee?"

"Ahh, yes. You named your Soother. I've been told that is customary."

He fell silent with head cocked to one side. Presently, he idmaged a note to Nishi. She plucked it from the air as it drifted past her eyes.

"With a Soother's help, I might control this body and not reveal our extraordinary situation," the note read.

Do you understand what he means, Wytee?

Wytee say spy things here.

But what does he mean that he needs you?

Lutt President sick. Nishi not sick.

Would you go with Ryll?

Nishi say Wytee go Lutt/Ryll?

Y–yes.

Wytee go.

I will be sorry to lose you, Wytee.

Wytee friend Nishi. Wytee friend Dreen. Wytee help sick peoples. Lutt President need Wytee. Ryll need Wytee.

Nishi looked at the man on the couch and nodded agreement.

Ryll stood and, once more, Lutt sought control, but a spasm of agony caused him to withdraw immediately.

That is a small taste of what you will get if you interfere, Ryll promised. He scooped up the Soother and bundled the creature beneath his suitcoat.

"What of our negotiations?" Nishi asked.

"I'll let the French share the secrets of Spiral technology."

And Ryll thought: *But I will misdirect them. You got that, Lutt? I told you I wouldn't let anyone attack Dreenor.*

Ryll turned toward the door and paused as a musical bell sounded from a vase on a table to his left. The vase opened along a vertical seam to reveal a vidcom.

Nishi crossed to the instrument and pressed the "answer" key.

Major Captain's face appeared on the screen. "There you are, sir," she said, addressing the figure she thought was the President.

"What is it?" Ryll asked.

"We have a first-class snafu on our hands, Mr. President." She looked pointedly at Nishi.

"You may speak in front of Mademoiselle D'Amato," Ryll said.

"I don't know, sir. This is pretty sensitive. I think you'd better call in the Secret Service with your communications box. This should be scrambled."

"Very well." Ryll went to the door and signaled one of the Secret Service men waiting in the hall.

Presently, Ryll sat with a scrambler hood over his head. Once more, he looked at Major Captain.

"Sir, your brother has gone berserk," she said. "He used a pass signed by you to enter the security area where Deni-Ra is held and, before anyone could stop him, he killed the Dreen."

"Morey? Morey killed Deni-Ra?"

"It's a mess! Yellow blood all over the place. A godawful stench. Even I threw up and I'm a doctor."

"But how could he do this? What weapon . . ."

"One of those damn blade guns! An anesthetic poison on it. We don't know whether it was the blades, the poison or what killed the Dreen. Some of our experts are coming in for the autopsy but we may not produce answers. The question now is—What do we do about your brother?"

"Hold him under protective detention."

"And what do we say if it leaks out?"

"What makes you think it'll leak out?"

"Your White House is a sieve, sir!"

"Say my brother struck a blow in the war against the alien menace, but don't release him."

Ryll broke the connection and returned the scrambler box to a Secret Service man.

Lutt? Why did your brother do that?

There was no response from his fleshmate.

I insist on an answer, Lutt. Do you want more head pain?

Morey's just conducted an experiment, I think. He's learned how to kill a Dreen.

Why would he want to do that?

He remembers us raving about an alien in our body. Morey plans to assassinate us.

How can he do that if he's a prisoner?

Don't be stupid, Ryll. He uses accomplices.

Alarmed, Ryll blurted: *We must go back to the Listening Post. We've missed something!*

There is a perfectly simple explanation for his calling her Nee-Nee and her calling him Rill. Lovers always have pet names.

—The prefect's report

It had been a rough two days for Ryll and he was in no mood for the trip to Dulles Airport where Phoenicia was to arrive shortly after midnight. No getting out of it, though. He picked up Wytee and girded himself for the ordeal.

During the long ride with Eola to Dulles, he thought about the problems he and Lutt confronted.

What had they missed at the Listening Post? It didn't seem possible for Morey to conduct a conspiracy under unwinking scrutiny. Unless you considered everything Morey did suspicious, probably the safest assumption, his actions before killing Deni-Ra appeared perfectly normal. The only untoward thing had been a visit to Nishi, but that had been arranged by Woon for a very good reason. Woon remained fearful Subiyama and Nishi would collaborate on more revelations.

"Subiyama's stories are dangerously embarrassing!" Woon had stormed. "It must be stopped! If this D'Amato dame won't take money, maybe that Subiyama bitch will!"

"Where would you get the money to pay her off?" Ryll had asked.

"How about Hanson Industries? Does your brother have a deep pocket?"

"Deeper than most."

"I'll look into it."

Phoenicia arrived at Dulles later than expected—well past midnight.

The damn French and their Concordes! Lutt complained.

Upset by the frustrating search through the Listening Post, he raged bitterly about the unreliable Concord IXs the French insisted on using to return Phoenicia.

An ordinary plane could land at Washington National. But no! They gotta show off their damn Concordes! And that drags us all the way out to Dulles!

Phoenicia, entering the VIP lounge to be met by the man she thought of as her son, saw him with his new wife, Eola, and tried to put the best face on this aftermath of what she considered to be her gaffe with Nishi. She rushed up to Eola, gave her a pecking kiss on the cheek and turned to do the same for Ryll but he had stepped back.

"Eola, how nice," Phoenicia said. And to Ryll: "So good of you to meet me, Son."

Ryll patted her arm, more to keep her at a distance than for any pretense of affection. In his best Lutt voice, he said, "Let's hurry it along. We have limousines outside."

Ryll and Eola had a White House limousine parked at the door of the VIP lounge with Wytee curled up on the back ledge but, at Eola's suggestion, they had brought the gaudy rickshaw for Phoenicia.

"Your mother always uses it and it will be a touch of the familiar to welcome her home. Besides, this way, you won't have to ride with her. I know how much you dislike it."

When they emerged from the lounge, Phoenicia took one look at the sprawled robocoolies in front of the rickshaw and thrust aside her Secret Service escort. "Take that damned thing away!" she shouted, pointing at the rickshaw.

"But, Mother," Ryll said. "I thought you always preferred the rickshaw."

"I rode in it to placate your father! He always insisted I use it. Couldn't you see that?"

Ryll waved for an aide to remove the vehicle. Still in his best Lutt voice, trusting excitement and jet lag to dull Phoenicia and prevent her from detecting any personality changes, Ryll said: "We are sending you to Blair House. I hope you understand. I can't spare you any time just now. And I have Eola as my hostess."

Phoenicia glared at him. "You're using her against me, aren't you?"

"Mother! This is my wife! The First Lady!"

Eola clutched Ryll's arm. "Phoenicia, please!"

"This is family business!" Phoenicia flared. "You stay out of it!"

"But I am family now," Eola whined.

Ryll patted Eola's hand. "Be still, dear."

"I knew you'd all turn against me once you won the election!" Phoenicia said.

Suddenly realizing this was precisely the spiteful pattern to be expected from Lutt, Ryll assumed a sneering grin.

"Think of it as retirement, Mother. You can go back to your parties and your friends."

"You are absolutely hateful! Where is Morey?"

"Morey is . . . ahhh, not here."

"I can see that!"

"He's doing some things with the Zone Patrol."

She leaned toward him. "What have you done with your brother?"

"Nothing at all, Mother."

"I want to see Morey immediately! We have Company business to discuss."

"Those matters have been delegated, Mother."

"I am still in charge of The Company!"

"Of course you are, Mother. Do anything you want with Hanson Industries."

"You're hiding something from me."

"State secrets can be shared only on a limited basis, Mother."

"What would Morey have to do with state secrets?"

"That's a state secret," Ryll said, enjoying the ease with which he fended her questions.

"Is it something about that horrible alien? Does this concern all the war talk I hear?"

"In a way, Mother."

"You're even more secretive than your father!"

"My new duties require it."

She studied him a moment, then, "Will The Company get any of the weapons contracts?"

"Only on a bid basis, Mother. I can have nothing to do with it. That would be unethical."

"Lutt, why are you treating me this way?"

"What way, Mother? I've just saved your life. The French would have executed you."

"Poppycock!"

"Your head in a basket," Ryll said. "I am giving the French what they asked. And you have not thanked me for saving you at great sacrifice."

An aide touched Ryll's arm. "Sir? The Chinese envoys at 8:00 A.M."

"I know," Ryll said. "Good night, Mother."

With Eola on his arm, Ryll followed the aide toward the White House limousine.

Phoenicia called after them: "Eola! What is he doing?"

"He is being President," Eola called back.

In the limousine rolling out of the airport with a full cavalcade of guards and aides, Ryll leaned back and closed his eyes. Mercifully, Eola was too tired to resume one of her interminable conversations about their "position in society."

You played that pretty well, Ryll, Lutt intruded.

I did, didn't I. You have been most instructive.

How about letting me have a little time with Eola tonight? You won't let me have Ni-Ni, so what about a roll in the hay with my wife?

You disgust me, Lutt.

Want me to fight for control?

Want me to hurt your head?

No! How do you do that? Is it really that cat on the back ledge?

That is not a cat. It is a Soother.

I don't find it very soothing.

You're right. Wytee seems to have absorbed strange ways from contact with Earthers.

The way you did?

Before Ryll could compose an answer, the cavalcade of limousines swung through the side gate of the White House, passed armed guards standing at attention, and rolled into the rear parking area. A Zone Patrol officer opened the door for Ryll. As he leaned forward to emerge, Ryll saw more ZPs guarding the dimly lighted rear entrance to the White House.

"Glad to see you home safely, sir," the officer at the limousine door said.

Ryll scooped Wytee into a soft bundle and stepped out. No one, not even the officer holding the door, gave any sign they thought it strange to see the President with a *cat* in his arms.

Zone Patrol man have many thinks lustful breeding secretary woman, Wytee offered.

This communication leaked through to Lutt.

What about my needs for "lustful breeding," Ryll?

Ryll ignored this but Lutt was not deterred.

Eola's not all that bad in bed, Ryll. A little prudish, but I find that stimulating.

If I permit it, will you stop interrupting me at crucial moments?

Anything, Ryll. Just watching everything is an awful bore.

Is it? I found it fascinating.

Except for sex.

That, of course.

Maybe you should stay in closer contact while I instruct you in the niceties. It might grow on you.

Stop it this instant or I shall not grant your request.

Okay. Okay. Just trying to help.

You are trying to entice me into your disgusting Earther pleasures. You think you can control me that way.

You seem to like basil.

No bazeel! You understand me, Lutt? Bazeel is over for good!

Anything you say, Ryll.

I mean it!

I see that. Just let me have Eola tonight. She's beginning to wonder why you're not humping her regularly.

Very well, but I shall hurt your head if you try any tricks.

I'll be good.

That is an impossibility for you, Lutt.

Never leave the Soother too long in contact with an extremely ill patient. Soothers not only take on characteristics of their patients but also are deeply influenced by others with whom they come in mental contact during the therapy period. For this reason, Soother applications must occur when there is only one sick mind within their range.

—Dreen text, for advanced education

Once more, Ryll and Lutt sat in the Listening Post to review its data. They had raced the sunset across country, using a military plane, the Humptulips Howler—"a rocket with wings," the media called it.

In the Post, Lutt dominated because of his more intimate familiarity with the place. They spoke openly, alternating voice control, certain that L. H. had provided a spyproof room.

"If you're right about a conspiracy to assassinate us, which I will go along with but not concede, the most suspicious events are those visits to Nishi," Ryll said.

"You saying she's in on it?"

Ryll managed a superb tone of Earther outrage. "Nishi? Never!"

"Then what're you driving at?"

"Woon is Morey's logical accomplice. After all, he conspired in your brother's plan to have us murdered on Venus."

"The fat-boy senator knows what'll happen to him if I'm not around to prevent it!"

"Perhaps an insufficient deterrent."

"Whatta you mean?"

"He may believe he could weather a spate of bad publicity if *you* are the focus of national animus. Make you look bad and he looks good by comparison."

"But he and Morey haven't met. There's only that one vidcom call and Woon merely asked Morey to go to the Madison with plenty of money."

"Which Nishi rejected."

"Let's look at the two visits once more," Ryll insisted.

"This is the last time!"

Lutt punched the Listening Post controls and a screen came alive with what was now a boringly familiar sequence, Woon entering Nishi's suite at the Madison.

"So he comes in and gives his hat and coat to Ebey," Lutt said. "Perfectly normal. It's winter, you know."

"He's not even carrying a briefcase," Ryll agreed.

"So whatta they talk about? Just what Woon told me! No more Subiyama revelations. And Nishi says she'll be mum. And Woon says Morey'll be along to 'recompense' Subiyama."

"Could Subiyama be the accomplice?" Ryll asked.

"Her? Nuts! That dame reports stories, she doesn't create 'em. Besides, there's no direct contact with Subiyama."

"Could there be more than one accomplice?"

"Who? We know everything they've said. Look. Woon leaves and later, Morey appears," Lutt said.

"Roll that one," Ryll said.

Lutt obeyed.

"Nishi must've talked to Subiyama in the meantime," Lutt said. "She's all ready with her answer."

"But Morey has a briefcase full of money."

"Which he never even opens!"

"And out Morey goes," Ryll said. "He looks happy about something, though."

"Morey always enjoys looking at beautiful women."

"Nishi gave him no encouragement."

"She's suffering symptoms of withdrawal from me."

"You've never . . . never . . ."

"But I want another go at my Ni-Ni, Ryll. As long as she's still in the capital, why not?"

"I will not permit it!"

"Look here, Ryll. We have to be partners. You have your pleasures and I have mine."

"I can read what you're thinking, Lutt."

"So you know what I want. What's wrong with that?"

"You will hurt Nishi and I am determined to protect her."

"Keerist! You are the world's biggest prude!"

"Shall we look at more of the Post's data?" Ryll asked.

"What's to see? Woon running campaign headquarters? Morey using his blade gun on that stupid Deni-Ra?"

"Do you now think you were wrong about a conspiracy?"

"Maybe. Let's still be cautious. No visits from Morey, not that he'll try. I've never wanted him close and he knows it. And we keep Woon at a distance."

"How long do we hold Morey in durance vile?"

"I hope it's vile. And we keep him as long as we can."

"The ZP appears amenable but your mother is becoming importunate."

"Let her import all she wants. It's good for her."

"I shall resume control now," Ryll said. "Let us call the guardians and return to Washington."

"You know," Lutt said, "I like being able to talk like this. With a little practice, we could shift back and forth easily. Might be helpful, because sometimes, you're not so good at imitating me."

"Good enough to fool your mother!"

"But what if she gets suspicious?"

"You may have noticed, Lutt, that I am improving with practice."

"You like being boss, don't you?"

"I like the practical application of knowledge."

"Well, let's keep this in mind if we need it."

"Your new spirit of cooperation is gratifying, Lutt."

"Will it make you more willing to grant me a few pleasures?"

"Since I see the pleasures you desire, we will judge each request on its merits."

Wytee stirred in the special pocket and blasted forth a thought that filled the minds of both Ryll and Lutt.

Pleasure make cure sick mans!

Ryll was a moment recovering from the force of the projection. When he gathered his wits, he protested.

Wytee! You promised Nishi you would help me.

Who you?

I'm Ryll . . . the Dreen!

A long pause, then: *Ryll Lutt mix. Cure Ryll cure Lutt.*

I don't need curing! You're supposed to help me control Lutt. Otherwise, he will attack Dreenor.

Lutt not hurt Dreens. Wytee hurt him's head.

Yes, Wytee. That's what you're supposed to do.

Wytee hurt many head they not make nice thought!

Again, the force of Wytee's thought stunned Ryll. Lutt took over their voice and spoke weakly, "What the hell's happening?"

"It's Wytee," Ryll whispered. "I don't know what's wrong with him."

Wytee not sick! Lutt sick! Ryll sick! Wytee fix!

Please, Wytee, Ryll pleaded. *I can't think when you do that.*

You Ryll? You go big white house now. You call Nishi. You tell Nishi see you.

Wytee! We can't do—

Ryll broke off, clutching his head in a flash of agony.

Wytee say you go Nishi now.

The tests of Vortraveler II *exceeded expectations. Orbited Venus in eighteen seconds, to Mars in another twenty-seven seconds, returned in twenty-two seconds. Total elapsed time one minute and seven seconds.*

—Sam R. Kand's report

"A terrible task falls on you, Jongleur," Habiba said, glaring down at him from a night-lighted platform in her mudbrick home.

He had sped through the dark in response to Habiba's call and had no idea of the exact time, but it was late . . . or early. Sleep had evaded him for days, and a presentiment of what the Supreme Tax Collector was about to say flattened his brow.

She looked terrible there, Jongleur thought. Deep dark shadows under her eyes, smooth areas beside her horn-tool nose. He had never before seen smoothing of Habiba's skin.

Jongleur trembled. All four knees ached. Why was she standing on that platform?

"The erasure ship must be sent," Habiba said. "It is fate, I believe."

Jongleur gaped. *Fate?* Dreens did not think in such terms. Creation, cause and effect, yes. Fate, never.

"But why have you summoned me?" he quavered.

"You must erase Earth," Habiba intoned. "I can entrust this terrible responsibility to no other."

For a moment, Jongleur thought he would faint. "Habiba," he croaked. "Please."

"The task is yours, Jongleur," she said. "You are *my* Chief Storyteller."

Her words filled him with painful pride. *Habiba's Chief Storyteller. But the consequences!*

"Could we not wait for Mugly's return?" he pleaded. "This whole thing was his idea."

"I fear Mugly will not return," she said.

Shock upon shock! Mugly . . . not . . . returning? What perilous task had Habiba given him?

"Are you . . . sure, Habiba?"

"I am sure."

"But . . . Mugly's helpers are still . . . I mean, there's Luhan. He could . . ."

"Luhan? This is no time for jests!"

"I was not—"

"That's worse! I give you a direct order: Take the ship to Earth and erase that hideous place. At once! If you leave now, I have calculated it will be over within forty hours."

"Habiba, you predicted catastrophe if we—"

"At once, Jongleur!"

"Will I, too, not . . . return?"

"You *may* survive but it is unlikely you will return." Her tone softened. "It saddens me for us to part this way."

She would not be swayed. He saw this. "May I have time for a few last words with my family?" he pleaded.

"That would only spread sadness and fear. Go to the ship. Do what must be done."

"And Ryll . . . my son . . . on Earth?"

"You're stalling, Jongleur! Earth must go! The fate of everyone in that dreadful creation is sealed."

That word again: *Fate*.

Habiba pointed to the door. "Go! Forty hours from now, there must be no Earth."

Trembling and faltering, Jongleur departed. He felt that he shed his past as some creatures shed their skins. But a heavier load replaced his past. Who would have thought a future could have such weight? The eternal now he once had enjoyed—erased. Future and past became alien.

Outside, Jongleur threaded his way through bands of the Elite huddled in the Control Cone's dim night lights, fearing to enter Habiba's presence without a summons. They called to him:

"Jongleur! What of Habiba? Why are you downcast?"

He could only shake his head.

But now he realized why Habiba had looked down at him from an elevation. *She could not bring herself to look me straight in the eyes.*

"Something is wrong!" one of the Elite shouted. "You must tell us what is happening!"

Sadness and fear. His very presence spread that awful mixture. *And I am powerless to do anything but obey Habiba. I am her Chief Storyteller. And this is the consequence!*

Great danger exists in the constant certainty that you have always made proper decisions.

—Graeco-Dreen aphorism

Ryll felt like a conspirator as he slipped into the tradesmen's door of the Madison where an advance party of the Secret Service detained a service elevator. Up they went to Nishi's floor, guards around him grinning. Some had seen Nishi. Word of her beauty and background on Venus had spread. They *knew* why he came here with such secrecy.

But Nishi herself had asked him to make "an immediate visit" and her message did not explain the reason.

The squirming presence of Wytee in his suitcoat pocket dictated that he obey the summons.

You not go Nishi Wytee hurt head.

Ryll had experienced enough of Wytee's enforcement to know he could not resist the Soother.

Nishi greeted him in her parlor, the bedroom door behind her open to reveal street clothes thrown over a chair. She wore a thin nightgown under a blue housecoat. Matching pom-pom slippers covered her feet.

"Is it Ryll or Lutt?" she greeted him.

"Ryll," he said. "What do you—"

"I am doing this for Mrs. Ebey. Lutt's father treated her shamelessly. You must correct this."

"Yes, but Wytee is . . . is . . ."

Ryll not talk Wytee! Talk love cure!

Ryll almost sagged with the force of the projection.

Nishi blushed. "Wytee . . . is . . . talking to me," she whispered. "It wants me to . . . I can't!"

You go Nishi bed, Wytee ordered.

Ryll shuddered and, as Wytee gave him a taste of enforcement, grabbed his head. *Please . . . no! No, Wytee! No!*

Hey! Lutt intruded. *If you don't wanta, I will.*

Wytee's response was immediate. A surge of agony shot up their spine.

"Ryll, what is it?" Nishi asked, seeing him stagger.

"Hurting . . . my . . . head."

"Mother of God!" Nishi put her hands over her mouth.

You go Nishi bed! Wytee repeated and emphasized the order with a brief shot of pain.

Ryll fell against Nishi. She held him with surprising strength. "Oh, Ryll . . . I'm sorry."

"What am I to do?" Ryll moaned.

That's a stupid question, Lutt offered. *Do it. And I wanta participate.*

Ryll tried to pull away from Nishi but she held him even more tightly. "No," he whispered.

At least let me share, Lutt insisted.

No!

You're nothing but a damn spoilsport!

What Wytee asks . . . it is not sport.

Lutt was amused. *Sure it is.*

Nishi put her lips close to Ryll's ear and stroked his head. "Do you still hurt?"

"Not . . . not much."

She put an arm around him and, supporting his faltering steps, steered him toward the bedroom.

"Where . . . where are we going?" Ryll whispered.

Nishi spoke with candid practicality. "I cannot remain a virgin forever."

"Ohhh, Nishi . . . no."

You not do Nishi love cure Wytee hurt head bad!

"I got that," Nishi said.

They reached the bedroom—flouncy Empire decor with a green-canopied bed. Nishi eased Ryll backward until he tumbled across a soft comforter. She began removing her clothes.

"It's all right," she said as he once more tried to protest. "I've sent Mrs. Ebey away for the night. We're alone."

Ryll tried to straighten. "What are you doing?"

"That's a foolish question," she said. "I will not make love to you through wads of messed-up clothing."

"Nishi . . . I can stand the pain. You don't have to do . . ."

Wytee make head hurt bad. Ryll feel hurt!

Ryll screamed in agony.

For Crissakes, do what Wytee wants! Lutt argued.

Dropping the last of her clothes, Nishi rolled him over, slipped off his suitcoat and shirt, removed his shoes, then his trousers and shorts. She stepped back and he had his first full look at an unclothed female Earther. It was oddly stimulating. Before climbing onto the bed, she turned down the lights.

Ryll closed his eyes and felt her nibble his right ear.

"You do nothing," Nishi said. "I know how from watching experts."

Wytee help! Both Ryll and Nishi received the words.

Immediately, Ryll became intimately aware of intense physical reactions. They surprised him.

"You see?" Nishi whispered. "You, too, know what to do."

Ryll began to lose control of himself in the deepest pleasure sensations he had ever experienced.

"Oh, Blessed Habiba," he whispered. "Why didn't anyone warn me?"

He could feel Wytee insinuated into every intimate fleshly contact, amplifying nerve responses and sharing the experience.

As pleasure climbed to ecstasy, their attention concentrated so intently that not even Wytee noted the return of Mrs. Ebey.

She hesitated in the doorway. Just what she had expected! That monster forcing himself on poor Nishi!

Well, a few minutes' work and I'll really be rich. And Nishi will be free of the Hansons forever!

	Captives	*Basil Addicts*
Adult Males	*59*	*53*
Adult Females	*46*	*37*
Male Children	*0*	*0*
Female Children	*0*	*0*
Totals	*105*	*90*

—"Dreens in Captivity,"
a Zone Patrol report

A strong southwest wind, spreading rain across southern Florida, drenched the mangrove swamp behind Osceola's hideaway shack for most of the day. She and Dood were kept busy for a time creating barriers to close gaping cracks in the windward walls. By dusk, the rain stopped and the wind eased, though it recurred in occasional gusts that rattled loose boards.

Raj Dood, resting naked on Osceola's bed after his labors, watched her at work in a corner of the room, preparing a freshly caught pompano for baking in the hot ashes of a firepit sheltered under the shack's eaves. She wore a brilliant orange dress with tie-dyed splotches of purple like squashed insects.

"You know, Osey," he said, "it sure takes a lot outa you to create even little things like those wind deflectors. I wonder how Dreens do so much of it and don't collapse?"

"They're probably bred for it," she said, tying leaves around the fish and hefting the bundle. " 'Bout six pounds. Gonna be hungry by the time this is ready to eat."

"How can Dreens be so much better at it than we are and yet so limited?" he asked.

"Said it yourself: idiot savants. Don't know about other dimensions. Just concentrate on what they have. Prob'ly answers your other question: limit themselves to what they know."

She went outside with the fish. When she returned, she found him sitting up on the bed, eyes open and with the glassy look of creative concentration.

"Thought you were wore out," she muttered, reclining beside him on the bed.

He did not respond.

Osceola sighed. Sometimes she wished her lover had never made his weird discoveries. Then again, she would not have developed Spirit Glass nor ways of scooting around the universe. She liked seeing new places but the boredom of long trips took the fun out of it. This way, they had the best of everything. Dood could play his games on Venus and spend his spare time here. And she could go where she wished—within reason.

Wonder what the old fool's making now?

She stared at him, squinting to tune in on what he was doing. The expected creative surge did not occur. He radiated a random smear of thoughts.

What the devil's he doin'?

She began to worry. It was not like Dood to take this long at his creative labors. She shook his shoulder.

Slowly, a somnambulist waking, he began to focus his eyes. He turned a frown toward Osceola.

"Sure hope I did the right thing," he muttered.

"What were you doin'?"

"Making an illusion."

"Everything's illusion, you old fool!"

"Osey, the Dreens are sending a ship to wipe out Earth."

She snapped upright. "Wipe us out? Whatta y' mean?"

"They'll erase us just as though we'd never been. Everything associated with us will vanish."

"We gotta do something!"

"Did. Just hope it's enough."
"What have you done?"
"I've set a sort of dimensional trip wire to flip their ship out of the Spirals in-between directly over an illusory Earth."
"Whatta y' mean, illusory?"
"It looks like Earth but it doesn't really exist except as a projection from another dimension."
"What's that supposed to do?"
"Dreens are peculiar animals, Osey. Ones we've studied all have that blind spot. Act like they don't know about other dimensions. But they must come from another dimension."
"What good's it do, us knowin' that?"
"They're compulsive passivists until something they've created threatens them. And that's us."
"We ain't threatenin' 'em."
"I'm afraid we are. Humans find it hard to share space with other animals. We've got this 'them-or-us' nature. If we can't cage or control it some way, we want to kill it. Dreens know that. Hell, Osey, they made this world!"
"That's what you keep saying, but I . . ."
"It's true, Osey."
"What's that have to do with this ship you say is . . ."
"That's it, don't you see? To stop us, they have to go against a basic instinct and eliminate something they've made. Violence!"
"So what happens when they blow up your illusion?"
"I'm not sure. But this gives us time to think about a more permanent solution. As long as they don't latch onto other dimensions, I can keep faking them out."
"How do you know?"
"That Habiba talks to herself a lot. And she keeps a journal and a diary."
"You been spying on them, you old fool! I thought we agreed that was dangerous."
"They're kind of distracted right now, Osey. Not as alert as they were."
"You went there?"
"No, just sort of looked through the keyhole, like we did when we stumbled onto them. Damndest thing! They've got this kinda crude illusion built up around Dreenor, a false Dreenor to make

the place look uninhabitable. That's what gave me the idea how to divert them."

"Just that one look was enough for me," she said. "They give me the creepy willies."

"Dreenor sure is one strange place. Not rightly a planet. Got roots into infinity. They call that 'ampleness.' Thinking about infinity seems to give them a pain."

"Gives me a pain, too."

"But you're mortal and know it. They've always thought they were sort of immortal . . . except for accidents."

"This one of your little jokes, Dood?"

"I swear, Osey. I had this bad presentiment and went looking for the cause. You know how I am."

"Yeah, you'd stick your nose in a cotton gin if you thought they was somethin' worth seein' there. You sure your illusion will stop the Dreens?"

"I keep strangers out of our swamp, don't I?"

"But Dreens ain't human."

"They still believe in what they see. No different from a hunter thinking he sees a swamp full of rampagin' boar 'gators or believing he's stumbled into a zillion cottonmouths."

"But if you're wrong, we'll have a worse problem than explainin' to some stranger how we come to live way out here."

"Trust me, Osey. Dreens may be better at making some things than I am, but they've no understanding at all about how to set up a con game from another dimension."

"Sometimes you make my skin crawl, Dood."

"I tell you what, Osey. While we're waiting for that fish to cook, why don't we get into some heavy skin crawling? Here! Let me help you out of that dress."

Life is full of decisions and there is no absolutely safe course. Reason and logic often create only the illusion of safety.

—Earther aphorism,
a Dreen
collection

Having seen what she expected, that awful Hanson monster having his way with poor Nishi, Mrs. Ebey lifted the blade gun she had purchased in obedience to the note crumpled in Senator Woon's hat. As the note had said, a mind-stunning amount of money was passed to her later in Morey's hat with the promise of even greater riches if she did as she was told.

She lifted the weapon, twisted the handle as instructed, aimed it and depressed the trigger. The blade gun performed exactly according to its accompanying manual: only a soft "slap" as the poisoned anesthetic dart struck its target.

Ryll, still gripped by the highest pleasure sensation of his life, felt a brief sting and clutched his buttock.

"Darling Ryll," Nishi whispered. "Was it good for you, too?"

"Something stung me," Ryll said.

His groping hand felt wetness. A hard object protruded from his flesh. A numbing sensation spread outward from his buttock. His Dreen senses reported poison.

Wytee, coming out of intimate concentration, became aware of Mrs. Ebey and, too late, read her thoughts.

Bad lady Ebey make poison thing in Ryll!

Ryll felt the Soother go completely out of mental contact.

Lutt intruded. *What's happening? Something's wrong. Why won't you let me feel anything?*

Ryll blocked him off and concentrated on stopping the slide into unconsciousness. He rolled off of Nishi, who murmured sleepily: "Only you, Ryll. Never Lutt."

Wytee? Ryll called. But the thought was weak and he felt no response. What was happening to the Soother? Had it been killed?

Wytee came back slowly from reflexive withdrawal. Nothing in the Soother's nature allowed for regrets that the dullness of Mrs. Ebey's mind had led to avoidance of mental contact with her. No recriminations about the fact that the assassination plot had been conducted only with notes and gestures entered the Soother's awareness. But millennia of breeding for benign therapeutic support of Dreens exploded in Wytee. The Soother went berserk.

Mrs. Ebey dropped her blade gun and screamed. She clutched her head and staggered around the bedroom.

Bad lady Ebey hurt Dreen! Wytee hurt bad lady!

Mrs. Ebey collapsed into a moaning ball. The moaning grew fainter. Her breathing faltered and stopped.

With his last consciousness, Ryll sent a call: *Wytee!*

Immediately, Ryll felt his consciousness reinforced.

Lutt intruded: *We're dying! I know we are! Do something!*

Ryll responded to the panic: *Wytee! Lutt's weakening me! Block him off!*

A wall went up in Ryll's awareness, silencing Lutt, then: *What Ryll want?*

I'm dying. There's a way to save me but I missed it in school. Do you know the way?

Wytee help Dreen.

Ryll felt probing tendrils in his mind, a twinge here, a prod there. He felt himself reliving school experiences with a more mature awareness. The path to survival unfolded—memories came into focus. At last, he had his answer!

The way in is the way out. But I need a new body!

Transformation required almost the full power of a Storyship . . . and he had to kill! Or accept flesh already dead.

Bad lady Ebey dead, Wytee offered.

Dismay threatened to sink him into oblivion. Where could he find a Storyship?

Storyship come, Wytee insisted. *Here!*

Ryll felt himself stretched along a thin thread from Nishi's bed, coiling outward to the perimeter of the solar system. Like a magnet, the thread's outer tip locked onto an approaching Storyship and he recognized the captain.

Father!

No time even to wonder if the elder Dreen recognized his son's thready presence. Survival required concentration. Ryll allowed his thread-self to tap the Storyship's power and felt infinitely strengthened, possessed of unlimited time.

His thread-self wound around Mrs. Ebey's body. What shape should he take? Without knowing Wytee supplied the data, Ryll realized Nishi admired dark, Irish types with tightly curled black hair. Holding fast to his thread-self, Ryll almost drained Storyship power to feed a voracious idmaging effort. Mrs. Ebey melted into oblivion, her cellular memories erased by Wytee in the interest of Dreen sanity.

A handsome Earther male took form on the floor of Nishi's bedroom. Except for Dreen eyes, the face echoed Legion Captain O'Hara but with stronger cheeks and chin.

As he felt his new body take shape, Ryll experienced a surge of reckless elation. Now! Now, he knew what had driven Lutt to risk his life in desperate gambles! What a marvelous sensation of life! So this was what it meant to be *alive!*

Jongleur, on the erasure ship, looked on what he thought was Earth and saw his instruments register a dangerous energy drain. *Earthers are fighting me!*

Using emergency power, he flipped through the eight stages of erasure and depressed the final trigger without once thinking about consequences.

Raj Dood's illusory planet vanished.

Jongleur fell to the deck in shock. *I have killed! I have committed mass murder in the name of all Dreens!*

His highly charged thought shot outward to be received by all but two of the Dreens in his universe.

Ryll, in the throes of transformation and tied to survival necessities, caught none of his father's message.

Prosik, at home in Texas and in the deepest bazeel ecstasy of his life, having drunk almost a liter of basil extract, remained a comatose copy of Lew Doughty. Subiyama, beside him in bed, stroked his forehead and wondered about that new liquor he was making.

But all Dreens captive on Earth and the massed throngs of Dreenor received Jongleur's signal. Instant amnesiacs, they responded to the ancient summons and fled to other dimensions, scattering like dandelion seeds blown on the wind.

It is done, Habiba thought and joined the exodus.

In Nishi's bedroom, Ryll completed his shapeshift and decided to gather his strength before idmaging clothes. He flexed his new muscles and sat up. This body contained less mass than his old one but Wytee soothed him.

Ryll safe.

What of Lutt? Ryll wondered.

Wytee save Dreen. Lutt Earther dead.

Ryll stood and looked down at the sleeping Nishi. Wytee was a curled ball of fur near her neck. A male form lay beside her . . . unbreathing. Ryll studied the familiar shape he had shared for what seemed eons. A pang of regret flashed through him.

Such a waste!

The lost potential of this Earther life filled Ryll with frustration. If the creature had only tried to learn!

A soft rapping sounded on the bedroom door.

"Mr. President?"

Ryll recognized the voice of a Secret Service guard.

With abrupt dismay, Ryll realized he stood naked in a bedroom with an assassination victim those Secret Service men would identify as the President of the United States. Stalling for time, he pitched his voice in the remembered Lutt tones.

"What is it?"

"The White House is calling, sir. There's a crisis call from the ZP. Something about Dreen prisoners escaping."

Fellow Dreens escaping? Ryll grinned with elation. But how should Lutt respond?

"Shit!"

"Sir, they're insisting," the Secret Service man said.

"Tell them to keep their pants on. I'll be with you fast as I can."

Nishi, awakened by voices, sat up and focused on Ryll's new body. She put a hand over her mouth. "Who are—"

"It's Ryll," he whispered.

She looked at the body beside her, back to the new Ryll.

He bent close to her and whispered, "Mrs. Ebey killed him. I had to make a new body."

She lowered her hand. "Mrs. Ebey?" She looked around the room. There was no sign of Mrs. Ebey.

"Wytee killed her," Ryll whispered.

Wytee help.

Nishi cocked her head to one side, then straightened.

"Wytee says you made a body I would like." She looked him up and down. "Very handsome. I didn't know you could do that." She looked at the door. "What now?"

The practicality of the question told Ryll she accepted the situation without more argument. Cross-examination would come later, he realized. Provided there was a later.

Ryll stared at the door, visualizing the impatience out there. What should he do? If he tried a new copy of Lutt, the smaller size would be seen immediately . . . unless . . . No! He would not make another merging with that remembered flesh. Some of Lutt might remain in the cells. One experience of Lutt Hanson, Jr., was enough!

Remove the evidence of assassination?

It would require time to cleanse that body of all poison and even then clever investigators would suspect foul play. He and Nishi would be required to explain the unexplainable. No. That was too risky.

Something clicked in the lock of the bedroom door. It opened a crack. A Secret Service man peered in at him. Seeing a stranger in the room, the guard threw the door open wide.

"Who are you?" He saw the familiar figure of his President on the bed, a very quiet figure not responding to this intrusion. The guard's hand darted into his jacket and emerged with a deadly stunner.

Wytee, reading new danger to a precious Dreen, attacked.

The Secret Service man dropped his weapon, clutched his head and fell to the floor. He was dead before Ryll could reach him.

Ryll took only a moment to make sure the Soother had killed for a second time. So the Soother learned quick violence.

Wytee! You must not kill people!

Not let bad peoples hurt Dreen!

Ryll stood. "Get dressed, Nishi. We have to run."

She glanced at the door, eyebrows raised.

Wytee, please. Just hurt their heads a little. Ryll pleaded.

The Soother did not respond.

Hoping the order would be obeyed, Ryll said, "Wytee will help us."

She accepted this and began dressing, taking the clothes she had left over a chair.

Ryll idmaged a tweed suit with black shoes, white shirt and a dark gray tie. He looked at himself in a bedroom mirror, seeing Nishi behind him already dressed.

"*Merde* in the fan," she said, looking at the body on the bed.

"Hey! What's taking so . . ."

Another Secret Service man stood in the bedroom doorway. He saw his fellow guard on the floor, the still figure on the bed, Nishi and Ryll in street clothes. The man's hand flashed toward a shoulder holster but did not complete the motion. He fell with a solid "thwock."

Nishi Ryll take Wytee go now!

The projection from Wytee stunned them.

Take Wytee go!

Wytee emphasized the order with a short jab of pain.

Knowing he could not resist, Ryll grabbed up the aberrant Soother and, Nishi in tow, plunged toward the door.

Screams of agony greeted them in the hallway. Guards lay writhing on the floor, hands clutching their heads.

"Where are we going?" Nishi demanded as Ryll, leaping over and dodging the incapacitated guardians, led her at a run toward the elevators.

"We will find an airplane," Ryll said. "We must get to France where the Legion will protect you."

The streets outside the Madison presented a larger repeat of the pandemonium in the upper hall. People lay on the sidewalk and street, some quiet, some screaming.

Ryll assessed the scene. Stalled cars straddled the curbs. Other cars sat smashed against buildings, dripping coolants and oils while their occupants moaned or sat silently immobile.

Please, Wytee! Hurt them just a little.

Nishi Ryll not talk hurt. Nishi Ryll run!

They could do nothing but obey the Soother.

Around a corner from the Madison, they found a car, its driver drooling out the open door, his eyes glazed in pain.

With Nishi's help, Ryll eased the man onto the sidewalk and appopriated his car.

As they sped toward the National Airport, cars ahead of them swerved aside, clearing a path.

The extent of Wytee's power over Earthers astonished Ryll, who urged moderation, but the Soother would not respond until they were in the terminal.

Go big flying thing Gate Six!

Nishi saw the gate sign and led the way. They found an Air France Boeing Rocketeer at Gate Six, prepared for final boarding, but everyone in the plane, including crew, unconscious.

Ryll stared at the interior of the plane in outrage. *Now what, Wytee?*

Ryll not make flying thing go?

How am I supposed to do that?

Ryll know how Lutt fly plane thing.

This is no Vortraveler!

Wytee help.

And Wytee proceeded to fill his mind with knowledge appropriated from the unconscious crew.

Saying a silent prayer to Habiba, Ryll closed the plane's doors, cleared the cockpit of its unconscious crew and made sure the dormant people were strapped into seats. Taking his place in the pilot's seat, he looked at the instruments and controls. Nishi slipped into the copilot's position.

Ryll Nishi do what Wytee say.

What else can we do, Wytee?

The irony of the question was lost on the Soother, who concentrated on getting them to safety.

We go France Legion make happy love cure place.

As the plane lifted from the ground, Ryll felt himself blushing but he dared hope Wytee's promise would be kept.

The extraordinary phenomena occurring around President Hanson's assassination have been traced to an alien attack on Earth. The combined military forces of our planet are repelling this infamous and underhanded viciousness. No matter how long it takes, we will overcome!

—Acting U.S. President
Jahoon Clanton

"Look at this, Osey!"

Raj Dood pointed to a display in a news receiver set up in the shade of a thatched sunscreen at the end of their rickety pier. The inlet and nearby hideaway shack baked in noon glare. The shiny receiver looked out of place in the primitive setting.

Osceola, in a pink and green muu muu, was pole fishing from the end of the pier. She concentrated on a red float bobbing suggestively in the sparkling water.

"Not now," she said. "Think I got a bite."

"But this is interesting. They say 'Fashion news was made today by Nishi D'Amato, the hottest couturier in Paris, when she unveiled her new *Venus Flame* line.' Calls herself D'Amato in her profession," he added, "but privately she's Mrs. Ryll. That was the Dreen's name, remember?"

"So that's what she did after she offed your nephew?" Osceola jerked the tip of her pole skyward but brought up a bare hook. "Damn! Got my bait."

"How many times do I have to tell you it was that damn Soother killed him?"

"And you couldn't save him?"

Raj Dood shook his head sadly. "I don't think anyone could've saved him after what old L.H. did to him."

"So the Soother killed him. But who told it to kill?"

"Nobody needed to tell it! What else could it learn there in Washington?"

Osceola spoke while rebaiting her hook. "You shoulda studied that critter more 'fore you threw it away."

"Hell and damnation! You are the most contrary female I ever met! I had to send it into another dimension fast as I could. The thing was wild crazy."

She reset the line below her bobber and lowered it gently into the water. "So we still got two Dreens on Earth, that one married to this D'Amato and the one they call 'the Basil King of Texas.' Should you do anything about 'em?"

"They're harmless, I tell you!"

"But Dreens can get Soothers and Soothers can kill."

"Only if they're shown the example. Soothers are sensitive to any madness around them. Can't cure more'n one person at a time, so when they can't function they go nuts."

"Yeah? Well, I was you, I wouldn't allow any more of those things on Earth. And I'd keep an eye on our two Dreens, 'specially ol' Basil King. He may be the biggest grower-shipper of that stuff, but he gets high on it, too. No tellin' what he might do when he's high."

Raj Dood abruptly leaned closer to the story unfolding on his display.

"Galloping gurus!" he muttered. "Know what those Dreens are planning next?"

"You're talkin' so much you're scarin' the fish," Osceola complained. "I'm tryin' to catch our dinner."

He ignored her. "It says here these 'old friends, the Subiyamas and the Rylls, are planning a daring hang glider vacation in the Himalayas.' "

Osceola set her pole in a wire holder and joined him under the sunshade. She looked at the display over his shoulder.

"Dammit all! I told you those Dreens were dangerous!" she said.

"If we're right about 'em, anything happens to those last two, this whole Earth and everything about it vanishes in a puff of smoke."

Raj Dood turned off his receiver. "We'd better get some warm clothing," he said. "Looks like we're going to spend our vacation in the Himalayas this year. Hey!" He pointed at the fishpole, which was bobbing violently in its hanger. "You got something!"

"I got a pain in the ass for a lover," she said. "But I guess you're the best available." She strolled into the sunlight, lifted her pole and admired the way it arched and jerked under the weight of a heavy fish. "But when you got 'em hooked, you got 'em."

PS 3558 .E63 M3 1985
(U18.95)
Herbert, Frank.

Man of two worlds

ECC/USF Learning Resources
College Parkway
Fort Myers, Florida 33907-5

ECC USF LR
DATE DUE
01.02.91
04.11.88